Cursed Legacies
Bound by Fate

Brent Miller

Other books by Brent Miller
The Z Virus: Outbreak
Cursed

Cursed Legacies: Bound by Fate

Cover by Anton Rosovsky
ISBN: 9798618710336
First edition, 2020

Aldric

Chapter 1

435 Years Ago – 21st Century A.D.

"You're not like them, Aldric," Silas explained. Aldric had heard this speech from his father more times than he could count, but it didn't make it any easier to accept. "You're better."

"I don't want to be better," Aldric sighed. "I don't want to be worse. I just want to be."

"Well, then it's for the best that you didn't get the choice. You may be ungrateful now, child, but one day you will recognize this for the gift it is."

"It's not a gift, father," Aldric spat. "Quit calling it that."

In a blur, Aldric saw his father's hand shoot forward. Unable to respond in time, he just braced himself as every nerve in his face lit up. Despite his best efforts to stay standing, the slap knocked him to the ground, and he landed on his back, dazed. The stinging in his cheek was almost unbearable for a moment, but it quickly faded away.

Every fiber of his being wanted to yell at his father. He wasn't ready to give up on the argument yet, but he knew no good could come from it. Longingly, he gazed toward the trees. Just on the other side of the woods, there was a town full of people – full of experiences beckoning to him. Somehow, it felt as though he could smell the perfume of the girls in town and hear the brakes as cars slowed down at intersections. The yells of children playing kickball on the streets as they warned others of approaching cars, or the laughs of children as the ferociously pedaled on the bicycles in an attempt to outpace one another. It was all so present to him, but just out of reach.

He yearned to know that world and couldn't comprehend why he couldn't be a part of it. There was no denying that his father was partially right – he was different. Aldric had broken bones, cut himself, stubbed toes – but nothing was ever lasting. There wasn't a single mark on his body, regardless of how many times he fell from trees or scraped himself on the rocks while roughhousing with his brothers. He'd seen what they all became on the full moons, and they'd told him it was only a matter of time before he was like them. The nagging voice in the back of his mind, though, hoped they were wrong. Aldric's fourteenth birthday was approaching, and he hadn't transformed yet. None of the others had been as old as him their first time. Maybe he'd escaped it.

Even so, his parents refused to allow him anywhere near town, despite phase of the moon, completely disregarding the fact that his first transformation would have to be on a full moon. All he wanted was to experience what everyone else had, but he hadn't ventured farther than a mile from his home in his entire life. How could his father see that as a gift?

Turning his back, Silas stormed back toward the house, and Aldric toyed with the idea of running. If he tried, he may have a hope of reaching the town before someone caught him. Fleeting as it was, the notion brought a deviant smile to his face.

Aldric heard crunching leaves from behind him, and his eyes darted toward the noise. His heart rate sped up as he turned to face the threat, raising his hands to cover his face. When he saw his mother's smiling face, he relaxed. For as long as he could remember, his father had trained him to be a warrior, explaining that there were people who would kill him if they found out what he was. Since birth, he had been caught in his father's war. At least, that's what they said. Having never actually seen any evidence of that threat, Aldric had started to believe that was just another excuse to prevent him from wandering too far from home.

"It isn't all you think it is," his mother comforted, kneeling down to look him in the eye as she nodded toward the woods.

Brushing hair from his face, she gazed at him lovingly. Aldric looked away.

"I know it seems almost mystical, but it's not. It's… loud."

"What's wrong with loud?"

"You'll get to see it some day, honey. But before your first change, it's just going to terrify you."

"I don't understand."

"I know. But you will."

"Why won't you just explain it?"

"Some things can only be taught by experience."

"Then why won't you let me experience the town?"

"Touché," she smirked, standing back up. "We all just want what's best for you. But if you try, I won't stop you, Aldric. But I doubt you can outrun Cade."

She nodded again, this time toward Aldric's older brother. Cade smirked knowingly at him, and Aldric's shoulders dropped as he followed his mother back inside.

Present
19 Days Until the Full Moon

"How was work?" Linda asked, smiling at Aldric as he walked through the door. Denying him the time to answer, she stepped in and kissed him, holding him in a tight embrace. After a moment, he pulled back and gazed into her eyes, losing himself in the love story they told.

"Sorry," she laughed, letting him go and stepping back. "I got excited."

"Oh?" He moved closer, closing the distance again. Aldric lifted her into the air, her dress flowing to her side. As he pulled her in, she wrapped her legs around him and draped her arms over his shoulders, lovingly looking down at him.

Finally breaking the moment, Aldric set her down and kissed her again before backing up. Loosening his tie, he turned away and walked toward their room.

"It was normal, I suppose," Aldric called back. "The design review went about as smoothly as we could have expected, so we're getting ready to move into production."

"Well, that's exciting!" she chirped. Aldric laughed as he unbuttoned his overshirt. Somehow, no matter how long they were together – or how many jobs he'd been through – she always found a way to be excited about his work. Aldric had taken a liking to Engineering – but he wasn't sure how much longer his current alias would last. He'd already been there for nearly a decade, and people were going to start questioning why he didn't age.

Tossing his shirt into the hamper in his room, he sighed and sat at the edge of the bed. It was getting close to time for another move – which meant a new career, new documents, and a new city. Over the years, he had become bored with most professions – having found the time to dabble in a majority of them. However, he was confident that it wouldn't be much longer before he'd built up the capital and investment portfolio that he'd be able to support himself and his wife without finding new careers.

"There's that look again," Linda groaned, leaning in the doorway.

"It's been a long time," Aldric shrugged.

"You know, plenty of people would be jealous of how much we get to travel."

"I love how you always find the silver lining," Aldric laughed.

"Just stop worrying about it and eat some dinner," she ordered. Aldric stood and followed her to the dining room. With her by his side, he knew he could face anything.

❖ ❖ ❖

"Any ideas for names?" Aldric pondered, staring up at the ceiling. Her head rested on his chest, and he held her with one arm. His other hand was under his head as he tried to get comfortable. They'd both been silent for a long while, and though he knew Linda didn't find the silence awkward, he himself was very uncomfortable. Aldric had never been good at dealing with things which weighed on his mind – he typically just resorted to brooding.

"I don't know, we always figure it out," she shrugged.

"I just think we should talk about it," Aldric responded, an unintentional harshness in his tone. He sighed as she pulled back and looked at him, confused. Although he'd expressed to her just how difficult their lives were going to become, he didn't think she could fully understand the consequences of their actions.

"Okay," Linda replied. "If it means that much to you, I think I like Miranda."

"Miranda?" Aldric inquired. Silently, he let the name swim around his mind for a moment. It wasn't something he would choose, but he wasn't opposed either.

"What about for a boy?"

"Come on, you can name yourself."

"I'm serious, Linda."

"I know," she sighed, clearly exasperated. Aldric had been under the impression that pregnant women loved talking about baby names. He wondered if media had just steered him wrong or if their case was just unique. Every movie he'd ever seen seemed to portray their roles as reversed – the man was always getting annoyed at the incessant discussion of the child. Given that any talk of the infant growing in her womb inevitably led to Aldric's speech concerning what a mistake they'd made, though, Aldric wasn't surprised that their case was unique.

Despite his best efforts, he rarely found himself able to avoid that trap his mind set. It wasn't that he didn't want a child – it was just that he was concerned for that child's well-being. There were too many people in the world that he didn't trust. More than one of his aliases had been prematurely ended due to hunters or other werewolves. Aside from that, if there was one thing he'd learned from his father, it was that a werewolf cub had to be kept separated from people. The difficulty growing up would only be accentuated by the pain of being different – and how was he going to convince a child to keep their lives a secret? There were just too many variables racing through his head.

Aldric caught himself spiraling again, though. It was exactly that reason that Linda had blown off his question, so he brought his mind back to the task at hand. For once, he was going to have a normal conversation with her about their child.

After a few moments of silence, she finally spoke up. "I haven't thought much about names for the baby. It's weird how easy it is to make up a new one for myself, but when it comes to naming our child my mind goes blank."

"It's a lot more pressure," Aldric laughed weakly.

"Like, I can be Miranda," Linda offered. "But would our daughter?"

"If we named her that, I suppose she would."

"But what if she doesn't feel like a Miranda?"

"I think whatever name we give this baby will feel natural after we use it for a few years," Aldric shrugged. "Anyway, we'll be too blinded by love to see if the name doesn't fit."

"I guess," she laughed before turning and staring up at the ceiling, apparently deep in thought. Aldric had thought about names for quite some time, but he was always embarrassed to suggest anything because he thought she wouldn't like it. It felt childish to even care about such trivial matters. It wasn't important if she didn't like the name; they'd just choose a new one. Nonetheless, he found it difficult for himself to verbalize his suggestion.

"I like Cailean," Aldric suggested, breaking the silence of a long pause.

"Okay," Linda hesitantly accepted. "If it's a boy, we will name him Cailean."

❖ ❖ ❖

Aldric signed a birth certificate, carefully comparing it to his current one as he searched for any perceivable difference. There had been plenty of political and social changes over his long life, but one good thing about the recent years was that forging had become much easier again. Regardless, he couldn't allow himself to make simple errors.

Stephen Kellick; born to parents Anna and Ethan at West Creek Memorial Hospital in Avalon, California. Aldric had grown accustomed to changing his name every few years, and he'd even began to enjoy creating backstories for the new personas. Stephen grew up in a small town, only leaving to go to a state school a few cities over. During his years at University, he met his wife Abilene. As he moved from marriage license to diploma, he pondered the career path he desired. Over his long life, he'd experimented in dozens of different fields from architecture to law enforcement to farming. He always tried to do something at least slightly different, pushing himself to avoid any semblance of a pattern. With his son on the way, though, Aldric wanted to accelerate his financial plans. In order to be there fully to protect his family, he had to have enough money diversified accounts routed through multiple aliases to ensure that the interest would provide for them but would also be relatively untracable. For that, he had to choose a career which paid well.

Over the past few decades, many odd jobs had faded out of existence as a large emphasis fell on jobs bathed in necessity. Farming, Medicine, and Engineering were his three major choices at that point for a stable career. Farming wouldn't offer him the level of income he needed at the necessary rate, and it had been years since he'd practiced medicine, so Aldric fell back on Engineering. Building and designing had always been a passion of his, and his long life gave him an edge in that field. He could remember products which existed long before anyone in his field was alive – understand how they worked – and replicate them.

Given that, he chose a Bachelor's degree in Mechanical Engineering. Additionally, he forged a Master's degree, Professional Engineer certification, and a resume with years of experience. As he wrapped up compiling decades of work experience from nonexistent companies, Linda walked quietly down the stairs, turning on the light and snapping him away from the task at hand. Aldric glanced at the clock, realizing he'd worked through the entire day. As he stood, he stretched his arms and rolled his shoulders. It had become a habit to pretend that sitting for too long tightened his muscles as it seemed to for humans. Although he himself had never actually experienced soreness or stiffness when standing, he had seen countless coworkers as they groaned and stood. Even so, stretching was still pleasant, and not entirely unnecessary. He wasn't sore, but he could still benefit from guaranteeing that he felt limber and ready to move at a moment's notice.

"Stephen?" she asked with a laugh. "Since when have you been one to go for what is historically one of the most common names?"

"I've never been a Stephen," Aldric shrugged. "I like it."

"I like Kellick," Linda added as she placed his birth certificate down. "That seems a little more like you."

"Well, I can't be too unoriginal."

"Who am I, then?"

"Abilene."

"Abilene Kellick. I can get used to that," she smiled. "I guess we couldn't both have common names."

"We need the contrast," Aldric explained. Although he'd explained his logic to her dozens of times, he found it impossible not to be thorough. Every time they changed identities, he had to be sure she knew exactly why. While he'd been doing it for far longer than she had, she was experienced in transferring aliases as well. Deep down, he knew he probably should stop repeating the information. Nonetheless, she always humored him, so he continued, "Everyone is hiding something, Linda. Everyone has some dark secret they try so hard to cover up, so they blend in. If you're part of the crowd, no one will ask questions, right? So if you truly want to hide, you can't use the same tactics as everyone else – relying on the darkness. If you illuminate every part of your life that you want the world to see, they won't think twice about the parts they don't see. They won't even think to ask. The best way to fit in…"

"Is to stand out," she finished. "I know, and I trust you. You haven't steered us wrong yet."

"I have practice."

"So, Engineering again?" She asked as she studied the new life he'd crafted for them. By then she was fully aware that she had to be as much of an expert in it as Aldric. She had to live the new life and give no one any reason to expect she didn't have her story straight. A hunter would catch a scent of doubt and latch onto it.

"It pays well."

"Maybe you've just found a job you like," she smirked as she peered into his eyes.

"I'm Biomedical now, focusing mostly on revamping a few medical devices which died off years back."

"Now you're transitioning into machinery?"

"It's just a little broader," he shrugged.

"Okay, that makes sense. Where are we going?"

"Arizona."

"Oh, that's bound to be interesting. When should I pack?"

"We're leaving in two weeks. I've submitted my notice to work. They believe we are moving to Colorado."

"I'll get some things together," she agreed, "but we can start later. First, come eat dinner."

Chapter 2

433 Years Ago

Clenching his teeth, Aldric refused to give in to the pain. Every fiber of his being wanted to scream – to fall to his knees and surrender. Instead, he stood tall, tensing his arms as if that would provide him any degree of strength. Regardless of how hard he fought, Aldric could feel the teeth sharpening in his mouth. He tightly balled his fists, digging his nails into his palms as if the pain would stop what was happening. All it did, though, was add to the pain he already felt.

"Let go," Cade growled as soothingly as his distorted voice would allow. "It makes it easier." Cade stared at the floor as he spoke, resting on his hands and knees. He was already partially transformed – his legs and arms slightly longer to allow him to stand as a wolf. His spine shattered and curved, correcting itself and allowing him to maintain composure. Cade looked up at Aldric, his yellow eyes glittering in the moonlight.

Aldric refused to give in. The transformation seemed inevitable, but there was no chance if he didn't try. Trying to push the pain he'd experienced out of his mind, Aldric focused on his dreams. His father had kept him locked in the house until his first change, but even after that he'd told Aldric he was too unstable to visit town. Aldric listened closely to the people wandering the streets. The girls his age laughing as they walked together – and the click of their heels against the cement. If he focused hard enough, he could almost smell the perfume, although it was overpowered by the gas of cars driving by. There was a life out there he could have if only he could defeat the beast which had ruled his life since birth.

"Please, Aldric," Lara, his older sister, pleaded as she gazed at him. She was still mostly human, but it was clear that she was in agony. Lara didn't hate what she was going to become – not like him. How could she? Since childhood, their father had ingrained a love of the beast into each of their minds. Aldric wasn't sure how he'd escaped the indoctrination. Maybe it was just a stronger fascination with the world outside, or maybe it was the general disdain for the kind of man his father was. Whatever the case, he couldn't blame Lara or Cade for accepting what they were. He just wished they wouldn't blame him for his own view.

Aldric felt his spine break, and the motor function in his legs was impaired. They felt weak, and he almost collapsed, but he managed to hold himself up. The bones themselves had broken, but he hadn't lost any nerves, so he was still able to fight the pain and stand tall. Aldric felt his left shoulder dislocate, but he tried to push it back into place. The second he did, it snapped back out, as if the beast were taunting him, countering his efforts.

Lara fell to the ground, finally overpowered by her darker side. She always tried to stay human for Aldric, just to convince him that it would be okay. Her drive wasn't as strong, though. She accepted the transformation, she just wanted to wait for him. With that level of resolve, though, she could never outlast Aldric. As she screamed in pain and her kneecaps shattered, Aldric turned away. Seeing anyone in his family like that pained him, but especially her. Lara deserved the pain the least, and yet her attempts to stay human long enough to comfort Aldric extended her transformation and made her hurt even more.

When he looked to his left, Aldric saw his father and mother in a fully transformed state. Although he hated the beasts, he couldn't deny that they held a certain majesty in their stance. Both stood tall, facing slightly away from each other as they surveyed the area. Aldric's father looked at him, hatred clear in the wolf's golden eyes. It turned away and Aldric felt as though he could see a scowl on the beast's face.

Aldric's right elbow broke, and he pitched forward, taking a step to catch himself. The pain was almost unbearable, but he'd fought through it every month for nearly two years. Aldric tried to think about the town – the life that he wanted – but his thoughts became cloudy. All he could remember were his father's words.

"The world out there isn't worthwhile, Aldric. They're nothing like you. They're weak and cowardly, and their lives are a mere blink to us. Association with their kind is a waste of time, as appealing as it may seem. You have nothing in common with them."

Aldric tried to shake his father's voice out of his mind, but it just grew louder as the beast continued to tear at his insides. Finally, the pain overwhelmed Aldric and he collapsed to all-fours. Aldric dug his fingers into the dirt as if holding the earth would prevent his hands from changing shape. Despite his efforts, he watched as the palms grew and the nails sharpened; his hands became paws before his eyes. A tear rolled down his face as he watched his father turn to walk away. All he could think about was that he was going to be just like him. No matter how hard he fought, Aldric Nystrom was destined to become the same beast he saw before him.

"You're not like them, Aldric," his father's speech continued in Aldric's mind. The words had been engrained into his mind since childhood, and he wasn't sure if he'd ever be able to forget them. "You're better."

Present
12 Days Until the Full Moon

"I don't suppose there's any way I can convince you to stick around," Kyle joked, leaning against the wall in front of Aldric's desk. Dozens of schematics littered the space as Aldric attempted to wrap up his projects and pass them on to the next person. Over the years, he'd had many employers, and he'd impressed all of them, so he was used to their disappointment when he left. Nonetheless, he wished he didn't have to leave this team behind. They would start to get suspicious, though, and he couldn't put his family at risk for some career.

"It'll be fine, Kyle," Aldric comforted, placing a hand on Kyle's shoulder as he stood. "I'm just going to lunch."

"And that's why we'll miss you," Kyle groaned.

"I have to admit, this place will be dry without my wit."

"Seriously, it has nothing to do with the work. It's all about the dry humor."

"Well, of course. I've managed to accomplish nothing in ten years."

"Go to lunch," Kyle laughed and rolled his eyes, walking back to his office. Aldric looked around the office as he stepped out. He'd been alive far too long to get sentimental anymore. He had memories with the coworker sitting at each desk, and in another life, he could have considered each of them friends. His curse didn't permit friendship, though. It didn't allow for connections. Aldric had to be ready to abandon any group, any city, and any job. That had made him cold for over a century, but he was finally beginning to trust his acting skills again. The other employees seemed to think more highly of him than he did of them.

Aldric found himself pondering their brief lifespan. Although he tried to fight the facts, he always found himself falling back on the fact that they wouldn't live longer than a few more decades. Even if he found himself forming relationships they wouldn't be lifelong. It wasn't worth wasting his time and safety for a blink. It wasn't worth wasting anything for humans.

As he stepped outside of the office, Aldric shook his head violently, pushing those thoughts out of his head. Regardless of his attempts at reprogramming his own mind, he often found his thoughts drifting back to those same ideas planted in his mind as a child. Every time he questioned himself, he had to fall back to the same justification which defended every action. Humans were short-lived, and their relationships were meaningless. Though he tried, he couldn't deny his father's ideology which was so deeply ingrained within him.

Aldric took a deep breath, sighing loudly as he started walking back home. The city seemed quiet to him, even though it was the middle of the day. There were people wandering around, and the lights were on in the businesses on either side of the street. Above him, the sun shone through a thin layer of clouds. He'd lived in much larger cities, though, and this town would never be as loud. By comparison to what he'd seen, it was a ghost town.

To his right, two young girls – probably no older than 17, were peering through the glass of a music store, pointing at something on the other side. Aldric hadn't paid any attention to the school schedule in over one hundred years, so he wasn't sure if they were ditching or just on vacation. As he passed them, the smell of perfume assaulted his senses, but he managed to avoid any reaction. When he was young that smell had always been so appealing, but he couldn't understand that thought anymore. Maybe it was due to the youth of the people wearing it, or maybe the association with his childhood. Whatever the case, Aldric was glad when he was far enough to avoid the scent.

Continuing along his path home, Aldric walked past another group of what he assumed to be high schoolers. There were four boys laughing and pushing each other lightly as they walked. No matter how many years passed, hearing their laughs brought him back to being a child and listening through the woods. Aldric shook his head, pushing the nostalgia deep down.

He only lived a few blocks from work, and the walk wasn't typically that painful. That day, specifically, though, something seemed off. Aldric hesitated, coming to a stop just before he rounded the corner to reach his house. The last dozen moves hadn't affected him like that, so why was he feeling so strange? He still had a week before he left anyway, so it didn't seem logical that those memories were forcing their way to his mind. Instead of stubbornly fighting them, Aldric accepted the possibility that his mind was trying to tell him something. Maybe the wolf had sensed something Aldric hadn't picked up on yet.

Taking a deep breath, Aldric closed his eyes. As he opened them, he exhaled and tried to relax. Aldric scanned the area, crossing the street and passing his house. To his left, back on the other side of the road, Aldric saw a face that he recognized. In that moment, his heart froze in place, but he forced his legs to keep moving.

Cade. Aldric would recognize the face anywhere. He blinked, shaking his head again. There was no way his brother could know where he had gone – his mind was just playing tricks on him. When he opened his eyes, his suspicions were eased. The figure had just been an apparition – a projection of his fears. Cade was nowhere to be seen, so Aldric turned in a full circle frantically.

Unsatisfied that he wasn't being followed, though, Aldric continued to walk straight. He turned left, taking a detour through a different neighborhood. This would lead him to the woods where he could lose any trackers and get back home. His heart still pounded as he walked, but he tried to calm himself.

Aldric crossed the tree line, looking over his shoulder to find nothing. Picking up the pace, he jogged through the woods and took a few rapid turns. When he turned one last time to head back home, though, the same face stared at him. It looked like Cade, but something was off. It looked exactly like Aldric remembered him – which made sense given that his aging would have halted – but it felt off.

"Aldric Nystrom," the young man greeted. Aldric sighed, unable to convince himself it was just his mind any longer. His hands drifted upward defensively but subtly.

"I don't know what you're talking about."

The man laughed. In a fluid motion, the man raised his hand and threw a hook punch toward his face. Aldric checked the attack as he weaved backward, but he didn't throw an attack back. That punch was either intended to miss or this wasn't Cade. It was slow and sloppy compared to what his brother could do, and Aldric had seen a twitch in the shoulder before he'd moved. Cade would never make such a rookie mistake as telegraphing his strikes.

"Well, you're definitely fast," the assailant granted.

"You're not," Aldric stated matter-of-factly. "Who are you?"

The stranger smirked and threw another punch. This one was aimed toward Aldric's solar plexus. It was a clear feint, though, because there was no intent behind the attack. Aldric gave his focus instead to the other fist, which shot out toward his nose. Aldric caught the fist an inch in front of his face. Twisting the arm, Aldric lifted his leg and kicked his attacker. His opponent's smile faded as he stumbled backward, glaring at Aldric.

With that anger he lost any sense of control. Predictably, he rushed toward Aldric with a flurry of punches. Aldric was able to consistently dodge, weaving and parrying the attacks. He leaned backward to avoid a hook, then ducked under a strike toward the temple. Taking a full step back, he avoided a few attacks aimed to his ribs. The attacker didn't seem to be tiring himself out.

Finally, Aldric ducked down and drove an elbow into the man's gut, knocking his breath away. The man stumbled back a few feet, and Aldric stood up straight and walked toward him. Regaining his composure more quickly than Aldric had expected, the man kicked at Aldric's head, but Aldric ducked under and lifted him, throwing him to the ground.

"Who are you?" Aldric repeated, glaring down at the man on the floor.

"I'm sorry," the man sighed. "I just had to be sure."

"What do you mean?"

"My name is Cyrus," he explained, presumptuously reaching a hand out. Aldric hesitantly grabbed his hand and lifted Cyrus to his feet. Cautiously, he took a step back. Cyrus clearly wasn't a threat, but that didn't mean he didn't want to be one. If there was one thing Aldric had learned through his years of training it was to never underestimate his opponent. A fight wasn't over until the end, and an opponent should always be treated as a danger.

"Is that supposed to hold any meaning to me?" Aldric growled.

"Well, Uncle," Cyrus smirked, dusting off his pants, "it would if you ever visited."

"You're Cade's son," Aldric sighed at the realization.

"I was sent to find you. I obviously had to test you before divulging any secrets. You know, since I had no idea what you actually looked like aside from a description from my father."

"How old are you, Cyrus?"

"Twenty-one."

"Great," Aldric laughed. "You're a child."

"I'm an adult," he defended.

"No, you aren't. You're a child. There are things seriously wrong with that family, boy. Your words will never hold the power to bring my decision to leave into question."

"I had that suspicion," Cyrus shrugged. "There's no point in trying to guilt you."

"Why were you sent?"

"Your presence is required."

"I decline."

"I didn't say requested."

"I. Decline."

"That isn't an option, Uncle. The family has summoned you – you're needed at home. You know you must return for your pack."

"Why?"

"They know."

"All the more reason to decline."

"Your alpha demands your return."

"I have no alpha," Aldric growled, carefully enunciating and emphasizing each word. In a flash, Cyrus's fist connected with Aldric's jaw. Aldric had let his guard down in anger, and he'd gotten too close. Popping his jaw back into place, he laughed and looked down at Cyrus.

"You're passionate. I'll give you one for free, child, because you have no clue who I am. Go home. Tell your pack I'm done. I would advise you to walk away from this. You don't get a second one."

"You think I was really trying?" Cyrus laughed. He threw another punch toward Aldric's face, but Aldric drove his forearm into Cyrus's bicep. He stepped in and drove an uppercut into the boy's jaw. Pushing against his shoulders with his arms and sweeping his leg with his own, Aldric threw the boy to the ground.

"Stay down, boy," Aldric ordered.

Cyrus growled as he rolled over and pushed himself onto his hands and knees. As he stood, he spat. Breathing heavily – more with anger than exhaustion – Cyrus glared at Aldric. Rushing in, he threw a flurry of blows. Aldric parried each of them. The last punch was aimed toward Aldric's gut, and Aldric deflected it, knocking the fist to the side as he stepped in and drove his elbow into Cyrus's ribs, breaking at least two of them. With his other hand, Aldric grabbed the wrist of the hand Cyrus had used to punch him. Aldric wrapped his arm around Cyrus's waist. Lifting his opponent, Aldric threw the boy over his shoulders, driving him head-first into the ground and audibly cracking his skull.

Cyrus froze for a moment, lying motionless on the floor. Aldric was fully aware, though, that it would take far more than that to kill a lycanthrope. Standing tall and exuding power, Aldric waited for Cyrus to regain consciousness. It wasn't long before the boy's eyes fluttered open.

"Stay down," Aldric commanded again.

Cyrus stood shakily once again. Aldric sighed, but he allowed the boy to be defiant.

Driven by anger and humiliation, Cyrus threw another punch to Aldric's face. Aldric leaned back, avoiding the attack with ease. Cyrus stepped in with a front kick, but Aldric stepped to the side and knocked Cyrus off balance. Cyrus quickly turned, throwing his elbow toward Aldric's head, but Aldric ducked down and drove a fist directly into the boy's armpit. His arm falling limply at his side, Cyrus stumbled backward. Recovering quickly, he stepped forward and kicked at Aldric's knee. Aldric stepped in a circle, avoiding the attack as he drove the ridge of his hand into Cyrus's neck, stunning him once again.

Realizing that Cyrus wasn't going to give up, Aldric finally put some force into an attack. As Cyrus rushed in once more, Aldric stepped to the side and covered his face with one hand, driving a fist into his ribs. As Cyrus pitched forward, Aldric caught his shoulders and pulled him down as he spun back toward him, raising his knee. Connecting the blow to Cyrus's nose, Aldric pushed the boy forward. Cyrus managed to stay on his feet and turn back toward Aldric. By the time he was facing his opponent, though, Aldric had already turned in a full circle, bringing his heel around to connect to Cyrus's temple. The blow would have been enough to end a normal man's life, and Cyrus dropped like a rock to the ground.

Aldric slammed his foot onto Cyrus's back, forcefully pinning him to the ground. When he felt Cyrus begin to stir under him, Aldric put more pressure, holding him still.

"Listen to me carefully, Cyrus. I will do anything to protect my family. I have no qualms ending your life right here and now. The only reason you're still alive is because you're still too young to understand the war into which you've been drafted. Now, this is what's going to happen: I am going to turn around and go home. You will lie here, face buried in the dirt, for one hour. You will stand return home with nothing more than this message: Aldric will not return, nor will he will not show this much mercy to anyone who comes for his family ever again. If you deviate from this in any way, Cyrus, I will end your life. Do you understand?"

Cyrus grunted angrily, squirming underneath Aldric's foot.

"Do you understand?" Aldric repeated, pressing his foot against Cyrus harder.

"Yes," Cryus spat, the shame clear in his voice. The dirt around his face was red as it absorbed blood from his nose, but he didn't move his face. Aldric sighed before lifting his foot. Slowly, he backed away a few steps, carefully monitoring Cyrus. When he was comfortable that the boy would follow orders, Aldric turned and rushed home.

❖ ❖ ❖

"What are you doing, Aldric?" Linda pleaded as Aldric emptied a can of oil over the couch.

"We don't have time to discuss this."

"Make time!" She grabbed his arm in attempt to stop him, but he shrugged her off. When he finished emptying the container, he set it to the side and turned to look at her.

"Our plan must be expedited. Grab a few sets of clothes and the documents. We will start over when we reach Arizona."

"What happened?"

"They found us."

"The hunters? Are they here?"

"No," Aldric sighed, shaking his head. "No, not them."

"What do they want from us?" Linda spat, concern washing over her face as the pieces fell together in her mind.

"Our child."

She froze, unable to formulate a response. Aldric had mentioned the possibility before, but it had never been so tangible. His family had come to claim his son.

"We have to leave. For our cover, we can't just disappear and reappear somewhere else. If my family found us, then the hunters will be able to as well. We have to ensure that we won't be tracked," Aldric thought aloud.

"So what's the new plan?"

"We have to die," Aldric shrugged. "There will be nothing left in this fire. It will be tragic, and we will be mourned, but not questioned."

"A body wouldn't completely burn," Linda argued.

"I need you to trust me. It's best you aren't involved. Just get your things together and meet me around the corner."

"Okay," she agreed. With the urgency in his voice, Linda knew better than to argue with him. They could have any discussion later, and he would explain everything, but in that moment he just needed a trusting partner to stand by him. Linda ran to their room and began packing a quick bag as Aldric rushed outside the front door.

It wasn't a pretty job, but he knew exactly what he had to do to survive. Nothing would stop him from protecting his family, regardless of the consequences.

The sun had set, and the entire town was asleep. The contrast between the panic and the noise in his mind compared to the quiet of the town was shocking to Aldric. He refused to allow himself to get lost along that train of thought, though, as he grabbed a shovel from his tool shed and raced to the graveyard.

Aldric sighed, searching his mind for any alternative before resorting to desecrating graves. In the end, though, he was willing to pay any price. Taking one more deep breath to steel himself, Aldric began exhuming the first corpse. Working tirelessly, he was able to remove the dirt within an hour, and he placed the body on the ground next to him before filling the grave and hiding evidence.

Repeating the process, Aldric found a woman as well. He carried the two bodies – one over each shoulder – back to his house. In the distance, he could hear Linda's car running and smell the gasoline. While he wouldn't hide anything from her, he was happy to protect her from being a part of what he had to do.

Aldric positioned the two bodies in his bed and poured some oil over them. Although the smell was one of the most powerful he'd experienced, his nose became accustomed to it, and he barely noticed that the entire house reeked of death.

After he had positioned everything properly, Aldric walked to the kitchen and opened the gas lines for all of the burners on the stove. As the smell of gas began to overpower the stench of decay, he lit a candle and set it on the floor. Silently, Aldric made his way back to the bedroom. The force of thc explosion shook the entire house, and flames erupted from the kitchen, travelling quickly to the bedroom. Aldric watched as the bodies burned, unwilling to leave the job half done. When he was confident that they'd been burned beyond recognition, he finally allowed himself to leave.

The flames travelled more quickly than he'd thought they would, and Aldric trapped himself in the living room as the fire rushed to the door. A spark found oil residue on his sleeve and lit his shirt aflame. He attempted to pat it out but the fire seared through his shirt and burned his skin before he managed to kill it.

The house burned around him, and the heat was becoming unbearable. Aldric gasped for air as the smoke filled his lungs. Breathing through his mouth, he could practically taste the mixture of smoke and burning flesh. Aldric rushed to the kitchen, kicking down the burning door which separated it from the other rooms. A support beam collapsed to his right, and the flame continued to grow. Aldric held his breath as he dove through the glass door leading to the back yard.

As he stumbled outside, Aldric was assaulted by sounds. The neighbors had been awakened by the flames, and he could hear a few of them as they desperately called the fire department. Behind him, one of Aldric's many lives burned to the ground. He stumbled forward and collapsed to his hands and knees.

Finally allowing his senses to catch up with him, Aldric processed everything he'd done. The nausea, remorse, and disgust all bombarded him simultaneously, and Aldric rocked forward, tears pouring from his eyes. He vomited, leaning forward as the sickness from the smells finally overpowered him.

Sirens approached, and Aldric knew he didn't have much more time, but his chest heaved as he sobbed, and he didn't have the strength to compose himself. After another minute, the sirens grew closer, and the commotion in front of the house was only growing louder. It wouldn't be long before someone discovered him.

Aldric wiped his mouth and struggled to his feet. With his other hand, he dried his eyes. As the fire truck pulled up in front of the house, Aldric jumped over the brick wall which separated his house from the neighbor's. Jumping over another wall, he made his way to the less populated street around the corner from his house. Linda sat in the idling car, waiting for him to arrive.

Aldric steadied his breathing and stood tall. He knew he had to be the strong one. Confidence in his stride, Aldric approached the car and opened the door.

"Is it done?" Linda asked.

"Yes," Aldric told her. "We'll be safe now."

Chapter 3
433 Years Ago

From far beyond the woods, Aldric could hear the town calling to him. It beckoned him; taunted him with the enticing lure of a world which he could never call home. Aldric tried to shake the perpetual longing from his mind; yet his ears remained tuned to the exotic sounds of life from the streets.

Locked behind his bedroom door, Aldric tried to focus on reading, but he was too easily distracted. Above him, the light bulb flickered a few times before stabilizing. Sitting on the bed in the corner of his room, leaning against the wall, Aldric stared at the light for a few minutes. He'd been told his entire life that he could visit the outside world when he was older, but he was tired of waiting. In the fifteen years of his life, he hadn't met a single person whose last name was not Nystrom. They told him he was a danger to himself and others – but he only transformed once every month. It didn't make sense that such a small portion of his life should define its entirety.

Glancing toward the window, Aldric toyed with the thought of escape for a brief moment. He wondered how long it would take anyone to realize that he'd left. Realistically, though, he knew there was no way he could be quiet enough to leave. If he could hear the town, he would be delusional if he believed his father couldn't hear something from within the house. Then, if someone saw him as he tried to make his way to town, they would catch him. Regardless of how hard he tried, Aldric knew he had no hope of outrunning Cade or his father.

Still, it was nice to pretend. He imagined himself climbing through the window and sneaking away. For just a night, he wanted to pretend he was a human.

A nearly imperceptible sound tore Aldric from his thoughts, and his eyes darted to the window. Just beyond it, a twig had snapped, so Aldric scanned the world beyond his bedroom walls. The sun was setting, but there was enough light for him to clearly see the emptiness outside. Cautiously, Aldric stood to his feet and walked toward the sound, ready for a fight. No one malicious had ever made their way to Aldric's home – but his father was consistently warning him of the possibility. The most likely scenario was that Cade was waiting to attack him – claiming that he wanted to train Aldric – but he had to be ready for any circumstance.

As Aldric approached the window, a hand peeked up into his field of view and signed the letters "O. K." Damien stood slowly as Aldric breathed a sigh of relief.

"What are you doing?" He signed to his younger brother. The only positive side of being trapped on their property constantly was that Aldric had plenty of time to read and to learn. He and Damien had learned American Sign Language in order to interact with each other under the radar. It was their own secret language. Their parents' support of Aldric's desire to learn had shocked him – they'd even retrieved books for them on a few dozen languages. Given how paranoid his father was, Aldric would have assumed he would stifle every attempt to learn anything which could be used to pass secrets.

Regardless, they had brought the books, and Aldric and Damien quickly gravitated toward Sign Language. Any other language still required sounds, so their family would be aware at the very least that they were communicating.

"I'm going to town," Damien replied.

"Are you serious?"

"Why not?"

"You'll never make it."

"Come on, Aldric, you know you want to see what it's like."

"Father won't allow it."

"Since when do you care?"

"I fear the consequences."

"So don't get caught."

"Easy for you to say. How did you get outside?"

"You just have to wait for them to be distracted. It's easy to hear anything when we're focusing, but even a werewolf can miss something if they aren't paying attention."

Aldric sighed, but signed nothing in response. Damien understood exactly what that meant, though. The two of them had fruitlessly planned their escape dozens of times. Maybe this was finally the night they got to see what was on the other side of their barrier of trees.

Aldric listened carefully, waiting for a moment that he could hear his father speaking. As soon as he did, Aldric carefully lifted his window just enough to slide through. Silently, he closed the window behind him. He and Damien pressed themselves against the cedar wall, desperately attempting to be stealthy. They inched their way to the back of the house where they were less likely to be noticed. Quietly as their panicked steps would allow, the brothers rushed across the open field and covered the short distance to the trees.

Breaking the tree line, they both collapsed. Despite their supernatural stamina, they were not immune to the effects of adrenaline, and their bodies needed a moment to adjust after their daring escape. After a moment, Aldric felt his heart slow to a normal rhythm, and he climbed back to his feet. The two of them regained their composure and wandered through the woods, careful to avoid leaving tracks as they headed toward town.

"I can't believe we actually made it," Aldric signed to his brother as the town grew closer. He hadn't heard any footsteps behind them and there were no shouts from the house to imply they'd been discovered. It was actually that easy for them to sneak out. Aldric wished he'd mustered up the courage to try earlier – but he was happy to share the experience with his brother.

"I told you it would be easy," Damien replied – a look of pure joy on his face. Aldric was terrified that the town wouldn't live up to his dreams after he'd been coveting it for his entire life – but it had to be better than being trapped in the same house for his entire life. He tried to convince himself that his parents meant well –

maybe they were actually concerned about their children's safety – but it was useless. They couldn't get away with hiding everything from him and then pretending it was for his own good.

Aldric beamed at Damien as he took a deep breath, steeling himself for the last few steps. Damien's smile faded more quickly than it had appeared, and a look of terror washed over his face. At first, Aldric thought he was joking, but the fear was too real. Aldric felt his own heart begin to pound as he turned around.

"You're both pretty sneaky," Cade greeted.

"We were just walking," Aldric tried to convince his brother.

"Right. To town."

"No!" Damien lied – sounding far too defensive to convince anyone.

"I get the appeal," Cade shrugged. "I always thought there was something mystical about it. When I actually went, though, I realized it doesn't live up to the expectation."

"Well why won't they let us go?" Aldric asked.

"You don't know control yet, and you're not prepared for the possibility that hunters show up. You have to learn to defend yourself."

Aldric didn't have a rebuttal. Cade had a way of making everything sound far more logical. Looking at Damien, he silently questioned whether the two of them were just being immature. Maybe it was for the best that they wait.

"I'll tell you what," Cade offered. "If you can beat me in a fight – both of you against me – I'll tell father that you're ready."

"Okay!" Aldric stood tall, accepting the challenge without hesitation. He'd trained with Cade enough times that he was sure he could get a single good hit. If all it took to convince his family to let him be his own person was defeating Cade, it was a small price to pay.

Not wasting a second, Damien rushed forward, throwing a punch at Cade. Cade effortlessly stepped to the side and drove an elbow into Damien's temple, knocking him out cold. Aldric sighed. Damien was always eager, and it clearly got him into trouble. If he'd taken the time to make a plan with Aldric, they may have stood a chance.

Despite the odds, Aldric lunged in and threw a round kick low, aiming for Cade's knee. Cade raised his shin to block the attack, but Aldric followed up with a jab to the nose as he landed. Cade leaned backward, narrowly avoiding Aldric's fist. Desperate to land a single attack, Aldric rushed forward with a flurry of punches. Not a single one broke Cade's guard, though, as he weaved through Aldric's offense.

Finally, Cade saw an opening and caught Aldric's fist. In one swift motion, he stepped in and drove his other arm into Aldric's elbow, shattering the bone. Aldric bit back the pain and kicked at Cade's knee once again, trying to break his knees. Cade lifted his leg and dodged the blow before throwing a kick to Aldric's jaw. Since he aimed for the side of the arm he'd already broken, Aldric was defenseless, and he felt his jaw crack open.

Dizzy, he rushed forward, throwing a punch with his good arm. Cade ducked down and executed the attack Aldric had tried to land twice already. In one smooth motion, Cade lifted his leg and drove it toward Aldric's knee, destroying his kneecap. Aldric dropped to the ground, but struggled to stand back up.

"Enough," Cade stopped him. "I think it's very clear to both of us that you aren't ready."

"I can't stay trapped in that place anymore, Cade."

"I know, buddy. So I'm not going to make you."

"What?"

"You can't protect yourself. That doesn't mean I can't protect you."

Present
6 Days Until the Full Moon

Sitting behind the wheel, Aldric followed the interstate without much of a plan. Beside him, Linda slept, resting her head against the window and breathing quietly and rhythmically. Even something as mundane as snoring had faded away with her transformation as her soft palate had reformed itself to allow more adequate air flow. Turning his eyes back to the road, Aldric searched for a mile marker. Eventually, he still wanted to make it to Arizona, but there wasn't a timeline anymore. He and Linda had been on the road for almost a week, trying to take the most convoluted route. Aldric wanted to be absolutely sure that no one was following them, so he had to avoid taking a straight shot to his final destination.

"Hey," Linda stirred. She looked toward him, slightly disoriented, before examining the road for any sign of their location. Blinking a few times, she adjusted herself and sat up taller in the chair. The sun had set, and the only light was coming from the headlights of Aldric's car, illuminating the asphalt in front of them. The plains on either side of him – aside from being a welcome change from the trees which had surrounded every home he'd had for most of his life – provided poor cover to anything which may be lurking in their path. That was part of the reason he'd taken such a circular path. Just to be certain that nothing could keep up with them, Aldric also drove well over the speed limit. He was confident that he wouldn't get pulled over in the middle of the night, but even if he did, he had enough fake licenses to burn one.

"Good morning," Aldric smiled. The sun had set hours ago, so Aldric assumed it was actually early morning. Apart from the occasional bathroom break, he'd driven for twelve consecutive hours, but Aldric was barely feeling tired. There was too much running through his mind for him to be distracted with sleep. His family had found him as soon as his wife had become pregnant, which had always been the reason he'd avoided having children. Aldric knew the rule about offspring, and he refused to put his child through that.

The more unsettling piece of information to Aldric, though, was that his father had been tracking him since he'd left. It couldn't possibly be a coincidence that he'd been found so close to Linda's due date. They'd just been waiting, and now they were trying to retrieve Aldric's family. They were trying to take his son.

"Where are we?" Linda asked. Aldric realized that she'd probably said something before to greet him, but he hadn't been paying any attention. Though he tried to focus on her, his attention had been divided since Cyrus had found them. The time she spent sleeping had become Aldric's respite because he didn't have to pretend he was calm and collected.

"Wyoming," Aldric answered. "We are almost there."

More likely than anything else, it was paranoia which drove Aldric to the vague answers. Regardless, it was better in his eyes to be sure no one could overhear. The plan was to circle around Arizona, drive through California and come back through the long way. That convoluted path would hopefully be enough to shake off anyone who had been following. Of course, along with that precaution, Aldric had been carefully listening for any presence which seemed suspicious. During the drive so far he hadn't noticed any reason to think someone had followed him. He clung to the unrealistic hope that they'd simply given up.

"I spy…" Linda started. They had exhausted every conversational topic Aldric could think of. Most things, though, went back to his family. They'd already discussed how the Nystroms had probably been watching Aldric since he'd left, and how they wanted to take Cailean back with them when he was born. Linda found it funny that Aldric had accepted the assumption that it was a boy. Then they'd moved on to attempts at making small talk, but they knew each other too well to bring up anything new.

"Linda," Aldric sighed.

"You lost them," Linda groaned, predicting Aldric's qualm. "They haven't been anywhere near us in a thousand miles at least. You need to try to relax."

"You didn't grow up with them."

"You've been away for over four hundred years."

"Not to them, apparently."

Silence hung in the air of the car as Aldric turned his complete focus toward the road. He searched his mind for the words to tell Linda to ease the tension, but he couldn't comfort himself – let alone someone else. Instead, he just let the quiet linger.

❖ ❖ ❖

Aldric stirred as the car rattled around him. Sitting up straighter as he fought off the fatigue, he observed his surroundings. He hadn't wanted to fall asleep but the constant driving had taken its toll on him. Somewhere in Nevada, Linda had insisted that she drive for a while, and he'd fallen asleep within minutes.

Searching behind the vehicle, Aldric scanned for any other cars or signs of life. They were driving across an unstable, rickety bridge which was probably even older than he was. There were wetlands beneath them, but Aldric couldn't detect much movement from within them. Most of the trees were dead and drying out despite the proximity to the river. Settling down, Aldric turned away from the passenger window to face forward.

"I haven't heard anything," Linda confirmed. She knew him well enough to know that it wouldn't have calmed him if she'd said anything before he performed his own search. It was still worthwhile to assure him that there was nothing he missed.

"Okay," Aldric nodded, breathing a sigh of relief. "No suspicious movement in the trees or anything either?"

"Aldric, you're paranoid."

"Did you notice anything?"

"A coyote or a fox here and there."

"A coyote or a fox?"

"Does it matter?"

"If you're uncertain, you can't guarantee it wasn't a wolf."

"I can to tell the difference between a five foot tall beast and a fox, Aldric," Linda sighed. She was exasperated, but she tried to hide it. Over the years they'd had to work through similar issues enough times for Linda to learn that Aldric wasn't going to change. He knew that his over-caution could be a burden at times, but he couldn't allow himself to lower his guard. He knew the measures his family would take to reach their goals. He had to remain vigilant.

"Linda," Aldric explained calmly. In the early phases of their relationship, his responses betrayed a hint of frustration, but he'd grown past that. Now he knew and understood her perspective. She hadn't shared past or grown up with a pack; there was no way she could entirely grasp the problem. "They will send the youngest. They'll take a thirteen-year-old who's only changed once and send them on a mission with a stockpile of wolfsbane and an old shirt. You can't imagine the lengths a young wolf will take to impress his father."

"So the wolf ages with you?"

"In a sense. Normally wolves would reach maturity far before thirteen years, but for a lycanthrope, the wolf… Wakes up, for lack of a better word. This happens around puberty, but the wolf isn't quite the size you'd expect from a young teenager. It starts off small – still a cub – the first change. After that, it matures rapidly, catching up with you in a few months."

"But if they send a young enough one, it would be about the size of a coyote," she acknowledged.

"So can you guarantee that you didn't see a wolf?"

"I can assure you that whatever I saw, it was hundreds of miles ago. The drive through California took us through sand dunes – there weren't places to hide. Even if they were following us – which I'm sure they weren't – they're gone now."

Aldric nodded and sighed as his form of acceptance. It was the best response he was going to get, and she made cogent arguments. Even without actively looking one would have been able to detect a wolf tracking them through sand in the middle of the day. Still, given the strong scent of gasoline, their vehicle left a trail a werewolf could track for miles, so Aldric was concerned that it wouldn't even be close enough to see.

"So this is it?" Linda spoke up after a few more moments of silence.

"Our new home," Aldric smiled, trying to focus on the moment. For the past week, he hadn't had a particularly good conversation with his wife. Since he saw Cyrus, Aldric had become a mess. While he was well aware of that, he hadn't been able to change anything. His unborn child was his top priority, and there was no doubt in his mind that his father would try to take it. Still, he had to accept that they'd done everything imaginable and there was no sign of his family. If they were to return, he would have to deal with it then. Until then, his pregnant wife still needed him to be present.

"Do you want me to take over?" Aldric asked.

"That's alright," she shrugged. "I like driving. It's relaxing."

Aldric twitched for a minute, but he pushed that sentence out of his mind. He knew it wasn't what she meant, but his mind instantly jumped to a concern that if she was too relaxed she wouldn't be on the lookout.

"Alright then. So… I spy…"

"Stop," she laughed.

"What?"

"I know you're not the car games type."

"I'm whatever type makes you smile."

"That was cheesy," she smiled, looking at him. "And I don't even think it's necessarily a good thing."

"Okay, cut me some slack, I was a hermit for the first twenty years of my life."

"Proportional to an average lifespan, that's less than three years."

"Don't math me," Aldric laughed. They both fell silent as they passed the first exit which led to a town.

"Want to check it out?" Linda asked.

"I suppose we can make a brief detour," Aldric responded as he glanced over his shoulder. There were no other cars – or movement of any kind – detectable to him.

Linda took the exit and slowed down as she entered a small town. Right off the freeway were a few gas stations which hadn't been used in well over a century. As she continued driving, there were still dozens of signs advertising restaurants long since closed. It wasn't more than a few minutes before they moved from businesses to what appeared to be more residential.

An old traffic light had collapsed, blocking the road to their left. Aldric tried to read the letters on a beaten-down green sign hanging from the other light, but the writing had faded ages ago. The buildings appeared to have lasted relatively well, but that made sense to Aldric. Without people, there wasn't much aside from the sun to wear down the buildings. The area was relatively devoid of natural disasters.

An eerie air surrounded the town. Aldric was in awe at the thought that this had once been a bustling town – something similar to the one he'd dreamt of just beyond his home. Children had gone to the school with the purple gates and broken marquee. People had lived in the houses which now stood with peeled paint and dead grass. The large, empty buildings used to be grocery stores selling food to citizens. Now, there was nothing but an aura of death.

"It's always amazing to see how time affects these places," Linda commented. "I know it's morbid, but I don't think I can ever get tired of looking at all of these ghost towns."

"There are a few around here a lot bigger than this one. Maybe we'll visit them some time."

"Yeah," she smiled as she turned the car around. Linda headed back out of town, driving down a street which had likely been one of the busiest in town. Now, they were in the only vehicle. She turned right and continued driving as both of them admired the peculiar vibe of the town. This wasn't the first time they'd found an empty town along the road as they looked for a new house, but it never stopped filling Aldric with a sense of wonder. It was a symbol of a past life – a relic to an era long gone.

"What's this on the left?" Linda asked, gesturing with a nod.

"I don't know," Aldric shrugged. "It looks like some sort of landmark."

"Let's explore."

"Okay, sure," Aldric agreed. He didn't have any specific timeline, so it was probably fine to spend a few hours wandering around.

They parked the car and walked out, looking around the area a bit. As they approached the building, it became more and more clear what the were looking at. A guard tower still stood tall over the entrance. The structure was crafted almost entirely of stone, implying to Aldric that it had been around even longer than he himself had.

Touching the stone, Aldric allowed himself to bask in the mysticism of something ancient. The corridors were open to the environment, and the cells lacked the most basic amenities. Wrought iron bars blocked the doors and the entryways to the corridors. As he turned a corner and passed through a gate, Aldric admired the building materials – mostly just impressed by the fact that they'd lasted so long.

An almost indistinguishable step on the stone around the corner made Aldric stop in his tracks. Silently, he motioned for Linda to stand still, and she froze. The sound didn't repeat itself, but Aldric focused intently for a full minute. Then, there was another step.

Aldric pressed himself against the wall as he waited for the person to approach. The second the figure turned the corner, Aldric grabbed him and pinned him against the wall. He recognized the face. Somehow, Cyrus had actually followed them the entire way.

"How did you track us?" Aldric asked.

"You're not hard to predict," he laughed.

"I warned you, boy."

"You wouldn't do it."

Aldric punched Cyrus in the stomach as he dropped him to the floor. Cyrus fell, coughing up blood. Before he could stand back up, Aldric kicked him in the face. Cyrus rolled over before pushing his jaw back into place and struggling to his feet.

Linda backed up, but Cyrus was now between her and Aldric, so Aldric rushed forward. He kicked Cyrus's shin, shattering the bone. As Cyrus pitched forward, Aldric caught his shoulders and drove his knee into Cyrus's nose. Stepping to the side, he tossed the boy behind him and moved to block his path to Linda.

Dripping blood on the stone floor, Cyrus stood and wiped his nose. He spat angrily as his body repaired itself. The narrow corridor didn't lend itself well to Aldric's fighting style – it inhibited his ability to move to the side much, limiting his options in dodges and counters. That, along with the anger, forced him to change his approach. Even though Cyrus was unrefined, Aldric didn't want to give him the chance to land a hit.

"You don't understand, do you?" Cyrus taunted. "I'm not here to hurt you. I'm here to save you."

"I think we have a different understanding," Aldric replied calmly, not dropping his guard. It was confusing to him that the boy hadn't thrown an attack yet, but he wasn't willing to walk into a trap.

"I told you before. I had to test you."

"You went a little far for that."

"Look, Uncle. I wasn't the only one sent after you. Maybe it's still my youthful ignorance, but I think you can be saved. My father is less inclined to bring you in alive. He only cares about the child."

"How have you managed to track me before an experienced hunter?"

"Father is amazing at a lot of things, but he doesn't know how to ask for help," Cyrus laughed. "A willingness to ask locals and an understanding of forgery got me a long way."

"Well, let it aid you in your long journey home."

"Fine," Cyrus groaned, reaching behind him. Aldric lunged forward, grabbing Cyrus's arm before he could draw the knife. Quickly, though, he reached back with the other hand and pulled the knife out, stabbing it toward Aldric. Aldric caught that arm as well, grappling with the boy. Cyrus brought a foot up, kicking Aldric in the groin, then plunged the silver knife into Aldric's arm. He pulled the knife out and tried to stab again, but Aldric caught his hand.

Not a full second passed as Aldric processed what he knew to be his best chance. He didn't like it, but it was the only way to end the fight quickly. Holding Cyrus's hand in his, he pulled the knife into his own shoulder. Using his shoulder as leverage, Aldric twisted Cyrus's wrist and broke it, forcing him to let go. Staggering backward, Cyrus growled. Aldric had intentionally twisted his opponent's wrist as he broke the bones. Although the bones would heal rapidly, they would not be quite perfectly aligned.

Aldric struggled to his feet and removed the knife, tossing it behind him. Linda quickly grabbed it and held it up, ready to provide backup if necessary. Cyrus muttered something as he broke the bones of his wrist back into place.

Cyrus threw a punch at Aldric's face, but Aldric ducked. The boy wasn't skilled enough to pull his punch back, so he drove his fist into the stone. Aldric rose with an uppercut, but Cyrus fell onto his back to avoid the attack. Rolling over his back shoulder, he jumped back to his feet.

Closing the distance quickly, Cyrus jumped and pushed off the wall, propelling himself higher as he drove his fist downward. Aldric stepped back, avoiding the showy attack and driving an elbow to the back of Cyrus's head.

Cyrus dropped to the ground like a brick, and Aldric followed up with a heel kick aimed to Cyrus's skull. Cyrus rolled out of the way, but he ran into the wall. That still gave him enough distance to narrowly avoid Aldric's kick. Cyrus used the wall for support as he climbed to his feet as quickly as he could. Aldric threw a punch toward his face, but he couldn't put much force into it as he fought through the pain of his multiple stab wounds. Cyrus crossed his arms above his head and blocked the punch.

While Aldric was distracted, Cyrus drove a knee into his stomach. As Aldric staggered backward, Cyrus rushed in. Aldric spun to the side and drove his palm into the back of Cyrus's neck. Cyrus turned and pinned Aldric to the wall, pushing his forearm into Aldric's neck. Throwing a punch toward Aldric's face, Cyrus smirked – not realizing Aldric had allowed him to do exactly that. Aldric parried the blow, directing it into the stone next to him. Aldric heard Cyrus's knuckles break as they connected with the wall inches from his head.

Aldric punched Cyrus's throat, and the boy stumbled backward, falling against the other side of the corridor. Following up, Aldric kicked Cyrus's face – careful to only hit hard enough to knock the boy out.

Struggling against his bleeding wounds, Aldric opened one of the doors to the cells and heaved Cyrus into it.

"Hand me the knife," he ordered.

"Aldric, you don't have to kill him," Linda argued. She didn't sound fully convinced herself. It was clear that he'd already followed them across the country, so there was no denying that he'd continue to do so.

"Linda, give me the knife."

"Okay," she replied hesitantly. She placed the blade in his hand, and Aldric looked down at the boy on the ground in front of him. Aldric's wounds were finally starting to close, but that meant it wasn't long before Cyrus was up as well. Still, Aldric couldn't allow himself to kill a defenseless child.

He slammed the iron bars closed. The cell doors had bars which extended to the side, attaching to a small hole meant for a padlock. Aldric drove the knife through the hole and grabbed the edge, bending it and locking it in place. The silver burned his hand, but he powered through it.

After a few minutes, Cyrus stirred and stood up. He grabbed the bars and shook them angrily as Aldric stepped back.

"Where is Cade?"

"I don't know!" Cyrus yelled angrily.

"Then you can rot here," Aldric taunted.

"You think these bars can hold a werewolf?"

"Do you know what happens to the starving body?"

"What?"

"When your cells run out of energy from food, they begin searching for anything to continue operating. First, they'll consume the fat on your body. You really don't have much of that, to be honest, so that stage won't last long. Then, it will move on to the protein. That's your muscle. You'll slowly degrade until there's nothing left."

"No," Cyrus started to argue, but Aldric cut him off.

"That's a human, of course. We're different, you see. Not in the process, but in the length of time. Your cells will also try to heal as you consume yourself. You'll feel every painstaking moment of yourself falling apart – becoming nothing. Even your wolf won't have the strength to break free from here."

Aldric was bluffing, at least to an extent, but all he had to do was be sure that Cyrus was terrified enough to tell him the truth. This was the only way he could guarantee an honest answer.

"No, I'll change in six days. The wolf won't be trapped in here."

"Silver is holding that door closed. A wolf can't break it."

"Please, let me out," Cyrus begged, his tone dramatically shifting.

"Where is Cade?"

"He's looking for you as well. He isn't far behind me, but we haven't been in touch. I don't know where he is."

"So he knows where I am? Then he knows where you are. Maybe he will save you."

"No! No if you leave me here, I'll die, Uncle. He won't find me. You can't do this."

"That's all I needed to know," Aldric said as he turned to walk away. Linda gave him a concerned look, but she didn't audibly argue. The two of them walked solemnly through the prison as Cyrus called to them, pleading as he shook the bars angrily.

Finally, they got in the car and started driving away. Both were silent until they were far enough that Cyrus's calls faded away.

"Are we really going to let him die?"

"If he doesn't break the bars on his own before the change, his wolf will. If somehow it can't, I'm sure Cade is close enough to hear the wolf howl as it calls for help. I wouldn't have left him if I weren't confident he'd get out. I had to scare him, though, to get an honest answer. Anyway, this gives us time to get far away without him tracking us."

"Okay," Linda accepted. "So where do we go now?"

"Find the nearest town."

"What?"

"The last thing they would expect is for us to stay close. They'll immediately fan out, trying to find us in some remote place. In reality, we will be within one hundred miles of this prison."

"The best way to fit in," she muttered as she nodded.

Chapter 4

433 Years Ago

Cade pushed a branch to the side as Aldric and Damien walked underneath. Anticipation grew and Aldric felt his heart pounding. The town was close – he could smell it. For the first time in his life, he was finally going to experience what it felt like to be human.

Never would he have guessed that Cade would be the one leading him to that. He had always assumed his older brother was too fond of their father to ever disobey his wishes. Cade was an enforcer – always pressuring the others into fulfilling their father's will. There seemed to be more to him than Aldric had thought.

Of course, there were plenty of times Cade had helped his brothers. He was always there to protect them and he was constantly training them to fight. Aldric wasn't a fan of that aspect of their lives, but he understood the necessity. At least, he understood why Cade found it so important. He hadn't actually seen hunters, but from the way his father talked about them he didn't assume they were a myth. It was vital to be prepared, and Cade was playing his role in ensuring that his younger siblings were.

Outside of that, Cade was still a brother. He'd still play games with the others, laugh and tell jokes, and partake in deep conversations in the middle of the night. Cade was rough around the edges, but he was still an older brother. Aldric never questioned the fact that Cade valued their relationship – family was the most important thing to him. It wasn't that he was necessarily afraid of his brother, he just saw Cade as an agent of their father to some degree.

In that moment, though, as Cade allowed Aldric to cross the tree line and admire the town in front of him, Aldric knew that his perceptions had been wrong. At the very least, there were more layers to his brother than he had assumed. Before turning to the town, Aldric noticed Cade's smile. His brother was overjoyed to be sharing that experience with him.

Cade had known for years how much Aldric wanted to see the outside world. He'd always given the same excuses their father had, though. They were a danger to everyone. If a hunter discovered them they could condemn everyone.

The possibility that Aldric hadn't been prepared for, though, was the fact that he'd be completely overwhelmed. That wasn't an excuse his parents had used before, but at a young age, someone may not be prepared for the transition into the outside world. Granted, Aldric probably would have shrugged that reasoning off as well, despite its logic. Even if it hadn't convinced him, at least that one wouldn't have been a paranoid lie.

As Aldric took in the view in front of him, he felt paralyzed. There were buildings made of steel – which he'd only ever read about. His own home was constructed of wood, and it lacked that metallic shine. There were cars driving by, and some of them had multiple people in them – as many as his entire family. In a matter of a second, Aldric could watch cars pass him and see more people than he could count.

The smell of gasoline assaulted Aldric, but he actually appreciated it. It was stronger than it ever had been, of course, but it smelled like freedom. The clear air of the woods had become a prison to him – and anything else just reminded him of his freedom, temporary as it may be.

Across the street was a movie theater, and Aldric stared as dozens – maybe hundreds – of people poured out of the building as their film ended. No two people looked the same – different ages and races all leaving that one area, united by something. Young men in T-shirts and jeans, others in slacks and dress shirts. Girls in flowing dresses, their hair curled and make-up bringing out a light in their eyes brighter than any he'd ever seen. The smell of their perfume overpowered the gasoline as he focused on it, and it was pure bliss.

Food was another powerful scent. Aldric couldn't sort out any individual scents because they were all things he'd never tried before. He could count the restaurants, though, on every corner. In the plaza with the theater alone there were at least five different places with completely different smells emanating from them. Some of those restaurants had tables scattered around outside of them, and there were people sitting at the tables, talking and eating. People spending time with friends unrelated to them, eating meals and bonding. Aldric could hear the laughter as groups told stories and shared memories.

The light flooded into Aldric's eyes as well, almost more than he could handle. It seemed as though everything in town radiated a light of its own. Headlights, streetlamps, phones, signs. The stars themselves were overpowered by the creations of man. Aldric wondered how the light didn't blind the humans within.

Signs were placed everywhere because there were far too many people to communicate verbally. Flashing lights seemed to direct the cars, and they had signs hanging from them. There were red signs at the end of some of the roads, and yellow signs other places. The sheer variation of color which painted the town was enough to mesmerize him.

Buildings towered over Aldric. He thought he was used to tall buildings because his home was two stories, but he was wrong. Some buildings there seemed as though they were reaching for the stars – trying to find them after they'd been hidden by the lights of the city.

"Aldric," Cade spoke up. His voice simultaneously seemed loud and distant, but he was directly behind Aldric. Aldric's mind, though, was somewhere else.

"Aldric," Cade repeated, placing a hand on his brother's shoulder.

"What?" Aldric finally responded.

"This is just a picture."

"What do you mean?" Damien spoke up, apparently being pulled from his own thoughts by Cade's strange statement.

"I mean," Cade answered slowly, searching his mind for the proper words. "What we're looking at is a piece of the town. Experienced from the outside. There's so much more."

"Let's go," Aldric chirped, excitement dripping from his lips.

"I don't know," Cade hesitated. "You both seem mesmerized by this. Maybe this is enough for one day."

"No," Aldric insisted. "Please Cade. I want to see more."

"Okay. Just please, stay close to me, okay?"

"Okay!"

Damien nodded his agreement as well, and the two of them followed Cade as he walked down the hill, finding a dark place to sneak into the town. Cade seemed to deliberately avoid crowds as he led them around a corner. The lights dulled rapidly as they left the bustling city center, but it was still far brighter than anything Aldric was used to. Street lights still illuminated the area, and Aldric could see rows of houses. He couldn't imagine how many people must live in those homes.

At the end of the street there was a small park with vibrant green grass. There was a structure in the middle with people standing around it. A few girls around Aldric's age were swinging back and forth on plastic seats attached to the structure by chains hanging from the top pole. Aldric couldn't understand how it was fun, but they appeared to be having the time of their lives.

"What are they doing?" Aldric asked.

"Swinging," Cade replied nonchalantly.

"Obviously. On what?"

"Swings?"

"There's no way they're called that."

"You swing on them."

"Apt," Aldric accepted.

"I want to try," Damien pitched in.

"No, we don't want to get too close to them," Cade declined, holding Damien back. Aldric rushed forward anyway, and Cade sighed as he followed him. He would do his best to follow Cade's wishes and stay as far away as possible, but he wanted to play at that park. There were plenty of things besides the swings.

Aldric found a bar suspended in the air by two other poles. He approached it, confused as he examined it.

"What's this for?" Aldric asked. Cade laughed, but he didn't answer. Instead, he jumped up and grabbed the bar, lifting himself above it. Releasing his hold, Cade dropped to the ground.

"What?" Aldric asked.

"It's a pull-up."

Aldric jumped back up and tried. It was far easier than he'd expected, so he did a few of them. He could feel the muscles he was using, but they weren't growing tired. Maybe this was just a way that humans exercised. It dawned on Aldric that they had to work in order for things like this to become easy.

After his fifteenth pull-up, he caught the eye of the girl on the swing. She glanced down, and he looked back away.

"Okay, that's enough," Cade whispered.

"It's easy."

"Don't make a scene."

Aldric groaned as he dropped down. Damien tried a few as well, but he dropped more quickly than Aldric, probably scared to upset Cade.

"I want to talk to that girl," Aldric told Cade.

"No," he laughed.

"I think she likes me. She was watching me, and she's really pretty."

He'd never seen a more beautiful girl, but that wasn't a very high bar. Still, he was confident that her beauty was unparalleled. She looked toward him again as her raven black hair swayed with her movements. She waved and he felt his heart skip a beat before he waved back.

"No," Cade repeated. "Trust me, she isn't worth it."

"What do you mean?"

"You can only love one person. What you're feeling right now is a chemical reaction, and you'll get over it. It's time to leave."

"How do you know who you love?"

"You'll choose the right person."

"When?"

"When you're older," Cade scolded, dragging them away. Distracted by Aldric, Cade didn't notice Damien rush ahead. He stood in the street, staring at something. Aldric turned to see the most beautiful painting strewn across the side of a building. Every color he could imagine was displayed, but he couldn't quite tell what the picture was supposed to represent.

A horn blared, though, and Aldric's attention was ripped from the picture. Just in time to see the car approach Damien, Aldric turned his head. Damien's small body was lifted from the ground and propelled forward with the impact and he rolled a few times when he hit the ground.

"Damien!" Cade yelled as he ran toward his brother. The car stopped, and the two people in the vehicle frantically jumped out. Aldric froze, completely unsure of how to respond. He looked behind him and the two girls from the park rushed toward them, concern on their faces. Lights from a few windows illuminated as people looked outside, apparently alerted by the car horn. Aldric felt his heart pounding. His brain screamed to move, but his legs refused to respond. He heard the horn blaring although the sound had long since faded. Finally, Cade's voice rang through.

"Come on!" He called. Aldric turned to face him. Cade was lifting Damien but looking at Aldric. The driver of the car was asking if he should call an ambulance. One of the girls was already on her phone. Aldric couldn't respond to all of them, and Cade wasn't saying anything.

"Come. Now." Cade started running, carrying Damien with him. Finally, Aldric's muscles responded and he followed after Cade, running as fast as he could. The people called after them, telling them to wait, but Aldric just ran faster.

Present
Night of the Full Moon

Aldric leaned back on the couch, watching the clock tick away the last few hours of his morning. Every month, the wolf took a full day from him – even though the transformation didn't begin until evening. Typically, he just spent the day dreading the change. Sometimes he would ponder different ways to fight the curse, but that had started to feel like a hopeless battle. Now, he just watched the clock, waiting to get the night over with.

"Aldric," Linda sighed, sitting next to him. She didn't follow with anything, though, probably because she knew that it would be futile. They'd been through too many full moons together for her to still believe there was a way to distract Aldric.

Even before the moon rose, Aldric could feel the wolf under his skin. He was irritable – so much so that he'd taken the day off from job hunting. His senses were in overdrive, and he felt as though he could perceive every sight and smell. There was a sense of longing, but it wasn't his own.

"Let's go," he broke the silence as he stood.

"What? We still have hours."

"Yes, but maybe it will be a distraction. I've never lived in a desert, so we can drive around until we get so far in the middle of the desert that we know we won't be traced."

"I guess that sounds like the most fun we can possibly have given the phase of the moon," she laughed.

"We'll just pretend it's sightseeing."

"It is sightseeing, technically."

"Alright, let's go," Aldric urged. He was mostly just excited to focus his mind on some task – even if that task was completely centered around the wolf.

"Hold on," Linda groaned as she stood. Pregnancy seemed to take its toll even on a werewolf. She seemed to be handling everything well, but she couldn't hide that the baby's constant kicking was wearing her out. Aldric wondered if the child could somehow sense the change coming and was reacting to it. That or his child was just already a warrior – kicking and fighting before he was even born.

She retreated to their room to start packing a bag. Aldric looked around the house, admiring the work they'd done over the past week. While he had spent most of his time submitting his application to local firms, Linda had managed to furnish most of the house. He'd helped a bit, but she had done most of the heavy lifting. The living room, kitchen, and guest bathroom were embellished with paintings and decorations.

On the mantle above the fireplace, Linda had placed a few framed pictures of her and Aldric. Candles adorned the coffee table which rested between a matching gray couch and love seat. The tile floor beneath the furniture was covered with a soft, white rug. The curtains on the window were draped open, so Aldric pulled them closed as he prepared to leave.

Before following his wife to the bedroom, Aldric moved to the family room adjacent to the living room. The brown carpet beneath his feet felt like fur, although he was sure it wasn't. A few chairs were placed near the window, looking out into their back yard. The water in the pool shimmered in the light of the sun. To his left, there was a bookshelf with a few dozen books stacked on it, and a desk rested to the side of that.

Linda had gone out of her way to make the house look "lived-in." Even outside of the obviously visible places, such as the bookshelf. In the cabinet at the bottom of the shelf were decks of cards and a few board games. She'd fully stocked the desk with paper, pens, and notebooks to look as though Aldric brought his work home with him. In the top notebook, she'd even scribbled a few pages worth of notes. It was nothing more than basic calculations, but it was enough to rid any possible suspicion someone may have at a quick glance.

She had become incredibly skilled at fabricating a long life. It appeared as though they'd accumulated years' worth of books and other items, but she'd purchased them all within a day. It wasn't the first time they'd had to move quickly and leave most of their things, so she had far more experience with that than she should have had. Aldric hoped that one day he'd be able to find a place they could settle down so she wouldn't have to keep up the charade. Deep down, he knew that he probably already had enough money saved away to perpetually replenish itself – he didn't particularly need a few more years – but he was cautious because he had to make sure he would be able to provide for his child as well.

A few minutes passed as Aldric pondered his financial plans, which granted him a welcome distraction. Absentmindedly, though, he found himself in the kitchen. He'd barely processed how hungry he was, but the wolf seemed to be ravenous. Aldric opened the fully stocked refrigerator and removed a few pounds of meat, preparing sandwiches for himself and his wife.

Even the kitchen was flawlessly assembled. Dishes were not only neatly sorted in the cupboards, but Linda had managed to intentionally chip a few of them to simulate years of usage. Every utensil imaginable was present somewhere, and everything had its place. Decorative towels hung from the door of the oven and a pair of oven mitts rested on a nail in the wall. This was a room Linda actually used, though, so it was logical that she'd want it fully operational.

Aldric walked through the house, carrying a plate with a very thick sandwich in either hand. No matter how many times he lived through the transformation, he always forgot to eat enough. His mind was just never particularly focused on the hunger.

Walking past the guest room, Aldric admired his wife's attention to detail once again. The furniture in the room was very minimal – just a bed and a dresser. The wooden dresser matched the bed frame, though, and the tan carpet beneath it. A white sliding door protected the closet, which was empty. A light blue curtain fell over the window, and the bed was made with sheets and a blanket matching that color. It didn't have to be anything particularly fancy given that they didn't actually plan on having guests, but it was something. Just in case anyone was to look around their house for any reason, it appeared that they had a purpose for the room.

The guest bathroom had matching towels on each of the rails – one closer to the shower and one near the sink. The blue shower curtain was closed, but it hid a shower with a bottle of shampoo, conditioner, and body wash. A bottle of hand soap rested next to the sink, and she'd poured a tiny bit out so it looked as though it was used.

The second bedroom was the last to be furnished. It had been a surprise one day when he got home from an interview, but she'd completely transformed the room into a gym for him. There was a pull-up bar, but that was mostly for aesthetics. A punching bag was set up in the corner, along with a wooden dummy for Wing Chun.

Just in time to find Linda zipping up the bag with their clothes, Aldric stepped into their room. It was the only room which hadn't been decorated. Finding the time had been difficult with everything else, but they also considered that the least important room to furnish. They had a bed, and there wasn't much else necessary in a bedroom.

"I made you a sandwich," Aldric greeted as he extended a plate toward her.

"Thanks," she replied gratefully. The two of them, apparently far hungrier than they realized, devoured the food in silence.

"Are you ready to sightsee?" Linda asked, setting the plate aside.

"I thought you'd never ask."

❖ ❖ ❖

Thirty miles past the end of the paved road, Aldric finally stopped the car. Nothing but desert surrounded them, and the setting sun illuminated the horizon. The orange hues lit the entire sky aflame.

"It's beautiful," Linda gasped, leaning back in her seat. As the sun fell, darkness overtook most of the sky, leaving a clear boundary between the dark, empty blue and the purple, fading into the orange of the sun. Aldric opened his door and sat on the hood of the car. Linda followed closely behind him. It was moments like that when Aldric appreciated his long life. There were still things he had yet to experience, regardless of how long he'd lived. Despite the darkness and pain that surrounded that night, there was still beauty to be seen.

The moon, surrounded by a vast ocean of stars, quickly replaced the sun, and the land fell dark. Without the light from the sun, the sky which had appeared void only moments ago now teemed with life from smaller lights. Even with the full moon shining above them, Aldric couldn't see much of the landscape around him. He could smell miles away, though, and there was no trace of humanity.

The low bushes and shrubs didn't provide any cover whatsoever, and the flat landscape would allow him to see miles away in better lighting, but it would also allow them to be seen. Aldric was fully confident, though, that they were far enough from any civilization to go unnoticed.

The dirt beneath him shifted as he removed his shoes. The sand was already cool, although the sun had barely set. That was probably the most impressive part of a desert in his mind. During the day, the heat was often intense, and walking in the sand could burn. At night, though, there was a drastic shift. Without the sun to warm the ground, the temperatures dropped rapidly, even below freezing during certain times.

Aldric felt the wolf pushing its way forward, just as eager to explore the new surroundings as Aldric was. As the moon climbed, the wolf scratched at Aldric's insides with an increasing ferocity.

"It's already starting for you, isn't it?" Linda asked. She didn't show any sign of the wolf yet, but she was probably hiding it well.

"It's faster for purebreds," Aldric confirmed once again. It wasn't the first time they'd had that exchange, and Aldric knew it wouldn't be the last.

Linda nodded. Her face betrayed the fact that she wanted him to give up fighting, but she would never tell him that. Although she hated seeing him hurt, she wanted to be supportive – and she hated the wolf just as much as he did.

Aldric wondered if the cacti surrounding them proposed a threat. Would the wolf be cognizant enough to avoid them? Of course, he'd been through worse, but Aldric still wasn't fond of the idea of waking up with dozens of needles protruding from his body.

The two of them stripped and placed their clothes in the bag. Opening the car door, Aldric tossed the bag, with the keys in it, inside. He was confident no one would try to steal their vehicle in the middle of the desert. To assure that they didn't destroy their transportation, Aldric and Linda wandered a good distance away.

Aldric bit back the pain as the wolf struggled for supremacy. Though he'd fought the change every month for four hundred years, he had never won. Nonetheless, he toyed with the possibility in his mind. It was evident to him that he was able to retain his humanity far longer than he had been as a child, so he was gaining time. Even if he only held the wolf back for one second longer each full moon, over the course of centuries that would accumulate to a full night.

Aldric's knees broke and he fell forward into the sand, which covered his fingers. He wasn't sure if it was better or worse that he couldn't see them as the bones shattered and the hands changed shape. He preferred to avoid watching as the claws forced their way from his fingertips, but he wondered if witnessing it gave him a bit of extra power to fight back. Maybe it was piece of motivation he needed.

Linda collapsed, but she kept silent. As her elbows shattered and her limbs took on a new shape, Aldric could see her clenching her teeth. Her nose grew and her jaw followed quickly after, forming her face into a snout. With the painful part of the transformation over, she breathed a heavy sigh of relief. Aldric wondered if the wolf felt the pain of the transformation as well.

His father had always told him that he and the wolf were the same, but that never made sense to Aldric. He couldn't remember what the wolf thought or did, and he blacked out when it had control. Maybe his father was right, and they were two halves of the same coin. Either way, Aldric wondered if that form could feel pain – because if it could, he couldn't remember.

Fur grew to cover Linda's new body, but Aldric continued to fight his own change. His spine shattered, but he refused to allow his back to bend. Mustering every ounce of strength he had, Aldric maintained the shape of his back to a human form. Eventually, though, his resolve lapsed for a second. That was long enough for the bones to begin healing, taking on a new shape.

Aldric's palms became paws, and face became a snout. Refusing to surrender, Aldric experienced every painstaking second of the transformation. He could practically feel the individual cells as they were chemically reverted to a stem cell state, only to grow once again into something new.

The reformation process didn't seem to hurt, but the degradation of every part of him was agonizing. Each nerve cell fired an impulse to his brain before it died, and he could feel his entire body decomposing.

Finally, the pain became more than Aldric could take. His vision blurred and the green of the succulents and shrubs around him melded into the brown of the ground. The colors seemed to blend together, darkening like two drops of paint slowly being integrated into one dark orb. Finally, Aldric could see nothing beyond the black.

Another minute passed where he was still aware of his surroundings. Although he couldn't see through the eyes of the wolf, he could feel the cool sand sifting through his paws. He could smell the plants and the wildlife around them. He could hear the chirping of the birds and the movement of creatures as the desert biome came to life – the animals finally moving from the burrows in which they hid from the sun.

A rattling sound startled him, but he couldn't control his reaction to it. Aldric felt a crunch as the wolf crushed the head of a snake. His mind raced, almost as if the wolf were trying to process what it had just killed. It had never seen such a creature before, but it was fascinated. Thoughts became difficult for Aldric, and they started to blur just as his vision had. Somewhere deep down, he knew the name for that type of snake. For some reason, though, he couldn't summon forth the knowledge. A moment later, he realized that he couldn't even think of what the creature was called. The fogginess overpowered his thoughts until he could think nothing at all, and the wolf finally had control.

Chapter 5
433 Years Ago

"Come on," Damien urged Aldric, signing with pleading eyes. "I have to go again."

"No! You almost died last time."

"You know I wasn't going to die."

"What if they had been hunters?"

"Have you ever seen a hunter?"

"Why would father lie?"

"To control us."

"I can't deny that," Aldric admitted. "But I also can't confirm it. It isn't worth the risk."

It had only been a week since the last time they visited town, and Aldric was still reeling from the events. It was amazing, of course, seeing so many people in one place, but last time had placed all of them in harm's way.

Their father had somehow known what they had done when they returned. Maybe he hadn't known, and he'd just heard the commotion and realized that his sons weren't home. Within the first few seconds of being questioned, however they all had given in. No one had the courage to lie to their father, especially when they had no idea how much he already knew.

Cade was still locked in the basement. From the books Aldric had read, being grounded sounded as though it were just staying at home all day for a set period of time. Really it was significantly more drastic than that. Cade, who had taken the brunt of the blame for his younger brothers, was locked in the same dark room for two weeks.

Aldric and Damien had been let off the hook surprisingly easy. Aldric wondered if his father assumed the fear – witnessing what had happened to Damien and then to Cade – would be enough of a punishment. For Aldric, he was correct. Damien, however, seemed only to be invigorated by everything he'd experienced in town. Every night he'd begged Aldric to go back with him.

Aldric turned and walked back to his room, closing the door behind him. He refused to entertain the idea any longer. It was his duty as an older brother to protect Damien, and at that moment, that meant not giving him everything he wanted.

For the next few hours, Aldric rested on his bed and read. He couldn't make much progress, though, because his mind was elsewhere. Aldric looked out his window, watching the sun set. Every second felt like an eternity, but somehow the minutes flew by. With each blink, Aldric could still see the flash of light and Damien's limp body flying down the street. He could still hear the car horn. How his brother was not completely petrified by that simply baffled Aldric.

In the shadows outside his window, Aldric saw movement. It was just a blur – a shifting shadow gone in a blink – but it was there. Panic set in as Aldric wondered if someone had found them. Maybe the hunters had just waited, stalking their prey for the past week. There wasn't a possibility in his mind that they hadn't heard of the chaos which followed the three boys who wandered into town and sprinted out after one of them was hit by a car. That is, if the hunters were a real threat of course.

Quietly, Aldric opened his window, trying to get a better look. He tried to convince himself that the movement had been just a trick of the light reflecting in the glass, but as he stared out toward the edge of the woods, he saw a figure standing there. It didn't seem large enough to be an adult, so he guessed it wasn't a hunter. It took a full minute for it to dawn on him that Damien was standing there, listening to the town as Aldric himself had done countless times.

Then, as if spurred by a sudden burst of motivation, Damien sprinted into the woods.

"No," Aldric muttered, hesitating briefly as he wondered what to do. If he told his father, Damien would only get punished. Maybe he could pull him back and talk some sense into him before anyone else had to find out. Aldric threw himself forward, awkwardly falling out of his window and stumbling to his feet as he broke into a run.

Following his brother's scent, Aldric pushed his way through the trees. When he saw Damien, though, he was ducked behind a bush. Barely able to stop himself from barreling into the boy, Aldric skidded to a stop next to him. Damien frantically motioned for Aldric to duck, so he obeyed.

"What is it?" Aldric asked.

"I heard footsteps."

"They were probably mine."

Damien just shook his head, disregarding the possibility. As if in response to his doubt, Aldric heard the footsteps as well. There was a slight rustling in the trees as branches were moved aside. Something felt strange about the movements, though. They were calculated.

"Do you think it's campers?" Damien signed – the fear apparent on his face.

"No. Go home. Get dad."

"What?"

"Just do it. Tell him I ran out here."

"We don't know that they're dangerous."

"We've never heard footsteps out here. You think the timing is a coincidence?"

"Probably not," Damien admitted.

"Now go. Run home. Send dad back."

"Okay," Damien hesitantly agreed. He backed away slowly.

"Damien," Aldric whispered. "Don't look back."

Aldric stood, feigning clumsiness as he stepped through the bush, pretending he didn't expect anyone there. The second he passed the shrubs, two men grabbed him, and a third stood in front of him. Aldric struggled, breaking out of their grasp, but the men grabbed again, restraining him to the best of their ability. Aldric gave up the fight. He knew he could break free, but it would only raise more suspicion for a fifteen-year-old to overpower two grown men.

Aldric heard Damien's footsteps as he finally turned, stumbling as he headed back to the house. Though he knew they could just yell loud enough for their father to hear, Aldric had to make sure Damien ran. Giving him a task was the only way to be sure he would.

"We don't want to hurt you," the man in front of Aldric said. Despite his words, he twirled a knife in his hands.

"Oddly enough, I'm having difficulty believing you," Aldric stalled.

"Oh, this?" The man asked, waving the knife. "It's for hunting."

"What are you hunting?" Aldric asked, weakly struggling against the men holding him back. "Children?"

The man didn't justify it with a response. Instead, he just squatted down in front of Aldric and moved the blade toward his arm. Aldric struggled more, starting to get concerned. Slowly, the man pressed the side of his knife against Aldric's arm.

He must have heated the knife somehow, because it burned as it touched Aldric's skin. He screamed in pain as he tried to pull his arm back, but the man tracked him, pressing the burning blade against Aldric's arm.

"Aldric!" Damien screamed, turning back around.

"I'm sorry," the man apologized with a hint of genuine sadness. "You failed."

Aldric pulled back, breaking himself free of the two men and trying to back away, but the man in front of him was fast. He turned the blade over and drove the knife into Aldric's stomach. The burning sensation spread through his whole body, overwhelming him with agony. Aldric collapsed to the floor, barely able to move.

Damien's footsteps grew louder as he ran toward his brother. Every neuron in Aldric's brain was firing, trying to force his mouth to move, but it was futile. His body felt as though it were burning from the inside out, and Aldric couldn't bring himself to speak.

The man stood back up, turning his attention to Damien. The other two drew knives which Aldric could only assume were heated as well. His mind raced, searching for an explanation, but his father hadn't actually told him much. Whatever his reasons were, he refused to give them any answers until they were "old enough." For a moment, Aldric wondered if Cade would know what to do. Maybe this was what they all were talking about when they said Aldric didn't know how to defend himself. That thought passed quickly, though, because nothing besides the pain lasted long in his mind.

Damien stood confidently while the men approached him, as if believed he had a chance in the fight. The first of the men reached for him, but Damien stepped back and dodged the attack. The other swiped his knife toward the boy. Damien intercepted the attack with a block. Trapping the arm, he ducked under it and lifted his shoulder up as he drove the man's elbow into it. In one motion, Damien snapped the man's arm.

The man in the middle stepped forward and kicked at Damien. He faked a round kick, so Damien moved to block it, but the man turned the kick into a front kick. Unprepared, Damien couldn't block the attack, and he took the blow to his face. He fell on his back and the man pinned him down. Aldric watched the man take a plant from his pocket and press it against Damien's lips.

"He isn't changing," one of the others observed. It wasn't near a full moon – why were they expecting him to transform?

"Give it a second," the leader barked.

"Do you think he's too young?" The other asked.

"Maybe. Give me your knife."

He pressed the knife against Damien's face and the boy screamed out in agony. He tried to wriggle his way out of captivity, but he was stuck. After a second, the man pulled the knife back with a sigh.

"I guess so. I'm sorry, child. You've failed as well."

He pulled the knife back and plunged it toward Damien's throat. Aldric struggled to move, but the pain was still overpowering. He reached for his stomach, trying to remove the knife. Finally, he found the hilt. It was too late, though; he wouldn't be able to save his brother.

A hand caught the hunter's arm, though, pulling it back. The hunter turned with the motion, carefully monitoring his own body. If he had allowed himself to be pulled back any more, his attacker could have broken his arm as well.

Lara slid her hand down the man's arm until she reached the knife. She grabbed the back edge and pulled against the opening in his fingers. Aldric could see the pain on her face as she fought through the heat, but she managed to retrieve the knife.

Aldric pulled the knife out of his own stomach and struggled to his feet, waiting for the wound to close. He started to feel dizzy, though, as blood poured from the open wound. It wasn't closing. Still, he fought through it, trying to think of a way to help his sister. The two followers approached him. Neither had their knives anymore, and one of them had a broken arm hanging limply at his side. Aldric was confident he could win this fight, but the blood loss would definitely be a struggle.

Lara kicked the head hunter to the ground. He rolled over his shoulder and jumped to his feet. As he rolled, he managed to find the knife the other had dropped and grab it. He lifted it by the edge of the blade, but he didn't even appear to notice the heat. Facing Lara, he waved the knife a few times, presumably gauging her reactions.

Aldric tried to force an intimidating pose, but he could feel himself wavering. He swung the knife weakly toward the hunter with the broken arm, but he dodged and the other stepped in with a hook punch to Aldric's jaw. Aldric stumbled to the side, barely able to maintain his balance. In a flash, that hunter had Aldric in a full nelson, and the other shoved a plant toward Aldric's face.

The hunter released him, but Aldric felt a terrifying feeling wash over him. It felt as though the wolf were forcing itself out, even though the moon wasn't full. He dropped to his knees, the knife skidding to a stop in front of him. The hunter with two working arms picked it up and stepped toward Aldric, who was too busy fighting off the wolf to move.

Lara turned, kicking the man's knee out from behind him. He fell down, but she caught his head in her arms as he fell. Twisting both hands, she broke his neck and dropped the body to the ground. Still holding the knife, she turned to the other hunter. Before he could react, she drove the knife into his throat, leaving it lodged in his jugular.

"Lara," Aldric coughed, trying to motion toward Damien. Aldric couldn't move as the wolf fought for dominance. He still felt the burn of the blade, although it was beginning to fade. It was something he had never felt before. The wound was starting to close, but it seemed to continually reopen.

She turned too slowly. The head hunter had already turned and knelt down next to Damien. He brought the knife across Damien's throat, cutting deeply. Lara rushed toward him angrily, but he was quick to his feet.

She threw a punch, which he ducked under. Swiping with the knife, he closed the distance between them. Lara lunged back, retracting her torso to avoid the blade. He followed up with a backward swing, but she ducked under. As she rose, she threw an uppercut which he narrowly avoided by leaning his head back. The hunter kicked forward and Lara deflected the kick, lunging to the side. Closing the distance, she punched toward his nose. He moved in to meet her, driving his hand forward with him.

The hunter's nose bled profusely, but Lara dropped to her knees with a blade protruding from her gut. He placed a foot on her chest and a hand on the hilt as he removed the blade, kicking her to the ground. Squatting down, he brought the blade toward Lara's throat.

Aldric felt the power of the wolf start to fade, and the stab wound began to close up. Finally, he was able to climb to his feet. As quickly as he could, he hobbled toward the hunter, hoping if nothing else to distract him long enough for his father to arrive and save them.

The hunter glanced at Aldric and Lara took the opening. She pushed the knife away and grabbed the hunter's head, pulling it toward her own. With the force she put into it, Aldric was sure he could hear both of their skulls crack. Lara dropped her head to the ground and the hunter fell back, dazed. Aldric kicked the man's head, knocking him off of his sister. The hunter lay stunned on the floor, but Aldric wasn't going to take any chances. He lifted his heel and drove it down on the man's forehead, shattering his skull. Instantly, the hunter fell limp.

Aldric dropped to his knees near Damien, listening for a heartbeat. The wound wasn't closing, and he couldn't understand why. Even something this bad should be healing.

After a few minutes, Lara was able to move, and she walked up behind Aldric, placing a hand on his shoulder.

"Come on, we have to find father," she ordered.

"We can't leave Damien. He's healing," Aldric cried.

"No, Aldric. He isn't."

Present
24 Days Until the Full Moon

"Do you really think this is the best idea?" Linda asked, leaning against the door frame. Aldric had spent most of the day training, so they hadn't talked much.

"They could find us," Aldric explained. That morning, he had finally decided not to search for another job. He'd been calculating interest from his investments and on interest alone he could easily support a family. Additionally, he didn't feel comfortable being apart from Linda for eight hours daily. His time would be much better spent training, and his presence would at least be a bit of a deterrent to someone attacking her.

"I understand," Linda agreed. "I think you could have stopped job hopping fifty years ago and been fine."

"I can't necessarily deny that," Aldric laughed.

"Don't get me wrong, I feel much safer with you here. My question was more focused on the wolfsbane."

"Oh," Aldric replied, glancing down at the stockpile of wolfsbane in the corner of his training room. "Well, that reasoning is admittedly significantly less sound."

"Try me," she smiled, trying to be supportive. She was clearly concerned about his well-being. Aldric had spent the better part of a week in that room, but it had really picked up the past couple days. When he'd finally decided to sacrifice the career search for more training, it had become almost an obsession. Aside from two breaks when Linda brought him food, he hadn't stopped shadowboxing all day.

He'd become complacent and stopped fighting, and without use, any skill was bound to suffer. His last fight with Cyrus had only proven to him how far he'd fallen, and he was certain that Cade hadn't slowed down at all. In order to adequately protect his family, Aldric had to hone his skills once again. However, he was concerned that even that may not be enough, so he'd fabricated an insane idea centered around wolfsbane.

"If I can control the wolf," Aldric explained, carefully selecting his words. "We can use that as a weapon."

"What do you mean?"

"I've been able to maintain my human state for longer and longer each full moon. Last week, I was able to think although my body was completely taken over by the beast. So I started wondering: if I use wolfsbane and force the change enough, maybe I can expedite the process. Maybe I can find a way to keep my mind in charge while in the wolf's form."

"And you think you can use that power to your advantage?"

"It might be the only advantage we have."

"So why haven't you started?"

"Well," Aldric hesitated. "Honestly? Because I'm terrified."

"Now you're making sense," Linda smiled.

Aldric nodded sadly. He knew he had to work up the nerve to finally start training, but he was afraid the wolf would be too powerful. Even if it was, though, the transformation would be relatively brief. He just had to be careful about the amount of wolfsbane he exposed himself to at any given time.

"Okay, I'm going to do it," Aldric nodded.

He picked up a small piece of the plant, and Linda shuddered at the thought of what was going to happen. There was a sense of conflict in her eyes as she seemed to debate following him on his futile mission.

"Wait outside," he told her – granting her the excuse she needed to leave. Nodding, she closed the door. Aldric heard her lean against the wall outside with a sigh. Clearly, she wasn't fully on board with his plan, but she was going to let him try. She had to be aware that there was no good option – so it was time to start trying the bad ones.

Aldric placed a small amount of wolfsbane on his tongue and closed his eyes. For the first time in his entire life, he didn't fight the change. The pain as his bones broke was dulled to a point that it was barely present. It was possible that it was just by comparison alone, but it was a welcome change.

Instead of focusing on struggling to keep his physical form, Aldric fought to keep his mind intact. He could feel the animalistic thoughts of the wolf creeping into his mind, but he tried to push them away. Within a minute his form had completely changed, but Aldric could still hear Linda's heartbeat on the other side of the door. He could still feel the ground beneath his paws.

"Okay," Aldric thought. Though difficult to even think that one word through the cloudiness of his mixed mind, it was a start. He tried to run through some math equations – simple addition – to keep his human mind thinking. When he was able to add two numbers under ten without a pounding headache, he was convinced it was working.

Finally, Aldric opened his eyes. He hadn't really thought about the fact that they'd stayed closed – he just figured his vision had faded when the wolf took over. However, when his mind sent the impulse to lift his eyelids, light flooded into them.

At first it was blinding – everything was white. Instinctively, Aldric blinked. Actually, it didn't feel like instinct – it felt like he chose to, but he knew he hadn't. The wolf seemed to decide to blink to try to wash some of the light.

A few blinks later, the light dulled. Everything was still bright and vibrant, but it looked different. The red punching bag in the corner looked dulled – a faint yellow. The blues of the walls stood out so much more, but most of the world seemed to be shades of gray.

Aldric felt proud for a second, but then his feelings vanished. As if hit by a sudden tidal wave, everything was washed away. Despite his struggles to maintain his rationality, he could feel his mind slowing down.

"Step," Aldric told himself, trying to command one of his paws to move. He wasn't sure how, though. Controlling a human body felt so natural, but every limb was foreign to him now. It was as if his brain didn't know where to send the signals to tell him to move.

His legs started moving as he ran toward the door and threw himself at it.

"No!"

The wolf pulled back and rammed into the door again, trying to break free. Aldric struggled, but he couldn't stop anything. The world faded to black as his mind moved back to its normal role of passenger. Just as the last bit of his mind faded away, the wolf seemed to get tired. It stopped fighting as hard, and Aldric was able to stay awake. It wasn't easy – as if he'd been awake for days straight – but he was able to stay awake.

The wolf fell back and for the first time, Aldric felt his body revert from the wolf's shape back to his own human body. Some of his fur retracted and some was shed. His paws shrank as human fingers began to protrude from them. As his mouth fell back, his teeth dulled. Aldric's knees broke as his legs fell underneath him, and they straightened out as he found himself on his hands and knees. His spine shattered, sacrificing its curvature in order to accommodate a bipedal form.

As the transformation ended, Aldric stood on shaky legs, reaching for the door handle for support. Once he'd stabilized himself, he pulled the door open to see Linda sitting against the wall, staring expectantly at him.

"For a first time," Aldric choked out. "I think that was a success."

The wave of exhaustion was finally too powerful, and Aldric collapsed to the floor. Before he even hit the carpet, he was already asleep.

❖ ❖ ❖

Linda pulled up, heaving herself over a ledge. Behind her, Aldric stood to offer support, but she didn't need it. Of course she wouldn't, but it still felt strange for him to watch his wife – who was in the third trimester of her pregnancy – climb a mountain on her own.

It had been her idea, though. She hadn't had much of an opportunity to explore in her life. Aldric had spent his entire life between being trapped in his family home and meeting his wife travelling. He'd explored mountain ranges, rivers and lakes, forests – basically every biome Earth had to offer. To him, a hike was just more of the same. Over the past hundred years, though, he hadn't done much of that. Instead, he'd taken to working in various towns and stockpiling funds for the future.

Aldric had tried to convince Linda to wait until they were settled down to experience the world. He didn't want her to push herself too far. He should have known, though, that with the physicality of a werewolf and the determination she'd always had, nothing would slow her down.

"Keep up," she joked, standing on the ledge. Aldric hadn't realized how long he'd been standing there watching her. Shaking his head as he returned to reality, Aldric jumped the eight feet to land next to her.

"Alright, show off," she groaned.

"Never skip leg day."

"You know what? Let me try."

"No, no," Aldric laughed, catching her arm before she jumped off the edge. "I'm sure you can, but there is a practically fully-formed fetus in there. How scared would you be if Earth just jumped?"

"I'd be impressed," she shrugged.

"Come on," Aldric turned as he released her arm. He headed up, working his way toward the peak. They'd driven for half a day to make their way to that mountain, but Linda had never been to Arizona, and she wanted to see the Grand Canyon. Rather than taking the easy path, of course, they'd decided to hike and watch the sunset over the mountainous desert. "We're going to miss it."

Linda glanced back at the ledge with resignation. "Next time," she accepted as she walked past Aldric. Together, they worked their way upward, managing to reach a perfect spot to look out over the state before the sun set. The purple and orange hues lit up the sky and painted the dirt on the ground so far beneath them. Aldric sighed happily, looking out at the landscape as Linda rested her head on his shoulder.

"It's going to be amazing," she assured him, as if reading his mind. Aldric couldn't stop himself from worrying about the life of his child. He didn't know how to be a parent – there was no question about that. His role models were lackluster, and he couldn't relate to any of the information he'd read. All he wanted was to raise his son well – to give him a better life. Deep down, though, he was terrified that he would make the same mistakes his parents did.

"You're going to be great."

"You have no evidence to support that claim."

"I have a pretty good feeling."

"One thing's for sure," Aldric pondered. "I don't want our child to ever feel trapped. I want him to know what the world looks like – to know he can explore. That there is so much more than he can see in front of him. I want him to hike, to swim. I want him to see the world from up here, and to watch the sunlight reflect from the ocean. To know how big the world is – but also to know how much he matters to it. To know that even with all of that, my whole world is inside of you right now."

"Like I said," Linda smiled, wiping a tear from her eye. "You'll be a great father."

A few moments passed by as they silently watched the sun set and darkness settle in. Aldric listened to his wife's steady breathing as the world around them fell asleep. He listened as other parts of it – the insects and the wildlife – woke up and sang their songs.

"What makes you so sure it's a boy?" Linda finally asked.

"I don't know," Aldric responded quietly. "I guess I just have a pretty good feeling."

Chapter 6
425 Years Ago

"I've been speaking with the other families," Aldric's mom started. The two of them sat across from each other in the study as she awkwardly began the conversation. Aldric looked around, wondering how many books on those shelves he hadn't read. He wasn't able to find a single one in a quick glance.

"What about, exactly?" Aldric asked. It wasn't particularly typical for his mother to associate with the rest of the werewolf families. They all tended to stay relatively secluded. If anyone had to discuss disputes or land trades, that was in his father's jurisdiction.

"Well, what do you think?" She laughed.

"I haven't the slightest."

"You, of course. The Valentines have a daughter near your age. The Laine girl is three years younger, but what's the difference of three years when you have an eternity?"

"What?"

"My preference is the Laines. We haven't been on the best of terms with them recently, since your father had that falling out with Keiran about the territory just south of here. Both families wanted to expand."

"I recall, Mother. This was only a decade ago. I think you missed my question, though."

"Well, if the Valentine girl is truly better suited for you then of course choose her, dear."

"What?"

Aldric was twenty-three years old but compared to his lifespan that was still incredibly young. He hadn't even left his father's home yet and had a chance to explore the world on his own. Ever since what had happened with Damien, he'd been too afraid to venture too far. He'd been to town a few times, but the thought of going out on his own was terrifying – even more so than the idea of being trapped under his father's control. Still, he wasn't sure where this conversation was coming from, but he wasn't prepared for an arranged marriage.

"Unfortunately the other families are farther off. I mean, I suppose you could wait another eighteen to twenty years…"

"I think I can find my own wife, thank you."

"Well of course. That's why I'm telling you the options. I'm not just going to pick for you."

"That's two options, Mother."

"That's all there are now. You're not marrying a human, after all."

"What do you have against humans?"

"They'll never love you like you love them. Anyway, it's futile. You'd be throwing away an eternity's worth of love for the blink of an eye."

"I'll take eighty years with a true love over a thousand with a forced partner."

"You've been reading too much fiction. That isn't how life is. You choose who to love."

"I would think I'd have to like them first."

"Well, Cassandra Laine will be here tomorrow. You can determine if you fancy her."

"Did you actually just set up a date for me?" Aldric scoffed as he stood, backing away. Maybe he'd allowed her to treat him like a child, and maybe it was just the multiple century-wide age difference, but he wasn't willing to go on a play-date because his mom wanted to play match-maker.

"You're over-reacting, Aldric, and it's unbecoming. How do you suppose Cade met Amelia?"

Aldric bit his tongue before he said anything rude to his mother. Regardless of their difference in opinions, he still intended to treat her with respect. Aldric sighed and pinched the bridge of his nose as he tried to determine how to react. Saving him from making that decision, though, Aldric's father walked into the room.

"Aldric," he commanded. "Come with me."

"Sorry," Aldric shrugged, looking back at his mother. "I guess we'll have to pick this up later."

Without another word, Aldric followed his father. Neither of them spoke as they left the house and walked quickly toward the trees. Aldric's father had never been a fan of communication, so it didn't surprise him that the man just stoically led him to an undisclosed location.

The quiet gave Aldric's mind a chance to race through all of the information. The political marriage that his mother was trying to arrange wasn't actually surprising to him. Somehow, werewolves all seemed to find one of their kind to marry, so someone had to be orchestrating those meetings. Although she pretended it was for his sake, he was sure it was more about keeping the bloodline pure. They all held some core belief that they were inherently better than humans.

Aldric didn't want to become like his parents – or even like Cade. They all seemed cold and heartless. He'd seen too many cousins leave the family only to be pulled back when they had a child, because a child is raised in the pack. He himself had considered leaving, and it only became a stronger desire as he uncovered more of his father's lies and secrets. He hadn't known about wolfsbane or silver until it was too late. Aldric couldn't help but believe that if he'd known, he could have saved Damien. If marriage meant bringing children into a family that lied to that child from birth, he wouldn't marry.

A quiet rustling on the other side of a few shrubs caught Aldric's attention, interrupting his thoughts. His father strolled straight through the bushes, standing tall and exuding an aura of power. Aldric saw three young men sitting around a pile of sticks and leaves. One of them was attempting to light the fire. His technique was off, but at least he was practicing his survival skills.

"What are you doing out here?" Aldric's father growled.

"What?" The one starting the fire dropped his sticks, startled, as he looked up at the intimidating figure. "Oh, hey man."

"Don't make me ask again."

"Calm down," another man spoke up. "We're just camping."

"Camping?"

"Well yeah, is that not what you're doing?"

"You know well what I'm doing."

"I think you may have us confused for someone else," the third man finally spoke up. Aldric just watched the conversation with confusion. He couldn't understand why his father was treating these men so harshly, but he knew too well to interrupt.

"What are the knives for?" He demanded.

"Hunting," the man replied cautiously.

"Exactly," Aldric's father growled. He grabbed the man's head before he could respond and snapped his neck.

Aldric gasped in horror, but he stood petrified. The other two men stood to their feet, screaming in surprise and anguish. The man who had been starting the fire responded violently – completely unaware of how outmatched he was. He rushed toward Silas, his hands balled into fists. The other, more cowardly but far wiser, turned and ran the other direction.

Before the camper made it to Silas, he'd already stepped in and thrown a punch to the man's liver, forcing him to lurch forward and fall to his knees. Silas kicked his ribs, shattering the bones as the man rolled over. Aldric heard his heart stop as pieces of his ribs pierced the muscle.

"Aldric," Silas called. Aldric remained silent, paralyzed.

"Aldric," he repeated, more forcefully. Aldric still couldn't bring himself to respond.

"Boy, go find that third hunter and end him."

"Hunter?" Aldric finally spat. "They were just men."

"In my woods."

"How could they have known?"

"We can't take chances here. You know what happens when we take chances."

"No," Aldric argued. "I don't. And I won't do this. If you want someone to blindly obey…"

"That is your job."

"No! If you want someone to murder innocent people…"

"They aren't innocent!" The two continued escalating their voices, speaking over one another. Though they were deep in the woods, Aldric was still mildly concerned that people would hear – but he didn't let that stop him.

"You brought the wrong son!" He finally yelled.

"No," Silas spoke in the silence. "I brought the one who needed to be tested. Now I know I cannot trust you."

He turned to run toward the third camper, but Aldric caught his arm. He threw a punch, but Silas turned too fast and caught it. Aldric followed up with another punch which Silas parried easily. Aldric kicked toward his father, missing once again. Silas elbowed Aldric's temple, dropping him to the ground instantly.

"You would fight your own for them?"

"You are not my own."

Silas kicked Aldric again, knocking him unconscious.

❖ ❖ ❖

Aldric wasn't sure how much time had passed when he finally woke up. All he knew was that his father was still standing over him. It took about a second for the fact to dawn on him that Silas had even left. Somehow, though, he knew that he'd blacked out for long enough for his father to find and kill the third camper before returning.

"You were emotional," Silas growled, trying to hide his anger. "So I will grant you one allowance."

"Yes," Aldric groaned as he stood, looking directly in his father's eyes. "I was emotional. But I was also right."

"Still you question me?"

"You've given me no reason to trust."

"You don't need one."

Aldric laughed and shook his head, backing away slowly. He had never trusted the man who stood before him, but everything was becoming clearer in front of his eyes. Though he had no idea where to go or how to lead a life without a pack – he knew he had to leave.

As he moved backward, a glint of sunlight reflected from metal on the ground caught Aldric's eye. He paused before reaching down and retrieving the knife, waving it in the air. Silas narrowed his eyes, glaring at Aldric. Finally, Aldric placed the flat of the blade against his wrist.

"You were wrong," he growled, pressing the knife against his arm angrily.

"I was right to defend my home," Silas argued.

"I'm gone," Aldric muttered as he dropped the knife.

"I have not granted you permission to leave."

"I don't need it. Nor do I want it."

"You disgust me," Silas spat.

"The feeling's mutual."

Aldric backed away more, his heart pounding as he realized exactly what he was doing. He didn't have any practical knowledge of the world, no skills to fall back on, and no idea where to go. Outside of that, he knew what his father did to traitors, and it wasn't even likely that he made it past the tree line. Regardless, he knew he couldn't stay.

"Don't follow me," Aldric threatened as he gained distance. "Or I swear I will tell everyone exactly what you are – come what may. I'll accept the consequences."

Present
22 Days Until the Full Moon

The meat sizzled on the grill as Aldric flipped it over and seasoned the other side. It had been too long since he'd cooked for the two of them. Recently, they'd fallen into a routine of Linda cooking by the time Aldric got home – which wasn't bad by any means, but he wanted to treat her too. With more free time on his hands, he'd decided to take a few hours off of training and prepare a nice dinner.

"Smells amazing," Linda complimented as she stepped into the back yard. She walked up behind him and wrapped her arms around him. Aldric laughed and gently moved her arms.

"This one's going to burn," he explained before flipping the second piece of steak.

"You can have that one. You basically like them charred to a crisp anyway."

"There's nothing wrong with some extra flavor."

"That's disgusting," she laughed and walked back toward the house.

"It's better than eating it raw."

"That was once!" She defended. "I was testing the waters."

"Just because you can do something doesn't mean you should."

"Well, I learned that lesson."

"Hey, can you get a few plates?" Aldric asked just before she closed the door. She nodded and returned a moment later with the dishes, and Aldric set the steaks down, turning off the grill. Linda smiled, about to say something, but Aldric held up a hand and she fell silent.

A quiet knocking resounded through the house. At first he thought he was hearing things, but it repeated. Someone was at the door. They hadn't been out enough to meet neighbors, so Aldric's mind naturally fell to the worst.

"Stay here," he ordered quietly.

"It's probably just someone trying to sell us something," she whispered hopefully. "Or welcoming us to the neighborhood."

"If it is, we can laugh at my paranoia later. For now, stay here."

The knocking grew louder, and Aldric moved silently to the living room. He hoped if he just didn't answer the door, they'd eventually leave, but that never seemed to work. The knocking just intensified, the visitor varying the pattern with no apparent purpose other than to irk them.

"I know you're in there," a singsong voice fell through the door. Aldric's heart skipped a beat. "Let me in, Brother."

Realizing there was no other option, Aldric took a deep breath and opened the door. Cade stood in front of him with a large smile on his face. While he didn't appear even slightly threatening, Aldric knew better, and he was prepared for a fight.

"It's been a minute," Cade greeted, extending his hand to his brother.

"Yeah," Aldric agreed, refusing to shake Cade's hand. "There's a reason for that."

"Don't hold a grudge, Aldric. It doesn't suit you."

"We don't have to do this, Cade. You aren't his slave."

"No," Cade agreed solemnly. "No, I'm just the good son."

"Just go home. Tell him you couldn't find me. Please, Cade."

"I can't do that. You know I can't."

"I won't bring him my child."

"You don't have a choice. Raising a child takes a pack. If he chooses you, you can take him back when he's of age."

"So there really isn't another option, then?"

"I'm afraid not."

"Then let's do this outside."

Cade nodded, accepting Aldric's terms. He stepped to the side and gestured for Aldric to pass him. Trying to muster his confidence, Aldric stepped outside.

"Follow me," Aldric instructed, leading Cade to the outskirts of town. The city faded away as they walked, and he found a secluded place in the desert. All he had to do was buy Linda the time she needed to run. They'd talked about it, and as much as she didn't want to abandon him, they both knew what was best for their child.

"Here," Aldric growled, trying to force power into his voice and conceal the fear. Cade nodded, inhaling deeply and stretching his arms. Removing his shirt, Cade tossed it to the side.

"This isn't training," Cade reminded. "I won't let you win."

"I'm well aware."

"Whatever you think of me, Aldric, just know that I didn't want it to come to this."

"Of that, I'm less convinced."

Cade nodded sadly, then lunged in with a strong hook toward Aldric's jaw. Aldric ducked under and countered with an elbow, but Cade lifted his knee and drove his shin into Aldric's arm. He brought a fist down over Aldric's head and Aldric lifted his other arm above to block. Cade threw a front kick, finally connecting and pushing Aldric a few feet back.

Cade rushed in again, faking a jab. Seeing through his technique, Aldric stepped in and threw a jab toward his brother's nose. With his front hand slightly extended, Cade parried the attack and reacted with a counter-punch which Aldric parried as well. Lifting his leg, Cade threw a round kick, but Aldric was faster. Connecting a low scoop kick with the underside of Cade's thigh, he intercepted the attack. Aldric took Cade's moment of weakness as an opportunity and landed a punch to his chest, driving him backward.

This time, Aldric was the one to rush in. He skipped toward Cade, driving his heel toward Cade's back. As Aldric had predicted, Cade weaved backward and then closed the distance with a jab. Aldric turned his hook kick into a round kick, aiming straight for the opening at Cade's stomach. Catching on to Aldric's plan, Cade dropped his hand and quickly caught Aldric's leg, dropping him to the ground.

As he fell Aldric swept his other leg under Cade and brought him down with him. Using the momentum, Aldric rolled over and pinned his brother down. He threw a few punches, but Cade kept his arms in front of his face. Finally, he bucked his hips upward to knock Aldric off balance and rolled over, trying to pin Aldric. Aldric kicked Cade back and rolled backward over his shoulder to land on his feet.

"You've improved," Cade smirked, standing in front of Aldric.

"Or you haven't," Aldric taunted. Cade's weak point was always his pride, and Aldric knew that his only hope was to target that. If he could aggravate Cade enough, he would make a stupid mistake, and that was all Aldric needed to win the fight.

Cade laughed before coming in again. Faking another punch, he closed the distance. Aldric tried to counter, but Cade threw a crescent kick, connecting the blade of his foot with Aldric's jaw. Stumbling backward, Aldric threw a retreating punch. Cade stepped to the side, but he wasn't able to follow up on his own attack. In a desperate attempt to maintain his advantage, Cade threw a hook punch, but Aldric ducked under and landed an uppercut in Cade's armpit. Cade's arm fell limp giving Aldric an opening to throw a punch at Cade's jaw.

Trying not to let up and give Cade a chance to recover, Aldric threw another punch. Cade parried the attack with his other arm and hit Aldric in the chin with an uppercut as his injured arm recovered.

Dazed, Aldric stumbled backward. Cade stepped in and drove his elbow into Aldric's temple, then punched his liver with the other hand. He drove his knee upward, trying to continue his combination, but Aldric was finally able to react. Dropping his arms, he was able to block the knee and push downward, throwing off Cade's balance slightly. That instant was all he needed, though. As Cade dropped forward, Aldric drove his fingertips like a spear at Cade's throat. Cade stepped back, gasping for air. Aldric stepped in a circle, out of the line of attack in case of retaliation, and brought his open palm down as a chop at Cade's jugular.

Aldric lifted his leg and aimed a kick at Cade's face, hoping to knock him out and end the fight, but Cade ducked down. Even as he struggled for breath, Cade was nimble. He swept his leg under Aldric's, knocking Aldric off balance. As Aldric fell backward, he regained his composure and turned the tumble into a roll, jumping back to his feet and block the punch that Cade threw as a follow-up.

Just before Aldric could kick in retaliation, a sharp pain shot through his entire body. Unable to control his legs, Aldric dropped to his knees. He tried to maintain his balance, but toppled onto his face.

His mind raced, searching for an explanation for the sudden unresponsiveness of his muscles. Cade hadn't landed any technique which could cause so much harm. As he thought, though, he realized that he'd heard the footsteps – he was just too focused to respond to them. In hindsight, everything was so clear.

Aldric reached his hand around, searching for the knife in his back, but he couldn't find it. Though he was fully aware that the odds were now stacked completely against him, he couldn't give up the fight. Finally, he found the blade.

"I warned you, Aldric," Cade taunted. There was a hint of sadness to his voice, but it was overwhelmed by the omnipresent sense of superiority. "This isn't training. This is a real battle. And nothing is off limits in battle."

Cade had always said that during their training sessions. He'd warned him that he wouldn't be as lenient if it were a real fight. Aldric had never thought anything of it until that moment.

Desperately, Aldric clenched his fist around the blade in his back. As hard as he pulled, though, the knife wouldn't budge. After a moment, he realized that the knife wasn't lodged into his back so well that he couldn't retrieve it, he just wasn't pullingHis arms were no longer responding to sensory input either, and all of his limbs were paralyzed. Cade had stabbed him just below the neck, rendering his entire body immobile.

Cade lifted Aldric's helpless body and draped him over one shoulder. As he did so, Aldric saw Lara standing solemnly off to the side. She refused to make eye contact with him, and she turned and walked off, leading Cade back to town.

Aldric's hopes that Linda had escaped were starting to fade, though. He hadn't realized that there had been another attacker. He'd been too concerned about defending his family from Cade to even consider that Lara would be helping her brother. Since she was there, it wasn't likely she'd left Linda behind.

Cade tossed Aldric into the trunk of a car and slammed it closed. As they drove off, he could hear struggling from the seat in front of him. Aldric tried to call out to Linda, but there was no strength left in his body. Blood still poured from his wounds, and the world started to fade around him.

Chapter 7
312 Years Ago

Confidently, Aldric pushed open the door to the dojo, stepping over the threshold as he tried to locate the person in charge. Though he'd been to many martial arts schools, he hadn't seen one with so many black belts before. Typically there were only a few, but it seemed that most people at that school had reached that rank. That alone was almost enough for him to turn and leave, but he decided to give it a chance.

"Hi," a stranger greeted him.

"Hello, I am looking for a place to train," Aldric greeted.

"Well, I'd be more than happy to introduce you to our instructor. We're just warming up for our black belt class now, but there is another class following it."

"I see," Aldric replied with an accepting nod.

"My name is Linda, by the way. Ms. Martin on the mat. In Tang Soo Do we refer to black belts by their last name. I've never been a fan of it, but maybe that's just because my last name is a man's first," she shrugged as she turned and walked toward an office.

Aldric didn't bother to introduce himself, but he did follow. Linda seemed overly eager, but that was probably why she was the one tasked with reaching out to new students. Since he was a child, Aldric had been learning martial arts, but he'd only gone to professional instructors recently. In that short time, though, he hadn't managed to shake the training from his father. Fighting was a necessity in life, and he wouldn't be able to survive without it, so he had to keep his skills sharp. That meant during training, though, he was expected to treat it as such. Finding someone smiling in such dire circumstances made him uncomfortable.

"What's your name?" She asked.

"Jason," Aldric replied coldly. He had already grown accustomed to lying about his identity and found no struggle with it. Although he didn't want to think about it, he found it easy to lie to someone when he realized that their life was a blink compared to his. Aldric avoided shaking his head, although that was his typical reaction when he attempted to force away such thoughts.

"You're not your father," he thought, scolding himself. The mindset was hard to break, though, and it made it easier to leave behind any minimalistic relationships he formed.

"Nice to meet you, Jason," she replied, turning back to face him as she stopped just short of the office. There was that smile again.

"Okay," Aldric replied, eager to end the conversation.

"That was wrong," he thought as he searched his brain for a more reasonable response. Human interaction still felt relatively new to him, although he'd been in their world for decades. The lack of exposure during his formative years made it incredibly hard for him to hold conversations with them, though.

"I mean, it's nice to meet you too," he stumbled as he faked a smile – which still felt wrong in a room where he was meant to train for his life. "Sorry, I'm a bit focused."

"Naturally," she replied with a smirk, narrowing her eyes at him. Aldric couldn't deny that she was attractive, but he wondered if that was exclusively due to her attire. He'd always found himself more drawn to women whom he knew could defend themselves, and the black gi and belt was a very clear sign of that. Regardless, though, he couldn't get past her overly positive attitude.

"Do you have any martial arts experience?" She asked, apparently trying to make conversation for one reason or another. Aldric surmised that in order to convince people to stay they tried to appear friendly and open. While that was the exact opposite of what he needed, he knew he was an anomaly. No business would be able to thrive if it catered only to werewolves perpetually on the run.

"No," he shrugged. Technically, his character never had, and playing Jason was vital to his survival, so it wasn't a lie as much as acting.

"Well, it's a lot of fun," she encouraged. Aldric's disgust was clear on his face, despite the fact that he tried to hide it. Quickly, he plastered on another fake smile, but she'd noticed the change in his expression.

"It's a great workout too," she quickly tried to recover, "and it's helpful for disciple and a perfect way to learn to defend yourself."

"It's okay," he comforted.

"I'm sure you'll find what you're looking for," she assured him with a pat on his shoulder.

"Thanks. I hope so."

She nodded and turned toward the office, waving down the head instructor and introducing them. Distracted, Aldric watched Linda walk back to the mat. A few of the students were sparring and Aldric observed their movements closely, already searching for weaknesses. Linda started fighting another student, and Aldric found himself impressed by her quick and powerful movements. For a human, she was surprisingly good.

"So, Jason, what brings you here?"

"I'm just trying to learn," Aldric replied, pulling his gaze from Linda.

"That's what I like to hear," the head instructor replied with a broad smile. Aldric couldn't understand why everyone there seemed so happy, but from watching their fighting, he could see that it was vastly different from anything he'd learned before. Every art had something it could teach him, and only by blending everything together into his own style would he become the most effective fighter he could be.

"When can I start?" Aldric asked.

Present
21 Days Until the Full Moon

Gasping, Aldric shot up as he looked around the room. In a moment of denial, he questioned whether the events of the previous day had been a mere dream. No pain or open wound were present to indicate that the fight had actually taken place.

As his eyes adjusted to the darkness, though, any miniscule hope of that possibility vanished. Even with the room practically devoid of light, Aldric recognized the basement of his old family home. Scanning the room, searching for any movement, he was able to make out a single figure – a mere shadow sitting in a chair not too far from him.

It wasn't until he tried to move that he felt a burning sensation overtake his entire body. Silver chains were wrapped around his entire body, binding his arms to his sides. The chains were buried in the ground and Aldric could only assume cemented there. Struggling to move his arms, he realized that his hands were bound as well – each cuffed to a small post on either side of him. Instantly, his mind began fumbling for a weak point. The bindings seemed like overkill, but they were pure precaution. Anything less and Aldric would have no difficulty escaping.

Still, everything had an opening. Sometimes it was just harder to find than others. He didn't bother pretending to still be asleep as he searched for his escape. The other person in the room would surely have heard his gasp, especially if, as Aldric assumed, they were a werewolf.

He took a moment to study the other figure. It was a feminine shape, but she wasn't pregnant. It looked like Lara, but he couldn't be complctely certain. Lara looked like her mother, and it had been hundreds of years since he'd seen them, and it was very possible it was another child of one of the two whom Aldric had yet to meet.

"You're finally awake," the figure spoke as she stood and turned on a single light. Aldric recognized the voice just before Lara was bathed in the dim light.

"Why are you doing this?" Aldric asked desperately.

"Me? Don't blame me, little brother. Your mistakes led you here. This is your doing, not mine."

"Oh, really? That's funny, I don't recall stabbing myself in the back."

"Had you been training for those four hundred years, I doubt you'd have fallen for such a simple trick."

"Lara, I know you've had children by now."

"I have."

"Where are they?"

"When they came of age, they chose to leave, to lead their own lives," she smiled sadly. "Of course, they'll always come back home when needed, as any wolf should, but it takes a special type of loyalty to stay with the family."

"But aren't you glad your children had that choice?"

"Every child has that choice, Aldric."

"No. Not mine."

"The newborn will be given the same choice as everyone else."

"Can you imagine one of your babies being forcefully ripped away from you?" Aldric tried to play on her emotion. If he could force her to picture herself in his situation, maybe he could win her favor. Lara was always the closest to him, so she was his best hope.

"That would never happen."

"Just picture it. Please, Lara. Don't let that happen to me."

"I told you, Aldric. I'm not letting anything happen. You chose this."

"Enough," a booming voice echoed from the top of the stairway. Silas, as powerful as ever, descended into the basement. Lara nodded and looked at the ground. With a wave, Silas dismissed her and she ran upstairs.

"You haven't aged well," Aldric taunted. Of course it wasn't true. Silas looked just as young and intimidating as he had four hundred years ago. The only difference was even more malice than Aldric had ever seen before.

"You haven't aged," Silas spat. "Still a whining child."

"Where is my wife?"

"She's safe."

"Where?"

"It doesn't matter, Aldric. You can have her back after our child is born."

"My child."

"All children belong to the pack. You know the rules, Aldric."

"I won't allow you to indoctrinate my son."

"You won't allow it?" Silas laughed tauntingly. "You aren't in much of a position to allow anything, are you?"

"We aren't your pack. We aren't your family. Just let us go."

"Stop begging, Aldric. It's pathetic."

"You misunderstand. It's not a plea, Silas. It's a demand – and a warning."

Silas laughed again before moving the chair in which Lara had been sitting as she waited for Aldric to wake up. He placed the chair just in front of Aldric and sat down in front of him, bringing his face within inches of Aldric's. Completely bound by silver chains, Aldric was unable to move, but he maintained eye contact as he tried to look more powerful than he was.

"You know something, boy?" Silas asked, malice dripping from every syllable. "You're welcome."

Pulling back, Silas leaned back in the chair, waiting a few seconds before elaborating. Finally, he stood, towering over Aldric, and kicked the chair back.

"There is one reason, and one reason alone, that you are alive right now. That is because I am merciful. I am forgiving. I have chosen not to kill you for your crimes, and even to offer you a chance to leave once again with your wife. You don't seem to appreciate just how generous my offer is. When someone disrespects me and then breaks my rules such as you have, Aldric, I should sentence them to death. I should make an example out of you. I should cut the child from your wife's womb with a silver blade. As she fails to heal, you watch her suffer until the moment that wound closes. Then, in front of your eyes and those of every wolf in the five clans, I should sever her head. That should be the last thing you see before I end your miserable waste of an existence.

"But I am merciful, and I am honorable. You spared the life of one of mine, Aldric. You could have killed Cyrus, but you allowed him to live. Now, I have chosen to return that favor. I am *allowing* you to live. Do you understand?"

"Yes," Aldric responded hesitantly.

"So watch how you speak with me, Aldric. Because I do have my limits."

Aldric clenched his teeth as he struggled against the chains to no avail. Nothing in Silas's tone implied that he was bluffing, and Aldric had no question that he would be exactly as heartless as he threatened. He was less confident, though, that Silas would keep his word and allow Aldric and Linda to leave. Regardless, Aldric wasn't leaving without his baby. Whatever he did, he had to find a way to break them free.

"Now, Aldric, maybe it's time for a father to teach his son one more lesson. What do you say when someone saves your life?"

Aldric growled quietly, his pride refusing to allow him to play his father's game. All he wanted was to spit in his face and order him to assemble the clans, because Aldric was finished with his games. He knew, though, that he'd be condemning not only himself to death, but also his wife. Instead, he had to play his father's game for at least long enough to find a way out of his prison.

"What do you say, boy?" Silas growled, slapping Aldric across the face. With the effects of the silver inhibiting his healing, Aldric could feel the sting in his face as his cheek turned red.

"Thank you," Aldric muttered, his eyes downcast.

"I can't hear you."

"Thank you for saving my life."

"Ah, that's better. Now, was that so hard?"

Silas turned and walked back up the stairs, each footfall a heavy assertion of his dominance. When he reached the top of the stairs, he slammed the door closed behind him and engaged multiple locks. Darkness and silence enveloped Aldric, filling his outside world before racing into his very core like a cancer, replacing any hope he had.

Chapter 8

309 Years Ago

Passionately pressing her lips against his, Linda leaned forward and wrapped her fingers in Aldric's hair. His mind racing, Aldric searched for an excuse to leave which he hadn't used yet, but that was becoming more difficult as time went on. Eventually, though, he stopped trying.

Lost in the moment, his control over his thoughts slowly slipped from his grasp. Aldric wrapped his arm around her waist and pulled her closer, matching and increasing the intensity of her movements. Retreating for a moment, Aldric gazed into her eyes. His heart burned with a mixture of desire and love.

Returning his gaze, Linda swung her leg over him and straddled him as he sat. Peering down at him, she slowly lowered her arms and lifted her shirt over her head, tossing it to the ground next to them. Aldric struggled against every instinct he possessed as he tried to muster the strength to stop her. Before he could bring himself to speak, she leaned forward, placing her hands on his shoulders and silencing him with her lips. As she kissed him, Aldric felt her arms slide from his shoulders as she slipped them behind her.

All of his senses continued to heighten as his heart rate increased. Every touch was a sensation he'd never imagined before that moment. He could smell the sweat dripping from her brow, separating it distinctly from the pheromones which pervaded the room. Aldric could hear her quiet breaths as she pulled backward, resting her forehead against his and focusing on the task at hand. The faintest scraping of metal followed as she unhooked her brassiere.

"Linda," he finally choked out against the protest of his body and mind. Instead of responding, she kissed him again.

"Linda, wait," he muttered, gently pushing her back.

"What?" She asked, breathing heavily as she sat up straight. Aldric forced his eyes upward, tearing them from her bare chest.

"I can't," he hesitantly added.

She sighed, dropping her shoulders with disappointment. After a moment of stillness, during which she presumably hoped he would change his mind, she finally stood and recovered her shirt.

"Do you want to tell me what this is about?" She groaned as she sat next to him.

"I…" Aldric attempted to find a reasonable explanation, but nothing came to mind. There was no doubt in his mind that he loved the woman in front of him beyond the emotion with which most people associated the word. Aldric would be ecstatic to spend the rest of her lifetime with her, consistently placing her needs before his own. In her, he had found everything he'd wanted and every reason he'd denied his mother's assistance in finding a partner.

The past two years had been the best of Aldric's life and he wanted to prove that to her. However, he couldn't deny that he had been lying to her. Aldric wasn't sure if it was fear that she'd leave him if she knew the truth, guilt about hiding facts from her, or the deep-rooted idea from his father that it was better if she didn't know, but something kept him from telling her every time it came up.

"Are you waiting for marriage?" She laughed nervously.

"No," he sighed, biting his lower lip. Breathing deeply, Aldric finally decided that he couldn't hide the truth from her any longer.

"Then what? You can talk to me about it, you know that."

"Linda," he began with a shaky voice, looking her directly in the eyes.

"What?" She asked when he hesitated another ten seconds before responding.

"Do you trust me?"

"Of course."

"I need you to remember that. To hold onto that, irrespective of anything that comes out of my mouth over the next few minutes. Set your disbelief aside."

"Okay," she accepted slowly.

"I have been lying to you since the day I met you," he explained. Tears forced their way into his eyes as he processed the implications of everything he was about to tell her. It wasn't right, though, to continue to waste her time – especially because she didn't have as much of it as he did.

"This world is so much bigger than most people know. Probably myself included," he continued with a sad laugh. "Just beneath the surface, there are things believed only to be nightmares."

"Like vampires?" She teased in attempt to cover the concern in her voice.

"No, not like vampires. Like werewolves."

"You're joking."

"No, Linda. I'm not. I've been horrified to tell you. The less you know the safer you are. It's not right, though, to keep stringing you along. I love you more than I can tell you. For a werewolf, though, we only get one chance at love."

"Wolves mate for life," she muttered.

"Yeah," he nodded. "It applies to us too."

"And I'm not the one?"

"That is not what I am saying," Aldric replied confidently. "I'm trying to say that you are. Lying to you, though, was wrong. This is your decision to make, and you deserve all of the facts."

Linda pensively stared at her hands which rested atop her lap. Tension filled the room, but Aldric didn't have any more words to add. He'd told her the truth, and she had every right and reason to walk out of the room.

"I want to see," she finally demanded confidently, looking back up at him.

"See what?"

"You. I want to watch."

"You mean…"

"Yes."

"No," he denied vehemently. Logically, Aldric understood why she'd want proof. What she was being told was completely insane from the human perspective.

"How does it work?"

"Scientifically?"

"I guess. I mean, most people can't just transform at will."

"It's not at will," he slowly explained. "From what I understand, it was a curse placed on my ancestors. When the moon is full, every cell in our bodies responds in a very specific way by being chemically stimulated to return to a stem cell state. Every cell has the DNA of both a human and wolf form, so it can differentiate to create organs and tissue associated with the other form."

"Okay," she nodded.

"I know it sounds crazy."

"No. I mean, yes, it does, but that isn't my concern. You told me to trust you, so I do. But I want to see, Aldric. I want to see you – to love you. All of you."

The fire in her eyes assured Aldric that he had no chance of changing her mind, but he refused to put her in harm's way.

"I'll put a small grate in my basement door. You can watch if you promise me that you will run the second it's over."

Present
Unknown Days Until the Full Moon

Darkness overpowered his senses, and the silver limited them to near human levels. Aldric could barely hear the footsteps as they bounded across the first floor, shaking the ceiling above him. No light had been allowed in the basement for ages, and Aldric lost count of the days. Everything began to blend together, and there was no routine by which he could measure time. Someone occasionally came down with food, but the time between those visits was inconsistent.

They had him caged up like an animal, and he had no hope of breaking free. A while back, they'd granted him the freedom to move around the basement, but he was still bound to poles cemented into the ground. He wore a silver collar around his neck and cuffs on each wrist, all of which held him near the poles and inhibited his mobility.

Silas was giving everything he could to break Aldric's will, and Aldric couldn't pretend it wasn't working. Starvation destroyed not only his ability, but his determination, to fight. Sensory deprivation overpowered his ability – so even if he tried, he couldn't think of any possible escape route. Completely powerless, he was at their mercy.

Suddenly, light flooded into the room, blinding Aldric completely. Managing to keep them open despite the pain of the overload, he watched a dark figure descend the stairs. The door stayed open behind her, allowing only a dim light from upstairs. That was enough, though, to be completely overwhelming. Aldric stumbled backward and dropped to his knees, retreating to allow his arms enough mobility to shield his eyes.

"Aldric," a voice spoke, deafening him. The sudden rush of sound left his ears ringing and his brain pounding. It was impossible for him to process so much new information simultaneously.

"Aldric!" She screeched, only making the agony worse. As hard as he tried to appear strong, he found himself cowering in the corner, his hands pressed tightly over his ears and his eyes clenched shut. Trying to steady his breathing, Aldric searched for anything else to focus on. His ears rang, though, and even through closed eyes the light seemed blinding.

"Pathetic," she spat. Aldric still couldn't place the voice, but he heard another loud clang as metal slammed against the floor. He forced his eyes open, and he was able to see his mother standing in front of him. It felt as if he were lying on the ground outside staring directly at the sun, then she stepped in front of him. Everything around her burned his eyes, but she was barely more than a shadow.

"It's so easy to break a man. To turn him into nothing more than a sniveling, groveling child," she laughed. Somehow, she had always been the most compassionate member of his family, but now she was the worst. Aldric didn't understand what had severed their bond, but maybe she was just painfully loyal to her husband. Wolves tend to be that way, so she must have started hating him because his father did. Coming down to leave a tray of food wasn't enough for her – she had to make sure to try to demoralize him as well.

She turned and stormed toward the stairs, each step an explosion of thunder as it resounded through the basement. The stairs protested, creaking loudly as she climbed them and he braced himself for the slamming of the door. After a few seconds, though, the door didn't slam, and her figure didn't move.

"Aldric," she added from the top of the stairs. The menace had crept away from her voice and only sadness was left. "You know I don't want to do this to you, right?"

"It may surprise you, but that was not apparent," Aldric choked out a sarcastic response, even as his brain yelped in pain – still overstimulated. The light was finally beginning to settle and the ringing died down. The silver kept his healing down, though, so it was taking longer than it should have – and he knew it was going to get just as bad soon.

"If you submit to him, you are free. You realize that? The rules have been there for lifetimes. Why must you cause the family such strife?"

"Tradition is a stupid reason to continue doing something wrong."

"Any time I look down here and think: 'That's still my son,' this is what I have to remind myself: My son died years ago. You're a carcass of what he was. Nothing more than a fool too proud to admit his faults."

"Like father like son."

The door slammed, plunging Aldric into darkness once again.

❖ ❖ ❖

Crossing his legs as he sat on the floor, Aldric closed his eyes and breathed slowly. He didn't have to let himself be beaten. Somehow, there was a way out. He'd almost accepted that he had been defeated, but that wasn't true. There was always an answer.

The cuffs weren't large enough for him to break through, even if he broke his own hands. Even if that did work, he would still be trapped by the neck. He didn't have the strength to pull the pole from the ground because they were cemented in and he couldn't channel much more power than an average human. He knew he could manipulate Lara or Cyrus into setting him free, but that was why they only sent his mother or Cade to bring food.

"Okay," Aldric thought, trying to push aside the idea that he was completely insane. *"I know you're in here somewhere."*

Aldric knew the idea was indeed preposterous, but he pushed that thought away once again. He couldn't use any of his strength or senses because the silver kept the wolf at bay. However, wolfsbane brought it forward and he was able to fight those effects. There had to be a way for him to find the wolf buried in his mind.

"If you can hear me, we're really stuck here. I know you can do this."

Aldric meditated for another five minutes before finally deciding that communicating with the beast was impossible. Surrendering his desperate last resort, he opened his eyes with a groan. His wrists started to burn more, and he felt his throat closing up as the silver burned. Since they'd attached them, he had felt the stinging. It was worse when he thought about it, but for the most part he'd grown accustomed to the pain. For some reason, though, it just kept burning worse, as if it were heating up. The pain was becoming unbearable, and Aldric instinctively tried to scratch them off, but it didn't work.

Sensing movement in the basement, he froze. The door hadn't opened in what very possibly could have been days. Had someone actually been down there with him that whole time? Maybe they'd snuck in while he slept.

Aldric looked around, searching for the other presence. Unable to see inches in front of his face, Aldric didn't know exactly what he was hoping to find. Something brushed against his leg and he jumped back. Whatever it was, it wasn't human. He'd felt soft fur tickle his leg when it ran past him.

A low growl emanated from behind him, and Aldric started breathing more heavily. Something in him knew exactly what it was, but that wasn't possible. Panic set in as he felt the beast's hot breath against his upper back. Focusing on his breathing, he tried to calm himself, but it was no use.

❖ ❖ ❖

Aldric's eyes shot open as he heard a wail from upstairs. Although her pain tolerance and determination meant that she rarely showed any sign of pain, Aldric knew her voice well enough to recognize Linda.

Jumping to his feet, Aldric rushed for the door. The chains pulled him back and he felt himself growl as an instinctive response. The floor in front of him seemed to be illuminated with a mystical light, and Aldric could see most of the room. Angrily, he thrust his left arm forward with all of his might – tugging against the bondage. The chains broke, shattering halfway down the line. Following suit, he tore the other arm free.

Still, his neck held him back. Aldric stepped forward, but he couldn't muster enough strength to free himself. Whatever burst of power he'd found was fading fast, but he refused to give up. Aldric grabbed the collar at his neck, attempting to pull it apart, but his hands burned and he released the silver. Determined, he turned and grabbed the chain behind him. Though his hands felt as if he was holding the rack of an oven, he held tight and pulled. Finally, the chain broke, and he stumbled backward.

Suddenly, Aldric grew very tired. He'd used up every ounce of energy his body had, and he could barely support himself anymore. The lack of food and constant connection to silver was draining him. Still, he couldn't give up yet. Though he hadn't heard another scream, he wasn't confident that was a good sign. Aldric had to find his way to Linda.

Another sound interrupted Aldric's thoughts, though. This one wasn't as loud, but it had a strange familiarity to it. It wasn't something he'd heard before, but he felt like he had heard it thousands of times. From somewhere upstairs, an infant cried.

Aldric froze as he heard his son's first cry. That cry brought him back to life and he felt as if he'd just woken up from a long sleep. The silver still burned, but the fog was lifted from his eyes and ears. More importantly, from his thoughts. His mind churned as he desperately considered his next course of action.

He knew he couldn't storm the house. Aldric would lose that fight and he knew it. He and Cade were evenly matched, but

Cade had help. If he did somehow make it past them, Silas was by far their superior. The only way he was going to get out of that house was to use his mind. No one knew he was free yet, and the second he sacrificed that knowledge, he lost his advantage.

He could lure them downstairs one by one and tie them up, but that was risky. The second one of them made too much noise, his efforts would be in vain. If he were to work quickly, he might be able to use the silver chains as a weapon to kill them one by one. It wasn't ideal, but he would do whatever it took to protect his family. Silas was the cancer plaguing the Nystrom family, but when removing a tumor, healthy cells nearby must die as well. Though he wasn't confident even that element of surprise would be enough to allow him the strength to overcome Silas, he was running low on options.

Aldric walked back to the corner, relieved to finally have some idea of how to proceed. He grabbed the chains and slammed them against the wall, causing as much commotion as he could. The moment he heard footsteps nearing the door, he ran to the staircase and pressed himself against the stairs, hidden from anyone descending.

The door opened and light flooded the room, but his eyes were able to adjust relatively quickly. He heard soft footsteps descend the steps and steadied his breathing as he awaited his victim.

"If you were more cooperative, you could meet my grandson," his mother sighed as she descended. "You know, he really is beautiful. A true –"

She froze at the bottom of the stairs when she realized that Aldric was gone. Before she responded, he stepped out from the shadows behind her and wrapped the chain dangling from his wrist around her throat, pressing tightly to keep her from making noise.

"Listen to me carefully," he whispered in her ear as he pulled her back out of sight of the staircase. "Make a single sound and I swear I will end your life now. I'm sure you're aware that this is silver as it burns your throat. If I pull hard enough, you won't have time to heal. Do you understand me? Nod for yes."

She nodded.

"Good. Now, is there a clear path to my son?"

She shook her head.

"Who is in the way? Lara?"

She nodded.

"Anyone else?"

She shook her head. That was good.

"You're going to lead me there."

She nodded, and he pushed her up the stairs, keeping the chain pulled against her throat. The two of them walked as quickly as he was able while still holding her hostage. They walked up the stairs, to find Linda holding Cailean on a bed in one of the bedrooms. Lara, so focused on the baby, didn't even notice Aldric enter and close the door behind him.

"Don't make a sound," Aldric growled at her when she looked up. Terror filled her face as she saw her mother's life being threatened, and she nodded her compliance.

"Step back and close the curtains," he ordered in an urgent whisper. She obeyed, shutting out the outside world.

"Where is Silas?"

"Father and Cade are in the woods, waiting for you."

"How far?"

"They're werewolves, Aldric. If they haven't already heard you, they're bound to soon," she answered, understanding his true question.

"Then I suppose we must move quickly."

"You won't escape, Aldric."

"Not alone."

"This path doesn't end well. Please. You are risking more than yourself. They'll kill her, Aldric. And the boy."

"Cailean."

"Cailean. They'll kill him."

"They'll try. That's why you're going to help me."

"I can't do that."

"I don't think you understand, Lara. I'm not giving you a choice. I will kill your mother at the slightest hint of noncompliance."

"She's your mother too."

"Well, what was it you said, Elena? Your son is dead. I'm a different man. Now, Lara, you're going to unlock these cuffs.

Then, you're going to run as fast as you can to the northern edge of the woods and scream at the top of your lungs. Do you understand?"

"Yes," she cried. "Just please, don't hurt her. She's still my family."

"And I'll spare yours if you help me save mine."

Lara nodded and walked toward Elena, who offered her a key. As Lara released Aldric from his cuffs and neck brace, he instantly felt more of his strength flowing back. He still had his palms pressed against the chain he held to his mother's throat, so the effects weren't completely negated, but it was a noticeable improvement.

Tears in her eyes, Lara rushed downstairs. Linda, without a word, stood and walked to the window, peeking through the glass. When Lara was far enough, Linda nodded to Aldric.

"Now, Elena, we are going to leave. If you've ever cared about me or your own life, you will be silent."

She nodded, and he released her.

"Linda, get behind me and head downstairs."

Linda did as she was told.

"They're in the house!" Elena screamed at the top of her lungs. Aldric lunged forward, pressing the chain against her throat and slamming her into the wall.

"Killing her does no good," Linda told Aldric. "We just have to go."

"My wife is kinder than I am. I swear if you try it again you will die," Aldric threatened. He released her and broke into a run. She just fell back against the wall, holding her hand over her throat with terror in her eyes.

Aldric and Linda ran toward the southern edge of the woods, but Aldric saw movement through the trees. He turned only to see a few more people on the other side.

"You have nowhere to run, Aldric," Cyrus taunted, stepping out of the woods in front of him. "You're a good man, you know? You spared me, and I'll be in your debt forever. So allow me this chance to repay you. Surrender now, and you can have your life, Aldric. The boy stays, but he can make his own choice at thirteen."

"Learn to speak for yourself, Old Man," Aldric called into the woods. Silas walked out with his perpetual smirk plastered on his face.

"You caught me," he shrugged. "Now, take the offer. You know you can't beat us all."

Cade stepped out of the woods to the east and Lara had already found her way back to approach from the west. Behind them, Elena walked out of the house. Lara's husband, Eric, and her son – whom she named after her younger brother – walked out of the woods as well. Cade's wife, Amelia approached from the other side.

"You're right," Aldric sighed, dropping the chains he'd been holding. "I can't run anymore. And I can't beat you all."

"Give me the baby," Lara demanded, stepping toward them. Aldric placed a hand in front of Linda and moved between her and Lara.

"No. I can't beat you all, but I don't have to."

"You're joking," Silas laughed, clearly the first to pick up on his meaning.

"I'm not. You're a cancer. A plague on this family. And honestly, I'm not a better man than you. I would have killed my own mother if my wife hadn't stopped me. I wanted to bring you each to the basement and kill you one by one. Because I'm a monster. Your leadership – your fatherhood – is a blight. So not just for myself, or for my wife and son, but for the Nystrom name. For this family. Silas Nystrom, I challenge you for the title of Alpha of the Nystrom Pack."

Chapter 9

300 Years Ago

"What happened?" Lara asked. She sat across from Aldric, sipping a cup of coffee in a local shop. She had managed to contact Aldric, but he'd refused to meet her at the house. She claimed she just wanted to meet his wife, but he was skeptical of anything related to that family, so he'd insisted that they all meet in public.

After the obligatory small talk and her subtle attempts to mention that she hadn't seen him in a century, she finally moved on to her actual question. Aldric didn't know how to answer it, really. He could recount one specific moment, a tipping point which had finally convinced him to leave, but there were far more than that – and just because he wasn't fond of his father didn't mean he should poison her perception.

Aldric just didn't understand the tradition. Outside of his questionable choices – which Aldric could understand – it seemed more of a personality difference. Silas had grown up in an even more traditional lycanthrope family, so he was trapped in his ways. He wanted children raised in the pack, only pureblood marriages, and tight-knit families. Children who left, in his eyes, remained part of the pack. To Aldric, it looked like a power play.

"So much," Aldric finally answered with a sigh. "Twenty years of differences."

"You've had five times that to move on," Lara argued.

"Thanks for making me feel young," Linda joked as she tried to change the subject. He and Linda had talked about his family, but not extensively. Mostly, all she knew was that it was a sore subject for him. Ever patient with her husband, though, that was enough for her. For Lara, though, it clearly wasn't.

"What do you mean, Aldric? I know what happened with Damien was hard for you –"

"You think that's what this is about?" Aldric laughed sadly. "Lara, there's so much more."

"Then talk to me, please. I'm your sister. When did you stop trusting me?"

Aldric sighed deeply, looking into her pleading eyes. There was no ill intention in her gaze. Looking around the building, Aldric knew it was too public a place to discuss anything specifically. That had been the point when he'd suggested it. Seeing her eyes, though, he knew she didn't want to hurt them. She was just a sister reaching out to her estranged brother, wondering what had gone so wrong and trying to repair their relationship.

"Let's go," he finally said as he stood.

"Aldric, wait," Lara begged, grabbing his arm.

"Come with us," Linda explained, clearly understanding Aldric's intention. Lara paused for a minute before nodding gratefully. Silently, she followed them to his house.

"It's a beautiful home," she complimented as she walked through the door.

"Thank you," Linda chirped. She was so proud of her work as a decorator and it always brought a smile to Aldric's face to see her so excited about anything. He motioned toward the couch and Lara sat down. Aldric took a deep breath as he sat in a chair near her.

"Okay," he finally opened up. "It wasn't you, Lara. I need you to know that."

"I hoped," she smiled weakly. "But honestly I don't think any of us were sure. You just disappeared one day."

"I know. Just, let me talk," he spoke slowly, careful about his word choice. He had never spoken in detail about his past before, so he was trying hard to work up the nerve. When he did, he knew he would have to just tell the story without interruptions.

"Linda," he added. "A lot of this I haven't told you. It's time that I finally open up, right? But I need you to just listen too, okay? It's hard for me to talk about."

"I understand," Linda nodded. She sat next to him, silently offering support by placing a hand on his back.

"Our father was always very traditional. He never wanted us to leave the family home. I couldn't understand that myself, but he claimed we were a danger to ourselves and others before we knew how to control ourselves. Therefore, before the first time we changed, we were basically prisoners. I had a younger brother – Damien," Aldric continued, starting to get choked up.

"Damien and I hated being trapped. Well, after my first change, my father still decided I wasn't ready. There was still more for me to learn before I experienced the world outside. So my older brother, Cade, took us outside. Damien got hit by a car and gathered a lot of attention, and hunters chased us down.

"This was the first time we'd ever encountered hunters, so we didn't really know what to do. Damien died because of me. I wasn't strong enough to help him, and I wasn't ready. But you know what my father said? He told me exactly that. He told me that as an older brother, I should have been a better example. It was my fault that Damien was dead. He wasn't wrong, honestly, but how do you put that burden on a fifteen-year-old?

"Over the years he finally started teaching me about the weapons they use – about silver and wolfsbane. He started to teach me exactly how to kill them. I gave him my rapt attention because I didn't want to fail again, and I didn't want anyone to get hurt because of me. He manipulated me into being exactly what he wanted.

"There was one part he couldn't control, though. You see, I blamed myself, yes. But I also blamed the wolf. If Damien and I hadn't been different, none of that would have happened. We would have been able to live in the city like normal kids. So I fought the change with everything I had. I'd always wanted to be normal, but that pushed me so much farther. The pain was worth it because I was fighting in Damien's memory. Father never liked that, and I felt like he hated me. Thought of me as a disgrace for wanting to be human.

"He told me my whole life that I was better than humans. They weren't worth our time. I mentioned wanting to date someone and he and my mother laughed. Humans would not have the capacity to love us the same, and their lifespans are miniscule, so what's the point? I tried to explain to them that love wasn't what they apparently thought it was, but they refused to listen. Instead, Mother decided to try to arrange a marriage with another werewolf girl to keep the blood pure. I just wanted to be my own person.

"Then I watched Father murder three men in cold blood. I wasn't sure what was happening in the moment, but they were campers, Lara. They were campers. They just wanted a good weekend with their friends and maybe to find some deer. It's so obvious to me looking back – I don't know how his long life didn't give him the experience he needed.

"I couldn't be around that. That isn't me. I won't let it be."

"I had no idea," Lara mumbled.

"I didn't want to destroy all of your perceptions."

"Everything he does, he does for a reason. You know that, right?"

"You're defending him?"

"I'm just saying, Aldric. You were young – and you were feeling guilty. Your perception is flawed."

"Maybe," Linda stepped in. "But it's his reality. Aldric knows what he saw, and I have no question in that."

"Thank you," Aldric nodded.

"I didn't mean to sound like I don't believe you," Lara defended. "I know he does things that are hard to understand. Honestly, there are things I don't support. I just have to trust him. If you don't then that was your choice to leave. Others have too. It doesn't mean we don't love you and we don't miss you, though."

"Really?" Aldric laughed. "You didn't find me for a hundred years."

"I didn't think you wanted to be found."

"I suppose that's fair."

"Aldric," Linda added cautiously. "I still think we should go with her."

"What?"

"Not to go back to that family, of course. I just think you need closure. Cade and your mother deserve to at least know why you left. And you can still have a relationship with them."

"That's not how wolves work," Aldric tried to explain.

"It won't be if you don't try to change it."

"Cade would like you," Lara complimented.

"We've been married for eleven years," Linda smiled, dismissing the compliment. "Don't you think it's time for me to meet the family?"

"Okay," Aldric accepted hesitantly.

"Great!" Lara cheered.

"But not today. We wait. It's a few day's travel, and I don't want Linda anywhere near that place on the full moon."

Present
Unknown Days Until the Full Moon

"Aldric, wait," Lara cautioned.

"Yeah, be careful here," Cade warned.

"Just back down," Elena added.

Aldric stood tall, ignoring the warnings of his family. Allowing himself a quick glance back at his wife, he could see the fear in her eyes. Nonetheless, she nodded, trying her best to provide him with any strength she could.

"No," Silas growled, holding his hand up as he commanded the three of them to stand down. He stepped toward Aldric, staring him down. "Once a challenge has been issued, there is no going back. I'm done making allowances for you, boy. You want a challenge? You have one. Do you remember the rules?"

"One on one battle. The survivor is the Alpha."

"The weapons are the challenger's choice," Silas added. "Choose wisely."

"You've trained in every weapon I could think of. To give you any of those is unwise, and to wield a weapon I don't know is even worse."

"Logical assessment. Then you have chosen unarmed combat?"

Aldric nodded, attempting to maintain his feigned aura of confidence. He wasn't wrong that Silas would be far better trained than him in any weapon, but the same applied to his fists. Nonetheless, that was Aldric's best option. Silas removed his shirt and tossed it to the ground. Aldric wasn't sure why the members of his family loved fighting without a shirt on so much, but he welcomed it. To him, it just made his targets that much clearer.

"Are you prepared?" Silas asked. "It's dishonorable to fight a weakened opponent. Have you had ample time to heal from the silver?"

"I'm fine."

"Then feel free to attack at your leisure."

Aldric took two steps closer, raising his hands to cover his face. Silas stood perfectly still, his hands down by his sides. Aldric had never actually fought his father – his training had always been with Cade. He wondered if this was the exact reason why. If the Alpha fought, he'd just be giving potential challengers experience fighting him. Instead, he could observe his children as they trained to try to learn their fighting style without compromising his own.

Aldric lunged in to fake a punch, planning to follow up with some sort of attack. Before he even noticed him move, though, Silas had lifted his leg and thrown a powerful side kick directly at Aldric's ribs. Aldric fell to the ground and rolled over his back shoulder, jumping to his feet. Silas placed his foot back on the ground calmly and didn't advance. Instead, he gave Aldric a second to recover and reassess.

Aldric lunged forward again, but this time he was ready for the kick. He faked a jab but dropped his hand to block the kick. Silas threw a jab to Aldric's jaw, followed by rapid punches to the ribs, kidneys, and chin. Finishing his combo, Silas drove his fist into Aldric's chest and knocked him back again. Stumbling, Aldric barely managed to maintain his balance. Silas still didn't move forward.

"Come on, boy. If Cade taught you, I'm starting to question his role as Enforcer," Silas taunted.

Aldric rushed forward, throwing a punch toward Silas's face. Silas weaved backward and countered with a punch of his own, but Aldric parried it. Aldric blocked the next four attacks and threw a combination, trying to raise Silas's guard before attacking low. He punched toward Silas's face, then dropped down and followed up with two punches to the gut. Silas lifted one hand to parry the high punch, then dropped it down to deflect the low punches. Closing his other hand, Silas dropped his fist toward Aldric's head. Aldric raised his hands to block and Slias kicked him in the face, knocking him to the ground.

"That was better," Silas offered. "A few more exchanges like that and you may hit me."

Aldric stepped just out of range for Silas, giving himself a moment to gather his thoughts. Silas, as overconfident as ever, allowed him to do so. The two of them stood and stared each other down for another minute. Aldric laughed under his breath before dropping his own arms to his sides.

"Giving up isn't an option here," Silas taunted.

"I'm not giving up. I'm changing my strategy."

Aldric stomped the ground beneath him, kicking dirt and leaves into the air. He dove forward, rolling to the side. As he landed the roll, he stayed low, kicking the side of Silas's knee. Silas pitched forward, balancing on his good leg. Rising, Aldric turned and drove his heel at Silas's nose. Silas stepped in and caught Aldric's leg, but he was still not supporting weight on his weak leg.

Silas stepped closer to Aldric to drop him to the ground and Aldric wrapped his hand around the back of Silas's head, pulling his face down. Driving his weight off of his planted foot, he flipped Silas over his other leg, dropping him to the ground. As he fell with him, Aldric made sure he pinned Silas to the ground.

In a temporary position of power, Aldric threw punches at Silas's face. Silas blocked them all, remaining defensive. Realizing that his onslaught wasn't effective, Aldric rolled backward off of his opponent and jumped to his feet. Before Silas could stand, Aldric stepped on his broken knee, placing enough pressure to keep it from pushing its way back into place.

Silas grabbed his leg, but he didn't have the leverage to pull Aldric down. He bit down the pain and rolled around, though, further breaking his own knee to bring his other leg around Aldric to perform a modified scissor sweep. Aldric fell to the ground, keeping his chin tucked to avoid hitting his head. Silas rose his foot and drove his heel down on Aldric's ribs, shattering one of them, and rolled over his back shoulder to jump to his feet.

He stayed back, avoiding direct conflict as he allowed his knee to heal. Aldric tried to get up in time to keep his advantage, but fighting through his own broken bone wasn't easy. After a few minutes, both of them were fully healed except for some blood from the minor scrapes which had already closed up.

"Impressive," Silas complimented. "This might warrant me treating this more as a game than a joke."

"Stop hiding and trying to distract me," Aldric groaned. "If you had the skill to back it up, you wouldn't need to talk so much about it."

"If you insist," Silas shrugged. He moved faster than anyone Aldric had ever seen as he lunged forward and threw five punches – none of which Aldric could properly block. The first hit Aldric's face, breaking his jaw. The next hit his kidney, then liver, then ribs. Finally, he drove an uppercut to Aldric's chin.

Dazed, Aldric tried to keep his guard up as he healed. Silas didn't hesitate, though. He faked a punch toward Aldric's face, tricking Aldric into keeping his guard high. Instead, though, he punched low, knocking the wind from Aldric's lungs. As Aldric's arms dropped, Silas punched him in the nose. As a delayed reaction, Aldric lifted his arms to block, but Silas quickly punched his armpit.

Blood poured from Aldric's mouth and nose and he could practically feel the internal bleeding as blood pooled around his organs. He staggered backward, trying to buy himself more time, but Silas was clearly ready to finish the fight. Closing the distance, he threw another flurry of punches. This time, Aldric was able to block or parry them all, but it kept him on the defensive. Silas bombarded Aldric with punches to the head, forcing Aldric to keep both hands up to cover.

Silas threw a front kick to Aldric's gut. With the close range, his kick was jammed so it wasn't incredibly effective. Nonetheless, it served its purpose as Aldric pitched forward. Silas grabbed the back of Aldric's head and drove his knee upward, completely destroying any bone in his nose. Aldric dropped to his knees as his vision blurred. Silas stepped behind him, facing him toward his wife and all of the other onlookers.

"Your challenger," he announced, his hand on Aldric's matted hair. Aldric could barely see the people in front of him, but he saw his son. He had to fight for him.

Silas wrapped his arm around Aldric's face and, in one fluid motion, pulled up. Aldric barely felt the snap of his own neck as he collapsed to the ground.

Chapter 10

300 Years Ago

Looming over him like a hungry beast, the family home stood exactly as Aldric remembered it in his nightmares. Every fiber of his being questioned his decision to return, but Linda and Lara had been right. He'd associated so much with that home which it didn't deserve, and he did still have a family who cared about him. Although Aldric still couldn't guess exactly what his father felt about him, he at least had siblings and a mother who anticipated his return. Something still felt wrong, though, and his instincts screamed at him to turn and run.

"Aldric?" His mother called out, surprised, as she stood on the porch step. She ran to him and wrapped him in an embrace. Hesitantly, Aldric lifted his arms and hugged her back.

"I'm so glad you came home!" She cheered, pulling back to look at his face. Confusion was painted across his expression, but he couldn't place exactly what was triggering his fight-or-flight instincts.

"I'm just visiting," he finally responded. He didn't want her to think he'd come back to stay. Some wolves would adventure in the world and decide it wasn't for them only to move back to the family home. Aldric was definitely not one of those people. Still, that seemed abundantly clear since he brought home a human. For some reason, though, it was all that came to his mind to say.

"It's been so long," she replied, ignoring his comment.

"Hello little brother," Cade greeted with a smile as he walked up behind Aldric and patted his back. "I've missed you."

"What's going on?" Aldric asked. No one was saying anything inherently wrong, but they weren't acting like themselves. Perhaps it was just because it was the first time they had an outsider in their presence, so they didn't quite know how to react.

"Who is this?" Elena asked as she turned to look at Linda.

"This is my wife," Aldric explained.

"Linda reached out her and as she introduced herself with a smile. Reluctantly, as if Linda were somehow made unclean due to her humanity, Elena accepted the handshake. Cade was avoiding looking directly at Linda too, for some reason. They'd all been around humans enough, so he couldn't understand their reaction to her.

"It's a pleasure to meet you," Elena lied through a clearly forced smile. "Come inside, I was just making dinner."

Linda followed Elena into the house. Aldric was a few steps behind, but Cade grabbed his arm and pulled him back. He nodded to Lara, who followed the others inside. As soon as they were inside, Cade's feigned smile faded fast.

"She's human," he panicked, as if it were some disease she had.

"I'm aware."

"Does she know?"

"I think she does," Aldric responded slowly. "Don't quote me on it. I don't think I have actually asked her."

"You know what I mean," Cade responded, his annoyance apparent.

"Yes, she knows."

"You brought a human into this. Do you realize what you've done?"

"Brought a human into this?"

"Father would have your head if he were home."

"Well, then I guess it's good he isn't."

"She doesn't love you."

"I beg to differ."

"You know what it feels like to love, Aldric. You wasted that on someone who can never feel the same for you. On someone who will die. Do you know what happens to a wolf who loses their love?"

"I'm going to guess they don't love someone else. I couldn't."

"I wish I could have protected you from this."

"There's a lot you could have protected me from," Aldric muttered as he pulled his arm away. "Most of it was a lot closer to home than Linda."

❖ ❖ ❖

Sitting at the table with his family, Aldric finally realized how much resentment he held toward all of them. Maybe it was merited and maybe not, but they had all allowed everything his father did to happen. They had kept secrets and they had lied. They were complicit in their father's crimes. It was because they didn't know better; They'd been raised their entire lives by a very controlling father, and they had just grown to believe that was acceptable. Still, a time should have come when they realized that their decisions were their own. It wasn't excusable to continue to allow their lives to be dictated by him.

"Where is the restroom?" Linda asked, breaking a tense air of silence. Aldric wondered if she was just trying to give him some time alone with his family. Maybe she thought that would give him a moment to speak up and to work through whatever bitterness he held. Instead, when Lara got up to show her the way, he remained silent.

"Aldric," his mother finally spoke up. "You brought a human here."

"Lara thought you'd all want to meet my wife."

"I could have found you a wife."

"Are you serious, Mother? You haven't even given her a chance."

"What's the point? By the time I give her a chance she'll be dead."

"I'd rather have eighty years of bliss than a thousand of complacency."

"I'm sorry," she sighed. "I haven't seen you in so long, I shouldn't be scolding you. I am just happy to see you. It's just hard to watch you throw away something so precious."

"And this is why I haven't come home," Aldric laughed. Cade awkwardly stood and walked away from the table, clearly trying to give Aldric and his mother a chance to work through their differences.

"Because there are people who care about your best interests here?" Elena retorted defensively.

"Because you're all slaves to ancient ways which have no realistic place in this world. You refuse to grow and change because instead of accepting any slight imperfection of yourself, you paint the world to be in the wrong."

"There's a lot you want to say, isn't there?"

"I've had one hundred years to rebuild my mind after father's brainwashing."

"Your father will be home tomorrow. Maybe you can stay, and we can all try to talk. We don't want to lose our son, Aldric."

Aldric paused. He wasn't prepared for the fear or the actual remorse in his mother's eyes. Their emotions were unpredictable, and he started to think that anything she was portraying was just a cleverly sculpted manipulation tactic.

Aldric heard a scream and his eyes shot in the direction of it. Everything fell into place in his mind. She was a distraction.

"What have you done?" Aldric asked.

"Saved you," Elena solemnly replied.

Aldric jumped to his feet and ran toward the source of the scream. Linda sat pressed against a wall on the other side of the hallway, blood pouring from an open wound on her leg. A large wolf stood between Aldric and Linda, and it was staring at her with murderous intent. Aldric recognized the yellow eyes of Cade's wolf. He had snuck away to use wolfsbane to attack Linda.

Aldric rushed forward and drove his body into the wolf, tackling it to the ground. It scratched at him, cutting deeply into his arm. He punched the wolf in the nose, but it continued to scratch. The sheer mass of the beast would overwhelm Aldric if he didn't think of something to do. Desperately, he drove his finger into the beast's eye. It yelped as it tried to scurry away from him. Aldric stood and backed up, standing directly in front of Linda.

With one eye closed, the wolf stared Aldric down. It growled at him, filling the small hallway with its massive form. Snarling, the wolf rushed forward. Aldric kicked it in the snout, stunning it slightly. It recovered, though, and it looked as though it was preparing to pounce again. It stopped, though, and began twitching violently. The wolf collapsed as it began to shift back into Aldric's older brother.

Lara, still human, came from the other side of the hall, looking onto the scene. Elena walked in from the kitchen so the two of them were on either side of the hallway. The shattering bones as Cade transformed reverberated through the building.

"You all planned this?" Aldric asked.

"I planned it," Elena offered. "Your brother and sister just obeyed their mother like good children."

"We're not children," Aldric spat, glaring at Lara.

"I wanted to give you a chance to love, Aldric," Lara defended.

"And if she died?"

"What's the difference between ten years and eighty when you live forever?"

"Seventy years," Aldric said. "You're all insane. I thought it was father, but you're all too broken to redeem. I'm taking my wife and we're leaving. Don't follow us. We aren't your family. We aren't your pack. You killed a chance for that tonight. Do you understand me?"

Neither responded, and Cade rested in human form on the ground in front of him. Aldric stepped forward, anger coursing through his veins. He pressed his foot against Cade's helpless neck.

"I want a verbal confirmation from each of you that you understand me or I break his neck right now."

"You wouldn't do that to your brother," Elena pleaded.

"You clearly weren't listening. We're not family. You killed your son."

"Aldric –"

"No, don't. You killed your son, and I will take another from you if you say anything other than: 'Yes, I understand.' So I will give you one more chance. I am taking my wife and we are leaving. You will never follow us, or you will be declaring war with my pack. Do you understand?"

"Yes," Elena muttered, swallowing her pride. Aldric turned to Lara, glaring at her.

"Yes," she nodded. "I understand."

Present
Unknown Days Until the Full Moon

Aldric lay on his stomach with his cheek pressed against the dirt beneath him. Unable to muster the strength to stand, he resigned himself to the cold. The light had faded and only a dim glow radiated from the sky. All of the spectators had dissipated, leaving him alone with his thoughts. Despite his desperation to stand and save his wife, he couldn't bring himself to move.

Aldric heard footsteps near him and wondered if someone had come to make sure the job was done. Nothing made sense to him. He couldn't remember hearing all of them walk away, and he definitely couldn't see it as he was unable to move his head. It felt as though it had been hours yet he hadn't healed. The pain had faded, but his mobility hadn't returned.

The footsteps grew closer, but they approached from behind him so Aldric couldn't see who was walking toward him. Had they realized that they'd left him alive? Maybe it was intentional, because Silas just wanted him to suffer as long as possible. Maybe they'd stabbed him with a silver knife again.

No, he knew this was different. Although he couldn't place exactly what was happening, it was different.

Listening intently, he heard the person circle around him. Finally, the furry legs stepped into his field of view. A wolf looked down at him with sadness in its pure blue eyes. It whimpered quietly.

"Who are you?" Aldric asked, although he knew the answer full well. Of course it didn't respond, but it didn't seem frightened by his voice.

Aldric tried to move, but the action reminded his body that it was broken. Pain seemed to be the only thing he could feel in that moment as his body cried out in agony. It was the worst torment he'd ever experienced, and his weak body collapsed back onto the floor.

The wolf whimpered again as it inched closer to him. Aldric knew he should be afraid, but he couldn't feel fear as the beast grew closer. There was something familiar about it, and it clearly didn't want to hurt him.

"Am I dead?"

It didn't have his answers, and Aldric wasn't sure why he'd expected it to. Sorrow mixed with pity in its eyes as it looked at him, but it backed away, standing tall. Aldric wondered if the animal was trying to communicate with him in some way.

"Can you help me?"

It barked, appearing to get excited suddenly.

"Please," Aldric begged, his eyes filling with tears. He didn't know if the wolf could actually understand him or if it even cared. Despite being completely aware that his experience was nothing more than his brain reacting violently to its sudden death, he refused to give up hope. It could still be active for three minutes after death, and that could be nearly an eternity in a dream state. This was a broken mind dreaming. Nonetheless, he begged.

"Please help me. I don't know if you can, but I swear you can have the moons. I won't fight you. Just please, save my son."

❖ ❖ ❖

The light of day flooded back into Aldric's eyes as they shot open. Silas walked away as Linda fell to her knees next to Aldric, still holding Cailean. Tears rushed through her closed eyes as she mourned her husband.

"Your alpha reigns supreme!" Silas called to the pack.

Aldric felt his hands burning as they twitched. Claws erupted from his fingertips, and he felt fur start to grow on his body. The shocked expressions of the pack were clear to him, but Silas seemed to mistake them as being impressed that he'd just defeated Aldric.

Opening her eyes, Linda stopped crying – probably from confusion more than relief. She backed up, giving Aldric room to stand. Growing as he stood, he towered over Silas. Aldric felt a tail form from the bottom of his spine as his ears grew to a point.

"Silas," he growled. As Silas turned, his triumphant smirk was replaced with a look of pure horror.

"What are you?"

"I've become something you wouldn't recognize. A father."

"You're a monster."

"I'm the end of your era."

Silas put his hands up, but they shook slightly. The others were still standing on the sidelines, completely stunned.

"Linda, I want you to go stand at the edge of the woods. Keep Cailean away from this. And cover his eyes."

"I… Okay," she nodded as she stood to run. Eric stepped in her way to stop her, and Aldric laughed. He intercepted the man, catching him as he ran, and grabbed his throat. Pressing with all of his might, Aldric crushed the bones and veins in Eric's neck, dropping Lara's husband to the ground.

Lara and her son, Damien, screamed. They rushed at Aldric blindly, and Aldric dodged a punch from Lara and slashed Damien's throat. The boy fell to the ground, instantly dead. Aldric kicked Lara, sending her flying across the clearing and into the side of the house.

"The challenge stands," Aldric growled.

"No, I won the challenge. What you are now is a monster, not an alpha," Silas stuttered. Cade tossed him a silver sword from a weapons cache on the side of the house.

"So be it."

He heard footsteps behind him, and his tail caught Elena's arm as she tried to drive a knife into his back. Wrapping his tail around her wrist, he snapped it and broke her wrist. Stumbling backward, she dropped the knife to the ground.

Lara, who had recovered, rushed toward him. Amelia rushed in from his left. Both brandished silver knives. Cade closed in from the front, holding a sword like his father. As he swung the sword, Aldric weaved backward. He spun out of the way as Lara and Amelia closed the distance. Catching the backs of their heads, he slammed the two into each other. Cade swung his sword at Aldric's back, but Aldric threw a back kick and sent Cade flying backward. Cyrus helped him up and the two tried to close the distance, but they weren't fast enough. Aldric took the knife that Lara had dropped and stabbed the back of her neck, driving the silver knife into her brain. He did the same to Amelia, and the two stopped moving instantly.

Silas swung the sword at his left and Aldric rolled away, only to find himself closer to Cyrus and Cade. Cade threw a punch to Aldric's face, landing square in the jaw, but Aldric didn't flinch. Cyrus, who had retrieved his father's sword, rushed forward with the tip of the sword pointed toward Aldric. Aldric punched Cade's jaw and stunned him, then lifted him and held him between himself and Cyrus. With too much momentum to stop, Cyrus plunged the sword into his father's stomach.

Aldric pulled Cade away, ripping the sword from Cyrus's shaking hands, and tossed him at Silas. Silas fell to the ground as Cade hit him. Aldric slashed his claws across Cyrus's throat, killing the boy instantly. Elena came from behind him again, but it didn't work any better than it had the first time.

Aldric turned, parrying her stabbing motion and leaving her open. Driving his palm forward, he hit her in the chest and sent her flying backward. Walking toward her, he was ready to finish the job, but Silas stood and ran toward him, leaving the sword behind.

Aldric threw a punch toward Silas's face which the man parried. He countered by ducking down and punching Aldric's stomach. Aldric stumbled backward and Silas closed the distance quickly, trying to keep his advantage. He threw two punches, which Aldric dodged easily. Aldric countered with a punch of his own, but Silas blocked it and kicked Aldric in the stomach. Moving in, Aldric fell right into Silas's plan as the man landed a powerful side kick to Aldric's ribs.

Elena approached from the left, driving a silver knife into Aldric's ribs. Instantly his power began to wane, but he turned and caught her arm. Silas stepped in and caught Aldric's jaw with a hook punch, knocking him to his knees and forcing him to release Elena. Moving in, Silas kicked Aldric in the ribs and knocked him to the ground. As he rolled, the blade twisted in his side and more blood rushed through the wound.

Struggling to his feet, Aldric retrieved the knife from his own body. In an attempt to confuse Aldric, Elena and Silas approached from opposite directions, planning to attack from both sides. Aldric stepped back, doing his best to stay out of the middle. They both changed their direction but he'd managed to get both of them in a line in front of him.

Aldric countered two attacks from Silas and slashed his forearm with the silver knife. It was barely more than a flesh wound, but it had done all the damage he needed. Using the surprise to his advantage, Aldric kicked Silas's knee and then his chest, breaking his knee and pushing him backward. Elena threw three punches, all of which Aldric avoided. With the third, she left a brief second of an opening with both of her fists too far to cover. Aldric drove the knife upward with an uppercut, stabbing her at the base of her neck. She dropped to the ground, lifeless.

Silas writhed on the floor – his weakened healing factor not working quickly enough to alleviate the pain. Pushing himself backward, he tried to give himself distance and time to heal as Aldric approached. The prideful part of Aldric didn't want to kill a weakened foe, but the practical side knew it was the easiest moment. He moved toward Silas, but he dropped to his knees as he felt another blade pierce him in the back.

Aldric grabbed the hilt of the blade with his tail, pulling it from the wielder. Reaching around, he pulled the sword out and drove it into the ground, using it to give himself balance. When he turned, he saw Cade, barely able to stand on his own. Blood still poured from the wound where the sword had stabbed him, but he'd managed to get to Aldric and stop him from killing Silas.

Cade collapsed in front of Aldric, the wounds getting the best of him after he'd completed his task. Though he was beyond mortally wounded for any human, Cade's heart still beat faintly. Aldric decided he'd deal with him later, though, because he couldn't allow Silas to surprise him.

Turning around, Aldric saw Silas stand up, completely healed. He groaned as he dropped the sword to his side, but he stood still. His own wounds still needed a bit more time to close, so he decided to allow Silas to make the first move.

Silas tried to bide his time, but he was clearly aware that Aldric was healing, and his temporary weakness was fading fast.

Finally, his resolve broke and he ran forward, throwing four punches, which Aldric parried. Silas kicked toward the open wound in Aldric's ribs, but Aldric raised his shin to block the attack. He drove an elbow toward Silas's face and the man weaved backward, then drove a hook punch into Aldric's wounded side.

Aldric stumbled backward and Silas stepped in with a barrage of attacks. Aldric blocked each one and managed to drive a knee into Silas's gut. As the man pitched forward, he caught his head and twisted, snapping his neck. Aldric dropped Silas's body on the ground next to him.

"Linda," he called, feeling his own power fading fast. She rushed to his side, pressing the infant's face into her shirt to shield him from the devastation. Aldric felt his arms and shoulders shrink. The muscles in his legs began to atrophy, returning to a human size.

"Let me hold him," he ordered, turning to face his wife.

"I… Yeah, okay."

She placed the child in his arms, and Aldric looked into the eyes of his son. As he accepted the baby, the claws in his hands retracted and he could feel his ears return to normal. Looking at that baby's innocent face, Aldric knew that everything he'd done had been worthwhile. None of it was pleasant, but he had protected that child from a life corrupted by that twisted family.

"I need you to do something," he told Linda without looking away from his son.

"Anything."

"Cade is still alive." He finally looked up at her to watch her expression change.

"No," she replied hesitantly.

"It has to be you, Linda."

"I can't leave you."

"You don't want this curse. You weren't given a choice, and this is your chance to be free. I can always give you the choice again, but for now, you need this."

"You need me," she argued. Linda clearly wanted her freedom, but her conscience wouldn't allow her to accept the escape so easily.

"Cailean needs his mother. You need to be there on the full moons because I can't."

"Okay," she finally agreed. She nodded, lifting the sword from the ground and walking to Cade, but she froze standing next to him. It was easy to talk about it with the destruction surrounding them, but actually ending someone else's life was another matter.

"It's okay," Aldric comforted her. Cailean looked toward his mother, but he was easily redirected as Aldric lifted him and pressed his body against his own. Cailean cried and Linda looked over her shoulder. Aldric looked down at his son, rocking him gently to sleep.

"It isn't easy. It never is. It never should be. Taking someone's life is a horrible thing. But if Cade wakes up, he will only come after us. We don't have another option. For Cailean, Linda, it has to be you. I'm sorry."

She had tears in her eyes, but she nodded. Lifting the sword, she closed her eyes. Blindly, she brought the weapon down and cut into the back of Cade's neck. Aldric listened as his heartbeat faded, leaving no activity.

Linda dropped the sword and stumbled backward, staring in disgust at what she'd done. Aldric stepped forward and wrapped an arm around her, spinning her around to tear her eyes from the scene. She buried her face in his chest and screamed.

At first it was for the emotional pain, but that was quickly overpowered by the sheer agony as her genetic code was rewritten, erasing all traces of lycanthropy. Aldric watched the wound on her exposed leg start to fade. The scar disappeared, and as it did the pain only seemed to intensify. Waking up, Cailean joined in her screaming. Linda clearly tried to stop herself, but she couldn't hold back the pain. She fell to her knees in front of Aldric and he held her in one arm and his son in the other, knowing full well he couldn't do anything to ease either of their pain, but embracing them anyway.

❖ ❖ ❖

Linda held Cailean, cradling the sleeping baby in her arms. Her back was turned to the large pyre Aldric had constructed. He'd gathered all of the bodies along with ample combustible material, setting it all down in a pile. The remnants of his torn family lay dead before him and he could barely bring himself to feel anything. He only felt numb.

Aldric lit a match and dropped it, burning the corpses in one large heap. He stepped back to stand with Linda, who was still looking away. Though he completely understood her aversion to looking, he couldn't tear his eyes away. The sight became more painful with each passing second, but Aldric needed the closure that it brought.

"With this," he spoke, partially to Linda and partially just to the air. "The Nystrom Line dies. We are something else. Something new."

He turned and looked down at his son.

"And this child will grow into a good man. Better than I have ever been. My legacy will not be his."

Aldric sighed. The peacefulness in his son's sleeping smile contrasted with the hectic battle his life had been for so long was a beautiful sight. He knew that he would give anything to prevent any harm from coming to that child.

"He will rise from the ashes of this broken family. Like a Phoenix."

Linda nodded, smiling down at her sleeping baby. Finally able to tear her eyes away, she looked at Aldric, gazing deeply into his eyes. He could practically see the thought forming in her tired mind as she tried to speak.

"Cailean Phoenix. I like it."

Cailean

Chapter 1

11 Years ago

Aldric

"I'll be alright, Aldric," Linda smiled, cradling her son in her arms. Aldric hadn't left her side for the past month, but he didn't have the option to stay. Theoretically, he could change in the basement, but he didn't want to risk anything. If he broke out, it would be disastrous, but even outside of that, he could make enough noise to attract attention.

"Are you sure?"

"He's a baby. All he does is sleep and cry, and I can handle those," she joked.

"He does so much more than that. He also eats and poops."

"Careful, you're going to make me panic."

"I wish I could help."

"You help every day, Aldric. Now stop dawdling or you'll run out of time."

She was right. The moon was already beginning its ascent, and Aldric could tell that the transformation was coming. A month ago, he had called upon the wolf for a strength he never could have managed on his own. He still wasn't quite sure how it had happened, but he remembered promising it that he would stop fighting. Aldric considered himself a man of his word, so he didn't want to break that promise – even if it was to a part of himself.

Anyway, he didn't particularly want to test the boundaries and see if he could infuriate the beast.

"Okay. I'll go to the woods; you know the place. I'll be back as soon as I can, okay?"

"I love you," she replied as she gently kissed his lips before nodding toward the door.

"I love you too," he smiled. Taking a few steps backward, Aldric kept his eyes glued to his son. The child was asleep so peacefully in his mother's arms. Aldric couldn't remember the last time he'd seen anything so tranquil in his entire life. The scene in front of him almost made the rest of his life seem like a dream. All the violence and death that had led up to that moment couldn't possibly exist in the same world as that baby.

Finally, he turned his head, tearing his eyes away as he opened the front door. Hesitating in the doorway, Aldric looked over his shoulder one last time. Linda chuckled and waved, silently telling him to hurry up. Cailean didn't wake from the noise, so he just rested atop one of her arms. Closing the door with a sigh, Aldric turned and began walking down the street.

Paranoid, he looked over his shoulder every few feet. Aldric exhaled deeply and relaxed his shoulders in an attempt to appear calmer. It wasn't likely that anyone would be following him, but if they were, he didn't want to give them a reason to be suspicious. It felt as though he'd forgotten everything he had taught himself over the past four hundred years. Of all the techniques to avoid being followed by hunters, staying relaxed and sticking to the shadows were the most basic. He had already caught himself breaking both of those.

Aldric turned, walking down an alley which wasn't on his path. After a few more intentional wrong turns, he managed to get back onto the path toward the woods. This time, though, he carefully avoided streetlights and any possible observers. He was distracted, but that wasn't a good reason for him to allow any of the basic defensive principles he'd established to falter. In fact, it was a reason to focus more on them if anything. More people depended on him now.

After a few more minutes of fast-paced walking, Aldric left city limits and wandered into the woods. The trees grew thicker as he pushed his way deeper into the woods. Aldric followed a walking path at first, cognizant of the signs. He'd walked the path a dozen times with Linda and Cailean over the past month, but he hadn't actually transformed in the woods yet, so he was cautious.

Aldric passed a campground to his right. There were a few tents set up not far from the path and a few people were gathered around a campfire. One of them waved at Aldric, who smiled and nodded back at him. As subtly as he could, though, he picked up the pace. He could see the moon climbing in the sky and feel the wolf beginning to assert its dominance – struggling for control.

When Aldric had gone about a quarter of a mile without seeing anyone, he started to jog. He had left too late, and he wanted to make sure he got as far as possible before changing. In less than two minutes, he'd managed to get a mile from the campground. The path turned, heading back toward town, but Aldric continued to run straight toward the dense foliage.

Confident there was no one anywhere near him, Aldric finally allowed himself to slow down. Although he'd stopped keeping track of time, he knew had had run for at least five minutes, so he was miles away from any other human. There was no doubt the wolf could travel that far if it desired, but he knew it wouldn't want to find people. If it was hungry or threatened, it may attack campers. Normally, though, it would prefer to hunt easier targets, such as deer.

Aldric removed his shirt and folded it nicely, setting it in the dirt near the thick trunk of a nearby tree. Stretching, he cracked his back before realizing exactly what that meant. Since he felt the need to crack his back, that meant the wolf was beginning to become uncomfortable in his skin, so it was trying to begin the process of breaking the bones and shaping them into something it was more used to.

"Alright, alright," Aldric thought. *"Just let me fold my clothes."*

Quickly, he removed his shoes and set them next to his shirt. He placed his socks within the respective shoe and pulled his pants off. Somehow, he felt as though he could feel the wolf's emotions. It seemed to be eager to be free, and it was pushing itself to the surface.

"I promised I wouldn't fight you," Aldric silently told the wolf. Part of him wondered how crazy he was. It didn't make sense for him to be talking to the wolf, but he still felt as though it was helping. He couldn't quite determine if he thought the wolf was just another part of him or a separate being which occupied his body. Either way, he felt as though he was talking to himself.

Aldric took his boxers off and set them in the pile before taking a few steps back. The moon was high in the sky, but he didn't feel the pain of the transformation. Every time in the past had been agonizing, even before his body fell apart. Before the wolf began to rend his flesh and bone to shreds, replacing it with its own. In the past, he'd been able to feel the pain as the wolf struggled to escape.

This time, though, there was nothing but a strange sense of comfort. If the wolf was a separate creature, it clearly knew that Aldric was planning on staying true to his end of the deal. If it was the same as him, whatever subconscious piece had finally stopped fighting Aldric. Either way, it was a welcome change from the transformations of the past.

Aldric felt the wolf pushing against him a bit, and his joints started to feel tight. With a sigh, Aldric popped his fingers. Eight of them were pushed from their sockets, leaving only the thumbs intact. That hurt, of course, but it still didn't compare to the past transformations. Aldric stretched his arms over his head, dislocating his shoulders.

His arms and hands reformed as he dropped to the ground. As new cells replaced the old ones, Aldric could feel the pain receptors begin to form. The typical agony was replaced by a mild discomfort. When that faded, though, a sense of peace seemed to wash over Aldric.

Aldric's knees shattered, causing him to grimace. They healed quickly, though, as if there had been no damage. His body quickly changed form, and he was a wolf within a few minutes. He'd never experienced such a quick and painless transition.

"Well, that was a pleasant surprise," he thought. He wasn't sure if he was just trying to have the thought to himself or share it with the wolf, but of course he didn't get a response.

The colors of the world faded as Aldric's eyes changed and he could feel the leaves under his paws. Aldric looked beneath him.

Most of the green colors around him had faded to a shade of grey, but still somehow everything seemed so vivid.

"Alright," he thought. *"Just don't do anything stupid."*

Aldric closed his eyes. At least, he tried, but the beast's physical eyes remained open. Still, his vision faded and his feeling dissipated as his control over his limbs was ceded to the wolf. It didn't feel much different than falling asleep except that his body was still moving.

For the first full moon in a long time, Aldric rested. The wolf ran through the trees, enjoying its freedom, but Aldric slept.

Present
Night of the Full Moon
Cailean

"Father," Cailean called as Aldric opened the front door. His father closed the door with a sigh, clearly gathering from his tone that it wasn't a quick question. Aldric squatted down in front of Cailean, dropping his bag to his side.

"What is it, son?" His voice was gentle, but Cailean could sense a bit of exasperation behind it. It wasn't the first, or likely even the tenth time that he'd stopped his father from leaving during the full moon. Patience was not a trait Cailean would associate with his father, especially near his transformation. Still, Cailean always managed to think of new questions just as he was about to depart.

Staring at Cailean expectantly, Aldric pasted a fake smile onto his face, failing to cover up the sense of urgency. Searching his mind for the reason he'd stopped him, Cailean came up empty. Maybe it had just been a cry for attention, or maybe he'd just realized that his questions wouldn't be answered anyway. It wouldn't have been the first time he'd tried, but for some reason his father was always very reserved when it came to lycanthropy.

Past conversations ran through Cailean's mind as he tried to find a question which he hadn't asked before. The one thing he didn't want to do was admit to his father that he'd distracted him without proper cause. Questions such as 'Why are we werewolves?', 'When will my first transformation be?', and 'Why can't I watch you turn?" had all been met with vague answers.

As a young child, Cailean had obviously believed anything his father had told him. Recently, though, he'd started questioning everything. His first instinct was to press Aldric for more information. All he wanted was some kind of proof that the story was true because the concept of werewolves seemed completely unreasonable to him. Nonetheless, despite his refusal to explain anything thoroughly or provide evidence, Aldric seemed very set in his convictions, and Linda supported him. It also seemed to be the only way to explain how his cuts would heal instantly or why he'd never been sick like the other kids.

Realizing that he'd been grasping for a question for a while, and the annoyance was becoming clear in his father's eyes, Cailean snapped his attention back to the present. Cailean opened his mouth, preparing to speak, but his breath caught in his throat. His mind raced as the amount of time he'd been silent became an increasingly pressing concern.

"Why can't you stay here? What if I change tonight?

"I've already told you why I can't stay," Aldric sighed heavily.

"But…"

"I really have to go, son," he cut him off. Cailean silently looked down at the ground as Aldric stood and retrieved his bag. He turned and reached for the door but hesitated. With a quiet groan, he dropped the bag and turned back around.

"Okay. If I'm here, I'll make a lot of noise. The hunters may find us because of it. Aside from that, though it's very unlikely, it's possible that if I changed in the basement, I could climb the stairs and break through the door. Sure, it's reinforced, but I'd rather be safe than sorry. In order to keep us all safe, it's best if I change in the woods."

"But how will I know when it will happen?"

"I wish I could tell you, but you won't see it coming too far in advance – the only signs will be within a few days. It won't be tonight, though. If I am somehow mistaken, your mother knows exactly how to handle the situation."

"Won't I be loud?"

"I'm bigger than you, buddy. I would make a significantly larger commotion. The hunters won't find you."

"Are you sure?"

"Yes," Aldric assured, turning back toward the door. "It's going to be okay, Cailean. I have everything under control. As long as you follow my instructions, the hunters won't be a problem."

Aldric opened the door and stepped outside before turning around and adding, "I promise." Cailean wasn't entirely convinced, but he felt a bit better after the conversation. Still, something told him that was going to be the night. In preparation, Cailean sought out his mother.

"Mom," he called, searching the lower floor for her. After a moment, he found her sitting on the couch in the living room reading. As he walked in, she closed the book and set it on the end table near her. Stretching, she stood and yawned.

"Is everything alright?" She asked calmly, walking toward him and squatting down to meet his eyes.

"I think I'm going to be a werewolf."

"Oh yeah?" She asked.

"Yes, I'm certain."

"Why is that?"

"I don't know," Cailean admitted.

"Well, if you don't know, it probably isn't tonight," his mom consoled.

"What if I want it to be?" Cailean questioned, annoyed.

"Unfortunately, that doesn't affect it much. Trust me, hun, there's no rush."

"I want to be like ."

"Oh, you are," she laughed, "far more than you know."

"Can you at least tell me the plan?" Cailean pleaded.

"Of course," his mother agreed, standing tall again. She nodded toward the hallway and started walking, so Cailean matched her pace. She led him toward the living room as she spoke.

"If you started transforming," she started slowly and seriously, "then there is a very detailed plan in place to keep us all safe."

"Yeah?" Cailean asked, not bothering to mask his enthusiasm.

"Of course," she affirmed as they approached the basement door.

"What is it?"

"Well, I would pick up your little wolf pup body and throw you down the stairs like dynamite," she informed him, her tone shifting drastically. As she finished the sentence, she picked him up and pretended to throw him down the stairs. Instead of releasing him, though, she just spun in a circle and brought him to the ground, tickling him.

Against his will, Cailean laughed as he struggled to break free. Despite his enhanced strength, his mother was able to hold him down with relative ease. Apparently it took more than the power of a werewolf to give an eleven year old the ability to break free from his mother's tickling. Finally, he was able to wriggle himself free and roll over his back shoulder, jumping to his feet.

"Your shoulder rolls are getting much better," his mom commented with a smile as she leaned back, placing her palms on the ground behind her.

"I've been practicing," Cailean admitted.

"Cailean, don't worry about tomorrow today," Linda added, the laughter draining from her voice.

"That's not how you plan," Cailean argued.

"No. But it is how you live. It's how you smile." She leaned forward and reached up, rubbing her hand on his cheek. "Be a child, son. Before you have to be a wolf."

Silently, he nodded and sat down in front of her. Cailean wasn't sure why both of his parents were so opposed to the idea of being a wolf. He thought it was an interesting idea, and it made him different from everyone else – even if he couldn't tell them. Nonetheless, he'd given up on arguing with them.

After a few minutes of quiet, Cailean's mom sighed and stood up, rustling his hair. He leaned his head against her leg in a half-hearted attempt at a hug.

"Do you want some food?" She asked.

"I'm not hungry."

"That's how I know it's not the night," she joked. Cailean didn't understand what she meant, but he could tell that it was intended to be humorous from her tone. Instead of asking for an explanation, though, he just let the meaning go over his head.

"Come on, let's go watch a movie," she offered.

"Maybe later. I just want to think a little."

"Okay," she accepted sadly. "I'll be here if you need me."

Cailean sat still for a few minutes after she walked away, staring blankly at the wall in front of him. He brought his hand in front of his face, staring at the back of it. Being a werewolf made him different, but he didn't feel different. He just felt like a normal person.

Angrily, Cailean jumped to his feet and looked toward the basement door. Closing the door behind him, he stepped onto the first stair leading down. To be cautious, he locked himself in before descending to the lower level of his house.

"Why?" Cailean muttered under his breath. "I don't get it."

Asking all the questions he could imagine to the wall, Cailean offered himself a moment of catharsis. All he wanted was to be like his father, but apparently that was too much to ask for.

Growling, Cailean punched the brick wall in front of him. His knuckles shattered, and he yelped in pain as he pulled his fist back, shaking it violently as if that would dull the pain. Staring at the back of his hand, Cailean watched the bones move under the skin, repairing themselves. As the anger was drowned out by pain and curiosity, he watched the healing process as he sat and leaned against the wall.

Cailean knew he was going to change that night. It didn't matter if either of his parents believed him, he could feel it. Something was changing within him, and he had to make sure he kept his mother safe. Tomorrow, he would be able to prove that he was right. Leaning against the wall, though, Cailean felt himself growing tired and drifted off.

❖ ❖ ❖

"There you are," Cailean greeted happily. In front of him rested a small wolf, probably still a baby. The cub looked in his direction, but its eyes were still closed. He'd seen the animal in his dreams for the past few nights, and he knew it had to mean something.

The wolf barely seemed able to stand on its own, but it inched its way backward as Cailean approached. For a reason beyond his grasp, Cailean felt afraid. The cub couldn't be more than a few days old, and it didn't seem to be the target of his fear, but they were alone and he was terrified. Regardless, Cailean cautiously inched his way toward the pup, holding his hand in front of him. When he was close enough to pet it, he dropped to his knees and held his hand in front of the dog.

It approached him slowly, and his heart pounded within his chest. Steadying his breathing, Cailean tried to keep himself calm as it sniffed the back of his hand. Slowly, the fear drained from him and was replaced by a sense of comfort. Finally, it began licking the back of his hand. Smiling, Cailean brought his hand up and gently pet the dog's head. Cuddling against the palm of his hand and using him for warmth, the cub fell asleep.

Chapter 2

11 Years Ago
Aldric

"What if we just stay here?" Aldric suggested, cradling Cailean and rocking him gently as he slept. Baffled by how tiny his son was, Aldric just stared at the baby. Of course, he knew in theory how small infants were, but it was something different entirely to hold one. The fragile being in his arms depended upon him and Linda for everything.

"This town has some bad memories for you, doesn't it?" She replied, concerned.

"They're just that – memories. Anyway, it was centuries ago. I think it's time to settle down and make some new ones."

"What about the last job?"

"We'll be fine," Aldric laughed softly, trying carefully not to wake the baby. For the first time in the conversation he was able to pull his eyes from Cailean and look up at his wife, only to find her staring at their son as well.

"I won't pretend it wouldn't be nice to have you around," she admitted.

"You know my tendency to overprepare. Let's just live here. We'll keep to ourselves. As much as we can, and no one will question us. For as long as possible, we can let Cailean live in one place."

"I like that," Linda agreed as she looked up and caught Aldric's eyes.

"I thought you might," he smiled as he handed her their son. Without another word, Aldric held up a finger to tell her to wait and wandered toward the basement. In one sweeping motion, he grabbed a stack of documents and turned back toward the door, bounding up the stairs.

"I already got started on our new identities, just in case," he informed her when he reached the top of the stairs. Aldric held the papers out toward her before realizing that she was still holding the baby.

"Trade," she laughed, handing him Cailean as she took the papers. All the motion jostled Cailean awake, and he started crying angrily.

"Just like his dad, he hates to be woken up," Linda teased.

"That happens to be a rather common dislike," Aldric defended. He wasn't sure when she'd fabricated that idea or why it was something about which he should be teased. To Aldric, it seemed obvious that he wouldn't like being awakened unnecessarily. As a child, Aldric's family had forced him to train his reflexes, and he had learned to wake up in a hurry to be ready for anything. He found that to be a hard habit to break, especially when he knew the dangers which surrounded their world, so Aldric was still a very light sleeper. Any time Linda would try to wake him, he'd jump up in a panic, and then be annoyed if there was no real reason, because it was impossible for him to get back to sleep after the adrenaline kicked in. Recently, though, Aldric had been having trouble sleeping at all. He couldn't distract his mind from the omnipresent danger of the hunters long enough to sleep.

"I know," she sighed, disheartened that her joke hadn't been received well.

"He's got plenty in common with me," Aldric tried to change the subject. His perpetual state of being tired since Cailean's birth brought along a level of irritability. Though he knew that Linda meant no harm with her joke, he was annoyed that she found it so humorous that he appreciated the little sleep he could get. Still, rather than making a scene about it, Aldric was happy to just move on to a different point of conversation.

"I'm pretty sure he has my eyes."

"I wonder whose eyes he'll have when he becomes a wolf," Linda pondered.

"That's not entirely how that works," Aldric laughed. The color of a wolf's eyes didn't particularly have anything to do with genetics. It was more associated with the development of the individual.

"What do you mean?"

"I'll tell you about it later," Aldric replied. The two still talked over Cailean's crying as Aldric rocked his son, trying to ease him back to sleep.

"For now, you check out those papers while I try to comfort this little guy," he offered. Aldric rocked Cailean back and forth as he looked down at his child.

"It's okay, buddy," he whispered. Soothing Cailean, Aldric continued to whisper and gently bounce him. Finally, Cailean's cries subsided and he drifted back to sleep in Aldric's arms.

"He's got your voice," Aldric joked, trying to return her attempt at humor.

"Original," she replied, narrowing her eyes at him. With a laugh, she looked down at the birth certificate in her hand. "I guess I can't argue with you though."

Aldric cradled Cailean, giving his wife a moment to look over all of the paperwork. He was confident that he would have the funds to procure everything they might need. Looking at his son's face, he knew the hundreds of years of hard work had been worth it. If not for the playful jokes with his wife, or for the ability to spend time as he pleased, then for Cailean.

"These look perfect," Linda praised with a smile. Though there was no sadness in her tone, she did sniffle slightly as she looked away from the paper she held.

"It will be the last alias in a long time," Aldric began, anticipating her question. "So I thought it was okay."

"Okay? I think it's great. We can finally use our real first names."

"It's our real last name, too. From this point on, we are legally the Phoenixes."

Present
29 Days Until the Full Moon
Cailean

Jumping out of bed, Cailean raced toward his calendar. In his haste, he barely even took the time to register the fact that he hadn't fallen asleep there. Instead, he turned his full attention to the countdown written in the boxes in front of him.

About a month ago, he had written the number of days remaining until school in each box. Since then, he had been crossing off the days as he woke up each morning. Only two weeks until he started sixth grade. Of course, Cailean wasn't particularly excited for school, but at least he was finally starting middle school. No one would be able to pretend he was just a kid anymore. Middle school was always the time which Cailean had assumed he would begin to transform – growing more like his father.

Eagerly, Cailean ran to the kitchen, bounding down the hallway. Beaming as he opened the kitchen door, he found his parents sitting somberly at the table. With the tension in the air his mood changed drastically.

"What's up?" Cailean questioned, gazing toward his mother.

"Nothing," she shrugged with a smile. "Did you sleep alright?"

"Yeah," he replied. After a moment of contemplation he added, "thanks for bringing me to my room."

"That's what moms are for," she smiled, squatting down to his level and kissing his forehead.

"Only two more weeks," Cailean cheered after his mom stood and walked toward the cabinets.

"For what?" Aldric asked, narrowing his eyes.

"Really?" Cailean asked, taken aback. Cailean knew his father was being facetious, but he still hesitated for a moment. Daily for the past month he had been reminding them that he was almost ready to start middle school.

"Of course I remember," Aldric laughed. "How could I forget?"

"Yeah!"

"Cailean," Aldric added slowly, as though carefully selecting his words. When he didn't follow the name with anything, Cailean began to feel concern. He'd never seen his father at a loss for words.

"What?" Cailean finally offered.

"After breakfast, meet me in the basement," he ordered.

"Oh, okay," Cailean shrugged, wondering why his father had struggled so much with that statement. They trained in the basement nearly every day, so it wasn't an irregular command. Without another word, Aldric vanished through the kitchen door.

"Is he alright?" Cailean asked his mom.

"He's just not ready for you to grow up," she teased, punching Cailean's arm. Cailean wondered if his mom was scared to hurt him, because she never put any force into her punches.

"I am," Cailean countered.

"I know," she laughed sadly. Clearly she was unwilling to accept that he was growing up as well. Cailean couldn't understand why it was so difficult for everyone around him to process the fact that he wasn't a child anymore. Growing up was normal; it didn't have to make everyone so uncomfortable.

"I'm going to make cereal," he muttered awkwardly after a moment of silence, motioning toward the cabinet behind his mother.

"Oh! Don't worry about it, I'll make it," she responded, apparently snapped out of her trance by his words. Turning around, she opened the cabinet and retrieved the box of cereal.

"Mom, I can make my own breakfast."

"I know you can. But it won't be long before you don't need me at all. Let me do what I can, huh?"

"Okay," Cailean muttered quietly before walking back to the table. Unable to grasp why his parents were acting so strangely, he just accepted that it was most likely just a result of their only child aging. Maybe they needed to have another kid. Cailean liked the idea of having a younger brother – even if he was quite a bit younger – and that would cure their early-onset empty nest syndrome. Cailean had suggested it before, but for some reason, his father seemed to be vehemently opposed to the idea. Deciding it was best not to bring it up again, he just remained silent as his mother added milk to a bowl on the counter.

He thanked her as she placed the bowl in front of him. Nodding with a smile, she sat across from him at the table and just stared at him. Ten seconds passed while Cailean waited for her to either say something or at least stop staring at him.

"Alright then," Cailean mumbled, turning his attention to his breakfast. Over his life, he had learned not to eat too quickly, especially when he trained in the morning with his father. Even with his metabolism, food took some time to digest, and fighting directly after inhaling any form of a meal was not in his best interest. Regardless, with his mother staring at him, the awkwardness drove him to eat far more quickly than he knew he should have.

"Alright, I've got to run," Cailean broke the silence as he pushed his chair backward and stood, retrieving the bowl.

"Don't worry about it," his mother motioned toward the dish in Cailean's hands.

"Okay, you're being really weird Mom," Cailean accused, refusing to hand over the dirty bowl. "You're the one who always taught me to clean up after myself."

"I'm sorry," she groaned, resting her head in her hands.

"What's going on? Is this about me going to middle school? Do you think I'm just going to stop loving you guys or something?"

"No," she laughed quietly.

"Then why are you both being so weird this morning?"

"Sometimes, you know that things have to change, but you just keep waiting, you know? I wish I could just keep you like this forever," she told him, gazing at him.

"You've taught me well, Mom," Cailean consoled as he rinsed the bowl. Walking back to her, he wrapped her in a hug. "I'm going to grow up, but I'm always going to be your son."

"Yeah," she smiled through tears.

"I'll stop talking about middle school if it makes you feel better," he offered.

"No," she shook her head. "It's not about middle school."

"Then what's up?"

"You should probably get to the basement. Your dad is waiting for you."

"Okay," Cailean hesitantly agreed. "Are you sure you're alright?"

"I'm fine," she replied with a kiss on his forehead. Leaving the kitchen, Cailean sighed deeply. His mother wasn't usually so emotional. Of course there were times that she'd respond to things, but to start crying for no apparent reason was unlike her. The entire situation made Cailean uncomfortable – and although he wouldn't admit it to her, he was excited to get away from it. Training with his father and learning to fight was by far the preferable option.

Cautiously, Cailean descended the stairs. The first lesson in self-defense that he'd learned was to never let his guard down. As his father always said – a fight begins before it begins, and it isn't over until it's over. It had taken Cailean a long time to understand that statement, but he believed that he finally understood what his father meant. An opponent could jump out at any moment – so even if the defender wasn't aware that a fight had begun, the attacker was waiting. The second half was far easier for him to wrap his young mind around. If he thought a fight was over, but the enemy got back up, he would be caught off guard. With that teaching running through his mind, Cailean was careful not to allow his father to catch him off guard as he reached the landing. To his surprise, though, he found Aldric leaning against the wall in the opposite corner.

"Good job using your training," Aldric complimented.

"Thanks," Cailean replied without attempting to mask his confusion.

"Don't worry, we can still spar," his father told him. Cailean never made it a secret that he enjoyed fighting, even though he had still yet to get a single hit in against his father.

"Is this a trick?" Cailean asked, watching the older lycanthrope with suspicion.

"No," Aldric assured him. "No, I just have to talk to you about something first."

"Okay."

"You're getting older. I think you're ready to hear this," Aldric started, turning a chair and offering Cailean to sit. Confused but excited to learn whatever it was his father had to say, Cailean sat silently and listened.

"What we are, Cailean, it scares people. You've always known that you're different, and I've done my best to explain that to you. You're not like the other kids, Cailean."

"No, I'm better," Cailean interjected confidently.

"No. You aren't."

"I'm faster. I'm stronger, I can hear and see better. I never get sick and my wounds heal instantly. I'm smarter than them too." The last part had nothing to do with being a werewolf, but Cailean's parents had taught him very well. Since he started school, they had supplemented his education. Cailean couldn't remember the last time he actually learned anything in school, but his parents told him that he had to continue going in order to keep appearances up.

"None of that makes you better," Aldric scolded. It had been a long time since Cailean had seen his father so angry, and he was taken aback. "It makes you different. Someone with strength should always use it to protect those without it, do you hear me?"

"Yes, sir."

"I wish I could teach you to do that, but it's an idealistic thought. Unfortunately, there are too many things preventing that."

"Like what?"

"Well, like I said," Cailean's father sighed, closing his eyes. Clearly, he was still working out the best way to organize his thoughts. "Some people are afraid of what we are, and fear, Cailean, is powerful. It can drive people to do monstrous things. There is an organization of these people called the Hunters.

"Hunters have made it their sole purpose to eradicate anything supernatural from this world. You see, we are stronger than humans. We could use that for good, but there are other wolves who would use that power to their advantage. Some of them hurt people with no discretion. Hunters, however, believe that we are all monsters and that we kill and hurt humans indiscriminately."

"Like when we're wolves?"

"Always. We can't control it when we're wolves, that's true. But that's why I take precautions. You always make sure you change on a full stomach, and you only change far from any humans. Still, sometimes people get hurt and because of that, hunters see us all as monsters."

"You said all supernatural creatures. Are we not alone?"

"This world is full of things you can't imagine, son."

"Like what?"

"Would you mind if we table that?"

"I guess."

"I'm sorry, but in case it isn't clear, this is difficult to me. I've never had to introduce a child to this before, and it makes it harder because you're my son."

Cailean had never seen his father struggle so much with anything, and he was unsettled. Something about the hunters clearly scared him, and to Cailean, that meant that he should take it seriously. If Aldric Phoenix saw something as a threat, Cailean refused to disregard it. Despite his curiosity, he agreed to be silent and allow his father to explain the situation.

"Each hunter has their own motivation – whether it's personal loss, religious zealotry, or just a desire to destroy what they don't understand. Whatever their motives, they are all dangerous. If they find out what you are, they will hurt you. Indiscriminately, they will kill you and everyone you love. They train their children basically from birth to notice any signs paranomality.

"Eyes will be on you as you move into this new school. Other kids will see you, teachers, parents. You're already strong, but it only grows after your first change. It will be evident, Cailean, just from looking at you.

"I will always be here to help you, but we need a plan. You won't be able to hide forever. So this is my advice to you: the best way to fit in is to stand out."

"What do you mean?" Cailean asked. Aldric knelt down in front of him, placing his hands on Cailean's shoulders and gazing intently into his eyes.

"Hunters will look for the quiet recluse. Werewolves wouldn't want to risk any attention. I want you to break that expectation. Try out for sports, spend time in the spotlight. Work out with your friends and give them a reason that you look the way you do."

"I think I understand."

"You can handle this," Aldric finished his speech, tapping Cailean's shoulder as he stood.

Cailean didn't budge. Instead, he took a moment to process the flurry of information which had been thrown at him. The idea that there was an entire group of people who wanted to kill werewolves just because of what they were sounded outlandish to him. If his father said they were out there, though, that was enough for Cailean. Still, to be as observant as he thought they were seemed to be another feat. Cailean surmised, though, if a person were trained from their youth, they would likely be able to notice how different Cailean was.

His mind raced, though, as he tried to work through the information. His father had implied that anyone at his new school could be a hunter. Suddenly, Cailean wasn't just walking into a rite of passage, but a gauntlet. For some reason, that idea was invigorating. For the first time in his life, Cailean was going to be able to fight something for real. Even if it wasn't an actual physical confrontation, every day was going to be a struggle.

Reading the situation, Cailean knew that his father wouldn't be very supportive of that mindset, so he kept it to himself. He didn't want to give the impression that he wasn't taking any of the new information seriously. It didn't feel particularly applicable to him, though. Cailean wasn't actually a werewolf, he was just the child of one.

"Father," he muttered unconfidently.

"Yes?"

"You say the hunters want to kill us just because of what we are, right?"

"I don't know their individual motivations, but yes, as a group, they intend to eradicate our species."

"But that's the thing, Father. This is your species, right? Mom and I are just humans."

"That's another story for another time," Aldric replied sadly.

"I'm old enough! I can hear it."

"That isn't the question," Aldric laughed, dropping back down to Cailean's level. Shaking his head and sighing, Aldric was for the third time that day at a loss for words. Silently glaring, Cailean waited for his answers.

"It's not about you, son. Your mother's is just a story that I'm not quite ready to tell yet."

"Fine, then what about me? Why can't I be like you?"

"What are you talking about?"

"I want to be a wolf! Like you, Father."

"You're growing up so fast," Aldric sighed, gently placing a hand on Cailean's cheek. Standing up, he turned and walked toward the wall. Cailean watched him, hoping there would be more to his response than that.

"Your mother and I weren't sure when to tell you about the hunters. We wanted to shield you from that truth for as long as possible. You deserved a childhood. The change will come, son. I wish I could stop it – because it's not something to be jealous of."

Aldric turned back to face his son and continued his explanation. Cailean could hear a tone of sadness in his voice, but there was a fire in his eyes.

"The beast consumes you. It's all I've thought about for years. Suddenly, life is about hunters and the next change. It's about survival. Once you see the world that way, there is no going back. So for as long as you can, Cailean, be a child. Go to school, make friends. Live, before living is all you can think about."

"I just want to be like you," Cailean argued, trying to bite back the tears. Aldric turned away, facing the wall. Defeated, Cailean stood and walked toward the stairs. Just as he was about to climb them, Aldric spoke up.

"Cailean," he called. "You're more like me than you'll ever know."

Chapter 3

10 Years Ago
Aldric

Stumbling with each step, Cailean slowly made his way toward Aldric. Patiently, Aldric knelt on the floor a few feet away, beaming as he watched his son. He held his arms extended toward Cailean, encouraging him with every motion.

"You can do it," Aldric cheered as Cailean took another wobbly step. He looked up at Aldric with a smile and giggled. The lack of attention directly on his feet caused him to lose balance, though, and he fell backward. Dropping to the ground, Cailean appeared to be ready to burst into tears. Instead, though, determined as ever, he stood back on shaky legs. Watching his feet carefully this time, Cailean took another step.

As he approached his father, his confidence seemed to grow. More steadily, Cailean continued his journey to his father's open arms. Finally, when he was just within Aldric's reach, he collapsed forward, trusting his father to catch him. Aldric moved his arms inward, intercepting Cailean as he toppled forward. Standing, he lifted Cailean over his head before bringing him back down.

"Good job, son," Aldric praised, gazing into Cailean's eyes. His face clearly expressed a sense of pride and accomplishment. A proud father, Aldric couldn't bring himself to stop smiling as he looked at his boy.

Tearing his attention away from the baby in his arms, a loud knocking reverberated through the house. The joy in Aldric's heart was quickly replaced with worry as he froze in place, staring toward the door. Silently, Linda approached him from the kitchen, reaching out and retrieving Cailean.

With his guard raised and every sense on high alert, Aldric walked toward the door. Linda stayed back, cradling Cailean in attempt to keep him as quiet as possible. Where she stood, she was just out of view from someone at the front door. The two of them had rehearsed the procedure a dozen times, but Aldric was confident that it hadn't been necessary. Linda was clever, and he trusted that she would sense the danger of any visitor. Regardless, as an engineer Aldric had learned the value of redundancy. Whether or not she was capable of improvising, it was best to have a procedure and a back-up plan.

Cautiously, Aldric glanced through the peephole in the front door. Outside, he saw a family smiling in at him. Nothing about them seemed particularly off-putting. They were a young couple, probably no older than their mid-twenties. The man was clearly well-built, but it was possible that just meant that he was concerned about fitness. The woman wasn't showing as much skin, and her clothes were a little baggier, so it wasn't possible to gauge her level of musculature, but from what Aldric could see, she was active, at the very least. In her well-toned arms, she cradled an baby – a young girl in a pink dress.

Aldric opened the door hesitantly, still refusing to completely trust these people. As he opened the door and was able to get a better look at the strangers, he only felt more uneasy. Aldric adopted a calm stance, relaxing his shoulders and sliding his hands into his pockets. Despite his appearance, though, he was on edge and ready for any attack the couple may throw.

The two stood in his doorway with slightly too much confidence, and with posture that clearly seemed rehearsed. Aldric could sense a level of tension developing between the parties, but he pasted a smile on his face, acting as normal as he could. While it was possible that they were just a spry couple with good posture, Aldric felt that there was something beneath their kind smiles.

"Hello," the man greeted, extending a hand. "My name is James."

"Nice to meet you," Aldric replied, giving a firm handshake by human standards. Looking at his visitor expectantly, Aldric waited for some explanation of why he stood on his doorstep. At the very least, he awaited further introductions. Instead James just stood smiling, holding onto Aldric's hand for a full minute.

"That's enough of that," Aldric finally broke the silence as he pulled his hand free. James held too tightly, clearly trying to gauge Aldric's strength.

"Sorry," James stammered convincingly. "I was just distracted, I suppose. You have a beautiful home."

"I fancy myself a bit of a decorator," Aldric lied, carefully avoiding any mention of his family. Of course there were plenty of people around town who knew him, so it was no secret that he didn't live there alone. Nonetheless, he resolved to keep mention of them to a minimum – at least with new people.

"This is my wife, Bree," James introduced. The woman carefully shifted the baby to her left arm and shook Aldric's hand with her right.

"And this little girl," James added, turning to face his daughter, "is Samantha."

"Pleasure to meet you Samantha," Aldric greeted, softening his tone slightly.

"Hi," Samantha muttered without turning her eyes to Aldric. Bree held her daughter a little too tightly as she faked a smile. Aldric assumed the girl was at least two years old. If he were taking Cailean to meet strangers at that age, he wasn't convinced that he'd be carrying him. That alone wasn't enough to make him suspicious, but everything seemed just slightly off with the couple, and Aldric wanted the conversation to end.

"We're moving in a few doors down, and we just wanted to introduce ourselves to the neighbors," James explained.

"Well, it's a pleasure to meet you. I'm Aldric Phoenix," Aldric responded curtly.

Bree attempted to discreetly look past him, probably searching the house for any sign of Linda. Aldric had no question that he was being overly cautious, but his paranoia had served him well thus far. Smoothly stepping to the side and leaning on the door, Aldric blocked her view into his home without sacrificing an appearance of comfort.

"Maybe when we get more settled in, we could have you over?" James offered.

"Keep me posted," Aldric replied in a noncommittal manner.

"Will do," James added awkwardly. As if waiting for more conversation, he stood for another minute at the door. Finally, he accepted that Aldric wasn't interested in continuing the exchange. Nodding, he turned and walked away.

As they stepped off the porch, Aldric retreated into his house and closed the door. Watching through the peephole, he waited until he was confident they were out of earshot before heading back to his wife.

"Did you have to be so cold?" Linda questioned.

"There was something off about them."

"They seemed nice. I think you're being paranoid."

"My paranoia keeps us alive."

"I know," she sighed. "I trust you. It's just hard to make friends."

"What? You want Cailean to have a playdate with Samantha?" Aldric teased.

"Maybe," she feigned offense.

"We could go on double dates," Aldric suggested.

"I'm sure we have a lot in common with them," Linda added.

"I'm sorry, I have trouble with human connection. My father basically saw all humans as hunters, and he ingrained that into my mind."

"It's been four hundred years."

"What can I say? Old habits die hard," Aldric shrugged.

"All I know is if you keep isolating yourself, it will start to get suspicious."

"I can invite them back," Aldric offered.

"I didn't say it had to be them. They were weird."

Present
12 Days Until the Full Moon
Cailean

Finally, the first day of sixth grade had arrived. Cailean had barely slept the night before, and for the past hour he had been lying in bed anticipating the alarm. If he'd tried to get up earlier than it went off, he knew his parents would try to tell him that he needed his sleep. Resolving that the argument wasn't worth it, he'd just rested. When the beeping radiated through the room, though, Cailean quickly pressed the button to silence it and jumped out of bed.

Excitedly, he crossed off the day on his calendar, officially marking it as the end of summer vacation. The smell of bacon and eggs wafted from the kitchen, which only made Cailean more eager to get the day started. He quickly changed and raced toward the smell, meeting his mother at the stove.

"It's almost ready," she told him, obviously sensing his overbearing enthusiasm.

"You know what's funny?" Cailean asked as he sat at the table, waiting as patiently as he could.

"What?"

"I'm pretty sure I will hate school in like, three days."

"Well, that's pessimistic."

"I don't know, I just don't think I'll meet anyone cool, you know? Still, I'm not a kid anymore."

"Okay," Linda replied, exaggerating the word.

"I'm not," Cailean replied defensively. "Middle school is the turning point. That's why it's called middle school."

"I don't think that's accurate," Linda teased.

"You're just jealous."

"Of being an adult?" She laughed. "Want to trade?"

She placed a plate in front of Cailean and kissed his forehead.

"You know you'll always be my kid, right?"

"Yeah," Cailean admitted. "But the rest of the world will have to take me seriously."

"No they won't," Aldric interjected as he entered the room. Linda set another plate on the table before returning to prepare one for herself. The playful tone died down as Aldric sat down, his expression stone-cold. "Caring so much about whether they take you seriously is only going to make you seem more like a child."

Cailean stayed silent, looking down at his food as his mother sat down. Aldric's harshness lingered in the air for a moment. His mother glared at his father, probably believing that he couldn't notice.

"I'm sorry," Aldric sighed. "I suppose there are better times for life lessons."

As the three of them ate together, the heavy air slowly thinned. Cailean's father was strict and often abrupt, but Cailean knew that it was just his way of expressing love. Aldric didn't talk much about his past, but he'd told Cailean enough to give the impression that it wasn't easy.

Wrapping up breakfast, Cailean checked his watch. If he planned to make it to school without running at his top speed, he would have to leave soon. As the actual start time drew nearer, Cailean began to question his anticipation.

"Well, I guess it's time to go," he stammered.

"You'll do great," Linda comforted, kissing his head.

Cailean stood to leave, but just as he reached the door, Aldric called to him.

"Remember the rules, Cailean."

"Stand out, but not too much. Don't tell the humans. I've got this, Father."

"I know you do," Aldric approved, nodding with a smile.

❖ ❖ ❖

Cailean approached his new school with awe. It was finally time for him to embrace a new life – a chance to start anew. For the first time, though, he began to feel vaguely intimidated by the new challenges he approached. The classes themselves would be simple, of that he was sure. The building itself, though, was frightening. At least twice the size of his previous school, this one sure housed far more secrets for him to learn.

As he crossed the threshold, Cailean was almost surprised to find a regular entryway. A long line of students had formed, and it wrapped around the corner. Glancing at the front of the line, Cailean saw a few teachers handing out pieces of paper. With a sigh, he walked to the back of the line and waited. One of the many differences to which he'd have to adjust was the fact that he was expected to change rooms between classes. Another, apparently, was that he'd have to wait for things. In elementary school, he'd never seen such a long line – even at lunch.

Impatiently tapping his foot, Cailean checked the clock on the wall. School was supposed to start ten minutes before, yet he still found himself waiting for a schedule. Though he questioned the efficiency of the system, he knew his complaints weren't likely to be heard.

"Last name?" One of the teachers, a young woman who couldn't have worked there for more than a year, asked as soon as Cailean stepped up.

"Phoenix," Cailean responded, agitated. He knew that to be rude to her would be to misdirect his anger but standing in the hall was starting to bother him. All of the chatter surrounding him was overwhelming. Cailean could clearly hear every conversation. A group of boys talked about what sports they played, a girl complained about her mother's refusal to let her wear makeup, and a dozen other groups complained about school starting too soon.

"N through P was supposed to be in this line," the other teacher reprimanded Cailean as she began digging through her pile of papers. This one was a much older woman, short and overweight with silver streaks through her hair.

"Sorry, I guess I didn't hear that," Cailean apologized, glancing around for a missed sign. Although annoyed with the teacher's tone, he tried his best to cover up his emotions.

"You should have read the sign," she groaned in response.

"Well, no need to be rude about it," Cailean muttered under his breath, stepping aside to let the student behind him speak with the younger teacher.

"Good morning! Please pick up your schedules and proceed immediately to homeroom," a voice blared over the loudspeaker. The noise screamed in Cailean's ears, leaving a loud buzzing long after the speaker turned off. The conversations only grew louder as more children arrived and everyone began talking over one another. Cailean felt his stomach churning as he wondered how a group of children had managed to behave more maturely than the mob which surrounded him.

"You're going to have to pay better attention to directions," the fat teacher scolded as she handed Cailean his schedule.

"Well, then you ought to get better at giving them," Cailean retorted, glaring at her. First, shock filled her eyes, quickly to be replaced by anger.

"You will treat me with respect, Mr. Phoenix," she spat.

"No, I won't. You don't earn respect for being old. You earn it by giving others respect."

"Stand back here. We're going to have a discussion after this," she ordered angrily.

"Sorry," he shrugged, pointing upward toward the loudspeaker, "I have to get to class."

"Get back here!" She yelled as he walked off. Ignoring her, Cailean wandered down the hallway, checking the paper in his hand for a room number. It was clear to him that the teacher would not chase him down – at least not with the still-growing line of people in front of her.

As he checked the doorways, searching for the correct room, his father's advice drifted back into his mind. While his primary purpose for that argument had been defending his own pride and standing up to a rude teacher, he was sure he'd be able to justify it. If starting a fight with a teacher on the first day didn't make him stand out, he had no idea what would.

The further he got from the entrance, the more bearable the sounds became. Still, he could hear a dozen conversations at once, and his head started to hurt a bit. Trying to distract himself from the conflicting noises, Cailean focused exclusively on the task presented to him. Checking the document to verify the room number, he scanned the numbers on the doors until he finally found his room. Walking through the door, Cailean was surprised to be the first one in the room.

"Hello," the teacher greeted, reaching out to shake his hand. "I'm Mrs. Cassidy."

"Cailean Phoenix," he responded, shaking her hand. Although her hand dwarfed his, Cailean attempted to give a firm handshake. When he noticed a subtle wince on her face, he quickly relaxed his grip.

"Firm handshake," she complimented.

"Sorry," he replied, embarrassed.

"No, don't be. A good handshake makes a good man," she smiled.

"Thank you, ma'am," Cailean replied awkwardly, looking at his shoes. He had never been great at accepting compliments. If he planned to go along with his father's ideas, he knew he would have to learn how to do so eventually. In that moment, though, he just wanted to find somewhere to sit. Cailean turned toward the desks but hesitated before he walked away.

"Is there a seating chart?" He asked her cautiously.

"I trust you to sit wherever you see fit," she told him with a smile. Cailean nodded before walking to a desk in the front row.

"The kids in the front learn the most," he explained as he dropped his bag near the desk.

"Well, I will do my best to make sure everything is useful," she laughed.

As other students began pouring in, she turned and greeted each of them, clearly working on learning names. Cailean was concerned that teachers would care less about their students when he moved into an environment where they weren't stuck together for eight hours a day, but he was grateful that his assumption was being challenged.

The class proceeded with mostly introductions and an overview of what to expect from the year. Cailean already found himself getting bored as Mrs. Cassidy spoke, but he was careful not to let that show.

Trying his best to give his attention to his teacher, he tried to tune out all of the other sounds. Each other teacher, though, seemed to be screaming to their classroom, as he could hear at least four other instructors giving similar speeches about what the purpose of homeroom was. Just as he was about to raise his hand to ask if she could close the door, footsteps drew his attention to the hall and he noticed that it was already closed. As he looked toward it, though, it burst open and the angry woman from the schedule table stormed in.

"Can I help you?" Mrs. Cassidy asked, pausing her monologue.

"I'm here for Cailean Phoenix."

"Why would that be?"

"We need to have a conversation about respect."

"I think you have the wrong student," Mrs. Cassidy defended. She gently placed a hand on the woman's back, directing her to the hall. Closing the door behind her, she probably hoped to offer some discretion. It didn't do much to stop every word from being audible, but Cailean appreciated the gesture.

"I handed him the schedule, I know who it is."

"Well, when I met Cailean this morning, he was very polite."

"That's wonderful, but it doesn't justify his behavior."

"Well, I didn't witness that, and I refuse to punish him for it."

"That's why I'm going to."

"No, you aren't. I'm not going to allow you to interrupt my student's class time."

"Listen, I get that you're new here –"

"No, you listen. It isn't healthy to carry a vendetta against a child. I would think someone with as much teaching experience as you would learn not to let things get to you, but here we are. Thank you for informing me of the incident – I will get his version of the story and handle it appropriately. Now, if you would kindly allow me to continue teaching my class."

Without another word, Mrs. Cassidy opened the door and walked back inside, closing it behind her.

"I'm sorry about that, class," she apologized before continuing teaching.

After another half hour, a bell rang to dismiss the class. Cailean instinctively covered his ears as the sound of the bell exploded, ringing through his ears and drowning everything else out. The other students stood and walked out, so Cailean tried to compose himself quickly. As he stood, though, his teacher stopped him from leaving.

"Cailean," she started slowly after the other students had left. "Do you want to tell me what happened this morning?"

"She was rude to me," Cailean sighed. "She insulted me and said I couldn't follow directions when they didn't provide any. I said that they should get better at giving instruction."

Mrs. Cassidy tried to look stern, but a smile broke out on her face as she started laughing. Leaning back in her chair, she sighed.

"You're going to be a little troublemaker, aren't you?"

"I don't make trouble, ma'am, but I'm not passive either."

"Very articulate," she assessed. "Alright, get out of here."

"Do I have detention?"

"Of course not. Just be careful. I won't always be there to defend you."

"Thank you, ma'am," Cailean replied, dumbfounded. Stepping into the hall, his senses were quickly overtaken by the rush of people and the sounds of confusion and conversation. He walked into the middle of the hall, searching for his own class, but the paper in front of him was blurry. The students around him seemed to talk louder and louder, and the footsteps resounded through the halls. Every clap as students greeted friends or scrape as someone failed to lift their shoes from the carpet felt like a gunshot. Looking up, Cailean tried to find a wall to lean on. He'd never felt dizzy before, but the world beneath him seemed to be spinning. Finally finding a wall, Cailean sat down and pressed his back to it, steadying his breathing as much as possible. As the conversations grew louder, though, Cailean failed to tune them out, and his heart started racing.

All of the words began to blur together and the lights started blinking in front of his eyes. Eventually, the sounds became a single buzz, overpowering any thought in his mind. Unable to rationally process the world around him, Cailean found himself hyperventilating. His arms and legs felt like anchors, binding him to the ground, as nausea set in. The buzz of noise only grew louder, deafening him to all else.

When he felt a hand on his shoulder, he wanted to jump away, but he couldn't budge. Barely able to process any new information, all sensory input began to blend together. Light blinded him, so he couldn't determine his surroundings, but he felt as though he was moving.

Eventually the sounds died down and he was able to regain control of his breathing. As he settled down, he realized that his environment had changed completely.

"Where am I?" He asked through gasps as he tried to replenish the oxygen in his deprived lungs.

"It's okay," a kind voice responded. Cailean felt a hand gently rubbing his arm. Normally, he would have been uncomfortable to feel a stranger touching him, but he couldn't deny that it was comforting. Anyway, he didn't have the strength to fight it, so he just allowed the well-meaning person to console him.

"Where…" he tried to repeat, but his voice trailed off. Cailean took another deep breath in attempt to calm himself down.

"Inhale for four seconds. Hold. Exhale for four seconds. Slow, deep breaths," he mentally instructed himself.

"You're in the nurse's office. You had a panic attack," the stranger answered. Cailean was finally able to turn his head to face the voice. In front of him sat a young girl with long, dark hair. As she brushed her bangs away from her face, he caught a glimpse of her brown eyes. Somehow, those irises reflected more light than any shimmering blue or green he'd ever seen.

Cailean had never looked at a girl and seen her as attractive before. He'd heard that people had girlfriends, but he couldn't understand why. Of course, on a scientific level, he understood the basic hormones which would cause it, but he had never felt their influence. Lying on the bed in the nurse's office, though, he could no longer say that was the case. As he looked at the mysterious girl who sat next to him, Cailean felt an unfamiliar fluttering in his stomach. When he realized where he was, though, any positive feeling was replaced with embarrassment. Sitting up quickly, he tried to brush away any sign of weakness.

When he saw her, he'd been briefly distracted, but as he thought again about what had happened, confusion set in. Cailean couldn't get sick, and low blood sugar couldn't have that type of effect on him – at least not without days of starvation. His mind scrambled for an explanation, but his efforts were divided as he simultaneously attempted to find a way to recover his image for the girl.

"Woah, slow down," she told him, placing one hand on his chest and the other on his arm to steady him. Cailean felt weak, but it wasn't from any illness.

"I'm okay," he replied, trying his best to sound masculine.

"Are you sure?"

"Yeah, of course," he shrugged.

"Anyway," Cailean added after a moment of silence. "What are you doing here?"

"Oh, sorry," she blushed. "I told them I was your girlfriend so they'd let me come back."

"Why?"

"You're weird."

"Thanks," he responded, defeated. Silence fell between them again, and the girl finally released her hold on him and sat back. She looked down, clearly searching for the words to say something.

"I used to get them," she told him – her tone shifting from playful to comforting.

"What?"

"Panic attacks. Have you never had one before?"

"No, I guess not."

"It's okay. Sometimes the world gets… loud."

"It's happened to you?"

"Yeah. My family moves a lot for my dad's job. The stress used to get to me. I've gotten better at dealing with it, I guess."

"Can you teach me?" Cailean asked.

"I can try," she smiled. Cailean looked at her, unsure of how to continue the conversation. He had never felt so stupid in his life, but he couldn't find the simplest words.

"I'm Cailean, by the way," he finally managed to say.

"I know," she laughed. "They said your name a couple times. I'm Brooke."

Chapter 4

10 Years Ago
Aldric

"Yes, I understand that you can fight, but you have to understand that a lot of your strength is gone," Aldric explained to his wife. She hadn't taken it well when he'd told her that she should train in case the hunters arrived, but he couldn't quite understand why. Regardless of the amount of training one had, it was always better to train a bit more.

"I did fine without it before," she defended.

"You didn't have to fight hunters before."

"Aldric, what makes you so sure these neighbors are hunters?"

"I'm not," Aldric admitted. "But even if they aren't, hunters will come. Werewolves rarely settle down in a town for this very reason. We just have to be ready."

"Okay, so you want to spar more often? Is that what you're getting at?"

"That would be a good start," Aldric acknowledged.

"Let's go, then."

"Now?"

"Cailean's sleeping, I doubt there will be a better time."

Aldric sighed. He wanted to teach her how to defend herself with a weapon and talk about a protocol in case they were caught off guard. They had to plan a rendezvous point in case the hunters managed to separate them. Knowing his wife, though, any conversation would have to wait until she'd made her point. She was a kind and loving woman, but her stubbornness was rivaled only by his own.

He followed her to the basement, both of them silently agreeing to put as much distance between them and the sleeping baby as possible. At the bottom of the stairs, Linda turned to him and raised her fists. Aldric shrugged and nodded, conveying that she should attack at her ready. Throughout all of their sparring matches, Aldric had never set out to humiliate Linda, and he'd always at least looked like he was trying. After she'd trained with him for a century, she'd actually been able to put up a fight. A hunter wouldn't grant her any courtesy, though, so Aldric resolved to do the same.

She stepped in and faked a punch. Aldric stood in front of her, not moving a muscle. Linda faked a kick to distract him and followed up with a jab, which Aldric deflected with ease. Following up from her attempt to raise his guard, Linda lunged in and punched with her back hand toward his stomach. Aldric stepped to the side, avoiding her advance, and pushed his palm against her back, pushing her forward.

Nimble as ever, Linda was able to roll forward, preventing herself from falling directly to the floor. Regaining composure quickly, she turned to face Aldric. Neither of them moved in – both waiting for the other to make the next move. Finally, Aldric lunged in and faked a punch to her face. Her guard didn't move, but he twisted his hips as he punched with the other hand to her gut. That too was a fake, but she dropped her guard for it. Twisting back, Aldric brought his front hand toward her with a hook punch. Within an inch of her face, he stopped completely.

Linda took advantage of his kindness and kicked his gut, knocking him back a bit. She closed the distance as she tried to continue a combination, expecting him to be phased by the kick, but Aldric surprised her with a counter kick. Once again, he stopped just before connecting the attack.

"Are we good?" Aldric asked.

"Okay, you've made you point," Linda conceded.

She threw another punch, trying to catch him off guard, but Aldric stepped in a circle. Her fist passed in front of him and he caught her wrist. With his other arm, he stepped forward, trapping her in an arm bar.

A cry distracted both of them, and Aldric released her with a sigh. Aldric walked up the stairs with his wife close at his heels.

As they reached the first floor of the house, Linda rushed to the crib. Walking back out to the living room, she was bouncing Cailean in her arms.

"Is he hungry?" Aldric asked. Though he was trying to be helpful, he was still not able to determine what Cailean needed as well as his wife.

"I doubt it; I just fed him," she denied. "I think he just wanted attention."

Cailean's cries quieted down as she rocked him. Not a minute later, though, he started reaching for her chest and crying again. Angrily, Cailean started pulling at her shirt.

"Well, he is your son," she laughed.

"He's a werewolf," Aldric shrugged. "He eats a lot."

"That went over your head," she smiled, handing him the baby. Cailean still gripped her shirt, refusing to let go. Carefully, she tried to pry his fingers away. After quite a bit of effort, she was finally able to free herself and walk to the kitchen.

"Sorry buddy, but we can't have you biting your mom," Aldric explained once again, as if his son could understand him. Aldric had never heard of a bite changing someone into a werewolf, but he assumed that was just because no one had survived a bite. There was a small chance that drawing blood, even in his human form, with his teeth or claws would be enough to infect Linda with the curse once again. It wasn't worth the risk, so they'd started weaning him from breast milk as his teeth came in. That was almost six months ago, though, and Cailean was still reaching for her breasts when he was hungry. Aldric was thoroughly convinced that it was just because he'd learned that the motion led to him being fed.

Linda walked back out of the kitchen with baby food and a spoon. Cailean cried and reached toward her, so Aldric set him on the ground and he shakily walked toward his mother, holding his arms out for the food. When he was close enough to her, he fell onto the ground and she sat with him, laughing.

"Do you want to eat at the table?" She asked, giggling at his determination to eat at that moment. Unable to process her question and provide a response, Cailean just struggled to get the food. Linda placed the container on the ground in front of him and opened it. She dipped the spoon in, but he grabbed the spoon himself as well.

"Oh, you're eager today aren't you?" She laughed.

"Mama," Cailean babbled.

"Yes, I am," she laughed. "Do you want Mama to feed you?"

"Mama," Cailean repeated, tightening his grip on the spoon. Linda let go with a shrug, and Cailean carefully lifted the spoon, watching the food with intense focus. Slowly, he brought it toward his mouth. Just before he was able to deposit the food, he tipped the spoon and it fell onto his shirt. Cailean froze for a minute, but then started giggling. Trying again, he was able to feed himself.

"Well, that's impressive," Aldric laughed. "At fifteen months, he can use a spoon better than I can."

"Well, that's not saying much," Linda teased.

"Okay, when I said it, it was a joke. Your agreement was just mean," Aldric feigned offense. She laughed and the two of them watched their son struggle to feed himself. Clearly, Cailean was going to grow into an independent young man faster than Aldric would have liked.

"When are we going to tell him?" Linda asked.

"What do you mean?"

"About everything: Lycanthropy, why he's different, hunters."

"I don't know," Aldric sighed. "I never want to hide what he is, but… I want to protect him for as long as I can. I don't want him to be afraid of hunters for his entire childhood."

"We can't just not tell him," Linda argued.

"Well right now he's eating apple sauce on the floor because he doesn't know what a table is. Can we figure it out as we go?" Aldric asked.

"I guess that's all parents can do," Linda admitted.

"For now, let's just enjoy spending time with our son. It won't be long until it's not funny anymore when he spills food on himself."

Linda laughed, and Aldric pulled her in for a kiss. She turned and he held her, placing her head on his shoulder. Cailean still had his back turned to them as he ate. Aldric wasn't sure what the best thing to do for his son was, but he was dedicated to spending his life trying to learn.

Present
11 Days Until the Full Moon
Cailean

"Hey, Cailean," Brooke called as he approached the steps. Waving, she trotted toward him. Cailean hadn't anticipated the way that he'd make his first friend in middle school, but it almost made the horror of his panic attack worth it.

"Hey," Cailean replied with a smile.

"Are you feeling better today?" The two of them stood in front of the school as other students arrived and shuffled into the building. Brooke clearly didn't understand how many layers her question had. Cailean still had trouble tuning out each individual conversation, and Brooke talking over them started to give him a headache. Her voice – pleasant as it may be – was high pitched and left a ringing in his ears. The smell of dozens of boys who didn't seem to understand that the changing in their bodies probably meant they should shower daily assaulted him – only to be rivaled by the conflicting perfumes of young girls trying to impress their peers. The iridescent lights from inside the building were already burning his eyes and he hadn't even entered the halls yet; he was only able to see them through the windows in the door. Even the hairs on his arms stood on end, and he could feel the slight breeze move them periodically.

Aside from that, because he had spent a good portion of the previous day in the nurse's office only to be escorted to his classes afterward, he hadn't had time to gain an understanding of his surroundings. As he checked the schedule that he'd folded up in his pocket, he realized he couldn't imagine a map in his mind. Even the location of homeroom was a mystery, because he'd only found it by chance the previous day. The task of navigating through the masses and finding his rooms was just as terrifying – if not more – than the previous day.

However, Cailean had learned from a young age to keep a guarded lock on his perceptions. Having no frame of reference, he couldn't be sure how much of that was because he was born different. Though he wasn't entirely sure why, his father had been very clear that he should never let other people find out about those differences. Brooke had said that she'd experienced something similar, but Cailean was still hesitant to pour out his heart to her. Instead, he pushed all of those thoughts aside and continued to smile.

"Yeah," he nodded. "Thanks."

While it wasn't the complete truth, it wasn't entirely a lie either. Cailean was confident that he was more equipped to handle the stress – if for no other reason than because he knew what to expect. With Brooke to give him a friend through it all and his own determination to pull his focus from the increasing noise, Cailean was confident that he wouldn't suffer the same fate as the previous day.

"What did your parents say?" Brooke asked, taking Cailean's hand and leading him to a bench. The second that she touched him, Cailean felt goosebumps race down his arm. Embarrassed, he wanted to pull his hand away to hide it, but he was also confident that would make it more obvious. She was cute, but he couldn't understand why he was reacting so strongly to her. She was just a girl, after all, and he'd been friends with plenty before.

Brooke sat on the bench, releasing Cailean's hand. A strange mixture of relief and longing flooded his mind as she let go. Careful to leave a reasonable distance between them, Cailean sat with her, leaning his side against the back of the bench so he could face her. His backpack still rested on one shoulder, so he slid it off and dropped it on the bench behind him. Cailean didn't want to leave her, and he didn't want to admit that he needed the few minutes they had before homeroom began to locate his class.

"About what?" Cailean finally responded, realizing that it was his turn to speak in the conversation.

"The whole thing yesterday," Brooke replied, carefully choosing her words.

"Oh, yeah. I didn't tell them."

"What?"

"I don't want them to worry. Anyway, I don't think they'd react too well."

"Oh, okay," Brooke accepted hesitantly.

"I'm fine, really," Cailean assured her. Unconvinced, she nodded and sighed.

"Well, just tell me if you need anything, alright?"

"Sure," Cailean stammered, his heart skipping a beat. The thought that she was so concerned about his well being made him feel strange, but he appreciated it.

"Do you know how to get to your class?" Brooke asked, standing back up and looking around. Most of the students had either made their way into the building or were bunched up at the door in confusion. A backlog of kids examining schedules standing in the doorway as they determined which direction to go slowed everyone else down.

Cailean didn't want to admit that he had no idea, but it didn't seem like something worthwhile to lie about. The indecision caused him to pause just long enough for her concern to shift to a knowing smile.

"Come on, I'll show you."

"How do you know where it is?" Cailean asked, standing and slinging his backpack over one shoulder.

"I know the school pretty well," she shrugged.

"Aren't you new here?"

"I'm pretty sure most of us are," Brooke countered. That wasn't exactly what Cailean had meant, but she wasn't technically wrong. He was just as new to the school as she was, even though she hadn't lived in town her entire life.

"Fair enough," Cailean admitted.

"My mom works here," Brooke explained, clearly having had enough of watching him struggle. "She's a teacher, so I had plenty of time to get to know the building while she was getting her classroom set up."

"Oh, so maybe you can show me to all of my classes today?" Cailean asked with a sly smirk. His pride made it difficult for him to ask for help, but it was significantly easier when he could convince himself it was just a way to spend time with Brooke.

"If you insist," she smiled knowingly, turning her back and walking. Following closely, Cailean tried to avoid staring at her. Logically, he knew he should have been examining the building around him. Even if she was going to be leading him to classes, it would benefit him to learn the layout of the building – in case she was sick one day. Despite knowing that, though, Cailean couldn't pull his eyes from her. There was something mesmerizing about the way her hips swayed as she walked, and he couldn't spare the attention on any other detail.

"Here we are," Brooke said as she stopped. Cailean almost didn't stop in time, but he was able to prevent a collision by stepping slightly to the side with his last step. He was grateful that his father had trained him in martial arts since a young age, because it allowed him the control over his own movement which protected him from making a fool of himself.

Before Cailean could respond to her, Mrs. Cassidy stepped into the hall to greet him. He understood being polite and trying to get to know the students, but it still seemed odd to him that she was going to such great lengths. It seemed like it would make more sense for her to just wait for him in the classroom.

"Is everything alright?" She asked. Cailean sighed. Clearly she had heard about the panic attack, and he just wondered how far the word had spread. He hoped he would be able to avoid obtaining that reputation. If he couldn't, at the very least it would make him stand out. Still, he'd hoped for a more appealing way to do so.

"Oh, yeah," Brooke interjected before Cailean could answer her. "I'm just showing Cailean around."

"Oh, okay. You worried me. Your class in on the other side of the school, right?"

"Yeah."

Cailean looked back and forth as they spoke, trying to understand what was happening. It was possible that she had Mrs. Cassidy for a later class, and he wouldn't be surprised that she knew the location of Brooke's homeroom. She seemed very friendly. Still, their mannerisms didn't indicate that they had just met the previous day. Finally, the realization hit Cailean and he felt foolish for the fact that it took so long.

"Do you need a hall pass?" Mrs. Cassidy asked.

"No, I think I can make it. Thanks!" Brooke assured her as she walked off. Turning and walking backwards for a moment, she added, "I'll see you later, Cailean Phoenix."

"You too," he called back. As soon as she'd turned back around, Cailean silently scolded himself. His response hadn't made any sense, but he had been distracted.

"I'm glad you two seem to be friends," Mrs. Cassidy told Cailean. "It's usually hard for her to make friends right after we move."

"She's just showing me my classes," Cailean defended awkwardly.

"Okay," Mrs. Cassidy replied slowly. "Well, thank you for being nice to her."

"It's easy to be nice when someone's so kind," Cailean shrugged. Not entirely sure what to feel or what to say next, Cailean slipped past her and found the same seat he'd been in the previous day. Suddenly, the front row felt far too close.

❖ ❖ ❖

At the dinner table, Cailean slouched in his chair and looked longingly at the food in the middle. His father was still bringing a few more things from the kitchen and his mother was setting plates out for the three of them. Cailean had carried the roast, but his job was complete, and he was left to just long for the delicious meal.

"How was school?" His mom asked as she placed a fork and knife in front of him.

"It was good," Cailean replied vaguely. She moved to her seat and placed her own silverware down before sitting. Aldric came from the kitchen with a pot of potatoes and placed it in the middle of the table. He hadn't been wearing any kitchen mitts, but the potatoes were still steaming, and Cailean was thoroughly confident that the metal pot was hot as well. To confirm his suspicions, he leaned forward and gently touched the silver. Pulling his hand back quickly, he waved it through the air.

"Why don't you just use mitts?" Cailean teased his father.

"It's conditioning. Anyway, I'm used to it by now," Aldric shrugged, glancing at his hands. They were red from carrying the scalding pot, but the color quickly began to fade and return to normal. Turning his gaze to his own finger, Cailean didn't seem to see a reaction from the pot. Still, he couldn't understand why anyone would intentionally bring themselves pain when there was an easily avoidable solution.

Aldric sat at the table across from his wife. Cailean's parents had taken up cooking after they'd retired. Sometimes they both helped prepare something extravagant and others they debated who would get to prepare the meal for the night. Cailean couldn't imagine enjoying cooking, but maybe if he had as much time on his hands as they did, it would make sense.

Listening to them discuss anything food related was hilarious to Cailean though. The science behind every decision, the specific temperature of each ingredient, and the competing flavors they worked with were all incredibly specific. Cailean had always figured cooking involved following recipes on a box, but his parents took it to a new level.

"How was school?" Aldric asked, waiting for Cailean and his mother to get their plates first.

"It was good," Linda replied in Cailean's stead. As if expecting elaboration, she looked at him and scooped vegetables onto his plate. Cailean just shrugged, staring at the plate. He wondered why they made such a big deal of eating well if Cailean's body would just continually get stronger regardless of nutrients. As far as he was aware, it was more of a calorie thing – it just required an adequate input of energy. He didn't have a full grasp on werewolf physiology, though, so he decided it was best not to question them.

"So I guess that's all we get," she laughed, serving food to herself and her husband.

"After counting down the days for three weeks?" Cailean's father teased.

"It was the second day," Cailean shrugged. "The second day is never very eventful."

"What about this Brooke girl?" His mother asked, nudging him playfully as she sat back down.

"What about her?" Cailean asked, blushing as he looked down. Trying to avoid continuing the conversation, he grabbed his fork and shoveled food into his mouth.

"Well, did you see her again? You didn't stop talking about her yesterday."

"She showed me where my classes were," Cailean admitted.

"That sounds romantic," she joked. Still trying to end the conversation, Cailean continued to eat as he searched for another topic. Glancing toward his father, he saw growing concern on his face.

"You really like this girl?" his father asked slowly. Cailean couldn't understand why his father was so concerned by that prospect. Was he that scared of his son growing up?

"No," Cailean defended, still embarrassed to be having that conversation with his parents. They had always been very open with him, so he wasn't sure why he had trouble talking about his new feelings, but he was very confident that he didn't want to.

"Okay," Aldric replied slowly, turning his attention to his food.

Silence filled the room for a moment and Cailean looked back and forth between his parents. Only a minute ago they'd been joking and laughing, but suddenly they seemed melancholy. Cailean had heard of empty nest syndrome, but he didn't expect them to be reacting so strangely so early. Even if he did like a girl – and he wasn't sure that was what was happening – it seemed like an overreaction to him.

"Cailean, I have to talk to you about something," Aldric finally spoke up awkwardly.

"Okay, hold on," Linda stopped him.

"What?"

"Really? At the dinner table?"

"I've never done this before."

"Done what?" Cailean pitched in.

"I'm just going to do it," Aldric announced, setting his utensils down with a sigh.

"As you get older, you're going to notice a lot of... changes," Aldric started.

"Yeah, I know. We've talked about it before. I'll be a werewolf when I hit puberty."

"See, he knows what puberty is," Linda added, desperately trying to ease the awkwardness they all felt. Cailean appreciated his mother's effort, but he had a feeling that his father wasn't going to drop it.

"That's not what I mean," Aldric continued. "I mean... changes. And you're going to start looking at girls differently."

Cailean had no idea how his father had lived for so long but hadn't managed to draft that typical parenting speech once. While he'd already heard quite a bit at school, Cailean had been dreading the moment that his parents decided it was time to try to teach him. It didn't have to be awkward – especially among them – but for some reason his father was making it weird.

"Father, I know where you're going with this. We really don't have to talk about it."

"It's important, Cailean. You see, wolves mate for life."

"Father! I'm eleven. I think her hair smells nice. Please don't be weird."

"Just be careful," Aldric said.

"Yes sir," Cailean muttered, turning back to his food.

Chapter 5

8 Years Ago
Aldric

With a heavy sigh, Aldric collapsed onto the couch, appreciating the brief respite he had earned by granting Cailean a way to distract himself. His son was sitting on the tile in the other room, finally having been introduced to finger-painting. Aldric wondered whether Cailean's erratic behavior and endless supply of energy came from being three years old or a young werewolf. Perhaps a mixture of the two was the culprit.

Aldric had not spent much time around young children – human or lycanthrope – so he didn't have experience to which he could relate. Still, if Cailean's liveliness was simply typical of children, Aldric couldn't imagine a human parent keeping pace. Even he found himself mentally drained after an afternoon alone with the boy. Despite that, though, he wouldn't trade places with his wife for anything. She'd spent the afternoon out with Bree in attempt to make friends with the neighbors. Aldric would prefer the company of his own rambunctious and exhausting son than any human he'd met.

Shaking his head, Aldric acknowledged the error in that statement. As he did, he sat up with a groan and dropped his head into his hands. Linda had been human when he'd met her, and she was again, so he couldn't accurately say 'any human.' That was simply another remnant of his father's mindset – a relic of an ideology against which Aldric struggled daily. Once again, he found it necessary to remind himself that humans weren't worse than him simply due to their shortened lifespan. In fact, there were enviable things about living in their world.

None of that changed his opinion on building relationships, though. It seemed pointless to him to establish friendships with humans who would leave their lives as quickly as they'd entered. Aside from that, the whiny and occasionally insolent child in the other room was his own flesh and blood. Whether it was right or not, a part of him did feel that that fact alone made him better than the humans. Cailean and Linda were his family, and he felt no remorse for holding them to a higher esteem than the rest of the world.

That familial loyalty was probably the only thing to which he still held dear from his childhood. Despite the stark differences in their beliefs which led to their fallout, Aldric was thankful for that core trait which was instilled into him. He was aware, though, of the irony which resulted from that quality. That was what had led him to put Cailean's best interests above those of his birth family. When he had chosen his new family over them, it had led to a brutal but unavoidable battle.

As Aldric's mind wandered, he tried to divert his attention from that scene. When he closed his eyes, though, he could still see the broken bodies of those who had raised him. His older brother, whom he had always admired in his own right, and sister, who had always been a bit of a protector. Their entire families, who were nothing more than innocent bystanders brainwashed by the cult of his father. Aldric envisioned the memory in third person, picturing what he must have looked like as some half-human, half-wolf beast. He'd made a deal with the wolf and somehow, it had listened. In exchange for his cession of his body to the wolf willingly on every remaining full moon, the animal had granted him the strength to defend his family in that moment. For the past three years, Aldric had held true to his word – no longer fighting the wolf and allowing it as much time as he could grant during the full moon.

Over time he had wondered, of course, what exactly the implications were of the state he'd taken during that fight with his father. Given that he had managed to control himself then, was there some possibility that reversing the transformation – or at least remaining in control during it – was possible? At the very least, he knew he could control the wolf's body when under the influence of wolfsbane, but he couldn't stop his mind from considering the possibility that there was more. He'd made a promise to the wolf, though, and if it had somehow understood him, he was terrified of breaking it. Disregarding his desire to be honest, if the wolf felt slighted, Aldric was afraid that it could seize more control. While that wasn't likely in his eyes, he didn't know enough about his own heritage to completely ignore the chance.

Aldric's father had never taught his children the details of the curse with which he was afflicted. Through time, Aldric had learned of wolfsbane and the strange sensation of the first transformation. He'd experienced the healing and functional immortality, as well as the immunity to sickness. Through Linda, he'd seen the scars from before a scratch heal – leaving only one. He'd learned the truth of the rumor that killing the wolf which inflicted the curse being a cure. None of that, though, was made clear by his father. Apparently, he was under the impression that knowledge would give his children the power required to revolt. He had, however, certainly made it a point to describe in detail the horrors of the hunters and the threat they posed. He had taught of their desire to eliminate Aldric's kind and painted himself to be their best defense. He had instilled a distrust and disdain for all of humanity through those teachings, which Aldric still struggled against in his thoughts. Over the centuries, Aldric had spent quite a bit of time pondering the fearmongering and brainwashing tactics of his father, but he found it terrifying that he was still piecing together new ways that the man had altered his mindset.

Hearing the doorknob turn slightly, Aldric was torn from his thoughts. In a flash, he jumped from the couch and turned to face the sound, his fists raised as he prepared for an attack. Aldric's heart raced as he glanced toward the hallway which led to Cailean's room. With his enhanced speed, there was no doubt in his mind that he would cover the distance faster than any assailant, although it was nearly twice as far from him as the door. Regardless, adrenaline rushed through his veins as his parasympathetic nervous system responded to the threat.

Slowly, the knob turned and the door creaked open. Linda stepped through the doorway, smiling and turning to wave at someone as she closed the door behind her. When she noticed Aldric's expression, which still hadn't quite softened from being startled, fear flashed over her eyes. As quickly as it had come, though, it was replaced with a comforting understanding.

"What were you thinking about?" She asked calmly. Though paranoia was Aldric's perpetual state of being, he didn't typically react so harshly to her return, and she knew him well enough to recognize that it meant she'd perturbed him while deep in thought.

"My father," Aldric admitted, finally dropping his fists as his heartbeat returned to a regular rhythm. Her eyes fell, clearly overwhelmed with the rush of emotion that the mention of the man brought to her as well. Taking a deep breath, she collected herself and turned her attention back to him in attempt to be supportive.

"It's hard," she acknowledged, moving closer and pulling him into an embrace. Stroking his hair, she whispered, "But it's in the past. You're not him. You never were, and you never will be."

"What if I'm too much like him?" Aldric mumbled, feeling like a scared child. His wounded pride still fought his vulnerability, but he needed to confide in his wife.

"You aren't."

"I think like him," Aldric countered. "They're fleeting thoughts, usually, but I do. His fatherhood is the only one I've known – what if I replicate it for Cailean?"

Linda pulled back, staring intently into his eyes. The flame in her eyes told him that she not only disagreed with his assessment, but she was angered that he himself believed it.

"You are already better than he was. Cailean thinks for himself. He is trying to learn, and you teach. You love our son, and you will always do what's best for him."

Aldric looked down – unable to accept her onslaught of compliments. Regardless, she continued.

"You would die for that boy, Aldric Phoenix. The only thing your father would fight for was power. For that – and that alone – you are better, stronger, than he ever was."

Aldric nodded, breathing steadily to avoid any display of emotion. Steeling himself, he finally looked at her and repeated the motion with more resolve. Running his fingers through his hair and washing away his lamentation and nostalgia, he moved back toward the couch.

"So, how was your day?" He inquired, desperate to change the subject.

"It was fun," she shrugged. "Shopping, lunch, and endless conversation about our babies. What more could a mother want?"

"Sounds incredible," Aldric sarcastically teased.

"It wasn't that bad. She's' just an excited mother. It did get a little tedious though."

Aldric smiled, silently staring at his wife. She laughed quietly but it was clear to Aldric that there was more she wanted to say. Something was on her mind beyond the conversation with Bree. At the very least, some point had trapped her deep in thought. Aldric assumed it didn't have to do with Samantha, but maybe that was just because he couldn't imagine caring that much about someone else's child.

"What are you thinking about?" He asked.

"Bree told me all about Samantha's school. What she's learning sounded so dull," Linda started, carefully choosing her words. Aldric wasn't sure where she was going, but he assumed it was something she knew he wouldn't like. Sheepishly, she looked away and brushed hair from her face.

"I just feel like school is not actually the place to learn things," she concluded.

"I don't disagree," Aldric admitted.

"Well, I was thinking, what if we home schooled Cailean?"

"No."

"Why not? Either one of us has more wisdom and experience than every teacher he would have through elementary school combined. You are just heartless enough to push him and make sure he learns. We would be able to cover so much more so much faster without waiting for all of the students to catch up. I just think we're more qualified to teach him than anyone else – especially given the sheer volume of knowledge we've accumulated over the centuries."

"You're right – and we will teach him. Just not exclusively."

"Why not?" Linda sighed, clearly annoyed at Aldric's lack of a true answer. Aldric sighed. Though he realized that cryptic was his perpetual state of being – and that wasn't healthy for his relationship – he found it difficult to fight. In his eyes, it should be enough that he said it was a bad idea. Still, he accepted that to be kind to her, he could at least offer an explanation.

"We're recluses," he began.

"You make yourself a recluse. I have friends; I make it a point to get to know the neighbors," she defended.

"You're friends with Bree, and yes, that's better than I'm doing. Still, you don't have a job. Your life, just like mine, is raising and protecting Cailean. Now, if he were to stay home all day, suddenly we become the family that doesn't leave home. We become mysterious. People will ask questions which should be avoided."

"What ever happened to 'the best way to fit in is to stand out'?"

"Exactly. To stand out – to make a scene and to draw attention to yourself. If you appear to be hiding, it's usually because you are. To seclude ourselves in this home – or even to join a small community of home-schoolers, would be to put a target on ourselves. Cailean has to go to school and be exceptional in every way because no one would expect that."

"That makes sense," she admitted softly. "I just don't want him growing up wasting his time with dull classes and getting picked on."

"Cailean has all of the time in the world, and he won't be picked on. He'll be revered."

"Well, I'm not confident that will be great for his psyche either," she groaned.

Interrupting their conversation, Cailean came running down the hallway. As he ran, he waved his hands, dripping paint onto the ground behind him. Skidding to a stop in front of them, he beamed up at them. When he saw the horrified look on his mother's face, he looked behind him at the trail of paint.

"You let him fingerpaint alone?" Linda accused.

"It's water based," Aldric assured her. Visibly, she breathed a sigh of relief. There was still a hint of annoyance on her face, but it mostly faded as the burden of cleaning became more bearable.

"I'm sowwy I pilled," Cailean apologized, looking up at his mother's disappointed gaze.

"It's okay," she told him. Her tone was apparently enough to convince him, because his eyes lit up once again. Aldric knew better, though, and he could sense the exasperation. After a moment, she added, "Just be careful next time, okay?"

"Otay."

"Cailean," Aldric spoke up, turning his son's attention to himself. "Spilled."

"Pilled?"

"Spilled," Aldric corrected again, carefully annunciating the word.

"Ssspilled," Cailean tried again, elongating the first syllable. Aldric accepted that as the best he was going to get, so he smiled and nodded.

"Come look!" Cailean cheered, bouncing and shaking more paint loose from his fingers. Linda leaned down and cupped her hands around his to trap the stray paint. She picked him up, wrapping an arm around him and resting him on her hip so she was able to maintain her grasp on his hands.

"Where?" She asked, forcing a bit of eagerness into her voice. Cailean tried to free his hand to point, but when she wouldn't let go, he averted his gaze toward the kitchen. Carrying him, Linda followed his gaze and Aldric stayed close behind her.

As he stepped into the kitchen, Aldric found the tile coated with a variety of colors. At first, it looked like a complete mess of disconnected drops of paint. Examining more closely, he found a hint of truth to that, but there was something more impressive as well. Cailean had spilled drops of paint around the floor and imprecisely misplaced certain colors, but as Aldric examined, he saw that his son had been mixing colors. He'd only been provided primary colors with which to paint, but there was a full pallet spread out along the floor. Multiple shades of grays and browns had been created as Cailean had clearly been searching for the perfect one.

Finally, Aldric's gaze fell to the painting in the center of the mess. Still drying, the edges of the figure dripped slowly. Still, the drawing was very distinct. To the best of his ability, Cailean had painted a wolf. Though it was mostly just a grey blob with four legs, Aldric could see the lightest of grays used for eyes and green for surrounding trees.

"What is it?" Aldric asked with enthusiasm, covering for his wife – who was staring at the floor with horror.

"I drawed my fwend," Cailean cheered.

"You drew your friend?" Aldric repeated, affirming that he had been listening while reinforcing the proper pronunciation of the words.

"Yup!"

"Well, since you used paint," Aldric said slowly.

"Painted!" Cailean corrected with joy.

"It looks incredible," Aldric complimented. "Now let's clean up after ourselves so Mommy doesn't have to, huh?"

"Yeah," Cailean agreed. As Linda put him down, he scooped some of the paint up into his hand and ran toward the sink.

"Don't worry," Aldric comforted, kissing Linda on the cheek and patting her back. "We'll handle it.

Present
8 Days Until the Full Moon
Cailean

With his eyes drooping, Cailean tried to focus as his teacher explained a basic equation which he'd written on the board. Normally, even when the teacher was covering something Cailean had learned years ago, he was able to stay awake and at least pretend to focus. For some reason, though, the past week had been incredibly difficult for him. Regardless of how much he slept, he still found himself drifting off in class.

Checking the clock, he saw that there were still twenty more minutes before lunch. Groaning quietly to himself, Cailean slid down in his chair and turned his attention back to the board. The students around him scribbled furiously, copying anything written on the board. Cailean glanced down at his blank notepad, wondering if he should be writing something to keep appearances up. He struggled to even feign interest, though, as he was assaulted with redundant information.

As his eyes grew heavy again, Cailean shook his head in attempt to break himself from the encroaching exhaustion.

"Cailean," the teacher turned toward him impatiently. "Would you like to tell the class the next step?"

"Four," Cailean muttered absently. The kids around him laughed, and the teacher scowled.

"Please pay attention, Mr. Phoenix," the teacher sighed.

"Divide both sides by two, subtract seven, multiply by four. X is four. I'll try to slow down for you next time," Cailean groaned. The room fell silent as a few of the other students checked his math. The teacher scowled, but he just turned back toward the board. Clearly, he had been hoping to catch Cailean off guard with his question, but he'd only managed to make himself look like a fool. Cailean was just grateful that he knew when to accept defeat rather than start an argument.

The rest of the class droned on as the teacher ran through a few dozen more basic algebra problems. Maybe it was just because it was the first week, but Cailean had been under the impression that the teachers were supposed to teach, not just demonstrate examples.

Finally, the bell rang to dismiss the class to lunch. Cailean clenched his teeth as the sound reverberated in his ears. The bells in elementary school hadn't been nearly as loud as those, and he couldn't help but wonder why they increased the volume so drastically. The classes weren't particularly louder, and the students or teachers shouldn't have been any harder of hearing.

Shrugging it off, Cailean stood and pushed toward the door, eager to get out of the classroom. When he stepped into the hallway, it was nearly empty. Walking down the hall, he navigated toward Brooke's class. Typically, he'd wait for her and they would walk to lunch together. Cailean was finally beginning to gain an understanding of the layout of the school, though, so he was able to find his way to her room.

"Wow, you're fast," Brooke greeted as she separated herself from the mob of students pouring through the door. Cailean smiled confidently, but he didn't respond. Silently, he turned and walked toward the lunchroom. After jogging a few steps to catch up, Brooke kept pace.

"How was class?" She asked, clearly trying to make conversation. Cailean appreciated that she liked spending time with him, but he didn't understand why she felt the need to talk the entire time. Silence had never been a problem for him.

"I fell asleep, but the teacher couldn't get me in trouble because I knew the answer to the question," Cailean laughed.

"Only the first week and you're falling asleep in class?" Brooke teased.

"What? All the cool kids were sleeping," Cailean replied defensively.

"Oh? So there were more than just you?"

"No," Cailean laughed. Brooke smiled, looking down as they walked. Cailean assumed it was wishful thinking, but as she turned her face, he was sure he noticed a hint of red in her cheek before it was covered by her black hair.

Watching her and searching for any sign of that potential blush, Cailean stopped paying attention to where he was going. Suddenly, she stopped moving and Cailean froze. Turning his eyes forward, he saw that they already stood in the lunch line. With his mind no longer completely focused on her, he was assaulted by the smells of hundreds of ingredients throughout the room. Somehow, he felt as though he could smell each student's food independently, and every individual stimulus was recognizable. Overwhelmed, Cailean didn't move forward with the line. His head darting around the room, he tried to locate the source of each smell. Scents of tomato, oregano, cumin, paprika, cheese, potatoes, chicken, and more than a reasonable amount of grease surrounded him.

"Cailean," Brooke prompted, snapping him away from the olfactory assault. "Are you alright?"

The concern on her face filled Cailean with a strange mixture of emotions. While he wanted to wipe the worry away, he was also honored that she felt it. It meant that she cared for him, which was exciting.

"I'm fine," he nodded.

"Are you sure?" She asked, placing her hand on his bare arm. Cailean felt shivers run down his spine and goosebumps race across his skin. His heart rate picked up, but it wasn't an entirely unpleasant feeling.

"Yeah, I'm okay," he affirmed. As an afterthought, he added, "I brought lunch though. I'll go get a table and wait for you."

"Oh, okay," she replied slowly.

"Maybe we can sit outside in the courtyard?" Cailean suggested. Her concern was clearly about his panic attack earlier that week, and Cailean was beginning to worry about the same thing. The chatter around him began to grow louder and the smells only grew stronger as more students arrived and began eating.

"Sure," she accepted. The hint of concern didn't leave her voice.

"Really, I'm fine. I'll see you out there."

Cailean backed away, almost running into the person behind him in line. There was no doubt in his mind that his clumsiness only furthered her concern, but he quickly turned and walked toward the door. The voices grew louder – almost deafening – and he could hear his own footsteps resounding through the cafeteria. As more students opened their lunchboxes, even more odors wafted through the room, confusing Cailean's brain even more. Trying to keep his cool, he avoided running for the door, but his pace increased as he got closer. Cailean could feel his heart rate increase, pounding in his chest as the sensory input overwhelmed him. The cafeteria lights seemed to grow brighter, burning his eyes. Everyone around him seemed to be screaming as they spoke to their friends.

Cailean pushed open the doors to the cafeteria and stepped into the courtyard. Above him, the sun burned brightly. For a moment, the light blinded him, coloring his field of view with a pure, white light. As the door closed behind him, though, the sounds started to quiet down and the smells faded. Of course, there were still plenty of students outside, but it didn't compare to the interior of the building. Steadying his breathing, Cailean could feel his heartbeat returning to normal and his thoughts clearing up.

Stumbling toward a bench, Cailean fell into a seat and set his backpack on the ground next to him. Cailean placed his elbows on the table and rested his forehead on his palms. He heard footsteps approaching him and assumed Brooke had already worked her way through the line, so Cailean sat up straighter and lifted his head. He didn't want to give her any reason to assume there was something wrong.

When he looked up, though, Cailean couldn't see Brooke anywhere. There were a multitude of student wandering around the courtyard, so it made sense that he would hear frequent footsteps.

Cailean looked around, examining his surroundings. To his left there was an open area with a few benches surrounding a large planter with a few green shrubs. Beyond that was a building which housed most of the classrooms. Cailean sat at a bench in the outdoor seating area which was covered from the sun by a large awning. The library was directly behind him and there was a dirt lot to his right. He was fairly certain that the school didn't own the lot, technically, but many students would spend their lunch playing sports out there.

Cailean exhaled deeply, trying to calm himself down a bit. He couldn't figure out why his nerves were on such high alert, but he hoped things would calm down as he grew more accustomed to the larger school.

"Hey," an angry voice spat from behind Cailean. Cailean turned to see an eighth-grader scowling down at him. Two other boys stood at his sides wearing similar expressions. All three of them were far taller and more muscular than most of the other kids.

"Hello."

"You're in my seat."

"Strange, I guess your 'Reserved' sign blew away," Cailean shrugged.

"You must be new. Clearly you don't know how things work around here."

"That's the line you're going with?"

"What?"

"I don't know, it just feels cliché. Wait, are you a bully?" Cailean laughed. "Am I getting bullied?"

"Get away from our table," he ordered, ignoring Cailean's sarcasm. Cailean stood, placing himself between the table and the bullies. Each of them stood at least a foot taller than him, so Cailean looked upward. Amusement forced its way onto his face as Cailean processed the situation.

"I don't think I will."

The boy in the middle – the one who had been talking – shoved Cailean. Surprised, Cailean almost stepped backward, but the bench was in his way. Barely able to maintain his balance, Cailean stood his ground.

"Pushing people isn't nice," Cailean taunted.

"I recognize you," the bully smirked, stepping backward and looking at Cailean. Cailean observed his face and his mannerisms carefully. "You're that weird kid who freaked out in the hallway, aren't you?"

"Hey!" Another voice called out angrily. Cailean heard a tray slam down on the table behind him as Brooke walked around the table. "Leave him alone."

"Oh, here's your girlfriend to protect you again. Look, guys, this little brat needs a girl to defend him."

Cailean held his arm in front of Brooke, keeping her behind him. Adopting the bully's smirk, he looked up intimidatingly.

"I don't need a girl to protect me," Cailean said menacingly, "but she may prevent me from killing you."

"Oh yeah?" The bully puffed his chest out and stepped toward Cailean in an attempt to intimidate him. Cailean didn't budge.

"Why don't you go walk away and let me and Brooke eat our lunch in peace?" Cailean offered. A crowd had begun to gather, and all eyes were pasted on Cailean. The bully's resolve wavered for a second. Clearly, he wasn't used to being challenged. Hardening his face, though, he stood his ground. With so many other students watching, Cailean knew that the eighth-graders wouldn't back down.

"Alright, Father," he thought. *"Time to stand out."*

As the bully took a step toward him, Cailean closed the distance, stepping off to the side and driving his fist into his assailant's ribs. The older kid clutched his stomach and fell backward, falling to a seated position. Rocking in pain, he was incapacitated in one attack. His friends looked scared, but they weren't willing to give up either. One threw a poorly aimed haymaker toward Cailean, who stepped in and drove his forearm into the attacker's bicep. Following up, he landed an elbow at the boy's solar plexus – knocking the wind out of him. To end his combination, he swept the boy's leg out from under him and pushed him to the ground. The third boy ran toward Cailean. Without hesitation, Cailean lifted his leg and extended it to his side, driving his heel into his opponent's stomach. The boy was launched backward a few feet and landed hard against the concrete.

Nonchalantly, Cailean turned away from the three boys writhing on the floor and back to his table. Sitting down, he fished through his bag for his lunch. Brooke, surprised, hesitated before taking her seat across from him. Cailean could still feel the eyes of all of the other students as they peered at him in disbelief.

"What was that?" Brooke asked.

"I know karate."

"Evidently."

"I'm sorry if that was too violent. I get it if you don't want to eat with me," Cailean quietly told her. Fear flooded his mind as he said it because he was terrified she'd actually leave. The moment before she replied was the longest he'd ever experienced.

"Are you kidding? That was awesome!"

"You really think so?"

"Of course. Those guys are jerks, they deserved it."

"Well, in that case, let's eat quickly. I don't think I have long before one of the teachers or security guards notices this."

❖ ❖ ❖

"Mr. Phoenix," the principal began slowly. Cailean and his father sat in the principal's office awaiting whatever discipline was deemed necessary. "Your son was in a fight with three eighth graders today."

"They started it," Cailean pitched in. "They pushed me."

"It doesn't matter who started it," the principal sighed. "There is a zero-tolerance policy for fighting on campus."

"So I was supposed to let them push me around, both literally and figuratively?"

Aldric, apparently satisfied with the way Cailean was handling himself, leaned back in his chair silently with his arms crossed over his chest. Cailean couldn't tell if his steely gaze was meant for him or for his accuser, but it was intimidating nonetheless.

"Of course not, but there is always an alternative."

"No," Aldric interjected. "There isn't. If Cailean is saying he didn't have a choice, then I believe him."

"Sir," the principal began slowly.

"Have you spoken with any of the witnesses?" Aldric asked.

"I have spoken with all involved."

"So you got three friends to corroborate stories and have chosen to blame the victim because you blindly accept the word of three eighth-graders with wounded pride?"

"I…"

"I don't understand why you called me down here."

"I'm going to have to suspend Cailean," the principal declared firmly.

"If you hinder my son's education for defending himself, rest assured that there will be a law suit in your near future."

"Sir…"

"No. Don't waste another minute of my time. Conduct an investigation – obtain actual witnesses – or drop it."

The principal's face twitched for a moment as he tried to regain control of the situation. Glancing between Cailean and his father, he tripped over his words and eventually stopped trying to speak. Sighing deeply, he looked down at the paper in front of him.

"They told me that you were sitting where they typically eat. They asked if they could sit there and you responded violently. Would you like to tell me your side of the story?"

"Okay," Cailean accepted, sitting up straighter. He was grateful for his father's forcefulness because he was confident that the principal wouldn't have even listened to him without Aldric's support. It was clear that the evidence looked bad for Cailean – there were three people who agreed on a set story and all of them were wounded while Cailean didn't have a scratch. Regardless, Cailean was convinced that if anyone took the time to ask Brooke or any of the students outside, he would be vindicated.

His reaction was intentional and excessive, of course. It would have been simple for Cailean to dissolve the tension by walking away or by using an arm bar instead of throwing strikes.

Still, he had allowed them to publicly shove him in order to build the perception that he was a victim.

"I was sitting there and they came up and demanded that I leave the table. I told them I wouldn't – I was there first after all. I stood up, just trying to talk. The guy who seemed to be in charge pushed me. I didn't even attack after that, but then Brooke came up behind me. I was concerned that they'd hurt us both, so when he took a step toward me, I punched him. His friends both tried to attack me, so I punched one and kicked the other. I only used the required amount of force to ensure my own safety and that of my friend."

"Mr. Phoenix, do you see my dilemma here?" The principal asked, turning his attention to Aldric. "Even your own son has admitted to attacking these boys."

"He has admitted to defending himself – and that is not a crime. Is self-defense disallowed on this campus?"

"No…"

"Then I don't expect to hear of this again. Please don't waste my time."

Aldric stood and walked toward the door. Hesitating, Cailean looked back and forth between his father and the principal. When Aldric opened the door, though, Cailean stood and rushed to his father's side. Aldric's cold gaze didn't lighten up, so Cailean began to worry about what was running through his father's mind. The two of them walked outside and found a place where they were out of earshot from anyone else.

"How badly did you hurt them?" Aldric finally asked.

"They'll be fine, they just had to catch their breath."

"How many people saw?"

"A lot," Cailean admitted.

"What do you think it looked like?"

"What do you mean?"

"What would you have thought if you saw it?"

"I think they would think I am a good fighter. I don't think they would guess what I am – they were just happy to see the bully dethroned. I think I stood out."

"That you did," Aldric nodded. Slowly, his stone-cold expression softened. Aldric rubbed Cailean's hair and pulled him in for a hug.

Chapter 6

7 Years Ago
Aldric

"Can we play?" Cailean asked, eagerly tugging on Aldric's pants. Sitting at his desk, Aldric sighed deeply. It had been quite a while since he'd had a moment to think. Even with his lycanthropic stamina, he found himself becoming fatigued. The problem wasn't that he didn't have the physical capacity to keep up with his son – who was quite possibly an endless stream of energy – but he had trouble with the mental component. He couldn't remember the last time he'd been able to think or have an actual adult conversation without hearing, "why?" every second.

Cailean's tugging became more forceful, threatening to rip a hold in Aldric's pants. With a quiet groan, Aldric rubbed his forehead with his thumb and two fingers as he rested his elbow on his desk. Realizing that any attempt to regain focus was futile, Aldric closed the book in front of him without bothering to mark his page. There was nothing supernatural about his ability to recall the information; he merely hadn't passed the first page before being interrupted.

"What would you like to play?" Aldric questioned, trying to sound more pleased than he actually was. He didn't want his son to notice his lack of desire to play and take that as a personal offense.

"I don't know," the boy shrugged, releasing the cuff of Aldric's pants. Tucked under his right arm was a stuffed gray wolf. Aldric had yet to tell his son much about his lycanthropy, but Cailean had selected that specific toy from the store and was unable to be dissuaded. Since then, he had carried the animal with him everywhere, and he slept with it nightly. Aldric had taught him not to fear the dark by refusing to grant him a nightlight, but Linda had insisted that he be allowed to sleep with his wolf. After all, it wasn't a security blanket as much as it was a connection to the item itself.

"Well, why distract me if you don't have a plan?" Aldric groaned, too coldly.

"Let's play something fun!" Cailean offered.

"Ambiguous," Aldric muttered.

"What's ambigagus?"

"Ambiguous," Aldric corrected. "It's when your answer doesn't provide any actual decision, so it's inexact."

"Oh," Cailean thought for a moment, placing a finger pensively on his lips. His eyes drifted upward as he searched his mind, making connections between the newly presented information and that which he already possessed. "So because I said I wanted to play a fun game, but it wasn't clear, it's ambigagus?"

"Ambiguous."

"Ambiguous," Cailean sounded out slowly.

"That's right," Aldric praised.

"I know!" Cailean added excitedly, quickly moving past his new vocabulary word. "Let's play Fight."

"Fight's not a game," Aldric informed him.

"It is if we make it up," Cailean reasoned.

"I suppose I can't argue with your flawless logic."

Cailean smiled, proudly standing tall and placing his hands on his hips. Aldric wasn't sure that he actually understood what he'd said, but clearly Cailean was able to discern at least the context.

"So, can we play Fight?"

"How do we play?" Aldric inquired, finally turning from his desk and looking down at his son.

"We fight," Cailean cheered. Without warning, he jumped forward, grabbing at Aldric's arm. Years of training taught Aldric to react instinctively, so he barely noticed as he dropped his hand

and threw a light back-knuckle at Cailean's chest. Connecting while Cailean was in the air, Aldric's counter was enough to redirect the boy's momentum and send him flying backward. Cailean collided with the wall on the other side of the room with a thud and slid to the ground. As he looked up at his father, tears welled in his eyes. Aldric sighed, standing and walking toward him to try to comfort him, scolding himself for his lack of control. He knew better, and he couldn't hide behind his past. He'd trained with countless humans, so Aldric had been forced to learn how to pull his punches. Still, it was far too easy to slip back into his basic instincts and become too violent for his child.

Cailean's chest began heaving as he sat against the wall. Aldric dreaded the moment of explaining to his wife how he'd hurt their son that time. Despite the fact that the boy was a werewolf and healed nearly instantly, Linda was very overprotective. Cailean's shoulders rose and fell as he cried silently. As Aldric got closer, though, he saw that Cailean's frown twisted into a smile and he jumped onto his feet, laughing hysterically.

"Yeah!" Cailean yelled excitedly, pumping his fist into the air. With a roar, he raced forward, ducking his head down as if it would increase his speed or protect him from a defensive attack. Charging blindly at his father with the wolf swinging wildly from one hand, Cailean barreled forward. Smoothly, Aldric stepped to the side and gently placed a hand on Cailean's lower back as he passed him, pushing the boy. With the extra force, Cailean tripped over his feet and dropped to the ground, rolling over his shoulder before falling to his side and tumbling into the wall.

Cailean stood shakily to his feet and placed the wolf at his side. "Wait here, Nina," Cailean ordered. Aldric couldn't recall whether his son had ever given an explanation for the name, but the boy had taken a liking to it.

Quickly learning from his mistakes, Cailean didn't charge quite as recklessly this time. Instead, he kept his head up as he ran. In an attempt to confuse his father, he skidded to a stop just before he reached Aldric. Of course, Aldric didn't budge, as he could predict the child's movements with near perfection. Cailean threw a punch toward Aldric's leg, but his short arms prevented him from reaching their target.

Aldric reached his arms out and lifted Cailean from the ground. Screeching with joy, Cailean flailed his arms and legs in the air. One stray kick connected with Aldric's elbow, forcing him to recoil a bit. The force would easily have broken a human's arm. While Aldric was concerned that his son may accidentally hurt someone – he was more impressed.

Aldric spun in a circle, giving Cailean the illusion of flying through the air. After a few spins, he stopped and placed the boy on the ground. Cailean dizzily threw a punch toward Aldric's knee, but his aim was far from accurate.

"I wanna go across the room again!" Cailean demanded as he straightened himself up, apparently becoming bored of actually trying to fight.

"What?" Aldric laughed.

"That was fun, I wanna fly again!"

"Okay," Aldric shrugged. Lifting Cailean, he placed his palm on the boy's chest and held him diagonally. "Are you sure?"

"Yeah!" Cailean exclaimed. Aldric pushed his hand upward, careful not to apply enough force to break the wall. Cailean soared through the air, slamming against the other side of the room. With the impact, the walls vibrated, shaking the house. Despite the fact that he should have been in at least some pain, Cailean stood, beaming and laughing. "Again!"

Aldric obeyed, fulfilling his son's wish for their violent game. As the room finished vibrating, Linda burst through the door.

"What's going on in here?" She demanded.

"I'm throwing Cailean," Aldric shrugged with a laugh.

"It's so fun Mommy! You should try."

"No," she replied coldly. "Aldric, you could hurt him."

"He's a werewolf," Aldric defended. That defense, he knew, wasn't actually a viable one. His son's lycanthropy didn't prevent him from harm – it only healed the wounds more quickly. While his pain tolerance was likely higher than other kids his age, and his bones were less likely to break, he wasn't immune to being harmed. Regardless, he wasn't as fragile as Linda seemed to believe.

"Still," she argued weakly. With a sigh, she softened her gaze, turning from angry to exasperated. Although Aldric didn't particularly like displeasing her, he couldn't think of better ways to play with Cailean.

"Just be careful," Linda ordered with a sigh. Aldric kissed her cheek.

Cailean retrieved Nina and ran up to the two of them, smiling up at his parents and clearly not sensing the slight tension. He tugged at his mother's pants, beaming up at her until she turned her attention to him.

"Mommy, want to play Fight?" He offered.

"Oh," Aldric interjected, squatting down to face Cailean. The image of Cailean accidentally kicking too hard and breaking his mother's arm raced through Aldric's mind. Trying not to make the panic from that idea too apparent, he gently suggested, "Let's only play Fight together. It's a boy game, okay?"

"Oh, okay," Cailean accepted. Slyly, he added, "No girls allowed."

Present
1 Day Until the Full Moon
Cailean

Sitting across from Brooke at the lunch table, Cailean could practically hear her heart beating. As he focused harder, he became confident that he was actually hearing the loud, rhythmic thumping as she twirled her long hair around a finger and gazed at him. Distracted, Cailean battled the urge to dart his eyes toward each sound around them. Every footstep was a roar of thunder and every conversation a resounding echo in his mind. Brooke spoke, but Cailean couldn't process any of the individual pieces as everything melded together into a cacophony of sound.

Unable to hide his discomfort from the situation, Cailean dropped his head onto the table in front of him. With Brooke nearby, he felt safe, so despite the overwhelming nature of the noise around him he didn't panic. Still, his head ached and his brain longed for a moment of silence.

Since Cailean had easily beaten three eighth graders in what the other students were calling a fight, no one had bothered him. Cailean struggled to acknowledge that altercation as anything more than an inconvenience – a fight typically involved at least a semblance of a threat on both sides. Regardless, rumors of the confrontation were spreading like wildfire through the school, and Cailean's name was on all of the students' lips. Lifting his head, he noticed other kids ducking their heads as they passed his table – which he'd taken over from the previously most intimidating group.

As he looked up, his eyes met Brooke's, and he detected a hint of concern. Her lips parted, but Cailean couldn't hear any sound. Wondering if it was because she hadn't spoken or her words had simply blended into the deafening roar of student life, Cailean narrowed his eyes in confusion. Brooke closed her mouth and gently reached out to touch his arm.

The sounds were momentarily washed away with her touch as goosebumps covered his skin. Everything in the world faded except her soft hand against his bare arm. Cailean stumbled for words, but he found himself lost, overtaken by emotions he hadn't experienced before. As she retracted her hands, the sounds of the world around him returned, but they weren't as overpowering as they had been before.

"Are you alright?" Brooke questioned, her voice nothing more than a gentle whisper.

"I'm fine," Cailean nodded with a feigned smile.

"Sometimes it takes a while to adjust to a new school. Especially when there are so many people," Brooke consoled.

"I guess," Cailean responded unconfidently. Though he didn't question her logic, he wasn't sure why the stimuli became more unbearable with each passing day.

"So, what do you think?" Brooke asked, a hint of hope replacing the concern in her voice. For the first time, Cailean noticed a red tint to her cheeks. Apparently, it was obvious that he noticed, because as he looked toward her, her eyes dropped to avoid eye contact. Cailean searched his memory, desperately struggling to find any statement she'd said which may justify her reaction. Thinking back over their conversation, though, all he could hear was an incessant buzzing as his ears rang from the screaming world around him.

"I'm sorry," he apologized slowly.

"Oh, no, I totally get it," she shrugged.

"I just didn't hear you," Cailean quickly interjected, a strange mixture of awkwardness and defensiveness polluting his words.

"Oh," she laughed.

The two sat in silence for a brief moment. Cailean's heart raced, but he couldn't quite understand why. The world around him didn't seem quite as terrifying, so there was no reason for the strange tightness he felt in his stomach. Regardless, though, the feeling was present, and it almost felt like nausea.

"I was just thinking," Brooke started slowly, hiding her embarrassment. Cailean wondered why it was suddenly so hard for her to speak to him. The two had been friends for two weeks, and they hadn't tripped over words before. Brooke especially was always able to say what was on her mind, which was one of the things Cailean found so appealing about her. For some reason, though, there was something different about the heavy thoughts on her mind.

Cailean wondered if she thought he was attractive. He found it difficult to talk to her sometimes, but that usually happened when his mind drifted to certain aspects of her body which particularly drew him in. He couldn't quite understand the feeling, but something about Brooke made him uneasy in the best way.

"Since it's the weekend tomorrow, maybe we could go somewhere."

"Where?" Cailean asked – completely missing her intention. Ignorant to her body language, Cailean just peered at her eyes thoughtfully.

"I don't know," she shrugged and laughed quietly.

"Then why do you want to go there?" Cailean wondered.

"I just want to hang out with you outside of school," she blurted out.

"Oh, okay," Cailean replied.

"Do you want to go swimming tomorrow night? I was thinking we could go to the river."

"That sounds like fun," Cailean smiled. Even with his lack of experience in the subject, Cailean was fairly certain that he had just agreed to his first date.

❖ ❖ ❖

"How was school?" Cailean's father questioned as Cailean took a bite of steak. Although the question itself was innocent enough, Cailean knew his father's tones well enough to understand that there was something hidden beneath the question. After the awkward conversation a week ago, he didn't want to talk to his parents about Brooke, but he assumed that was what his father was asking about.

"It was good," Cailean shrugged.

"Nothing special?" Aldric asked with a laugh. Cailean shrugged off the question. Part of him wanted to ask his father what it was that he was actually trying to find out, but a larger part knew better than to question his father. Instead, Cailean quietly ate another piece of meat as he brushed away any conversation regarding school.

"Are you noticing any changes?" His mom asked slowly, more bluntly approaching the subtext behind his father's line of questioning. Cailean's mind jumped to the moment Brooke had placed a hand on his arm. He sifted through all of the confusing thoughts he harbored for her. Cailean had never been so interested in being around a girl before, but it was beyond that. Something about the way she walked made him feel odd – and he was far more excited to swim with her than he thought he should have been.

"What do you mean?" He shrugged the question off. Rather than talking through any of his perplexing thoughts, he elected to pretend they didn't exist. It was something Cailean would much rather work through on his own than deal with the painful conversation as his parents tried to explain anything.

"Well, as you get older," she began slowly.

"Okay, Mom, I know what puberty is," Cailean groaned. That wasn't an entirely accurate statement, but he hoped it would be enough to avoid the conversation. All he knew was what he'd heard and what he'd read in one book as he tried to better understand his strange symptoms. It was all very limited knowledge, but at least he'd managed to retain the word, because as he uttered it, his mother's expression changed slightly.

"That isn't what we're talking about this time," Cailean's father interjected.

"Then what are you talking about?" Cailean couldn't help but wonder why his father was always so cryptic.

"Loud noises, stronger smells, anything like that," Aldric explained.

"Oh, I don't know," Cailean shrugged. "I think it's all pretty normal."

While some of those things applied to him, Brooke understood how he felt. As much as Cailean wanted to be like his father, there was no reason for him to believe that there was anything abnormal about what he had experienced.

For a moment, Cailean toyed with the idea of ranting – complaining about how much louder middle schoolers were than elementary schoolers – but he decided against it. There was no reason to concern his parents over nothing, and Cailean didn't want to relive the most stressful parts of his school days. Instead, he chose to stay silent as they both examined his face for any sign of hidden information. Slowly, Cailean took another bite of his meal, chewing as he looked back up inquisitively at his mother, meeting her gaze.

"Well, I'm glad you're not getting in any more fights," his mom teased.

"That was barely a fight," Cailean replied. "Anyway, I think I may be the scariest guy on campus now."

"What makes you say that?" Aldric inquired, concerned.

"I just hear a lot of people talking about how I beat up the bullies."

"So you're a local legend, then," Aldric laughed.

"Yeah, I guess," Cailean acknowledged quietly. "I think it's fair to say I'm standing out."

"You're doing well," Aldric praised. "I'm sorry that you have to focus so much on this, but I am proud of you."

"I'd still prefer you not get in fights," Linda muttered.

"Mom," Cailean sighed. "I'm not going to lose a fight to some bully."

"It doesn't have to make sense, I'm a mother," she defended.

Cailean considered his own word choice for a second. When he thought of those three eighth-graders, they were no longer simply humans in his mind. For the first time in as long as he could remember, Cailean didn't separate himself from humanity. Though he wasn't sure if that was because he was beginning to doubt whether he'd ever take the form of a wolf as his father did or because he was happy to associate with Brooke's species, Cailean wasn't sure, but it was a novel feeling either way.

As dinner proceeded relatively uneventfully, Cailean continually bit his tongue about Brooke. By no means was he embarrassed of her, but he wasn't ready to try to defend his reasons for spending so much time with her. Carefully, he avoided mentioning how excited he was to meet with her the following day or how his stomach had been tied in knots when he'd noticed her red cheeks. Instead, Cailean focused his conversations on the topics covered throughout his mundane classes as if they were the highlight of his day. In reality, Cailean was just counting down the minutes to the following evening.

Chapter 7

7 Years Ago

Aldric

Uncomfortable, Aldric shifted to the side slightly as he sat on James's couch. The last thing Aldric wanted was to be sitting in that room trying to be friendly with neighbors, but his wife had insisted. Of course, there was logic behind her argument. First, if they were attempting to appear normal, playdates for their children and friendships for adults were a necessity. Also, the main reason Aldric hadn't wanted to raise Cailean in his pack was because he didn't want the brainwashing that came with exclusively interacting with werewolves throughout childhood to affect his son. Despite Aldric's own hesitation to interact with the world, it was good parenting to allow Cailean those opportunities to socialize.

Linda sat next to him, leaning on his shoulder and laughing at something Bree had said. She and James sat on a sofa adjacent to Aldric and Linda, and Cailean and Samantha were playing with blocks in the middle of the room. Building intricate structures from the geometric shapes, Cailean appeared focused on his creation. Aldric and Linda were careful in their decisions of toys to provide for Cailean. Anything which provided mindless entertainment was intentionally avoided in exchange for something more stimulating. Partially because of that, Cailean's intelligence had developed impressively well for his age. Although that wasn't a sign of lycanthropy, Aldric had been paranoid that it would be mistaken for one. However, Samantha seemed to be able to keep up with Cailean fairly well, and she was working on her own small city built from logs.

Dividing his focus, Aldric closely monitored his son while watching every move from his hosts from his peripheral vision. Leaning back on the couch, he smiled and attempted to appear relaxed. The role of a calm father watching his son play was a simple one to play, so Aldric slowly slipped into it. Breathing deeply, he was able to force away any evident sign of his uneasiness.

Before much more time had passed, Cailean had finished laying out blocks across the floor. Samantha was placing the finishing touch on a roof of one of her houses and Cailean reached forward to start moving another structure she'd built. The two of them worked together to transport her houses, lying them next to Cailean's interconnected blocks.

"They make a great team," James observed, turning his attention to the children. Both of them were too focused on their creation to notice the eyes moving toward them. Meticulously, they positioned Samantha's buildings around the streets Cailean had laid out in a pattern which vaguely resembled the town.

"Maybe they'll get married," Bree joked.

"That seems premature," Aldric muttered quietly.

"I don't know, it's never too early to plan," Linda shrugged.

Aldric couldn't understand their eagerness to plan for the children to grow up. Especially Linda, who was nearly daily mentioning how it felt like no time had passed since Cailean was in diapers. Rather than risk making a scene about the joke, though, Aldric just bit his tongue.

"At the very least, they could open an architecture firm," James suggested, either agreeing with Aldric about the joke or at the very least sympathizing.

"No, Cailean," Samantha argued, her voice rising above the adults' conversation. She had her hands firmly wrapped around one of the buildings, but Cailean was trying to move it elsewhere. Panic forced its way into Aldric's mind as he fought the urge to pull Cailean away. Instead, Aldric just tried to think of ways to explain it in case Cailean accidentally broke some of the toys.

"The school goes here," she concluded confidently.

"No, if your house is there, then the school is this way," Cailean debated. Releasing the school, he moved his hand to an empty place on his street, patting the floor beside it.

"If you walk from my house, you have to go up this way and then over that way," Samantha explained, moving her fingers along the street to simulate a person walking.

"That's backwards," Cailean disagreed.

The two of them argued back and forth for a few more moments. Due to the relative civility of the conversation, none of the parents interjected. Finally, Cailean groaned and walked away, storming toward the couch.

"Father," he complained, grabbing Aldric's pant leg. "Samantha said the school goes there."

"If you're being creative, the school can go anywhere," Aldric told him.

"Not if it's wrong."

"Alright," Aldric sighed, picking Cailean up and setting him on his lap.

"I think he's probably getting hungry," Linda defended.

"Oh, do you want us to get some food?" Bree offered, standing up and motioning toward the kitchen.

"No," Aldric jumped in. Silently, he cursed himself for speed and brevity of the response. In attempt to cover it up, he added, "That's alright. We should get home, I think. He's going to need a nap soon too."

"I don't want a nap!" Cailean whined.

"Are you sure?" Bree asked.

"Yeah," Linda nodded, rubbing Aldric's back to inform him that she would handle their escape. "We should do this again sometime, though."

"Any time," James smiled.

"Mommy," Cailean argued. "I'm having fun!"

"I know buddy. Don't worry, we'll be back. It's nap time though."

"I'm not tired! I want to play!"

"Cailean," Aldric scolded firmly. Instantly, Cailean fell silent and dropped his face against his father's shirt. After an awkward exchange of goodbyes, they were finally outside and heading toward the street. The two walked across the road and up their porch steps in silence.

"You know, I'm really surprised that you aren't better at talking our way out of these things," Linda teased Aldric when they were behind their closed door.

"I spent my formative years in isolation," Aldric defended.

"That was centuries ago."

"Well, I don't like people anyway," Aldric groaned as he set Cailean down.

"He's kidding," Linda told Cailean, who looked up at his father with confusion.

"I'm not," Aldric denied. "That's why you have to be an especially good boy, you've got to make up for your old man."

"That's not fair," Cailean complained.

"It never is," Aldric laughed sadly. Although he was joking for the most part, his words still reminded himself of his own father.

"He's just playing with you, Cailean."

"Okay," Cailean shrugged, clearly losing interest in the conversation. Turning, he ran off toward his room. Linda glared at Aldric, but eventually laughed. He knew it had been a long while since she'd given up hope for his social skills to match that of a normal functioning human.

A moment later, Cailean returned with a foam sword. Rushing at Aldric with a battlecry, he held the sword high in the air.

"His attention span is miniscule," Aldric observed. As Cailean approached him, he stepped to the side, avoiding the attack. Cailean, unprepared for his target to move, pitched forward and plummeted to the floor.

"He really is your son," Linda laughed. Aldric had convinced her long ago that it wasn't worth making a scene if Cailean fell or hurt himself. Even if he had scraped something, the wound would be gone before she had a chance to get him a bandage anyway. "He can go from building to whining to fighting in minutes."

"I will choose not to be offended by that," Aldric laughed.

Cailean stood back to his feet, releasing another loud cry as he swung the sword at Aldric. Aldric moved his leg slightly, avoiding the strike completely.

"I was serious about the nap, though," Linda sighed.

"Don't worry," Aldric smiled, cracking his knuckles. Cailean lurched forward again, but Aldric dove forward and grabbed the boy, lifting him into the air. "I'll just have to tire him out a bit first."

Present
Morning of the Full Moon
Cailean

Cailean counted down the hours, waiting for the sun to set. Every time he thought about meeting Brooke that night, a strange feeling washed over his stomach and he felt nervous – even though he'd already seen her every day at school for the past two weeks. Cailean checked his alarm clock again to find that the time hadn't even ticked past noon yet.

Standing up, Cailean paced the room, restless. Even when his mind drifted from Brooke, there was an uneasy feeling in his gut. Anxiety was the only word Cailean could conjure as description, but that didn't feel quite accurate. There was no reason for him to be anxious, and the feeling persisted whether he was thinking or not.

Wishing the day away, Cailean stood in the middle of his room. Despite how hard he willed the knots in his stomach to flee, there was no change. It felt almost as though he were forgetting something, but Cailean hadn't left his house, so there was no reason to feel as though he had left something behind.

Finally, he accepted that his subconscious was attempting to tell him something, so he dropped down on his bed and ran through a mental checklist. He'd done all of his homework already. He had finished his chores within an hour of waking up just because he had needed something to do to help kill the time. He hadn't taken the time to give his parents an excuse for where he wanted to go, but he didn't assume that would be a problem. He was absolutely positive that it was the correct day. No obvious answer seemed to present itself to him, despite how hard he searched for a logical reason for his body's reaction.

As one last verification attempt, Cailean checked the calendar hanging from his wall. The bottom page listed all of the days while the top page was merely a photograph of a different natural landscape each month. Fittingly, the picture in front of him was a stream running through a forest. Cailean glanced downward to the day, but his eye was caught by the lunar chart in the middle of the calendar.

"No," he muttered under his breath. How could he have forgotten that it was the full moon?

Cailean panicked as he dropped back onto his bed. Even if he wanted to, he couldn't cancel on Brooke. If he did, he was concerned that she'd never want to speak with him again. Cailean was certain that his parents would refuse to allow him to leave the house, though. His mind raced for a solution, but his thoughts became cloudy as the trepidation set in.

For the first time in his life, Cailean was grateful that he wasn't like his father. Regardless of what his parents claimed, Cailean hadn't transformed into a werewolf, and he was severely doubting that would ever happen. Maybe he had inherited the healing and strength from his father and the humanity from his mother. Whatever the case, he knew that he wanted to spend time with the cute girl who was expecting him.

Cailean wondered if he'd be able to convince his mom to let him leave after he proved that he wasn't going to transform. If he just waited for the moon to reach its place in the sky, he could manage to make it in time if he ran full speed. That was a risk, though, because if she didn't allow it then he sacrificed his chance.

As Cailean's mind raced through his limited options, a knock on his door resounded like an explosion. Cailean leapt from his bed and lifted his hands to cover his face. Adrenaline raced through his veins as his heart pounded from the sudden sound. Breathing slowly, Cailean dropped his hands to his sides.

"Come in," he called.

"You alright?" His father asked as he pushed the door open.

"Yeah," Cailean shrugged. "Why do you ask?"

"Well, you're just standing in the middle of your room, I heard you jump, and I can hear your heart now."

If Cailean tried, he was able to hear his father's heartbeat as well. Cailean couldn't remember a time when he couldn't hear so well. Consciously, he knew that he hadn't actually noticed the enhanced ability to hear until middle school, but just as a sick child selectively forgot the feeling of health, Cailean had trouble remembering what it felt like to not hear every minute sound.

"You just startled me," Cailean admitted.

"Sorry, I forget how jumpy you are," Aldric teased. Typically, Cailean would have responded to that type of comment with some type of defense, but he couldn't bring himself to do so. Instead, he just feigned a laugh and then allowed silence to fill the space.

"Anyway, I have a few hours before I have to start getting ready for tonight. I thought you may want to do something."

"You want to fight?" Cailean surmised.

"No," Aldric laughed. "Your training is important, of course, but it isn't our entire lives. I thought we'd play catch."

Cailean laughed quietly as his father tossed a ball in the air. "Is it for my reflexes?" He asked.

"Well, fun things can still have a purpose," Aldric shrugged. Cailean smiled and followed his father outside.

❖ ❖ ❖

For the first time in years, Cailean didn't ask his father to allow him to accompany him to the woods. He wondered whether that was suspicious and considered asking just to maintain a sense of normalcy. However, if his father agreed for some reason, Cailean would have to cancel on Brooke last minute. It was better for him to simply appear to be accepting the fact that he wasn't going to transform.

"Alright," Aldric sighed heavily, standing at the door with a small bag at his side. Hesitating before exiting, he turned around to face his family. Squatting down in front of Cailean, he narrowed his eyes and investigated Cailean's.

"Are you sure nothing has felt weird?" Aldric asked cautiously.

"No. I mean, yes, I guess," Cailean stuttered, tripping over his words.

"Okay." Turning his attention to Linda, he added, "Be safe."

"We'll be just fine," she smiled. "You be careful out there."

Aldric nodded solemnly as he stood and turned toward the door. Cailean wasn't sure why it was always such a spectacle when his father left to transform. It happened monthly, so it was nothing new to them. If he was ever able to experience the transformation, Cailean couldn't imagine himself treating it as a bad thing. His father seemed to think it was nothing more than a side-effect of the powers he had, but to Cailean, it seemed like the most interesting part. The fact that his entire body could simply become something else was baffling.

Aldric opened the door and stepped through. With a sigh, he looked back toward his family and nodded before closing the door behind him. The setting sun shone through the door for a brief moment, and Cailean suddenly realized how late it was. His stomach twisted into a pretzel as he thought about keeping Brooke waiting.

"Want to play a board game?" Linda offered.

"I'm alright, Mom," Cailean told her. He was not answering the question she'd asked, but rather the one hidden in the subtext. For the past year, Cailean had been impatiently awaiting his first transformation. Every month, he had complained to his mom about how he wanted to be like his father. That night, though, he wouldn't trade being himself for anything.

"Okay," she accepted quietly. The two of them had come to an unspoken agreement to avoid pressing Cailean for information concerning his desire to be a lycanthrope. His mom knew that he would talk to her about it if he felt the need, but she was also aware that he sometimes needed to process things internally.

"I'm tired," Cailean told her, breaking the fleeting silence. "I think I'm going to go to bed early."

"Are you sure?" She asked, concern flooding into her voice.

"Yeah. I'm okay, Mom. Really. I love you," Cailean hugged her tightly. He felt horrible lying to her, but he knew she wouldn't allow him to leave. Though he'd never changed before, she always thought it important to keep him locked away in his room. Anyway, Cailean was sure that he'd feel differently if he were about to transform into a wolf. There was no logical reason for him not to meet Brooke.

"I love you too," his mother replied sadly, hugging him. As Cailean pulled back, she held him for a second longer. Finally, she released him and Cailean retreated to his room. With the sun rapidly setting, he was sure that Brooke would be at the river soon if she wasn't already. He didn't have much time to spare if he didn't want her to think he'd stood her up.

Rapidly getting to work, Cailean slipped a few pillows under his covers and changed into a swimsuit. Quickly, he put his shoes on and slid on a new shirt. Checking the mirror, he examined his hair and ran a comb through it to try to get it to keep its form. Cailean flipped his light off and quietly moved toward the window. Lifting it gently, he attempted to keep all of his motions as silent as possible. Cailean slipped through the window and lowered it behind him, just in case someone noticed it had been moved.

Looking around him, Cailean watched for any observers. When he was confident no one had noticed his exit, he snuck around the house, sticking to the darkest corners. When he reached the other side of the building, he checked one more time for any onlookers before breaking into a run for the tree line.

As he crossed into the forest, Cailean picked up the pace. He changed his direction slightly, heading toward the river which ran along the town. The further he got into the trees, the more confident he became that no one was watching and so the faster he ran. Within a few minutes, Cailean found himself barreling toward the river. Stopping suddenly, he tripped over his feet and rolled onto his shoulder, jumping back to his feet.

Brushing off the sticks and leaves, Cailean exhaled deeply and allowed himself a few seconds to catch his breath. Brooke sat on a rock not too far in front of him, mindlessly tossing pebbles into the water. From his position, Cailean could see her at an angle, so he was able to make out her stance. One leg was extended in front of her, her heel resting on the ground, while the other was firmly planted on the floor. On her bent knee, she rested her right arm and her chin rested in that open palm. With her left hand, she tossed a small rock and caught it again before sacrificing it to the lake.

In the light of the moon, her black hair seemed to glow, reflecting the shine. Her loose shirt caught in the slight breeze, flowing gently. Her shorts barely reached the middle of her thigh, so her exposed legs seemed to glow. As she breathed slowly, her chest rose and fell rhythmically.

A quiet thumping filled the world around him as Cailean listened to the calming beat of her heart. He carefully observed the sounds of her breath as it passed her slightly parted lips. The occasional splash of water was thunderous, but not entirely unpleasant.

Finally, Cailean was able to snap himself out of his trance and approach the majestic figure before him. Stumbling over his words, he was unable to formulate a proper greeting, so he froze. As he did, he dug one foot into the ground, accidentally breaking a stick beneath him. Brooke's head turned rapidly toward him, fear painted on her gentle features. As she recognized him, though, that was washed away by an enticing smile.

"You startled me," she greeted with a quiet laugh. Standing, she dropped the rocks from her left hand and faced him. Cailean searched through his mind, grasping for any way to break the increasingly awkward silence, but he couldn't find words.

"I was starting to worry you weren't coming," she told him.

"Sorry, I had to wait for my father to leave," Cailean shrugged.

"Oh, where was he going?"

"Long story," Cailean laughed it off, realizing that he'd already been careless with his words. What he had said wouldn't have been anything too incriminating, but he had no follow-up, so that was problematic. Although he was confident Brooke wasn't a hunter, he also knew that he had to be more careful.

"Alright, then," Brooke replied, confused. "Well, are we going to swim?"

"Yeah," Cailean smiled.

Brooke turned from him and grabbed the bottom of her shirt with her hands. Lifting it over her head, she tossed it to the side. The thin string of her bikini was the only thing keeping her back from being completely bare. Dropping her hands, she unbuttoned her shorts and pulled them down. As she stepped out of them, she kicked them to the side. Cailean watched her hips sway until she descended into the water.

"Are you coming?" She questioned, turning back to face him. A drop of water reflected from her breast, but Cailean tried to force himself not to look. The feeling in his gut started to become painful, as if the butterflies frenzied and searched for a way out.

"Yeah," Cailean choked out, fighting back against the emotions and hormones that raced through his brain. He pulled his shirt off and tossed it with her clothes before running and jumping in the water. The rush of cold didn't do much to quell the tingling in his stomach. In fact, the sensation seemed to spread like a cancer, overtaking most of his body. As the water rippled, the reflection of the full moon in the center of the sky seemed to vibrate.

"What are you looking at?" Brooke asked, approaching him slowly and following his gaze. "Is there something in the water?"

"No," Cailean shook his head. Too many thoughts raced through Cailean's mind for him to take action upon any of them. A large part of him wanted to look up and admire Brooke's body as she stood in the waist-deep water with him, but he wondered if that was considered impolite. Either way, for some reason, he couldn't tear his eyes from the pulsating reflection of the moon. Suddenly, the moon dissipated in the water beneath him and something jumped out from it. Reacting quickly, Cailean stepped to the side and caught whatever had jumped for him. Less than a second later, he realized he was gripping Brooke's wrist and quickly let go.

"Sorry," he quickly apologized.

"You have good reflexes," she laughed, rubbing her wrist. Both of her arms in front of her seemed to press her breasts together and draw his attention to them even more. More mesmerizing than the moon had been a moment ago, Cailean couldn't take his eyes from her. Before he noticed her move, Brooke had thrust her hand through the water and splashed his face.

"Hey," he complained, wiping the water from his eyes.

"What are you looking at?" She teased.

"I… Umm…" Cailean stuttered, terrified that he'd ruined any chance he had with her.

"What?" She asked, leaning toward him.

"The moon?" Cailean tried to answer, but it came across more as a question. As she leaned forward, he found his eyes instinctively drifting back toward her. A strange feeling washed over him – as if his entire body were being stabbed by small pins.

"Oh, really?" Brooke asked, leaning backward and placing her hands on her hips, pushing her chest forward as she did. "The moon."

"What can I say? It's hypnotic," Cailean shrugged.

"There's that confidence I found so attractive," Brooke complimented.

"You find me attractive?" Cailean asked. Brooke glanced at Cailean's chest and then admired his arms. Cailean felt his muscles tense in response to her gaze and his arms seemed to grow larger as if to impress her.

Cailean stepped toward her and the pins grew to blades, stabbing his body painfully. With as much confidence as he could muster, he wrapped an arm around her waist and pulled her toward him. Their faces inches apart, Cailean gazed into her eyes for a moment. Adrenaline coursed through his veins as he felt her skin against his. The discomfort in his body grew into agony, and he wondered if this was what people meant when they talked about how love made someone feel.

For a reason he couldn't quite understand, Cailean felt a growing urge to be closer to her. Hoping drawing nearer would kill the butterflies in his stomach, he stepped toward her, moving his face within inches of her. His father's words echoed through his mind, though, and he reluctantly stopped himself from pressing his lips against hers. If he could only love once, he had to be careful with his decision, and he knew he couldn't make it based on the feelings flooding through his mind. Fighting the urge only twisted his stomach into knots, though, worsening the pain. With a sudden gasp, Cailean stumbled backward.

"Are you alright?" She asked.

"Yeah," he shrugged. "I think I just stepped on something."

Trying to catch his breath, Cailean peered into the water beneath him. Searching for whatever had caused the pain, he tried to see past the surface of the river, but all he could see was his own reflection in the moving water. In the bright moonlight, his eyes seemed to adopt an entirely new color – glowing a bright golden-yellow.

Chapter 8

6 Years Ago

Aldric

"Thanks for coming!" James greeted, opening the door seconds after Aldric knocked. Cailean stood next to Aldric, holding the gift he'd insisted on carrying. Linda stood on his other side, firmly holding his hand. Aldric wondered if his relatively relaxed attitude concerning Cailean or Linda's overprotection was normal. Every time he crossed the street, she insisted on holding his hand just in case. To Aldric, it didn't seem particularly problematic for the boy to walk on his own. The worst case scenario was that he got hit by a car and Aldric had to come up with some explanation for how he wasn't hurt.

Of course, as the door opened and Cailean rushed inside, Aldric and Linda switched roles in an instant. Linda relaxed, allowing Cailean to go search for his friends, but Aldric cautiously tried to peer around James, unwilling to take his eyes off of his son. While they had known most of the neighbors for years, Aldric couldn't shake the fear that there were hunters hiding amongst them. When it came to hunters, Aldric was very concerned for his son's safety. A hunter could actually cause permanent harm and therefore was a significant threat.

"Of course," Aldric replied, attempting to sound as friendly as possible. Every instinct warned him to be overly cautious, but he forced himself to relax, at least slightly. Even in the relatively unlikely event that James and Bree were hunters, it would require either extreme confidence or stupidity to attack him at their daughter's birthday party.

As Aldric crossed the threshold, he was surprised to see only Cailean and Samantha playing in the living room. Hesitantly, he stepped further into the room, allowing James to close the door behind him. Although he'd been to that house countless times, something felt particularly wrong about that time, but Aldric couldn't quite decide what it was.

"First family here. I guess there are benefits to living across the street," Aldric laughed, carefully concealing his question as a joke.

"Yeah, more people should be coming by soon," James assured with a nod. "At least, I hope they do. I have a lot of cake for just the six of us."

Something about his host's tone made Aldric's skin crawl. Smiling, he took a step away, turning toward the children and hoping that his avoidance of further conversation wasn't obvious. In attempt to better understand his situation, Aldric inhaled deeply. Something smelled strange, but he assumed the cake was just some flavor he had never smelled.

"Can I get you both some water?" James offered. Aldric, squatting down next to Cailean, declined the offer absentmindedly.

"What is it, Father?" Cailean asked, turning from his friend.

"What do you mean?" Aldric questioned, concealing the panic in his tone with feigned confusion. His son had always been perceptive, so he should have known that using him as an excuse to turn from the other adults was a bad idea.

"Something is wrong," Cailean replied firmly.

Aldric hesitated, hoping James would leave soon. The last thing Aldric wanted was to give away his suspicions. Apparently interested in the conversation, though, James lingered over Aldric's shoulder.

"You know what, I think I'm just thirsty," Aldric laughed. "Maybe I will have that water after all."

"Two waters, coming up," James announced. As he walked away, Cailean looked back toward Aldric, confusion on his face. Moving toward them, Linda placed her hand on Aldric's shoulder.

"Alright, what's going on?" Linda whispered.

"I don't know. We shouldn't be here," Aldric told her.

"Why not? It's fun," Cailean argued.

"Yeah, don't make Cailean go home," Samantha chimed in.

"Who's going home?" Bree asked with concern as she entered the room from the other direction.

"Unfortunately," Linda answered, turning to face her friend. "I think Cailean needs a nap. He's being a bit grumpy."

"I'm not grumpy," Cailean whined.

"See?" Linda shrugged.

"Oh, at least stay for cake," Bree begged, just as the doorbell rang. Holding a finger up to tell them to wait, Bree turned and raced toward the door. Aldric listened as she exchanged pleasantries with new guests, but his nerves weren't calmed like he had thought they would be. Despite the lack of logic, he could practically smell their intention.

Distracted, Aldric barely noticed as James walked back into the room. Accepting the water, he thanked his neighbor and smiled. Aldric took a drink, hoping hydration would ease the tension in his nerves. Bree, leading another family, walked into the room.

"Aldric, Linda, this is Kieran and his son, Darren," she explained, introducing everyone. Darren seemed to be quite a bit older than Samantha, so Aldric wondered why he was there. His thoughts grew foggy as he tried to listen to Bree's introduction, searching for the reason for their presence. The other guests began speaking and shaking hands, but it seemed as though they continually tried to speak more loudly and less intelligibly than the previous person.

"I'm sorry," Aldric muttered, stumbling toward the hall. "I have a bit of a headache. I'm going to run to the restroom."

"Do you need medicine?" James offered, but Aldric ignored him. The question left his ears ringing as if he'd screamed directly in Aldric's ear. Safely down the hallway, Aldric paused as the puzzle fit itself together. Lifting the cup to his nose, he breathed in the scent. Wolfsbane.

The realization dawned on him that he'd smelled it from the moment he entered the house, but it had been so long since he'd been exposed to it that he hadn't remembered. As the wolf tore at his insides, though, clawing its way out, he recognized the smell far too well. Aldric lurched toward the wall, using it for support as he tried to continue toward the bathroom.

"Are you alright there, Aldric?" James asked tauntingly, appearing at the other end of the hallway.

"At a party?" Aldric spat, turning toward him. "Our families are here."

"You are a hard man to isolate," James countered. "And desperate times, right?"

"I'll kill you – and everyone you love," Aldric threatened. Turning to face James, he stood tall and bit back the pain.

"If left unchecked," James nodded. "That's why I will stop you now."

James drew a knife from where it hid tucked into the back of his pants. Adopting a fighting stance and holding the knife between himself and Aldric, he waited for Aldric to start the transformation. Groaning, Aldric shook his head. He knew that if he allowed himself to transform, he'd be vulnerable. Instead, he held back the wolf with all of the strength he could muster.

Charging toward James, he caught the man by surprise. James swung the knife wildly, but Aldric weaved back to avoid the strike. Stepping in, he drove his forearms into James's arm on either side of the elbow. Grabbing his wrist with one hand, Aldric pulled the other back and pushed it against James's elbow, breaking the bone out of place. James screamed in pain, but Aldric slammed him forward and pressed his head against the wall, muffling the screams.

"Kill me, then. It won't stop anything," James spat.

"The other two," Aldric realized.

"Darren is in training, but Keiran can end you. Your family passed the test, but he'll hurt them anyway if it makes you give in. So kill me, you're just dooming everyone you love."

"I've been told that before," Aldric growled in his ear. Surprising him, James thrust his other arm backward, plunging a second knife into Aldric's gut. Turning to face Aldric, James threw a punch with his good arm, connecting with Aldric's jaw. Using that moment of confusion to his advantage, James dove forward and knocked Aldric to the ground.

Lost in the moment, Aldric felt the wolf pushing its way forward. Despite the fact that the knife was still lodged in his stomach, the beast clawed its way to the surface in attempt to protect its human half. Ceding some control to the animal, Aldric felt pressure in his eyes as the colors faded from his vision. Lifting his head, he bit down on James's neck, ripping open his vein.

Collapsing to the ground next to Aldric, James futilely covered the wound in his neck. Aldric grasped the hilt of the blade lodged in his ribs and removed it, trying to give the wound time to heal. As it closed, he finally allowed the wolf to take over, unable to control himself any longer.

Through the eyes of the beast, he saw a seven-year-old girl, staring in horror at the sight of her father bleeding on the ground. Bree rushed in front of Samantha, charging the wolf to defend her daughter. Aldric jumped forward, pinning her to the ground and biting into her ribs. As he felt the bones break beneath his teeth, he released her and stepped backward.

Samantha wailed, screaming likely in both terror and sorrow. Aldric inched toward her, but his mind was barely present. Fear filled his mind as he wondered what the wolf would do to the girl. Gently, it pushed its nose against her, forcing her to the ground. Clasping its jaws around her shirt, the wolf lifted the girl into the air. Defeated, she didn't struggle much – she just hung limply from its jaws. Aldric could feel the wolf's hunger as it smelled prey, but he fought to convince it to leave her unharmed.

Turning the corner, Aldric found Keiran and Darren, each holding a knife to the throat of one of his family members. Rage flooded the beast's blood, but Aldric's mind fought to soothe it. Inching forward, he maintained eye contact with Keiran.

"I'll kill your son!" Darren threatened.

"No! It will hurt the girl. We don't want to lose her today too."

"It will kill her anyway. It's a monster!"

Keiran released Linda from his grasp, motioning for Darren to do the same for Cailean. Reluctantly, his son obeyed. Linda picked up Cailean and ran, standing behind Aldric. Carefully, Aldric set Samantha on the ground in front of the hunters. After cautiously lifting the baby, Keiran backed away, leaving the

Phoenixes on their own. As the effects of the wolfsbane wore off, Aldric felt the pain of the wolf retreating into his body, but his mind never lost consciousness.

Present
Night of the Full Moon
Cailean

"Quit being all pensive," Brooke teased before jumping onto Cailean's back, pushing him underwater. Distracted, Cailean didn't have time to react as he felt her weight bearing down on him. As his head was submerged, Cailean instinctively closed his eyes and held his breath. The water felt far colder as it rushed around his face, and it numbed his muscles. For a brief moment, the pain left his body and Cailean felt weightless as he floated in an empty void.

In an instant, all sensation was returned to him and agony overtook his body. Cailean's eyes shot open as he tried to see through the water. Beneath him, he saw his own hand, but it was almost unrecognizable. In an attempt to stabilize himself, he had absentmindedly dug his fingers into the mud beneath him. As he released his hold, he saw that his fingernails had grown and become pointed, and hair had begun to grow from the back of his hands.

Cailean spun around, looking above him to see Brooke smiling down at him. Her hair flowed behind her, carried in the river like a majestic wind. Seeming to shine from an internal light, her eyes sparkled as she peered down at him. She smiled and laughed, forcing bubbles from her nose as she saw the surprise in his face, probably assuming it was a response to her attack.

His mind racing, Cailean desperately searched for explanations. He wanted an explanation for Brooke to keep her from thinking he was a monster, but also for himself. Cailean had never experienced anything similar before, but he knew he had to be transforming because there was no other logical explanation. As he finally made that connection, Cailean stopped considering excuses or explanations. If his father was right, he was about to become incredibly dangerous, and all that mattered was getting Brooke out of there – even if she never wanted to see him again.

Cailean reached upward with his human hand and placed it on her sternum. Thrusting his arm upward and diagonally, the threw her from the water. She flew backward, landing on her back as she collided with the riverbank not too far away.

Pushing the dripping hair from his eyes, Cailean stood and caught his breath. Pain exploded from his lungs as the oxygen filled them, expanding them within his chest. Biting back the pain, Cailean looked toward Brooke, who was rubbing her butt, which had probably hit the packed sand first, with a confused and pained expression.

"What was that?" Brooke called out angrily.

"I need you to run, Brooke. As far as you can," Cailean instructed.

"What?"

"Just do it," he growled, glaring at her with his golden eyes. His shoulder tensed and the nerves down to his arm tingled. Cailean felt his legs seizing but struggled to stay standing against the current which fought to bring him under.

Brooke stood as the pain in her eyes was replaced with concern. Cailean held a hand toward her in attempt to force her to stand back. Thrusting his arm forward, he felt his shoulder dislodge from its socket. Though he attempted to accompany the action with an order, no words escaped his mouth as his vocal cords broke.

Unable to bear the pain, Cailean finally collapsed and succumbed to the current. Falling to his knees, he felt the water encompass him once again. The hand he'd shown to Brooke was beginning to change shape as well, and he watched as the fingers broke and cracked, shrinking back as the palm extended.

Lifting his head, Cailean saw two smooth, radiant legs as they were submerged in the shallow water near him. Brooke cautiously approached him, displacing water as she stepped toward his broken body. Cailean heard a loud crack and pain shot through his back. Stifling a scream to avoid allowing water to flood his lungs, Cailean bit his lip until it bled.

Brooke's legs moved steadily closer to him as he dug his hands into the mud below. The ground appeared to grow closer as Cailean's arms caved in. the bones in his forearms broke and dissolved, shrinking his arms down slightly as they reformed without the joint of his elbow. The current felt more powerful as Cailean's legs shattered and his knees were no longer able to support him.

Brooke's hips crossed the water as she drew closer to him. Cailean could hear her calling his name, but nothing within him had the strength or ability to respond. All he wanted was to tell her to run before he hurt her but warning her became an impossibility. The current pressed hard against him, forcing him to dig his paws further into the mud beneath him. One last option forced itself into Cailean's mind as her toes neared the tips of his claws. Her hands pushed through the water as she moved, and her torso was easily within his reach. Mustering all of the strength he could manage, Cailean pulled his hands upward, thrusting a good amount of mud into the waves and obstructing Brooke's view. With no weight holding him to the ground, Cailean felt the current sweep him away, and he watched as Brooke's legs grew further from him with each passing second.

Agony overwhelmed Cailean as he felt more of his bones shatter and nerves reconnect. When he collided with a large rock protruding from the ground, Cailean's motion stopped and he instinctively let out a yelp. The water rushed into his mouth as he panicked. Aside from the slight soreness from the impact with the rock, the pain slowly faded from his body.

Brooke moved toward him again, much more quickly this time, and Cailean tried to flee from her. As he tried to move his arms, though, he felt no motion. Regardless of how much effort he expended, none of his muscles would respond to his commands. Brooke grew closer and the bottom of her chest was submerged as the river grew deeper. Cailean struggled to move, pleading with himself to get away before he hurt her, but he found himself stuck against the rock. She grew closer, propelling herself forward with her arms and kicking as she switched from walking to swimming. Finally, Cailean was dislodged by the current, and he felt his body being pulled to the side. Just as he was beginning to float away, though, Brooke's arm lurched forward, wrapping around him. She pulled him close, planting her feet into the wet mud as she turned and struggled against the current.

"It's going to be okay," she assured him, taking another step and lifting him above water. Cailean coughed, spitting up liquid as he struggled to breathe. She continued walking, holding him close to her chest as she forced her way to the riverbank. Cailean heard the rapid thumping of her heart as she exerted herself by carrying him from the waves.

Finally, her foot landed on the moist ground of the riverbed. After a few more steps, she collapsed and gently placed Cailean on the ground in front of her. Coughing, Brooke fell forward and rolled over onto her back.

Cailean stumbled to his shaky feet. Looking around, he examined his surroundings for what felt like the first time. Everything had taken on a new grey tone, and it appeared much larger than it had moments before. Cailean took a step forward, wobbling and almost falling over. More confidently, he moved his other paw to catch up with the first.

Cailean's brain begged for his body to stop moving – or at least turn the other direction. He had heard stories from his father, and there was a reason Aldric always transformed in the woods. If the wolf managed to make its way to Brooke, he couldn't imagine any good outcome. Despite his pleas, though, his body seemed to act of its own accord. His legs continued to work their way forward as he inched toward her.

Finally, the wolf was within reach of her. She rested on the sand, her chest heaving as she tried to catch her breath. Gently, Cailean pushed his head forward and pressed his nose into her side. With a whimper, the wolf moved closer to her. Curling up next to her, it pressed its body against hers as she regained her breath.

Suddenly, Cailean felt a soft hand press against his head, rubbing his scalp. His ears perked up and he jumped to his feet, wagging his tail vigorously. The wolf's tongue fell from its mouth as its breathing increased. Excitedly, it licked Brooke's arm, lapping the water from her skin.

"Cailean?" Brooke asked quietly, choking up with fear so the name was barely audible. He cocked his head, confused. Cailean's own thoughts were growing cloudy, but the wolf seemed to recognize the sound. "Is that you?"

In response, Cailean barked happily. Whether it knew its name or not, the wolf seemed happy to have one. The cub pressed its head against Brooke's leg, nudging her as she sat up. The wolf jumped into her lap, licking her face as she smiled down at him.

"Okay, okay," she giggled. Confusion and concern were apparent in her voice, but her tone was happy – and that was all the wolf seemed to understand. Cailean, a passenger in his body, watched the scene unfold through the eyes of the wolf. He tried to tell her to leave, or at least to stop the wolf from jumping on her, but he had no semblance of control over the animal he'd become.

She climbed to her feet, searching around for something. Finding a large stick, Brooke picked it up and dangled it in front of the wolf's face. Excited, it jumped and tried to grab the stick from her hand. Lifting it above his reach, though, she pulled it away from him. Throwing her arm forward, Brooke released the stick. The wolf's attention darted toward the motion and it raced after the lost toy.

Retrieving the stick with its mouth, the wolf carried it back to Brooke triumphantly. It wagged its tail as it dropped the stick next to her again. She bent over to pick it up, but the wolf pushed against her and she stumbled backward, barely able to maintain her balance. Cailean pleaded with the wolf to be gentle, but it didn't seem to notice. He didn't feel any anger from the wolf, but he wasn't sure how in tune he was with that part of himself.

Brooke lifted the stick again, and the wolf jumped after it. Pushing itself against her, it tried to grab the stick before she was able to throw it. Clumsily, the wolf stumbled forward, pressing its front paw against her. Its sharp nails pierced her upper thigh as it stood on its hind legs and searched for support. Stumbling backward from the pain, Brooke failed to provide the stability the wolf needed, and it fell toward her, dragging its claws down her thigh. She fell to the ground, dropping the stick next to her and inhaling deeply as she pressed her hand over her bleeding thigh.

Without noticing her pain, the wolf moved a few inches to retrieve the stick. Cailean could feel confusion coming from the animal, as if it wondered why she hadn't thrown it as far the second time. Regardless, it placed the stick in front of her and wagged its tail. Finally noticing the pain on her face, though, it stepped toward her and gently pressed its nose against her hand.

"It's alright buddy," she told the wolf through clenched teeth. "I know you didn't mean to."

The wolf licked her fingers, cleaning the blood which continued to pour from her leg. She kept one hand pressed firmly against her thigh and brought the other up to push his face back. The wolf tried to move in again, but she pushed his face away. Losing his resolve to lick her wounds, the wolf simply curled up next to her leg.

After a moment, Cailean – or the wolf, he was starting to become unsure – heard a rustling in the bushes a few feet away. It jumped up, growling quietly and standing between the sound and Brooke. A large figure moved aside some branches and took a step toward them.

The intruder was a man whose gait hid a great deal of pain. The wolf recognized the smell, but it couldn't find a name for the person in front of it. The man inched forward, struggling against some unseen force. His face lit up as he stepped through the foliage and neared the river, moving into the moonlight.

Cailean recognized his father, still a human as he walked on two legs toward Cailean. Every step was slow and deliberate as he clearly fought against his own animalistic side. Aldric neared Brooke, glowering down at her and the wolf which stood guard. Cailean felt the wolf relax slightly as it recognized the father of its human half, but it still felt unsettled.

Silently, Aldric reached the two children and stood over them. Leaning forward, he grasped the fur and a flap of skin on the back of Cailean's neck. Lifting the young wolf, he held him in one hand and took a step backward, still looking down at Brooke.

"Can you walk?" He asked. His tone was not hard, but his voice was a low growl nonetheless.

"I think so," she affirmed, standing to her feet shakily. Blood trickled down her thigh and continued down her leg, leaving a thin trail behind it. Brooke clearly favored the other leg, but she was able to stand. She stepped toward Aldric, but he held out his open hand, telling her to stay back.

"What's happening?" She asked quietly – the curiosity clearly overshadowing the pain.

"Did he scratch you?"

"He didn't mean to," Brooke defended the young wolf Cailean.

"I'm so sorry," Aldric choked up. Cailean could smell his pain, but he could also sense a confusing flurry of other emotions.

"He didn't mean to," Brooke repeated. "What's going on?"

"There's a lot to that story," Aldric muttered, clearly biting back pain. "Go home. Clean that up. I'll explain everything tomorrow."

"But..."

"Listen," Aldric ordered. Despite the pain, his tone was filled with a new sense of power. The girl standing before him dropped her head, clearly afraid of the anger in the voice of the adult scolding her. Cailean found himself terrified of what the conversation would entail the next day, and the wolf whimpered in reaction to his tone.

"Brooke, right?" He questioned. She nodded sheepishly. "Listen, Brooke. I can't stop myself from this transformation much longer. You saw what happened to him? Well I'm much larger. Go home. Walk – run if you can. Tomorrow, you will get your answers."

"Yes sir," she muttered quietly. Starting slowly, she walked away from them. Turning over her shoulder, she made eye contact with the wolf and Cailean found himself longing for her to come back. Aldric didn't put him down until she was well out of their sight.

"I'm so sorry," Aldric whispered under his breath, staring into the darkness into which Brooke had vanished.

Chapter 9

6 Years Ago
Aldric

Waking up naked in a stranger's house, Aldric carefully struggled to his feet. His internal clock was completely devasted – as it always was after a transformation – so he had no idea how long he had been unconscious. Judging by the fact that Linda stood, holding a crying Cailean, in the exact same place as she had the last time he'd seen her, though, Aldric guessed that it wasn't long.

Dazed, Aldric used the wall for support as he balanced on shaking legs. With each passing second, he felt his strength growing back and his vision stabilizing. Confrontation was by no means a new phenomenon for Aldric, but there wasn't a single time in his life that he could remember actually killing someone as the wolf. The memory of tearing into another person's flesh coupled with the sight of the mangled corpses in the hall made Aldric's stomach churn. Steeling himself, he stood up straight and took a deep breath.

Silently, Aldric walked down the hallway, trying to focus as much on the path ahead as possible. Despite his best efforts, he continually found his attention drawn to the bodies on the floor beneath him. Behind him, Linda barely moved. Aside from gently bobbing her arms in a futile attempt to comfort Cailean, she was completely motionless.

At the end of the hall, Aldric found a large bedroom. Physically, he had completely recovered from the change, but emotionally that was far from the case. As Aldric caught sight of himself in the mirror, he fell forward, leaning on the tile counter for support. Aldric choked back vomit as he tried to tear his eyes away from his own visage. Wondering how much human blood he had swallowed, Aldric was finally able to direct his eyes away, looking at the sink below him as his stomach heaved. Steadying his breathing, Aldric was able to calm himself down and pull his thoughts away from the darkness.

Aldric reached forward, turning on the water. Before looking up again, he splashed his face and deeply scrubbed the scruff on his face, working any blood out. Rinsing his mouth, Aldric swished water vigorously before spitting it out. Confident that he'd at least addressed the blood on his face, Aldric granted himself another glance at the mirror. Any trace of blood had been removed from his face and hands, but there were still spots of red covering his arms and abdomen. For the moment, though, that would have to do. The hunters had left, but there was no doubt in Aldric's mind that they'd be back with more manpower.

Aldric found his way to the closet and found a pair of pants hanging up. After retrieving them, he pulled them on to cover himself. He grabbed the first shirt he saw and pulled it over his head before walking back to his family. When Aldric reached them, Linda's head was downcast and Cailean had cried himself to sleep in his mother's arms.

"I know," Linda whispered under her breath, not giving Aldric the chance to speak. The thought would probably be as painful for her to hear as it was for him to say, so he appreciated her sparing him from verbalizing it. Verbal or not, though, it was clear to both of them that they were no longer safe. They were no strangers to moving, of course. Over their long lives, they had lived in at least a dozen different states. Their son, though, hadn't been forced to experience that side of their lives, and they'd hoped he wouldn't have to. Aldric knew it was an unrealistic hope, of course. For werewolves living in a society, discovery was imminent.

Nodding solemnly, Aldric turned from her and walked to the door. Careful not to wake Cailean, she followed him closely.

As Aldric led the way back to their home, he listened for the slightest sound. At any disturbance in their surroundings, Aldric would ball his fists and prepare for a fight. When they reached their porch, he held up his hand and instructed his wife to wait outside while he searched the house. Even though he couldn't hear anything from the inside, a quick look helped ease his mind.

Confident that their house was empty, he motioned for his wife to join him. As she crossed the threshold, he closed the door behind her. Gently, she laid their son on the couch in the living room, quietly stepping backward with a sigh.

"He won't remember," Aldric offered. It wasn't much, but it was the best consolation he could find.

"He'll see it again," she countered sadly.

Aldric searched the depths of his mind, but there was no rebuttal. She was right. Regardless of how hard he tried, Aldric would never be able to shield his son from the life into which he was born.

"He won't have a home," Linda added quietly.

"Plenty of humans grow up moving around. As long as we're together, it's a home."

"I suppose it is," she accepted.

Aldric turned to walk back to their room to begin packing. The hunters knew exactly where he had been less than ten minutes ago, they knew what he was, and Aldric found it extremely unlikely that they didn't know which house was his. If they didn't, they were likely to simply attack each house until they found him. Aldric wished he could save his neighbors from that fate, but his family came first – and that meant leading them to the next temporary spot of safety.

Just before Aldric took his first step toward the other room, though, a thundering footstep reverberated from outside. His paranoid ears were tuned to hear any slight disturbance, but that particular step seemed intentional. Aldric couldn't imagine anyone's gait being so heavy – which brought him down to two options: Either the hunters were arrogantly announcing their presence, or someone was warning him.

"Mr. Phoenix," Aldric heard a whisper permeate the room around him. His eyes darted to either side as he desperately searched for the source of the voice. Linda, noticing his reaction, appeared confused but remained silent. If she couldn't hear it, that meant the voice was farther away than Aldric had assumed.

"I come alone, and I come in peace." Although Aldric had only heard Kieran's voice a few times, he recognized it well. A hint of sincerity was present in his words, but Aldric knew that the hunters were trained to deceive.

"I am aware that it's hard to believe me, but this alone is a show of good faith, is it not? I will knock on your door in just a moment to announce my presence. Please, grant me one conversation."

"Stay here," Aldric whispered to his wife. "If anything happens, I want you to take Cailean and run."

Linda clearly wanted to argue – no wife wanted to abandon her husband – but she bit her tongue. Both of them knew that Cailean's life was far more important than either of theirs. Linda nodded and inched toward her sleeping son, ready to grab him and run if the need presented itself.

"My son is sleeping," Aldric whispered as he opened the door to find Kieran with one hand poised for a knock.

"Then I shall continue with the whisper," Kieran offered.

"What are you doing here?"

"I would like to speak with you."

"Why should I trust you?" Aldric growled quietly.

"You shouldn't. Just as I shouldn't trust you. But I ask, Aldric, that you would set should aside and walk with me."

"The second I step outside, I will be ambushed."

Without another word, Kieran lifted his hands above his head. Aldric adopted a modified fighting stance, shifting his weight to his back foot to gain distance and prepare himself for a counter kick if necessary. Slowly, Kieran reached his hand behind his back, drawing a knife from a sheath on his belt. After retrieving it, he effortlessly flipped the knife, holding the blade in his hand and offering Aldric the hilt. Maintaining his stance suspiciously, Aldric made no move to retrieve the knife. Regardless of how confident Kieran was, it was a risky play. Aldric was faster and stronger, and even if Kieran managed to pull the knife back before Aldric grabbed it – which was incredibly unlikely – he would be in no position to defend against the impending attack. Still, Aldric remained on the defensive – in case there was something more sinister awaiting him.

Kieran bent his knees, squatting down and placing the knife at Aldric's feet. With a flick of his wrist, he slid the knife past Aldric, sacrificing any chance he had at retrieving the weapon. While in a squatted position, he removed a blade from a sheath hidden beneath his right pant leg. In one smooth motion, he did the same with that weapon.

"I am now unarmed," he explained. "Even if I have an ambush prepared, if we walk together, I will not be able to outpace you. I may take you down, but I'll die myself. Now that I have adopted a daughter, I'm not quite ready to die."

"What makes you so sure I won't kill you anyway?"

"I'm willing to take that risk."

Aldric fell silent for a moment, allowing himself to consider Kieran's request. Even if the man's intentions were malicious, he made a valid argument. Still, it was possible that he was ready to sacrifice himself to take down a wolf as skilled and powerful as Aldric. Something in his eyes told Aldric that wasn't the case, though. Aldric relaxed slightly with a sigh. Turning his head toward Linda, he nodded toward her, communicating every required piece of information.

"Let's walk, then," Aldric accepted.

Following Kieran outside, Aldric kept his senses on high alert. No ambush was apparent, even as they made their way to the streets. Aldric listened carefully for any heavy breathing, fidgeting, or loud footsteps, but there were no signs of human activity outside of families who populated the neighborhood.

Kieran led silently for a while, seemingly searching his mind for the proper words. The two of them reached the edge of the woods near Aldric's house and Aldric froze. Sniffing the air and listening closely, he carefully searched for any sign of life.

"I saw something in your eyes," Keiran finally spoke up, witnessing Aldric's hesitation. Instead of persisting, he stopped with him and turned to face Aldric.

"What?"

"The wolf. It eliminated the threat mercilessly, as any beast would. But then it lifted a child and carefully carried her to my feet, placing it there. Now, we had hostages, yes, but a beast can't process that fact rationally."

"No, it can't," Aldric concurred.

"So I think there was something more to this," Kieran continued. "This shows me that you didn't want to kill her. There was no malice in that wolf's eyes. In the eyes of that animal, I saw more. I saw humanity."

"What are you saying?"

"Walk with me," Kieran instructed. Reluctantly, Aldric followed the hunter into the woods. As the two continued along the trail, Kieran resumed his speech.

"I hunt monsters. My duty in life is to put a stop to the beasts which feed off the innocents in our world. The wolf that I saw in that room – it wasn't a beast. It was a defender. So you see, Aldric, I have no desire to kill it.

"I know that you've become accustomed to running, but I also know the toll that takes on a family. Aside from that, even if that wolf isn't inherently violent, every time you change in an unfamiliar place, there is a new risk."

Aldric knew that Kieran wasn't understanding the situation completely correctly. He could feel a certain level of violence within the beast when he changed. Just because he'd managed to curb it with his own human mind for a brief moment didn't mean it wasn't there. He chose not to share that fact, though, and remained silent instead. The two of them walked for a while longer before arriving at a very official-looking sign.

"I believe it to be not only in your best interest, but in that of the hunters and of society if you stay. I lead the hunters here, and I can assure you safety if you stay in this part of the woods. We have marked it very clearly, as you can see, and the local government will be notified of my decision to restrict this area. Humans who break these rules put themselves at risk, but as long as you stay in your part of the woods, I can grant you immunity."

"Why?"

"As I said, Mr. Phoenix. I hunt monsters. I don't believe you are one."

"My pack," Aldric pressed.

"Stay in your part of the woods. You and yours will not be bothered by me or mine," Kieran offered once again. Extending his hand, he looked into Aldric's eyes with confidence. Cautiously, Aldric searched Kieran's face for any sign of dishonesty. There was the possibility that he was setting up an elaborate trap, but if he wanted to attack him, there were many more direct ways. Finally, Aldric reached forward and accepted Kieran's hand, grasping just firmly enough to cause enough pain to remind the hunter of what would happen if he was betrayed.

"I accept your terms," Aldric agreed with a shake of his hand.

Present
29 Days Until the Full Moon
Cailean

With the sun beating down on him through the canopy, Cailean struggled to open his eyes. Blinded even by the few rays which filtered through the leaves, he groggily raised an arm to cover his eyes. Every muscle in his body felt heavy as Cailean tried to sit up, so he allowed himself another moment of rest. Cailean extended his arm toward the sky, examining it for any remaining side of the wolf. Spreading his fingers apart, he turned his palm toward himself. Nothing appeared out of the ordinary, and there was no sign of what had happened the previous night. All that assured him of its validity was his memory.

Feeling a breeze pick up, Cailean realized that he was completely naked lying on the dirt. Embarrassed, despite the lack of any human presence around him, he turned his head as he looked for his clothes. He was in an unfamiliar part of the woods, though, so he had no idea how he would find his way back to the river.

Suddenly, the light of the sun was extinguished from above him, relieving him of the necessity to squint. As Cailean's eyes widened, his field of view expanded. After realizing what had provided the shade, though, Cailean would have preferred the light.

Silently, Cailean's father dropped a pair of shorts next to him. Crossing his arms, he turned to face the other direction. Cailean struggled to his feet, fighting off the stiffness of his muscles.

As he stood, he quickly felt the symptoms of fatigue begin to fade. His muscles became re-accustomed to movement in their human form and the weariness dissipated. Quickly, Cailean pulled the shorts up, grateful that his father was able to find them.

His mind raced as Cailean searched for the proper explanation to give to his father, but no words presented themselves. Confusing thoughts polluted his mind as he tried to gather his feelings. While he was excited to finally have had his first transformation, the circumstances were far from ideal. He felt horrible for what had happened to Brooke, but he was also terrified of his father and the punishment he'd receive for disregarding his direct order. In spite of that, Cailean felt a strange sense of power that he never had before.

The silence bore down on him as his father continued to stand with his back to Cailean. In the early hours of the morning, the songs of the threshes and mockingbirds melded with the clicks of cicadas to form a soothing melody. It took the music in the otherwise stillness of the woods around him to awaken him to the dissonance which had defined the last few weeks. Even with the looming fear of the conversation with his father, Cailean was able to appreciate the momentary respite.

Cailean glanced toward his father again, but the man remained silent, an immovable stone statue before him. When he tried to speak, the words caught in his throat. Instead, he remained silent, trying to find his own peace in the serenity.

Finally, Aldric began to move. Without words, and without a glance to verify that Cailean followed, he walked forward, moving toward what Cailean assumed to be the edge of the woods. Cailean could feel the fire burning from his father, so he carefully kept a safe distance as he followed after him. Aldric didn't break from his long, powerful strides, so Cailean struggled to keep up without breaking into a jog.

"Father," Cailean finally whispered, working up the courage to break the silence. Aldric stopped so suddenly that Cailean plowed into his back. Aldric didn't budge from the impact, but Cailean stumbled backward. He watched as his father's shoulders heaved a few times with deep breaths. Slowly, he turned to face his son. Betraying his anger, his eyes glowed with a light flame. His face, though, was not twisted into a scowl, but rather thinly concealed pain.

"Yes?" Aldric asked. Cailean found himself more taken aback by the forced soft tone in his father's voice than he would have been by an explosion of anger.

"I… I swear I didn't know."

"Did you try? I asked you about the signs," he retorted – disappointment dripping from his words.

"I was embarrassed," Cailean defended.

"Of what, exactly?"

"I didn't know what I was feeling. I just…"

"You thought it was Brooke?"

"I guess so."

"When did I tell you the change would begin, boy?"

"When… When I reached puberty."

"Your feelings are confusing. I know. But those feelings were your warning. The earsplitting sounds, the powerful scents, the fits of emotion. You didn't talk to me."

"I'm sorry," Cailean stammered.

"No. Apologies are useless now. You disobeyed me. You failed to heed my orders and your actions have consequences."

"I'm sorry," Cailean repeated.

"Don't apologize to me. It isn't my life you've selfishly ruined."

❖ ❖ ❖

Brooke's front door appeared far larger to Cailean than he would have expected. Becoming the embodiment of his fear and pain, it grew in his mind into an impenetrable obstacle. The wooden door loomed over him, and as he raised his fist to knock, it seemed to angrily and judgmentally stand above him.

Cailean's hand froze inches in front of the door. He had begged his father to allow him to face her alone – it was his responsibility and his alone. After reaching her home, though, he had very quickly grown to regret that decision. It was becoming increasingly apparent that his father's unspoken judgement was correct – Cailean was not by any means mature enough to own up to his own mistakes. It wasn't something as trivial as saying the wrong thing or forgetting a date. Cailean had put her very life at stake and ended up dramatically altering it.

A few hours had passed, but his father hadn't cooled down much at all. They hadn't discussed the previous night to any useful extent. Cailean's father had continually pushed off the conversation until Brooke was there. He insisted that every affected party should be together. Cailean was confident that it was merely an excuse to grant himself more time to cool off before discussing Cailean's disobedience and utter failure. If that was the reason, though, Cailean appreciated it. Although the wait for the conversation and the punishment which would result was overwhelming, he was grateful that it gave him a couple hours of peace.

Unable to work up the resolve to actually knock, Cailean just fell forward onto the door. His closed fist collided first, followed by his forehead. Resting his head and fist on the door, he closed his eyes and waited for a response. After a few seconds, no sound erupted from the other side of the door, and Cailean dropped his hand, already feeling defeated. Then quiet footsteps radiated from the other side of the barrier and Cailean straightened himself up, standing before the door.

Brooke opened it slowly, meeting his eyes as she did. Averting his gaze, Cailean dropped his eyes to the ground and avoided her glance. Though he had already been through the conversation a dozen times in his head, Cailean couldn't find the proper words to begin his apology.

"Cailean," Brooke slowly started. Her tone had a completely unfamiliar tone buried within. Because it was something he had never associated with her, it took him a moment to recognize it as fear.

"What's happening?"

"It's… hard to explain," he stuttered.

"Well, you can try," she retorted, choking up. Cailean sniffled quietly, fighting back the tears welling up in his eyes. For him, lycanthropy was an exciting gift. He'd been so excited to be like his father. Despite his feelings, though, it wasn't something he wanted to force upon someone else – especially after he realized how painful the transformation was. As he tried to compose himself, Cailean nodded and finally looked up at her.

The water in her eyes reflected the light from the sun, shining brightly at him. She blinked, forcing away the tears and covering up her overwhelmed concern with a determined look. Cailean wondered how long she had been awake, because she was already wearing a t-shirt with a pair of jeans. She typically wore shorts, so the sight was confusing to Cailean at first. Cailean listened closely, but he couldn't hear her heart beating. He barely even noticed the footsteps as another person approached.

"Who is it, honey?" Mrs. Cassidy asked as she approached the door. When neither of them responded, she stepped into view and smiled down at Cailean. "Oh, hi Cailean."

"Hello, Mrs. Cassidy," he greeted, trying to paste on a charming smile. Though he was confident that he had failed miserably, she didn't acknowledge that fact.

"Mom, can I go for a walk with Cailean?"

"You are more than welcome to come inside," Mrs. Cassidy offered.

"Thank you, ma'am," Cailean replied, unsure of how to proceed.

"It's just really nice out," Brooke interjected.

"Okay, well whatever you prefer," Brooke's mother shrugged as she turned and walked back into the house. Brooke nodded her head forward and Cailean backed up. Following him, she closed the door behind her and sighed heavily.

Silently, Cailean started walking down the street, careful to stand next to the road to allow Brooke to walk on the inside. They walked slowly along the pavement, both of them waiting for the other to speak first. At the end of the road, Cailean turned to the right. Just around the corner, she finally grabbed his arm and pulled him to a stop.

"Cailean," she stammered. "I thought I had a really weird dream when I woke up this morning. I dreamed that we were swimming and you… you turned into a wolf."

"Brooke…"

"No, wait," she interrupted. Silently, he nodded his acceptance. Standing in front of him, Brooke unbuttoned her pants as she recalled her dream. Cailean worked hard on focusing on her eyes as he heard the zipper fall.

"You scratched me. We were playing and the little wolf got too excited, I guess. Then some guy showed up and yelled at me to go home. It was such a weird dream, Cailean, but when I looked at my leg, I had this."

She dropped her pants, revealing her thighs. Torn, Cailean turned his glance toward the scar on her thigh. The healed scar tissue appeared as though it was from a wound inflicted years ago – not something which had been pouring blood the previous night. Cailean's guilt as he looked at the scar was actually enough to distract him from the fact that he was basically staring at her in her underwear.

"I don't understand, Cailean," she continued. "I mean, even if that wasn't a dream, how is it closed up already? How is it not bleeding? That should have needed stitches."

"Brooke," Cailean took his turn to interrupt her, placing his hand on her shoulder as she spoke faster. Her muttering slowed to a stop as she released the one hand which held her pants, allowing them to fall. Instinctively, Cailean reached his free hand out to catch them. Breathing heavily, she looked eagerly to him for answers. With a sigh, Cailean began pulling her pants back up until she took over.

"I'm a werewolf," he told her bluntly. Cailean saw no point in sugarcoating the truth, especially after everything she had been through.

"That's ridiculous."

"Ridiculous or not, it's the truth."

"How is it healed?"

"Brooke… I'm so sorry," Cailean muttered.

"For what?" She asked, anger creeping into her voice as she raised the volume.

"No one should have this forced upon them. But you did. I shouldn't have gone out with you. I swear I didn't think I would transform. It was the first time, but I didn't think it would be so soon."

"What?"

"We don't transform until we reach puberty. I didn't think I was… old enough for that… I guess?"

"I… Okay?"

"When I scratched you, Brooke, I gave you whatever it is I have. You're like me, now."

"Then why didn't I transform?"

"It takes a little longer than that," Cailean laughed sadly. "That's why your wound healed, though."

"I don't get it," Brooke told him, breaking down and sobbing quietly. Cailean realized that he was not doing a good job introducing the topic. For him, it was something he'd heard since childhood. Brooke was learning of the existence of lycanthropes and all of the ways that affected a person as well as her new identity as one. It was a lot for her to take in, but he didn't have an established way to break the news to her.

"I'm sorry," Cailean sighed. "I'll try to start over."

❖ ❖ ❖

Cailean sat with his parents and Brooke in his living room. It was far from the circumstances in which he'd imagined her meeting his parents. Cailean and Brooke sat next to each other on one couch and Cailean's parents were on the other. Resting his head in his hands, Cailean didn't bother hiding the shame he felt for his mistake. Brooke sat with her hands intertwined and resting between her legs, which clasped them tightly as she sat hunched forward. Cailean's mom looked sympathetic and pensive, sitting back with one leg over the other and her hands folded in her lap. His father was tall and powerful – his posture far better than anyone else in the room. Still, his concern was as easily distinguishable as anyone else's in the room.

Cailean had already introduced everyone and awkward greetings had been exchanged. He had explained to his parents everything which he had informed Brooke. After failing to explain anything properly, he had insisted that she obtain the information from someone with far more expertise than himself.

"Brooke," Aldric opened slowly. Cailean had never heard such a lack of confidence in his father's voice, and he wondered what could possibly have driven him to that point. Judging by his tone, Cailean expected him to continue. However, the single word hung in the air for almost a full minute with no continuation.

"Yes?" She asked, confused as she clearly shared Cailean's interpretation.

"Have you ever.... Have you.... Started?"

"What?"

"Really?" Linda laughed sadly. "Weren't you a doctor for years?"

"Well, this is a strikingly different situation," Aldric defended, annoyed.

"I know it's awkward, honey," Linda spoke up. "But trust me when I tell you it's important. Have you had your first period yet?"

"I... What?" She asked, startled by the question. She looked to either side, clearly dumbfounded by the invasion of privacy from complete strangers. Cailean placed a hand on her thigh. To his surprise, she freed her hands and placed one of them over his, closing her fingers around his tightly before taking a deep breath to respond. "No, I haven't."

"Okay, so you have time before you really have to worry about any of this," Linda comforted.

"Why?" She asked.

"Well, you see, a werewolf's first change doesn't occur until after puberty. For young women, starting your cycle is a clear indicator of that," Aldric jumped in – apparently shedding any sense of awkwardness surrounding the topic since it had been brought up.

"Oh, okay," she whispered. Silence fell within the room again until she finally added, "Will it hurt?"

"Yes," Aldric answered earnestly.

"Oh."

"It's brief, though," Linda tried to console her. "Then you fall asleep."

"What?" Cailean asked.

"What she means is that the human part falls asleep, basically. The wolf takes control for a night, but you won't remember any of it. It's a burden, but it's only one night a month," Aldric tried to explain.

"What do you mean you don't remember?" Cailean asked.

"Ah, yes," Aldric muttered, opening his eyes wide and leaning back. "I'm sorry, son. I had forgotten. It's been quite a while since my first change."

"What?" Cailean repeated.

"You remember the first time, you see," he explained. "The wolf is still young, and it doesn't have the power to take complete control. It seizes control of your body but it isn't quite able to completely overtake the mind yet. After the first time, though, that stops being a problem."

"Oh," Cailean responded quietly. He wasn't sure if the news concerned or relieved him, but he knew there was nothing he could do to change it. Anyway, it was better to avoid throwing too much unrelated information at Brooke. Brooke sat in silence, absorbing the information and tightly clenching Cailean's hand as she looked around the room.

"What is it like?" Brooke interjected.

"We have a while before you start to change," Aldric told her slowly. "Take it slow. Digest, think things through. We are here for questions, and we will help you through this. For now, though, I think it's best to just take your time."

Cailean completely understood why his father avoided the question. While no one wanted to lie to her, Cailean definitely didn't want to try to explain to her everything he'd gone through the previous night. His father had apparently made the decision that it was best to keep her from facing that terror – at least for the time being.

"You're not alone in this, Brooke," Aldric added. "Cailean and I are here for you. We're a pack now."

Chapter 10

4 Years Ago
Aldric

"Quarter turn left. Low block," Aldric instructed. As he spoke, he demonstrated the movements for Cailean, who followed him with rapt attention. Since his son had been able to walk, Aldric had taught him as many basic principles of self-defense as possible. For the first time, though, he began a formal instruction of his art.

"Step forward, center punch, land in front stance," Aldric continued, executing the steps himself. Cailean followed along as Aldric continued with the next step, turning in a half-circle and blocking again. With Cailean positioned in front of him, Aldric was able to watch his son's movements. As they both stepped forward and threw another punch, Aldric sighed.

"Alright," he groaned, standing straighter. Clearly, Cailean heard the displeasure in his voice. He brought his feet together and turned, facing his father somewhat defiantly.

"Why are we doing this? It's boring."

"You will train because I deem it important," Aldric answered bluntly. A flash of his father passed before his eyes, and he closed his eyes with frustration. Although being questioned was annoying, he consciously fought to avoid becoming that man. With a deep breath, he tried to regain his focus and provide his son with a more satisfying answer.

"Humans use forms to strengthen relatively unused muscles with stances. It's also a great way to practice balance, for which you also have a natural skill. Though those uses are diminished to us, there is still much to learn here. First, you will learn discipline. Secondly, it is a mechanism by which you can practice your blocks and strikes."

"Huh," Cailean accepted with a nod.

"So, use this to practice everything," Aldric ordered. "Punch like you mean it. Block like your life depends on it. Because one day it may."

"Father," Cailean began quietly. Aldric could practically watch his brain work as he tried to formulate his question. "If I'm the strongest, why do I still have to train so hard?"

"You're not the strongest. There will always be someone stronger. Even if you were, raw strength will never be enough. Skill, speed, and efficiency are everything."

"All I have to do is punch them, though," Cailean argued.

"Tell me, boy: What if you fought me?"

"I wouldn't have to."

"Then someone as strong as me."

"No one is."

"I have met plenty who were."

"I guess I'd just punch them, then."

"One punch? That's all it takes?" Aldric taunted, squatting down in front of Cailean. "Prove it. I will give you one free punch. This is the only opportunity you will ever get. Prove to me that you're the strongest."

Cailean hesitated, so Aldric turned his cheek and kept his hands low. Raising his fist shakily, Cailean growled as he tried to work up the nerve to attack his father. Aldric rocked back on his heels, impatiently awaiting the attack so he could finish proving his point. Eventually, though, Cailean's hand dropped back to his side.

"Good. Now then, your punches are weak. Aim with the front two fingers," Aldric explained to his son.

Covering the basics in excruciating detail, Aldric worked on building a firm foundation for Cailean. He showed him the kata, good form when punching and kicking, strong stances, and even a basic combination to practice. After working tirelessly for hours, he finally decided Cailean deserved a break. When training humans, stamina was a factor, but for his son, it was exclusively his receptiveness to new information. After being presented with so much at once, it was only natural that his attention would start to waver.

Still, Aldric knew that he needed to be completely sure that his son was ready to defend himself. Aldric himself had started formal martial arts training even younger, but he wanted to make sure Cailean was more mature than him when he started.

"That's enough for today," Aldric instructed, nodding as a way to acknowledge Cailean's good work. Cailean, actually breathing heavily from the workout, hesitated in the middle of the room. He took a moment to catch his breath and settle his heartrate before straightening up and facing Aldric confidently.

"Father," he argued. "I can learn more."

"We have to space things out, otherwise you won't properly internalize the information," Aldric explained. There was no annoyance in his tone, although he recognized that any type of questioning would typically spark such a reaction. Aldric quickly realized that it was simply because the annoyance was overridden by pride. Cailean's desire to learn and improve his skills, even though he'd only barely begun to formally learn them, made Aldric proud. Aside from that, it made him hopeful. His son would eventually be a good fighter, able to defend himself against the hunters.

"Yes, sir," Cailean replied, disappointed. It had taken time, but he'd finally learned not to go against Aldric's decision. Sometimes, such as in that moment, he tried to argue once. However, when Aldric affirmed his statement a second time, Cailean typically accepted it as reality.

"If you want to continue practicing," Aldric conceded slowly, "you can practice what we've gone over today. Your technique will always need improvement and honing. Focus on your kicks and your balance."

"Yes, sir!" Cailean repeated with a new vigor in his voice. As he walked away, Aldric heard the snapping of Cailean's pants as he kicked into the air. Reaching the bottom of the stairs, Aldric turned to watch his son. Cailean's front kicks were still weak, and they weren't aimed with the ball of the foot. His side kicks weren't folding deep enough to his side, which would sacrifice power for speed. The round kicks were fast, which was the main goal, but he was powering through them too much, throwing off his balance. Aldric worried that he'd already thrown too much at Cailean for one day and was concerned that the boy was mixing up the reasoning behind each of the kicks.

Sighing deeply, he turned back toward Cailean and moved back into the basement. More days than Aldric could count had been spent training for more than twelve hours, so it wasn't anything new to him to continue longer than a traditional class. If his son was showing such enthusiasm, that was something he wanted to foster.

Just as he was about to say something, though, Aldric watched as Cailean folded for another side kick. This time, he slowed down, focusing on each step of the kick. His knee drew further across his body and his heel pointed directly in front of him. As he thrusted that heel forward, he turned his hips into the kick and audibly snapped the fabric in his pants. For a moment, he left his leg extended fully, balancing on his back foot. Slowly, he withdrew the kick, pulling his knee back across his body before placing his foot back on the floor in front of him.

"Good," Aldric praised.

"Thank you, Father," Cailean beamed. The child was nearly bouncing with excitement having received a positive remark from his father and teacher. Nodding triumphantly, Aldric leaned against the wall behind him. Cailean turned back to continue practicing his kicks and Aldric could see his balance and technique improving with each subsequent attack. There was no question in his mind that his son was going to be a warrior.

Present
3 Years Later
Cailean

"Mom," Cailean whispered, hesitating with his hand on the doorknob. The questions racing through his mind screamed for answers but once again, he found himself too uncomfortable to ask. As he felt her gaze turn toward him, he quickly fumbled for another topic. While he had time before he had to leave, he wasn't sure he wanted to spend that time in an awkward conversation with his mother.

"What's up?" She asked, concern clear in her voice.

"I love you," he responded, forcing a jovial tone into his voice and smiling as he turned back to face her.

"I love you too," she smiled, though her response was skeptical.

"I'll see you after school."

Escaping the uncomfortable air which he'd created, Cailean quickly stepped outside and closed the door behind him. Shuffling off toward Brooke's house, he left his home and his questions behind him. Somehow, spending time with Brooke made him believe everything would be fine. Even though the uncertainty in his mind exclusively revolved around her – she was somehow able to dampen its effects. As he briskly walked toward her home, everything else seemed to dull in the world around him. Barely registering the footsteps behind him, Cailean jumped in surprise when he felt a hand on his shoulder.

Turning quickly, Cailean backed away, trying to remember his father's training. Since he was a child, he had been taught to prepare for a surprise attack. When the actual possibility arose, though, all he could think about was his heart pounding in his chest as the adrenaline killed his capacity for rational thought. Lifting his hands, Cailean faced the aggressor.

"Calm down, slugger," his mom teased, completely unfazed by his stance. Cailean wondered whether her confidence was around the hope that he'd recognize her before reacting or the idea that she could easily dodge his attack if he didn't.

"What…" Cailean stumbled, wondering what to ask as his fists fell to his sides. "Did I forget something?"

"Not exactly," she laughed, waving her hand at the ground in front of Cailean. Without waiting for his response, she continued walking past him. Confused, Cailean caught up with his mother and walked by her side.

"So, do you not want to talk to me about it or are you scared your dad will hear?"

"Father does hear everything," Cailean chuckled.

"Well, I think it's safe to say we're out of earshot," she observed with a shrug.

"It's not that I don't want him to know," Cailean stumbled.

"Sometimes a boy needs his mother. Let me relish that a bit," she encouraged, stopping and placing her hands on his shoulders. Smiling down at him, she gently kissed his forehead. Instinctively, Cailean pulled back and wiped his head as if that would have any effect. Exhaling deeply, he tried to collect his thoughts.

"How do you know?" He finally asked. The confusion on her face told him that he hadn't been clear enough, so he forced himself to add detail. Uncomfortably, he clarified. "How do you know when you're in love?"

Silently, she looked up and pondered his question. Simultaneously burdened by the weight of the silence and comforted by the fact that he finally asked the question, Cailean anxiously awaited her response. The two began walking again as she placed a hand on his back and directed him forward. He didn't want to be late to school, so he was grateful that she continued walking with him toward Brooke's house as she spoke.

"I wish I had a better answer for you, but you just know."

"But Father says I can only love once. Is it my choice? How will I know when I've chosen?"

"Oh, you'll definitely know that one," she coughed, laughing and appearing equally uncomfortable and entertained by her own response.

"What do you mean?"

"Love comes in so many different forms. Honestly, we don't have enough words for the diversity of meanings it actually has. You see, you never choose the perfect person to love, Cailean.

It's a choice, though. A decision to always put this person before yourself."

As her words resounded in Cailean's mind, he wondered if he ever truly loved anyone. His desire to be near Brooke had led him to put her in danger. Though she didn't seem to resent him for her transformation, he still bore the burden of that selfishness. Love sounded difficult, and he wasn't confident he was actually capable of it.

"Of course, we're all human. Even you, most of the time," she smiled, rubbing his hair as she seemed to read his mind. "We're selfish and we all make mistakes. But love is also accepting each other's mistakes and caring for them in spite of them."

"If love is a choice, why can I only choose one person?"

"Well, that's where other definitions come in. Sometimes, love is also an emotion. It isn't enough to rely on, because emotions change, but that is an undeniable aspect. That's all your father is talking about. A werewolf chooses a mate and they can never feel that emotion for someone else. You can still choose to show people love, but you can never feel the same way. It's a deep, all-encompassing feeling."

"That sounds scary."

"It's terrifying, but it's also beautiful."

"I've been scared to get too close to Brooke. I really like her, but I don't want to accidentally love her if I'm not supposed to."

Stopping on the sidewalk, Cailean's mom laughed and shook her head. After taking a moment to compose herself, she placed a hand on his cheek and smiled down at him.

"Trust me, that isn't going to happen by accident. Your father can be very strange about certain information, that's for sure. This is a conversation we can have after school, alright?"

"Why?"

"Because I need some time to prepare," she stumbled awkwardly. "For now, I promise you, it doesn't happen by accident and you have nothing to fear. When you find the person you want to spend your life with, whether you're a human or a werewolf, you just know."

"Yeah, okay," Cailean nodded. "Thanks Mom."

Embracing her tightly, Cailean tried to decompress all of the information. Though he was still confused, he was becoming more confident that he wasn't meant to spend his life with Brooke. Over the past three years, they had spent every day together and she was constantly on his mind, but if he had to ask that meant he didn't know. At least, it felt like he didn't know. Resolving to wait until his mom was ready to have whatever conversation she felt too uncomfortable to partake in before school, Cailean just stepped back and turned back toward Brooke's house.

"I love you, Mom," he smiled, turning over his shoulder. As he said it, hundreds of selfish acts raced through his mind and he wondered if it was true. Still, he knew that he couldn't live without his mother and if that wasn't love, he didn't know what was.

"I love you too. Now get to school. You don't want to be late."

She turned and quickly started walking back home. Though he was confused by her sudden shift in tone, Cailean shrugged it off and walked up the pathway toward Brooke's house. The two of them had walked to school together every day since she'd turned. Sometimes Cailean found himself wishing he could walk alone to process his own thoughts, but he knew that Brooke hated to be alone. Barely even considering the fact that granting her that company would limit his ability to interpret his conversation with his mother, Cailean gently tapped on her front door.

"Cailean's here," Mrs. Cassidy called from the other side of the door. Cailean heard scuffling from the inside of the house as all of them shuffled around. After a moment, the door opened and Brooke's mom stood in the doorway smiling at him.

"Sorry, Brooke is still getting ready, she shouldn't be much longer. Do you want to come in?"

"Thank you," Cailean accepted, stepping past her as she closed the door behind him. Normally, she had already left by the time Cailean picked up Brooke, but she was clearly running late. Her wet hair was still tied up in a towel and she had raced to the door before finishing with her make-up. Make-up wasn't something Cailean understood. Usually, women looked just fine without it. His rationalization was that it was just the human way of covering up their scars or any imperfections on their skin, but it didn't seem worth the effort.

Her dress, which fell loosely around her body, dropped past her knees. Brooke's mother found a way to remain fashionable while dressing appropriately for her job. Watching the fabric flow behind her as she returned to her room to finish applying the make-up, Cailean found himself wondering why seeing Brooke in a dress was so rare. Her mother wore them nearly exclusively, and plenty of girls in his class did the same. Of course, the high schoolers' attire typically didn't cover quite as much skin and were often less tasteful, but they were still dresses. The unique aspect of Brooke's fashion decisions was endearing to Cailean, though.

On the couch, Cailean waited for a moment as everyone else in the house continued to prepare for the day. He wondered whether it was more difficult for humans to be on time for something or if his father had simply taught him well. Aldric was always prepared for everything and being early was his general state, so that attitude had passed to Cailean. Waiting on Brooke to get ready didn't bother him, though. In fact, he found the commotion comforting in a strange sense.

"Hey Cailean," Brooke's dad greeted as he walked in, adjusting his tie.

"Hello Mr. Cassidy," Cailean greeted, jumping to his feet and extending a hand instinctively. For some reason, being around Brooke's father always made him uncomfortable. The man was by no means intimidating, but he was still someone to whom Cailean went out of his way to act respectfully toward.

"How many times do I have to tell you to call me Josh?" He asked, laughing softly. Shaking Cailean's hand with one arm, he reached over and jostled his hair with the other.

"If my father found out I disrespected you that way, I'd probably be grounded," Cailean countered. He was fairly confident he was hyperbolizing but it wouldn't have surprised him. One of Aldric's rules had always been to respect his elders and failure to meet those rules was never met kindly. Cailean's father never seemed able to deem which of his rules were more important than others. He seemed to believe that any slight slip-up would alert the hunters and put their lives at risk.

"One could argue that it's more disrespectful to use a more formal title when granted permission for informality."

Cailean fell silent for a second as his eyes widened. Dropping his hand, he desperately listened for Brooke as he waited for his escape. Speaking with humans had never been one of his favorite pastimes, but he had never felt so awful at it.

"I'm messing with you, bud," he consoled, patting Cailean's shoulder.

"Are you ready, honey?" Mrs. Cassidy called, dropping her purse strap on her shoulder and tossing the car keys to her husband.

"When you are," he smiled, barely managing to catch the keys. Cailean wondered if her throw had been weak or his reaction too slow. He surmised, though, that it was both as he watched them walk toward the door. Even their walking seemed slow to him, but he was sure that was just a predisposition against humans he was still working through.

"Are you sure you don't need a ride to school?" Mrs. Cassidy offered. She had given them the option every day for the past three years – even after Brooke and Cailean moved to high school so the stop would be out of her way. Every day Cailean declined, but he never stopped appreciating the thought.

"No thanks," he replied. "I like the walk."

"I know you do," she laughed, walking out the door as her husband opened it for her.

"Behave yourselves," Mr. Cassidy added, turning to face Cailean before he left. Already standing straight, Cailean tried to straighten his back even more as he nodded. The moment the door closed, he collapsed onto the couch with a sigh.

"When are you going to stop acting so weird around my dad?" Brooke teased, stepping out of her room. Wearing blue pants and a black brassier, she stood before him with a shirt draped over her shoulder. Struggling to compose himself, Cailean searched for an adequate response. Instead, he found himself babbling, so he fell silent.

"It's not like you haven't seen them before," she scolded as he stared at her. She pulled the shirt over her head and pulled her hair out from where it was trapped between the shirt and her body.

"Sorry," Cailean stammered, dropping his eyes. Since Brooke had started her transformation two years ago, they had changed together every month and while he tried not to look, he hadn't managed to avoid it every time. She was far more open and comfortable with her body than he would have expected, which made it easier for her. For him, though, he found himself feeling strange every time he saw her less than fully clothed.

"You're too easy," she sighed.

"Yeah, yeah, yeah," Cailean groaned, standing up and leading her to the door. Even when she was intentionally making him feel uncomfortable, Cailean still somehow felt more himself around her than anywhere else. Smiling despite her teasing, he added, "Let's just get to school."

❖ ❖ ❖

Feigning an obnoxious smile, Cailean laughed as Adam, one of the upper classmen on the varsity team, punched his arm. Realizing that the force of the blow would have caused a reaction from the majority of humans, Cailean swung to the side a bit. Cacophonic cackling erupted from the rest of the group as if any form of physical assault was the most humorous thing they'd experienced all day.

"You can't pretend she isn't hot," Adam whispered with a surprising degree of urgency as he insisted upon the validity of his flawed argument. Turning his attention from Cailean, he watched as Kristin turned the corner, revealing more of her shapely figure. The senior had drawn the eyes of every male in the hall as she paraded past them suggestively swinging her hips and accentuating her practically bare legs with each movement. To Cailean, nothing about her desperate plea for attention was enticing.

"Whatever man," Cailean shrugged. "She's just not my type."

"How?" Ryder, Adam's right-hand man, asked in shock.

"She can probably hear you," Cailean groaned in a futile attempt to change the subject.

"Who cares? She knows she's hot," a forgettable junior on the team piped up.

"Hold on, I'm really curious, is human perfection not your type?" Ryder asked, pushing Cailean into an answer. Cailean knew it was his job to blend in with the jocks around him, but he found that increasingly difficult. Their minds were guided by nothing more than girls and sports – and babbling about their human interests was dull. Over the past few years, though, he had grown significantly better at unashamedly objectifying and insulting the people around him. While it wasn't a difficult mindset, it simply failed to entertain him.

"Not particularly," Cailean muttered. Sighing, he tried to turn the attention from himself by providing an actual explanation. "She's just too… boring. You know, there's nothing for me to chase."

"You calling her easy?" Adam spat.

"Look at her," Cailean retorted.

"Alright," Adam shrugged, punching his arm once again. "Then what is your type then, Freshman?"

Only one name came to Cailean's mind, but he pushed it away despite it burning through his other thoughts. If for no other reason, simply because he couldn't tolerate the idea of his peers objectifying her like they did the others. Suddenly, as if summoned by his will alone, Brooke sauntered past them and Cailean instinctively followed her with his eyes. A quiet teasing befell Cailean as the others followed his gaze.

"Hey, hot stuff," Ryder called out to her, overshadowing the whistles which erupted from his friends.

"She does have certain… assets," Adam admitted in a hushed tone as Brooke turned over her shoulder.

"Why don't you come over here baby?" Ryder continued to tease.

"Who, me?" Brooke asked, her voice raising an octave as she expressed a clear interest. As she moved toward them, Cailean felt as though he'd been punched in the gut.

"I don't know why you cover up those legs of yours," Ryder winked at her as he lowered a hand to slap her butt. Before he made contact, though, she caught his wrist and twisted his arm. Falling to his knees, Ryder gasped in pain and tried to follow the direction of the lock. Releasing him, Brooke pushed backward and he stumbled away. The group around Cailean began spurting profanities and insulting her as if truly believing their friend had done nothing wrong.

"You're more than welcome to look," Brooke coquettishly murmured, silencing their stammering. "But only one of you is actually good enough to touch."

Cailean froze as she winked at him, clearly having heard the entire exchange. Sensing his discomfort, Brooke had stepped in to make a scene for him. With a flourish, she turned and walked away, intentionally walking as seductively as possible. Once again, she had been the rock he needed. As much as he'd grown accustomed to faking his friendships, Cailean still found feigning humanity difficult and Brooke was always there to make it easier. If nothing else, simply by distracting them from his momentary lapse in acting ability.

As she walked away, Cailean found it impossible to avert his gaze from her. His mind drifted to the moment he'd scratched her – which he could barely remember. The following days had been terrifying as he expected her to hate him, but she had never wavered. Brooke had been by his side through everything.

"Brooke," he called out confidently.

"What's up?" She asked, turning back around. By the time she faced him, he had already covered the short distance between them. Without another word, Cailean wrapped his fingers in her hair and moved toward her. As his lips met hers, every doubt he'd ever had faded away. He wasn't sure exactly what his father meant about only loving once, but he knew there was no one with whom he'd rather share it.

"So this is love?" He whispered, gazing into her shining eyes.

"Took you long enough," she laughed, throwing her arms around him. Nothing about him regretted his declaration. In that moment, Cailean Phoenix knew he would never want to live a life without Brooke Cassidy in it.

Hayden

Chapter 1

6 Days Until the Full Moon

Cailean

Thanks to years of training with his father, Cailean found it simple to feign entertainment as he stared at the pieces of the broken picture before him. Sitting on the floor across from him with her elbows resting on her knees, her legs crossed, and her chin firmly planted in her open hands, River Cassidy stared blankly at the puzzle. After a moment of silence, she reached forward only to change her mind and retract her hand again.

Pretending to be human had become so natural to Cailean that most of the thoughts were subconscious. Between his slightly enhanced senses and the painstaking hours he'd poured into practicing his perceptive skills, puzzles were trivial to him. As he helped Brooke's mother piece one together, though, he carefully monitored his speed to avoid betraying his secrets. Running automatically, though, he was able to allow his mind to drift as he occasionally slipped a piece into place.

"How do you do that?" Mrs. Cassidy muttered as Cailean gently placed another piece on the table in front of him.

"What?" He asked, caught off guard by the sudden influx of volume and human voice.

"You're just exceptional at puzzles," she complimented.

"Oh, I don't know about that," Cailean shrugged, laughing charismatically while simultaneously making a mental note to himself to slow down. Though the past three years had thoroughly convinced him that Brooke's mother was not a hunter and there was no reason to believe she would assume he was a werewolf for any reason, his general stance was to err on the side of caution. Mimicking a behavior he'd seen from her, he picked up a piece and tried to fit it where it didn't belong.

Listening to Brooke's shuffling as she changed and put on her make-up, Cailean tried to gauge how much longer she'd be. He had grown very accustomed to spending time with her parents over the past few years, but puzzles were still dull. Something about the tediousness was appealing to him, though. At home, he felt as though he was wasting any time he didn't spend training. Even if perpetuating that mindset wasn't his father's intention, it was a side-effect from his actions. Watching an hour pass as he sat on the floor with Brooke's mom while he waited for her to meet them felt normal. It almost felt human.

Instinctively, he whipped his head to the side as he heard a quiet movement from the doorknob. A key turned and the knob slowly followed, assuring Cailean that it was Brooke's father. Exhaling deeply, he relaxed his shoulders and turned back to the puzzle in an attempt to conceal his over-reaction.

"A little on edge today?" Mrs. Cassidy teased, clearly noticing Cailean's apparent reaction. Silently, he scolded himself for his carelessness while outwardly trying to laugh off the situation.

"I was just really focused," he laughed defensively. With a shrug, Brooke's mother accepted the answer and stood to meet her husband.

"Hey, River," Brooke's father greeted, embracing her in the entryway. Releasing her, he turned his attention to Cailean. "Hi, Cailean."

"Good afternoon, sir," Cailean answered respectfully, rising to his feet and turning toward him as he spoke.

"You don't have to 'sir' me," he told Cailean warmly. Though Brooke's parents had been attempting to convince him to refer to them by their first names for months, Cailean still felt uncomfortable with the concept. Especially since he'd met Mrs. Cassidy in the context of school, where she was his middle school teacher. Switching to their first names was a hurdle for Cailean.

Generally, he tried to simply avoid referring to them by any name. For the most part, he was able to achieve that goal without any tension, but it was awkward to get their attention.

"Sorry," he apologized, dropping his gaze a bit.

"River and I are going to get something to eat, would you and Brooke like to join?" Her father offered. Having resigned slightly to Cailean's awkwardness regarding using their first names, he just moved past the subject. Any topic involving finances made Cailean uncomfortable too. Brooke's parents would never allow him to pay for a meal for the four of them, but he hated passing that responsibility to them. After centuries of properly handling finances, Cailean's father had built up a small and relatively untraceable fortune, so Cailean hated the prospect of good people spending money they worked hard for when he had a practically endless supply. Not for the first time, Cailean silently acknowledged that human interaction was still not a subject with which he was comfortable. Dating Brooke felt natural but navigating the relationships with her parents was a burden – despite the fact that he occasionally enjoyed spending time with them as well.

"I appreciate the invite, but we already have reservations," Cailean politely declined. After allowing his words to hang in the air for no more than a moment, he forced himself to add, "Thanks, Joshua."

"You know what?" Brooke's father laughed, walking toward Cailean and patting his shoulder gently. "It's an improvement, and I'll take it."

"Progress, not perfection, sir," Cailean joked. Shaking his head with a laugh, Josh loosened his tie and walked toward his room.

Cailean heard him exchange greetings with Brooke and tell her how beautiful she looked, so he assumed she had finally emerged from her room. He had intentionally arrived early, so Brooke was actually ready right on time, but his discomfort made it seem as though it had been ages. His lack of ability to interact with her parents was something he knew he'd have to work through if he and Brooke were going to spend their lives together, so he'd made it a point to force himself to get more used to their presence.

"So, when do you want to help me finish the puzzle?" River joked as they waited for Brooke to turn the corner.

"Let me know when you want me here," Cailean shrugged.

"I'm joking, Cailean. You don't have to humor me for my daughter's sake."

"It's fun," he told her, only partially lying.

"I'll keep that in mind," she smiled. Suddenly, her attention turned to Brooke. Following her gaze, Cailean rotated his head to watch her stride toward them. As if he'd been punched in the stomach, Cailean felt the breath escape his lungs. Though he'd felt it since they had met, he had expected that feeling to fade, but it had only grown more intense when they actually started dating. Watching her walk toward him with her hair flowing past her shoulders and blending into her black dress, he found himself just as smitten as he had been the day he'd awakened to her brown eyes.

"What's wrong?" Brooke asked. For some reason, she always became self-conscious when wearing a dress. Ironically, Cailean's staring, lost in her beauty, probably only served to fuel her insecurities. Composing himself, he pulled his eyes from the job they'd assumed of tracing her body and pinned them to her eyes.

Wanting nothing more than to wash the worry from her eyes, Cailean smiled lovingly and dropped his guard. For the first time that night, he allowed himself to tell the whole truth. "Nothing. Nothing at all."

4 Days Until the Full Moon
Hayden

"Hayden, don't forget to bring tampons!" Her mom called from across the house. Sitting at the breakfast table with her brother, Hayden felt her face burn as it flushed with embarrassment. Frozen, she hesitated with her fork over her eggs for a moment before turning her eyes away from Caleb. Silently pretending it hadn't happened, Hayden returned her attention to her breakfast. Placing the fork down, she awkwardly took a sip from her orange juice. Peeking her head into the kitchen, her mother added, "Did you hear me honey?"

"Yes, mother," Hayden muttered, gritting her teeth and glaring at her. "I think the entire neighborhood heard you."

"It's nothing to be ashamed of," her mother defended, moving forward to share the room with them. "You're becoming a woman."

"Alright, enough of that," Hayden quickly interjected, desperate to change the subject. Laughing quietly, Caleb just shook his head sipped his coffee with a smirk. Hayden appreciated the fact that her brother was mature enough to avoid teasing her or making a big deal of the conversation, but it didn't ease the tension.

"Okay, okay," her mother shrugged as she backed away. "I'm just saying you shouldn't be ashamed of your body's natural processes."

"You know, if it helps," Caleb whispered after she had left. "She told me the same thing around your age. Different meaning, but equally mortifying."

"Oddly enough, that thought does not help much," Hayden laughed weakly, standing and emptying her plate in the trash before placing it in the sink.

"Well, it's not a big deal if you don't make it one," Caleb comforted.

"Thanks," she sighed as she picked up her backpack and walked to the living room. Collapsing onto the couch, she dropped her head and stared at the ceiling. Though she logically knew they were right, her emotional reaction refused to agree. Forcing herself to her feet, Hayden walked to the bathroom to finish getting ready.

Examining her face in the mirror, she leaned forward and groaned as she scanned a few small bumps on her face. One particular blemish, a pimple which had erupted overnight, was guaranteed to draw attention. In attempt to lessen the redness, Hayden rubbed foundation across her face. Turning her attention to the pimple she blotted concealer over it and attempted to blend the makeup into her fair skin. Satisfied that she'd minimally hidden her acne, she turned her attention to digging through her earrings. Absentmindedly massaging the hole in her ear with a cotton ball, she searched through her jewelry. Finally settling on a simple pair, she slid the stud through her ear and secured the back.

"Are you ready?" Caleb asked, appearing from the hallway and drumming his fingers on the frame of the open door.

"I don't know, I wanted to curl my hair," she pondered, twirling the ends in her fingertips.

"Doesn't that take like an hour?" Caleb groaned comically.

"It'll be ten minutes, tops. How much longer do we have?"

"You have time," Caleb admitted, checking his watch. The two of them often walked through the front gate of the school as the bell rang and Hayden couldn't deny that she was quite frequently the cause. Caleb had taken to alerting her twenty minutes before they actually had to leave that it was time to depart. Though she found the gesture slightly patronizing, she couldn't argue his intention behind it.

"I'll be quick," she promised, plugging in the iron.

"Yeah, yeah yeah," he muttered, walking away. Before the iron had even heated up, though, he appeared in the doorway again. "Don't be too quick, though. I don't want you to burn yourself."

"That was once!"

"I'm not making fun of you, I'm just legitimately concerned for your well-being."

"Right," she rolled her eyes playfully as she closed the door on him. She began loosely wrapping small sections of hair around the iron, working carefully but quickly. When she finished, she set the tool down and unplugged it before running her fingers through her hair to give it more body and a wavy look.

A knock on the door spurred her on and she rushed to brush her teeth and glance over herself one last time before rushing to school. Confident she wasn't forgetting anything, she opened the door to tell Caleb she was ready. Instead, she saw her mom leaning against the wall near the door frame.

"I put a few in your bag," she greeted without context. Hayden responded with a brief, confused glance before she realized that her mother's earlier warning had fallen on deaf ears. Chuckling quietly, she dropped her eyes and nodded.

"Thanks, Mom," she smiled, hugging her tightly before scurrying off to the living room to meet her brother. Waiting for her, Caleb sat on the couch with his feet propped up on the coffee table in their living room. Leaning his head back, he intertwined his fingers behind his neck.

"That was the longest ten minutes ever," he complained as he moved his feet and fell forward. Using that momentum to stand, he grabbed his backpack and swung it over his shoulder.

"I'm sure it's not the longest," Hayden argued.

"Far from it," Caleb admitted, shrugging as he walked around the couch. Retrieving Hayden's bag from where she'd set it, he added, "I suppose usually ten minutes is closer to half an hour."

"I'm glad you're starting to understand the math," she told him, accepting the teasing rather than trying to argue. Caleb tossed the bag to her and turned toward the door. Reaching both of her hands out in surprise, Hayden wrapped them both around the backpack as it collided with her chest. With a pained exhale, she stumbled backward and narrowly avoided falling over.

"Caleb, there are books in there!" She complained after she recovered. Carefully, she pulled the straps over her shoulders and met him at the door.

"Sorry, I forgot you were a girl."

"That has no bearing on this situation," she mumbled defensively. Feigning anger, she added accusingly, "Are you saying that I'm weak because I'm a girl?"

"No, of course not," Caleb countered as he opened the door. "I'm just saying that you have a higher center of gravity. I should have tossed it lower and you would have been fine."

"Women have a lower center of gravity than men," she informed him, narrowing her eyes as she followed him outside.

"Well, that just doesn't make sense," he debated.

"It totally does. It's hips versus shoulders."

"Fine, it was a girl joke," he admitted as Hayden reached for the doorknob.

"Have a good day at school," their mother called from inside. "I love you."

As Hayden closed the door, she and Caleb both called back to their mother to express their undying affection. Climbing into the passenger side of her brother's car, Hayden dropped her head against the seat behind her and closed her eyes. Caleb chuckled softly, clearly amused at her perpetual state of fatigue, but he was kind enough to allow her to rest as he drove.

❖ ❖ ❖

Tapping on the table gently, Hayden attempted to cure her boredom by creating a rhythm. Subconsciously, she found herself replicating the song which had been on Caleb's radio that morning. Waiting for Chase, she watched the clock as her lunch hour ticked away. His class was across campus, so it wasn't fair to expect him to arrive at the cafeteria at the same time as her, but she still found herself slightly annoyed. Fully aware that the reaction was from a mixture of hormones and a lack of food, though, she refused to acknowledge it.

Silently approaching her from behind, Chase leaned over her shoulder and kissed her cheek. Startled, she jumped in her seat and almost hit the table in front of her. Turning to face her boyfriend, she tried to cover up her annoyance with a smile.

"Sorry," he apologized earnestly.

"It's fine," she laughed. "I appreciate the gesture. I was just really focused on my song."

"Oh, right," he nodded, straightening up and leaning back as she stood. "It was truly magical. You should play the drums."

"Alright, I said it was fine, no need to kiss up," she chuckled.

"What, I liked it," he shrugged. "You're far above average when it comes to rhythmically tapping on tables."

"It does happen to be one of my lesser known talents."

Stepping closer, Hayden wrapped her arms around Chase's waist and hugged him. As she rested her head on his chest, she silently thanked him for reminding her how much she liked him. He was a constant source of light – always shockingly upbeat and friendly. Chase never failed to put a smile on the faces of the people around him.

"So how was class?" She asked, backing away and walking with him to the lunch line.

"Oh, incredible," Chase retorted. "We're reading a book in English class, but the teacher came up with the novel idea called: 'popcorn reading.'"

"Okay," Hayden nodded, giggling as he over-emoted throughout his story, waving his hands as he spoke.

"So it's this system where one person reads a section and then calls on another student to continue where they left off," Chase explained the process as if it weren't a tactic employed by every teacher since elementary school. "You see, my entire existence has been preparing for this moment. The best side-effect of being forgettable is that no one calls on me. I get to skate through class without putting in any effort whatsoever. It's like being read a bedtime story."

"Whatever," Hayden groaned sarcastically. "Everyone loves you and you know it."

"That's the trick, though," Chase winked. "I carefully monitor every conversation in order to leave just a good enough impression on everyone that they like me enough to avoid calling on me as a cruelty, but not quite enough to do so because it would be funny."

"You're a mastermind," Hayden teased.

"It's not hard, I can teach you my ways. You just have to be cold and calculating," Chase began. Interrupting himself, though, he squatted down to retrieve something from the floor. Hayden hadn't even noticed its presence, and by the time she identified the object, Chase was already tapping on the shoulder of the person in front of him. With a smile, he returned the wallet to a grateful peer.

"That was so cold I'm shivering," Hayden teased.

"Okay, so that was poor timing," Chase admitted.

"You read a lot, didn't you?"

"I… Yeah, I read so much."

As the two of them reached the front of the line, they both chose chicken sandwiches from the limited selection of meals provided by the school. Leading Hayden through the checkout line and back to their table, Chase remained very focused on pleasantly greeting each person they passed. Hayden was far from an introvert, but she still found herself exhausted on his behalf when she finally fell back into her seat and unwrapped the sandwich.

"Anyway, how have your classes been so far?" Chase asked, turning his attention back to her as she greedily bit into her lunch. Setting it back down on the tray, she quickly chewed and swallowed as she pondered an answer to his question. She didn't want to answer with a single word, so she searched for anything interesting to share.

"Well," she started slowly. "I guess I learned some more algebra."

"That's cool, math is fun," Chase shrugged.

"I'm sorry, I'm not as good at finding humor in mundane things as you."

"Oh, don't worry about that, that just happens to be one of my lesser known talents," he smiled. Laughing, Hayden dropped her eyes and subconsciously twirled her hair. When she caught herself, she wondered if that had anything to do with how quickly her hair became greasy throughout the day. Not thinking about the fact that there was someone else at the table, she pulled her hand from her hair and looked at it to see if her fingers looked dirty from the food.

"Hey, Hayden," Chase broke the brief silence, startling Hayden and pulling her eyes back toward him.

"What's up?" She asked, dropping her hand and covering it as if that would hide the thoughts which had polluted her mind. Realizing that he clearly had no idea what she was thinking, she tried to relax. She and Chase had been dating for a few months already, so she wasn't too concerned about scaring him off by running greasy fingers through her hair. Determining that it was simply her aching stomach which made her uncomfortable, she took another bite and looked intently toward Chase.

"My family is going camping this weekend. Just in the woods near town. I was wondering if you wanted to come out with us."

"Camping?" Hayden grimaced.

"Yeah, it's where you go out into the woods and set up tents," Chase began jokingly explaining. Playfully, Hayden leaned forward and hit his arm. Feigning pain, Chase rubbed his arm and scooted back before taking the first bite of his own lunch. Though he tried to act calm, Hayden could clearly see the anticipation on his face as he awaited her answer.

"That sounds like fun," she lied, pasting a smile on her face. As much as she wanted to spend time with Chase, camping was one of the last things she considered enjoyable. Nothing about the outdoors had ever particularly appealed to her. Hayden preferred the comforts of her home to the harsh environment. Unwilling to disappoint her boyfriend, though, she decided it was worth trying. Still, her brain raced as she searched for a way to provide herself an escape in case she changed her mind. "I do have to ask my mom, though."

"Of course," Chase accepted. His face lit up as if she'd already given him confirmation, though. Hayden ate a few more bites in silence, trying to convince herself that camping would be enjoyable. At the very least, she would get to spend a few days with Chase and his family and get to know them better. She had never been outside of town, either, so even just a journey into the nearby woods could actually prove to be an adventure.

"What about wolves?" Hayden asked as her brain presented every possible concern which had kept her from venturing into the woods before. Her mind drifted to all of the howls which she had heard from the safety of her own bed.

"Wolves don't really attack people. They may come for our food, but that's about it. Bears are the scary ones."

"That's comforting," she sighed sarcastically. Seeing past his own excitement and reading her fear, Chase dropped the smile from his face.

"I've never seen a wolf or a bear. They don't usually like to come near people. Anyway, my parents have been into camping and hiking their entire lives, so they know how to keep a clean campsite."

"That's closer to what I wanted to hear," she nodded, smiling weakly and continuing to eat her food.

"If you're scared, you don't have to go," Chase offered. Hayden was once again impressed with his selflessness. Despite the fact that he clearly wanted her to accompany him, there wasn't an ounce of disappointment or dishonesty in his offer.

"No, it'll be fun," she replied, trying to convince herself that it was the truth. Talking herself into it as she finished her food, Hayden found herself growing excited for the trip. The weather was perfect to be outdoors and every new experience was a chance to learn something. With veterans in regards to camping, she knew they'd be safe.

"It's going to be great, Hayden," she thought, believing it more with each passing second. *"Nothing will go wrong."*

Chapter 2

4 Days Until the Full Moon
Cailean

Ducking under a hook, Cailean stepped in and countered with a punch to Brooke's ribs. Pulling his punch, he only drove forward with enough force to drop her to the ground. Still, the bones cracked under the force of the impact. Brooke stumbled backward, clutching her ribs before falling to a seated position. Silently, she bit back the pain and placed her hands behind her, leaning back on them and breathing through the pain.

Straightening up, Cailean waited for her broken bones to piece themselves back together. While he felt bad for hurting her, he knew it would only disservice both of them to train poorly. Practicing was always meant to be more difficult than the actual game if his coach was to be believed. That was all the more applicable to fighting. If she didn't break anything during sparring her pain tolerance wouldn't increase as much as his had. The hunters – if they ever encountered them – weren't likely to hold back.

"I think that was the first time you didn't scream," Cailean complimented.

"Wonderful," Brooke groaned, stumbling to her feet. "If nothing else, at least my crowning accomplishment from this fight can be that I took the pain well."

"It's important," Cailean assured her. "If one broken bone debilitates you, you'll go down after a single hit. If you become numb to it, you can continue fighting. Damage incurred isn't scored in a true fight. The only winner is the one left alive."

"That's dark," Brooke teased, stretching as her ribs fell back into place. As she lifted her arms, Cailean could see the definition in her stomach and biceps. She had never been out of shape, but since her first transformation she'd slowly been shedding the little bit of adipose tissue that she did have. Cailean wondered how their bodies determined the point of stability, though. He himself, though he'd been a werewolf for his entire life, still calculated at least eight percent body fat. Watching her arms fall back to her sides, Cailean was grateful that their werewolf bodies seemed to settle on healthy proportions rather than continually building muscle forever. While his childhood training had probably taught him to value a strong woman, there were still a few areas where he appreciated the fat. Interrupting his thoughts, Brooke asked, "What are you staring at?"

"Umm…" Cailean hesitated, pulling his eyes up toward her face. Something about training with her made him want nothing more than to be closer to her. Cailean couldn't understand the feelings from experience, but he could easily put words on them based on the physiology he'd learned. Exercise was boosting his testosterone levels, slowly stealing his thoughts from him.

Mercilessly, Brooke lunged forward and threw a kick toward Cailean's abdomen. Though she tried to take advantage of his moment of hesitation, his instincts led his reaction. As she extended her leg, he pivoted, catching her attack and lifting her off the ground. Dropping her, he dropped to a knee and punched her solar plexus, knocking her breath away.

"Where did I tell you to watch during a fight?" He asked, standing and stepping back. After a moment, she caught her breath and stood a foot away from him, attempting to stay out of his reach.

"The chest," she answered.

"Why?"

"Watching your eyes would limit my ability to respond. It would take longer to see movement in your feet, so I'm less prepared for kicks."

"Exactly."

"So that's your reason?" She prodded.

"I won't argue the pleasant side-effects," he admitted. "But you're the one who insists on training in a sports bra."

"I don't have to," she shrugged, stepping forward and gazing seductively into his eyes. Recognizing the trap, Cailean tried to maintain focused, but his young body refused to cede control. As she moved toward him, he felt his stomach churning. Gently, Brooke placed a hand on his cheek. Cailean winced with the touch, concerned for the inevitable attack. Instead, her lips came forward to meet him. Stumbling backward, Cailean eventually found a wall behind him and leaned on it for support.

The offense, aside from an onslaught of kisses, never came. Cailean felt as though the wolf were rushing forward, dictating his actions and leaving him as a passenger. In that moment, though, he had no desire to stop it. When she pulled her head back and kissed his neck, Cailean took a deep breath and pushed her away gently.

With a sigh, she stepped backward and intertwined her fingers behind her head. Regretting his decision, Cailean watched her chest rise and fall rhythmically as she caught her breath. For a while, Cailean had believed kissing Brooke would result in his giving her his lifelong love. However, after one kiss and an awkward conversation with his parents, he had learned that there was more to it than that. No part of him questioned whether Brooke was the woman with whom he wanted to spend his life, but there were a lot of variables which he didn't feel qualified to take into account.

"You are confusing," Brooke sighed, dropping her hands and turning from him. Retrieving her shirt, she slid it on and stretched.

"I just don't want us to make a mistake," Cailean whispered.

"Why do you think it's a mistake?"

"I don't," he laughed. "But I'm fourteen. I just think we're a little young to be making this kind of decision."

"It's a bit of a special circumstance."

"Which is why we should treat it with even more scrutiny."

"Fine, fine," Brooke accepted. She slid down and sat against the wall. "I just love you, you know? More than I know how to express. If there's any possible way that I can feel that even more, I want to know what it's like. I already know I want to be with you forever, and I just want the wolf to know that too."

"You make a compelling argument," Cailean admitted, sitting on the floor next to her. "But I just think we need to take some time to think and discuss."

"How romantic."

"Anyway," Cailean added, lowering his voice to a near imperceptible whisper. "I'm fairly confident my father can hear everything we say or do in this house."

4 Days Until the Full Moon
Hayden

"Camping?" Hayden's mom laughed. It took half of a minute for her to realize that Hayden wasn't sharing her laughter. Finally grasping that it was a real question, she contained her amusement. Hayden couldn't blame her for her response. She herself was completely shocked that it was even something she'd consider.

"It's his whole family," she reiterated.

"I just thought you hated nature," her mom defended, surprised.

"I don't hate nature," Hayden mumbled defensively. Realizing that she was unintentionally shutting her mother out, she tried to elaborate. "I mean, it's pretty. I just don't like being in it."

"So why do you want to go?"

"I don't know, I feel like I should branch out. Anyway, Chase told me there's nothing to be afraid of."

"Right," her mother said slowly. Sitting down on the couch, she patted the cushion next to her to encourage Hayden to sit. Reluctantly, Hayden moved toward her and fell onto the couch. Clearly, getting permission was not going to be as easy as she'd assumed.

"We need to have a talk about something," her mother started slowly.

"What's that?"

"I know you're growing up. You're becoming a woman."

"I don't know about that."

"There are going to be changes in your body," she continued, ignoring Hayden's interruption. "You may feel certain urges."

"Mom," Hayden started slowly. Though she didn't want to be rude to her mother, she had no interest in continuing that conversation. Having gone to public school her entire life, she had already heard enough about the topic. Anyway, it wasn't even something that had crossed her mind in the slightest, and the idea made her uncomfortable. It couldn't be what Chase was expecting.

"I know it's awkward, but it's important that we are able to talk about anything."

"I don't think that's going to be an issue with you," Hayden laughed.

"That means I'm doing my job," she chirped proudly.

"I'd sleep in the tent with his mom and sister. The whole weekend will be supervised. You have no reason to be concerned."

"That's comforting, but I still think this is something we should talk about."

"Honestly, Mom, I'd really prefer not doing that. I know I can, and I appreciate that. Right now, though, I just want to go camping for the first time."

"No you don't," her mother teased with a smile.

"True," Hayden admitted.

"Do you want me to say no? I can ground you or something," she patted her knees and stood to her feet with a groan.

"That's okay, Mom. I think I'll enjoy it, honestly."

"And his parents do this a lot?" The concern which she tried to hide slowly crept into her voice. Hayden's mother didn't share her fear of the woods, but it was only natural to be slightly concerned. Neither of them had left town for the greater part of their lives, so Hayden wasn't surprised that her mom was slightly unsettled by the idea too.

"He said they go camping all the time. He even told me that they've seen a bear. Which I guess doesn't make me feel any better, now that I think about it, but it does prove to me that they have some experience. I mean, they're alive, right?"

"As far as I know," her mother nodded.

A moment of silence hung in the air between them. Hayden began to feel awkward as she realized how far out of her comfort zone she was willing to go for her boyfriend. Waiting for a response from her mother, she slowly began to grasp the concept of having butterflies in her stomach. She felt nauseated as the fear that she would refuse crept into her mind. Equal to that, though, was the fear that she would agree. Hayden tried to appear confident, but she was afraid of whatever roamed those woods at night.

"Just promise me you'll be careful," her mother finally whispered.

"What do you mean?"

"I don't know, I just get worried. Anyway, it's a full moon, and people get crazy."

"I think that's a myth," Hayden laughed.

"Maybe, but I've worked at the hospital on full moons. The crazies come out."

"I'll watch out for the crazies. If the tree people come for me, I'm fairly sure Chase's dad has a shotgun."

"Don't mock me," her mother playfully complained.

"I love you, Mom," Hayden smiled, pulling her into an embrace. As her last excuse disappeared, she tried to accept the fact that she was going to leave town that weekend.

❖ ❖ ❖

With a suitcase open on her bed and clothes strewn out around it, Hayden held two shirts as she cursed her lack of any attire appropriate for the outdoors. Teetering on the balance of looking nice while also being willing to wear the clothes outside proved more difficult than she'd expected. Apart from determining which clothes were worth dirtying, there was also the question of appropriate attire. She had no idea what to expect in terms of weather, given that she'd never slept in a tent. Unable to make a decision, she rolled both of the short sleeve shirts in her hands and placed them next to each other in the suitcase, cramming them between four pairs of pants and two separate sets of pajamas.

"Hey there," Caleb greeted quietly, casting a shadow over her disorderly bed as he leaned in the doorway.

"Hey," she replied absently as she searched for a skirt which she was sure she'd set on the bed earlier. Lifting a small pile and sifting through the clothes, she grew more frantic as she failed to find the article.

"What have you got here?" Caleb asked gently. His shadow grew as he walked into the room.

"I lost my skirt."

"Hayden, you're camping."

"Yeah, I may need it, I don't know."

"It's also in four days."

"I have to be prepared."

Finding the skirt, she reached over her suitcase to grab it. When she pulled her hand back, it snagged on the bag and pulled it toward the edge of the bed. Lunging forward, her brother caught it and minimized the damage to her organization. Desperately moving to reorganize everything and find a place for the skirt, she lifted the bag back onto the bed and sifted through it once again.

"For an apocalypse?"

"It's not that much," she defended.

"Hayden, you'll be gone for like two days. You have at least sixteen outfits."

"Some are for hot and others cold. I have a swimsuit in case we go to the lake."

"And another swimsuit in case that one tears?"

"I… I have a backup for the second one too," she admitted, dropping her hands. Moving to her side, Caleb wrapped his arm around her and she dropped her head onto his bicep.

"Will you come for a walk with me?" He asked. Since she was a child, Hayden had always enjoyed walking to calm herself down. Before her mother had been comfortable allowing her to do so alone, though, he had always accompanied her.

"Where?"

"Who cares?"

"Okay," she nodded somberly. A slight smile tugged at the right side of her mouth, fighting against her inclination to mope.

Leading her with his arm still around her shoulder, Caleb moved to the door. When he opened it for her, she moved ahead of him and aimlessly wandered down the road. Caleb quickly overtook her with his longer strides before slowing his pace slightly in front of her on the street side. Rounding the corner, both of them remained silent as they walked a path they'd travelled hundreds of times before.

"Have you ever read that book about the lobsters?" Caleb finally spoke up, breaking the silence. Confused, Hayden turned toward him and tried to hide the tears brewing in her eyes. She had assumed he'd wanted to give her some sort of brotherly advice or calm her down, but he was clearly burying the lead. At the very least, she was interested to see how he turned his random comment into something meaningful.

"As vague as that was, I would like to tell you that it wasn't enough information, but honestly I think I'm comfortable saying no."

"Huh," he muttered, falling silent once again. As he turned another corner, she followed closely behind him. The quiet lingered for a moment and the song of the crickets reverberated off the concrete and asphalt beneath them. The path seemed to glow a dull orange as the setting sun lent its light to the earth. The peace of the world around them was almost enough to drain the anxiety racing through Hayden's mind.

Searching for a logical explanation for her emotion, Hayden distracted herself for a few moments. Despite her best attempts, she was unable to explain the feelings. Camping was a new experience, and she was somewhat afraid of the woods, but that wasn't enough to justify her reaction. That knowledge, unfortunately, was nowhere near enough to overcome the dread. Her brother's lingering comment, though, combined with the peaceful environment, pulled her out of her stupor for a moment.

"What about the lobster book?" She laughed.

"I don't know," he shrugged. "I was just wondering if you'd read it."

"That's it?"

"I don't know, do you want a review?" He teased. "It was surprisingly funny. The character is a little bit shrimpy at the beginning."

"Oh no," she groaned.

"He runs into some fishy characters."

"Please stop."

"Honestly, though the whole book is oceans of fun, it's pretty deep."

"This is clearly intentional."

"It left me thirsty for more."

"There's no lobster book, is there?"

"There are a lot of books, Hayden. I can't possibly answer that for certain. But this particular book was invented for the craft of a pun."

"I expected some type of moral or something."

"Oh, I suppose a fable would be the most likely genre for a novel about sea creatures."

"No, from you," she chuckled, looking up at him as the sun fell behind his head. "Usually your random musings contain some sort of brotherly wisdom."

"I do like to pretend I'm wise," he acknowledged.

"I don't know, you usually have some pretty good advice," she dropped her eyes. At some point, they had wandered off of the main streets and the ground beneath them was no longer paved. Shadows covered most of the dirt beneath her, but the setting sun still streamed through the darkness. Rays of light were visible as they reflected from the dust particles in the air around her.

"Well, you're setting the bar pretty high," Caleb hesitated, slowing to a stop. Hayden stood next to him and he placed his hands on her shoulders as she turned to look up at him. "I can try my best to come up with something, if the lobsters didn't already say it all."

"I'm sure you can beat those hard-headed guys."

"You tried, and I'll give it to you," he laughed, moving his hand to her cheek gently.

"I'm right here," Caleb told her, his tone changing drastically. "I'm with you. You know that?"

"Obviously," she replied slowly.

Gently, Caleb rotated her shoulders. Spinning in a circle, Hayden saw nothing but trees around her. Their leaves mostly blotted out the sun, but there was still just enough light to see their low hanging branches like arms reaching toward them. Her pulse quickened as she wondered how far she'd wandered and where she was.

"Hayden, you have nothing to be afraid of."

"We…"

"We left town," he smiled.

"For the first time," she choked, laughing as the fear dissipated. While she was still concerned about bears and wolves, the irrational fear didn't seem as insurmountable.

"You know it isn't because he left, right?"

"What do you mean?" She asked. The tears in her eyes told her that her body – and some subconscious part of her mind – already knew the answer to her own question. Still, she didn't try to search for it. Part of her wished she hadn't asked at all.

"Dad. It isn't because he left."

"It was right when he got back," she countered, tears filling her eyes.

"He was sick, Hayden. That trip didn't make him sick, and staying wouldn't have helped either. I know you were pretty young, but he went to get the best treatment. He was sick before he left, and he was still sick when he came back."

"How do we know?" Hayden broke down, surrendering to the fight against the cathartic rain of tears.

"Because I remember. And because people camp – they go out there and they come back. Because people live outside of our small town. There isn't some disease out there, Hayden. It just seemed that way when you were young. It seemed like the outside world took him away, but it didn't. Now, if I'm being honest, I don't really like the idea of you camping any more than you seem to, but I have my own reservations as your brother. If there is a reason you don't go, though, I don't want it to be because your fear held you back."

Hayden dropped her face into her brother's chest and he wrapped his arms around her. Quietly, she wept until the sun went down around them, plunging them both into darkness. Finally, she composed herself and stood shakily on her own feet.

"You have nothing to be afraid of," she assured him. "You know, concerning your brotherly reservations."

"Oh, Hayden. The fact that you even know what I'm talking about proves that you're wrong," he chuckled quietly, gazing down at her. "Just know that I have no morals. I will kill him."

"I don't believe that for a second."

"I've deceived you for too long with my empathy."

"I love you," she told him, pulling herself toward him again.

"I love you, too," he replied, gently rubbing her hair as she grabbed his shirt and burrowed her face against him. Caleb was silent for a moment and Hayden just took a moment to spend with her brother. Though Caleb wasn't much older than her, he had been forced to take on far too much of a parental role for her. When their mother worked, Caleb had been the one to prepare dinners and do most of the chores. Over that time, he had developed an uncanny ability to know exactly what she needed. Hayden wanted to tell him how much she appreciated everything he had done and become for her, but instead she started laughing.

"Hey, Hayden," Caleb nudged her, apparently mistaking the movement for sobs.

"I'm okay," she assured him, smiling as she pulled away to look at him.

"Oh no, I know," he shrugged. "I was just going to tell you that I hadn't actually planned the timing of this whole thing well. We should probably head back before it gets too dark to see."

Chapter 3

Night of the Full Moon
Cailean

Eager to get the transformation over with, Cailean tossed his bag onto his shoulder and hovered near the door. He and his wolf had gone through a difficult few years, but Cailean was beginning to reach a copacetic medium. As a child, he had wanted nothing more than to transform and be like his father. He'd always felt different from everyone else and he hadn't lived a day where he wasn't forced to hide a secret, so Cailean had taken to the transformation as an excuse to feel like an outcast. When Brooke had come into his life, though, she drained that feeling from his heart and negated the necessity of using the transformation as a crutch. For the first time in his life, Cailean had not actively willed himself to transform. Of course, that was the first night he did, and Brooke paid for it. After that, Cailean hated the wolf for a while – blaming it for his childish decisions. Over the past few months, though, he had come to terms with his own mistakes.

Brooke had taken well to the transformation, so that had helped lessen his guilt. Though there were struggles with lycanthropy, they both seemed to agree that one night every month was a small price to pay for the benefits it carried. Their senses and reflexes were far superior to those of their peers and their strength unparalleled. Aside from that, the healing rendered any injury negligible and kept their skin flawless.

The only potential concern was posing a threat to others. Slowly, though, Cailean had accepted the fact that he wasn't doomed to be a monster or a menace. With his father's guidance, he hadn't caused any damage whatsoever since scratching Brooke. Since his father had found a secluded place deep in the woods which was off limits to the public, that risk was significantly reduced. Even if they did harm humans, they wouldn't be to blame. Any nosy people wandering around in restricted areas of the woods were responsible for their own fate. Given that it was nearly impossible for Cailean to harm anyone he cared about anyway, he wasn't particularly concerned.

Bouncing on the balls of his feet, Cailean anxiously waited by the door. Though the fear, both for himself and others, had mostly faded with experience, he was still antsy to get through the night. Surrendering control of his body still made him uncomfortable, so he just wanted to get through the night and get back to using the wolf's strength to live his own life.

Long before Brooke approached the door, Cailean heard her footsteps down the street. As she drew near, he met her outside and greeted her with a hug. When he stepped back, he gave himself a moment to admire her in the orange glow of the setting sun. Wearing the same flowy shirt and loose-fitting pants which she wore every month, she still looked stunning. Her wavy hair fell unevenly over her shoulders and she stood with most of her weight on her left leg, leaning to the side slightly. When she raised her eyebrows and waved her hand in front of him, Cailean realized that he had been staring for longer than he'd intended to. Shaking his head, he lifted his eyes to meet hers.

"Are you ready?" She asked, nodding toward the street. Cailean started to assert that he was waiting for his father, but as he followed his gaze he saw Aldric already standing at the foot of the porch steps. Simultaneously, he was impressed at his father's stealth and embarrassed of his own distraction. For him to completely fail to hear the door open and sense the movement of another person behind him clearly meant he was far more distracted than he had realized.

"Yeah, of course," Cailean stammered. Moving quickly, he hopped down the stairs to catch up as his father began confidently leading the two of them down the street. Within moments, they had crossed the tree line and the asphalt beneath their feet was replaced with soft dirt and scattered leaves. The orange and red hues painted the world around them as the sun slowly fell from the sky. As they walked, the luminosity of the sun faded and was replaced by the dim shine reflected by the full moon rising to take its place.

The scent of meat roasting over a campfire wafted with the breeze, assaulting Cailean's nose. Turning his head to the left, he tried in vain to locate the source. Continuing to move forward with his father, he kept his eyes trained in the general direction from which the scent came. Finally, through the darkness he saw a flicker of orange and a modest plume of smoke.

"Do you smell that?" Cailean asked the group. Though the answer was obvious, he was more concerned with addressing the issue of the campers than actually receiving a response to his immediate question.

"Let's pick up the pace," Aldric responded, indirectly answering Cailean's question. "We are still a few miles from our usual space, but they are too far into the woods for my comfort. As a precaution, we will push out further."

Although his father wasn't looking at him, Cailean instinctively nodded his approval as the three of them sped up. In the darkness, Cailean found himself stumbling over roots and hesitating as he tried to avoid low-hanging branches. Watching his father expertly navigate the trees, though, he eventually gave up on trusting his own eyesight and blindly repeated Aldric's movements. Impressed, he wondered how long it would take for him to find the confidence and the ability to move so masterfully through the darkness.

Passing one of the many signs embedded in the ground around the perimeter of that section of the woods, Cailean wondered why the town had chosen that specific area to restrict from the campers. He assumed it was due to a high risk of aggressive fauna, which was far more fitting than city officials likely understood. The werewolves who had made those woods their home were far more dangerous than any potential wildlife. By trying to protect humans from a minimal threat, they'd allowed a larger one to move in.

"I can still smell the campfire," Brooke sheepishly informed the others as Aldric slowed to a stop. "Should we keep walking?"

"We won't be able to walk far enough to completely avoid the scent," Aldric explained. "Wolves are territorial creatures, though. They tend to spent most of their time in the center of their territory, and they won't venture too far – especially near humans – except in search of food. Smells of humans and smoke tend to scare them off. That said, I know Cailean and I won't be an issue, but did you eat enough, Brooke?"

"I don't know," she shrugged. "I definitely ate more than anyone else. I didn't want anyone getting suspicious."

"Are you hungry?"

"Not really."

"Not really or no?"

"No, I'm not," she assured him, standing taller as a response to the urgency in his voice.

"Here," he took the bag from his shoulders and retrieved a small container and removed the lid. Dropping the bag on the ground near a tree, he pulled a large piece of brisket. Hesitantly, Brooke accepted the protein as he extended his arm and offered it to her.

"I'm really okay," she affirmed, although she was already holding the food. She knew as well as Cailean that her words no longer mattered, and Aldric would order her to eat simply to be safe. With that mutual understanding, Aldric merely widened his eyes in a silent order. With an embarrassed sigh, Brooke slunk back toward the trees and ate quietly.

"Do you always bring extra food, Father?" Cailean asked.

"You can't smell it?"

"I suppose I can," Cailean pondered, trying to think back to the past. Cailean had likely subconsciously registered the scents, but his mind was always elsewhere. As he allowed himself to think, he began remembering previous full moons and the subtle aroma of meat emanating from his father's bag. He wondered if those memories were accurate or simply fabricating themselves as he tried to confirm his father's suspicions.

"It serves two purposes. Moments like this are the first and most obvious. However, the subtle scent of food at my bag will keep the wolves nearby. If they get hungry they will be more likely to dig through the bag than to go near a camp. Of course, they're even more likely to hunt a deer because werewolves seem to enjoy the hunt and the kill more than simply acquiring food, but it serves as an extra layer of defense for any nearby humans."

Cailean nodded, greedily consuming the information as if it were a meal of its own. Brooke, wiping her fingers on her pants, rejoined the group. Aldric turned his attention to the sky and Cailean saw a brief flash of pain wash over his father's eyes.

"It's time," he sighed, affirming what they already knew. "I'll be close, just past these trees."

Without another word, Aldric turned away and removed his shirt. Before stripping down, he took cover in the nearby foliage. Cailean assumed his father was trying to avoid making Brooke feel uncomfortable, but he didn't seem to understand how difficult a feat it was to find the limits of her comfort zone. Of course, it was also possible that he himself was the uncomfortable one, but Cailean doubted it. As old as he was, it didn't seem likely that his father was concerned about social norms.

Cailean could practically feel the wolf scratching at his intestines, clawing its way out at the expense of his internal organs. Hearing a grunt from Brooke, he turned his eyes toward her to see that she was clearly experiencing the same pain. She slid her shirt off, revealing her bare chest. Without a chance to brace himself, Cailean found his mind to be completely useless and his muscles vehemently opposed to the idea of turning away as every part of him was enraptured with her body.

"I don't understand boys," Brooke teased, dropping her shorts to the ground. Folding her clothes, she walked toward him. "Can I put these in your bag?"

"Yeah," Cailean nodded, pulling himself free of his trance and bringing the bag toward her. Gratefully, she unzipped the bag and stowed her clothes before giving him space and backing away.

"Your dad seems confident that we won't run that far," she whispered, looking back toward the fire.

"Father has been doing this a long time," Cailean assured her.

"I just hope he's right."

"I trust him," Cailean affirmed. "Anyway, he's right. Can't you feel a bit of inexplicable fear as you smell that fire? The wolves won't go anywhere near it. As long as the campers stay by the fire, I can't imagine the wolves will want anything to do with them.

Night of the Full Moon
Hayden

Droning on about a time he'd hiked across some nearby mountains, William, Chase's dad continued another of his stories as they sat around the campfire. Given the diversity of experiences he'd had, Hayden wasn't surprised that he enjoyed telling those stories. She hadn't heard of many people who travelled quite as much as he did, and he was overflowing with knowledge and experience of the world around them. Although the stories in themselves were somewhat interesting, she slowly became exhausted listening to the same person dominate the conversation. Hayden tried to be polite and attentive, but she eventually found herself dozing off and dropping a marshmallow into the flame. She couldn't help but wonder if his dad was simply trying to impress his son's girlfriend or if he actually loved hearing himself talk.

Chase's young sister sat on the floor between her father and Hayden. More than once, Hayden caught the child curiously examining her. When Hayden turned her attention to the girl, though, she cowered behind her dad. On the other side of the fire, Chase's mother sat on a blanket with her knees pulled up and her arms draped over them. Watching the intrigue on her face as her husband told a story she'd probably heard countless times, Hayden believed she had found the perfect picture of love.

"You'd be surprised how many caves are around here, too," William continued after a brief pause.

"Oh, yeah?" Hayden asked.

"One time, during a camping trip, I was looking for a place to set up camp. I didn't realize until I heard the bear that I had wandered into its territory. Of course, this was back before I had a lot of experience, so I didn't know what to do. My first thought was to make myself bigger, but it didn't seem intimidated when I puffed out my chest.

"The next best thing, though, was to run. I ran to a nearby cave. A little ironic, isn't it? Hiding from a bear in a cave. I saw an entrance small enough for me to squeeze through, though, so I tossed my bag in and crawled through some mud. The bear growled at me for an hour before it finally gave up. I bet it had just had babies or something.

"Anyway, with the bear on that side of the cave, I decided to explore a bit and see if there was another exit. Luckily, I did know how to start a fire. I wrapped a spare shirt around a stick and made a torch, which lasted about as long as you'd think. Still, it gave me time to look around for a while and explore a few passages. I must have wandered around that cave for hours before I finally found an exit. When I crawled out, everything looked familiar.

"I had just gone in a huge subterranean circle. Which, obviously, meant that the bear was still around. I decided to just set up camp in the cave. I wouldn't recommend that – at least not this one. You never know when it's going to rain, and it's mostly just mucky anyway. It kept me alive until morning, though. Then I just left and continued on my way, carefully looking for any bear activity."

"Was that close to here?" Hayden asked, failing miserably to conceal the horror in her voice. Paranoid by the slightest sound, she looked around the campsite and tried to see into the woods beyond.

"Oh, don't worry about that. This was before I moved here. Oh, one thing that I did see here though," he started, excitement perpetually residing in his voice.

"Dad," Chase interrupted. "I am excited to hear that story, but maybe not on Hayden's first time camping."

"Oh, are you scared of bugs?" His father asked, his eyes widening with a legitimate sense of concern. Hayden lowered one eyebrow as the confusion set in. Unsure of how to respond, she remained quiet.

"I don't think it's the bugs," Chase answered for her.

"Oh, then don't even worry. This one was just about a weevil."

"The fire is getting low," Chase's mom interrupted, standing and reaching toward the sky as she stretched.

"Hayden and I can go get some more firewood. You guys just stay and relax," Chase offered. Hayden carefully concealed the joy on her face and simply nodded her agreement.

"Do you want to come, Chloe?" She offered, turning toward Chase's little sister. Silently, she shook her head and hid behind William. As Hayden followed Chase away, though, she could feel Chloe's eyes drilling a hole in her back.

The two of them walked in silence for a while. After listening to two hours' worth of stories, she appreciated the reprieve. As they put more distance between themselves and Chase's family, the sound of his father's next story eventually became lost in the trees, leaving only the quiet chirping of crickets.

"Sorry," Chase chuckled quietly when they were well beyond earshot of his family.

"For what?" She asked.

"I know my family can be a bit overwhelming. My dad just likes to talk and I think he's scared you won't like him."

"Why would he think that?" She asked. Whether or not it was logical, she was slightly offended that he felt he had to try so hard to earn her favor.

"Humans tend to be self-conscious. I would argue that any denial of that is simply an attempt to cover up that embarrassing feeling with something else."

"That was pretty profound. Spoken like someone who has experience," Hayden teased, stopping in a clearing and holding Chase's hand tightly. For the first time during their walk, she could actually see the features on his face, and she wanted to cherish that moment.

"Oh, did I forget to tell you? I'm not human," he shrugged. "I just live with them so I know a lot about them."

"Is that so?"

"Yeah, I hope that's not a dealbreaker."

"The lack of humanity isn't a big deal, but living with them is a little weird to be honest."

With a laugh, Chase turned and gently tugged on her hand. After a moment, he stopped again to reach down and pick up a particularly large branch. Having completely forgotten that they were searching for something, Hayden hadn't bothered to look around. To make up for that, she tried to be hyper-vigilant for the rest of the gathering experience. She and Chase ventured deep into the forest, and, though she would never admit it to him, she appreciated the break from his family. Chase confidently strode past a "no trespassing" sign, so she didn't bother to ask about it. Devoting her full attention to finding adequate firewood, she kept her eyes glued to the ground and, as if silence would aid her eyesight, her lips sealed.

Instead of being useful, though, she ended up succumbing to her paranoia. A cracking branch from the trees to her right pulled her eyes toward it. She heard another come from the foliage to her left, though, and she turned her eyes in that direction.

"Did you hear that?" She whispered, grabbing Chase's forearm and pulling him to a stop.

"We probably scared an animal off," he whispered comfortingly. As if in disagreement, though, a loud howl erupted from somewhere nearby. Hayden's ears rang after the beast fell silent once again. Barely able to stand, Hayden found herself petrified with fear.

"It's okay, just stay calm. Wolves don't tend to attack people," he assured her. Low hanging branches broke from a tree to her right, though, and she stumbled backward, dropping to the ground. First, the snout poked into the dimly lit clearing around her. Slowly, the beast continued to move closer.

There was no question in Hayden's mind that Chase was right. Whatever it was, it clearly wasn't wolves. While it stood on all-fours, they were far too large and there didn't seem to be quite enough fur. If anything, it looked like a mangy bear staggering toward them. Baring its teeth, it snarled at Chase, who stepped between it and Hayden. An angry fire burned in its mystical golden eyes and it confidently strode toward him. Chase slowly squatted down and pulled a knife from a holster on his leg. With his attention focused on the animal in front of him, Chase didn't seem to register the movement to his left. Stealthily, another animal emerged and walked to join the battle.

"Are… Are those bears?" Hayden stammered, her voice cracking with fear.

"I… Just stay behind me," he told her calmly. Hayden wasn't sure how he could be so collected, but she appreciated that one of them was. The creature's friend approached from the left and Hayden could see a murderous glare as its light green eyes shone against the darkness of the forest.

Chase waved his knife in front of himself menacingly. When that failed to produce a result, he stood taller and tried to tense the muscles in his arms and chest. Still, the beasts continued to approach. Chase growled at them, but they only hungrily returned the gesture.

"Hayden, I want you to back away slowly," Chase whispered. "Go get my dad. They aren't far, just go directly away from us. I'll keep them from following you."

"I can't leave you with these things," she argued urgently.

"I'll be okay. They're just animals."

"They're huge," Hayden argued. The next moment happened more quickly than she could process. Suddenly, Chase's left hand was on the center of her chest and she felt herself falling backward. At the same time, Chase stepped to the side and dodged as one of the animals lunged at him. As he avoided the attack, he pulled the knife across the torso of the beast. To Hayden, the cut seemed as though it would be enough to kill it. Still, she pushed herself backward and debated following Chase's orders.

With Chase distracted, though, the other animal jumped at him from behind and viciously dragged its claws across his back. Agonized, Chase dropped to his knees and the beast seemed to be rearing back for a second attack. Finding a rock on the ground, though, Hayden procured a weapon of her own. In a sudden burst of courage, she threw the rock at the green-eyed animal. Snarling, it snapped its head toward her.

The yellow-eyed assailant barely seemed hindered by the gaping wound in its side. In fact, as Hayden searched for a mark, all she could see was the blood matting the bits of fur and skin which surrounded the deep laceration.

Supporting its pack mate, the other wolf growled at Hayden as well. Both of them apparently decided to eat her first, because they began trotting toward her. Struggling to his feet behind them, Chase whistled loudly to pull their attention back to himself. Before taking the chance to gauge the efficacy of his distraction, he charged the green-eyed monster and jumped onto its back, plunging the knife into its spinal cord. Violently shaking him off, it pulled his grip from the knife. Snarling, it pinned him to the ground as the knife slammed into the dirt a few feet away.

Unable to contain her fear, Hayden screamed as Chase fell. Both of the monsters turned toward her as the shriek reverberated throughout the woods. Utilizing the adrenaline pumping through her veins, she rushed forward and drove her foot into the nose of the beast pinning Chase. The shock forced it to release him and stumble backward, but the other animal angrily rushed toward Hayden.

Fighting against the apparent pain, Chase struggled to his feet and tackled it before it could reach Hayden. Surprised, it flailed its head and gnashed its teeth. Without too much effort, it was able to launch Chase backward and free itself. Vengefully, it crawled toward him with drool falling from its snout. The other one had recovered as well, so it began circling the two of them.

"Run, Hayden," Chase commanded, choking on blood as he tried to encourage her to leave.

"I won't leave you," Hayden stammered, miserably trying to sound confident as she searched for any other weapon. Any sudden movement would without a doubt result in both of the animals rushing forward, so she tried to stay controlled. Still, she could feel her chest heaving with terror and her hand twitching as if reaching toward any rock she could see.

Suddenly, Hayden was deafened by a blast not too far from her. As she saw the flash, she dropped to the ground and instinctively covered her head. The ringing in her ears lasted a full minute before finally subsiding. As the world around her quieted down, she finally found the courage to look up.

Their attackers had fled, leaving a trail of blood behind them. Chase was on the floor a few feet from her, barely conscious as blood continued to pour from his back. His father was crouched beside him with a shotgun leaning against his leg. Scrambling to her feet, Hayden rushed toward Chase.

"How can I help?" She asked, talking slightly too loudly.

"Turn him over," Chase's father ordered. Nodding, Hayden placed one hand on the side of his knee and the other on his hips. Together, the two of them turned Chase onto his stomach. As they did, he groaned in protest.

"How bad is it?" Chase coughed when neither of them responded. Hayden fumbled for words but holding back the nausea became her sole function. The creature's claws had scratched into Chase's trapezius muscle and left four gashes trailing down his back. In the two central ones, Hayden could see pieces of white which she was convinced were bones.

"That bad, then?" He tried to lighten the situation, but it was clear in his voice that he was even more scared than Hayden.

"Can you shoot?" His father finally asked. As he spoke, he pulled Chase's shirt off. Realizing that it was coated in dirt, he tossed it to the side and removed his own as well. Before Hayden could process any of the information, he pressed his shirt against the scratch.

"I… I don't think he can move," Hayden stammered. Chase's dad gently placed one of his hands on hers and moved it toward the cloth absorbing some of the blood pouring from Chase's back. When her hands were on his back, he pushed against them, silently instructing her to firmly hold it in place.

"Not him."

"Oh. Oh, no. No, I've never even held a gun." The idea of holding a gun didn't even have a chance to scare her as she was distracted by the blood seeping through the shirt and covering her hands.

"It's easy. Point and pull the trigger. They probably won't come back, but if they do, I need you to be ready. I'll leave this with you and I'm going to get the first aid kit and the others."

"Don't leave me here," she begged.

"I'm sorry, Hayden, but we don't have a choice. I have to clean the wound. Just keep pressure on it and if they come back, all you have to do is shoot. They'll run."

"Okay…" She muttered as tears formed in her eyes. He stood and ran back toward the camp. Hayden's chest heaved as she leaned against Chase, trying to stop the bleeding. With time, she was able to slowly compose herself. The blood flow seemed to be slowing down, but the shirt was drenched.

Hesitantly, she pulled it back to check the wound. Though his entire back was red, the scratch itself wasn't nearly as bad as she had originally thought. In her panic, it had appeared far deeper and more threatening. When she looked at it again, though, it was clear that it hadn't cut to the bone. In fact, she wasn't even convinced it would need stitches.

Chase grunted, stifling a scream. Looking over him, she caught a glimpse of his face. Though he tried to remain silent and not frighten her, she could see on his face that he was in terrible pain. Finally, the anguish broke loose as he howled in agony. Hayden wondered if the claws had severed nerve endings, because the depth of the wound didn't seem to warrant what he was experiencing. Of course, she only knew the minimal first aid her mother had taught her, so she was far from an expert.

"Chase," she tried to comfort, but his wails drowned out her soothing voice. Finally, it clicked and Hayden realized that the pain had started after she removed pressure. Chase's father's shirt was too soaked to be of much use, so she removed her own and pressed it against his back. The force didn't seem to be enough to end Chase's suffering, though, as he just continued to scream and writhe. Desperately, Hayden leaned against his back and used all of her weight to press against the wound.

She could feel her shirt dampening in her hands, but the process was significantly slower than it had been just a few minutes prior. Relieved, she surmised that the blood was clotting. As she saw the deep red color begin to absorb into her shirt, though, and spread slowly, she wondered how much blood he'd lost. The garment on the floor was saturated with the viscous liquid and she was still mopping up quite a bit. Even if the wound stopped bleeding, the blood loss alone would be enough to cause issues.

"How can such a small wound be bleeding this much?" She thought. It was possible that she had been correct the first time. Maybe it was nothing more than a blind hope which had tricked her into thinking that the wound was insignificant the second time.

"I'm sorry," Chase grunted through gritted teeth.

"For what?" She laughed, despite the circumstances. The only person she knew who could possibly apologize for being a burden while struggling against apparently immense pain was Chase. Most people would at the very least wait until they were stabilized to ask forgiveness.

"This isn't exactly the best first camping experience," he replied. His words became clearer as he spoke, so she was hopeful that the pain was somewhat subsiding. Leaning against him more, she tried to apply even more pressure.

"You can apologize for that later."

"It doesn't hurt as much," he mused. Somehow, any trace of suffering had crept away from his voice. Confident that it was due at least in part to her pressing against the wound, Hayden exerted as much energy as she could muster to increase her efforts.

"It's weird," Chase muttered quietly, trying to roll over. Hayden, sitting next to his side, refused to let him move. Locking her elbows, she held her weight down over his back.

"You can't move, I won't be able to push as much."

"That's okay, Hayden," Chase comforted, reaching his hand back and searching for hers. When he realized he couldn't reach it, he gave up and let it fall back to the ground.

"I have to make sure to stop the bleeding."

"I'm sorry to ask," Chase said slowly, ignoring her desperation. He took a deep breath as if the question concerned him. "Can you check?"

"Check?"

"Is it still bleeding? How bad is it?"

"No. No way. Last time I let up I thought you were going to die."

"I think the bleeding has stopped, Hayden. Anyway, you're kinda hurting me."

"I'm sorry," she replied quickly, pulling back slightly.

"I just need to know if it's still bleeding," he reiterated.

"Okay," she hesitantly agreed. Slowly and unsurely, she pulled the shirt away from his wound. Blood stuck to his skin surrounding the wound, limiting her ability accurately gauge the severity of the wound. Gently, she tried to wipe away some of the blood. As she did, no more came to replace it.

"I think the bleeding has stopped," she sighed, relieved.

"Well, that's good."

Hayden continued to brush the blood away. Somehow, the wound seemed even more shallow than it had moments ago. As she cleaned the area a bit, more forcefully rubbing off some of the stubborn spots with her hand, she was unable to find any break in the skin. There was a clear mark where he had been scratched, but beyond that, she couldn't locate any source of the bleeding.

"Chase…" She muttered, unsure of what exactly to tell him. Confusion overwhelmed her and she struggled to formulate a sentence, but the concerned tone was clear.

"What? Tell it to me straight," he responded, attempting to sound confident and masculine but unable to hide the fear in his shaky voice.

"It's… gone."

Chapter 4

29 Days Until the Full Moon
Cailean

Groggily, Cailean shielded his eyes from the sun shining through the canopy above him. With a groan, he pushed himself up and sat, leaning forward and squinting as he examined the area. At first, he remembered nothing and wondered how far he'd run from the spot where they changed. Nothing seemed familiar, and typically the wolf seemed to return to somewhere near where it had transformed. Thanks to that penchant for territorialism and familiarity, Cailean recognized most of the areas around their usual spot. As his brain woke up, though, the fogginess began to clear up. Cailean remembered smelling the campfire and walking further into the woods. Wherever he was, he was probably closer to that new spot.

Climbing to his feet, Cailean stretched and then rubbed his eyes as he tried to convince his body that he was awake. Glancing around the area, he couldn't see the others. Without too much effort, though, he was able to find his bag. Opening the bag, he grabbed his pants. When he looked down at his legs to put them on, he noticed a bit of blood on them. With an annoyed groan, he pulled his pants on. Buttoning them, though, he saw significantly more blood dried onto his stomach.

"I bet the deer was delicious," Cailean muttered, sarcastically talking to the wolf as if it were a separate entity. "But could you be less of a slob next time?"

Returning his attention to the bag, he reached in and retrieved Brooke's shirt. Bringing it to his nose, he inhaled deeply. As he dropped the shirt to his side, Cailean smelled the air around him. With his senses enhanced due to the recent full moon, Cailean followed his nose and searched for Brooke. Finally, he found her shamelessly sprawled out in a bed of leaves.

"Brooke," he greeted, trying to gently wake her. When she didn't respond, he repeated her name and shook her a bit. Brooke was absolutely covered in blood as well, but Cailean still hadn't seen any sign of their kill. Shaking her shoulder more violently, he finally got a reaction out of her. With a moan, she rolled onto her side and turned her back to him. Despite the fact that she was clearly in perfect health, Cailean felt a flash of concern as he saw the blood crusted onto her back.

"Alright, Brooke, let's get up."

"No," she protested, elongating the word.

"Why not?"

"Weekend," was the only word she spoke. Cailean was fully aware of her fondness of the full moons which fell on a weekend because it allowed her to sleep in. Regardless, he would feel more comfortable if she weren't lying completely naked in some unfamiliar part of the forest. Though he had no doubt she was more than capable of defending herself, his natural protective instincts steered him away from leaving her in any situation which may present any possibility of conflict.

"I don't know where we are," he explained. "I don't want to leave you here alone."

"Then lie down with me," she suggested.

"You're covered in blood."

"What are you afraid of?" She laughed quietly, finally forcing herself to sit up. Cailean averted his eyes as she did, but eventually gave up on trying to respect the privacy which she wasn't concerned about. "It's not like you're going to get sick."

"Fair enough," he admitted. "I just want to go wash up."

"Fine," she grunted, dragging out the vowels to display her discontent. Brooke stood and took the shirt from Cailean, resting it on her shoulder. "So where's the river?"

"I just figured we'd follow the sound of running water."

"Alright," she agreed. Both of them fell silent as they tried to listen for any motion. A quiet trickling pulled Cailean's attention and he led the way. Ducking through foliage and pushing aside branches, Cailean navigated toward the river.

"Wow," Brooke muttered, grabbing Cailean's arm and pulling him to a stop. She nodded toward the ground to their left, which was covered in fresh blood.

"I guess it got away," Cailean shrugged.

"Are you kidding? Nothing could lose this much blood and walk away. No, I think we ate it."

"Gross."

"Yeah, bones and all. It's the only logical conclusion."

"I really wish you were wrong."

Cailean tore his eyes away and continued his voyage toward the river. Though he knew the wolf occasionally hunted animals at night, he had never known it to crush and consume the bones as well. Of course, he had no doubt that it would be able to.

"I've heard that bone marrow actually tastes really good," Brooke continued, staying close to Cailean.

"Maybe, but what about the actual bones?" Cailean shivered, nauseated by the idea of eating a bone.

"I mean, they're dogs."

"I can't argue with that," Cailean accepted. "But I'm going to convince myself that you ate the intestines."

"Oh, why'd you have to make me think of that?" Brooke groaned.

"Hey, I'm just saying, logical conclusions and all."

"Yeah, yeah. Just be quiet, I can't hear the river."

"I'm sorry, you can't play your own game anymore?"

"Shut up," she laughed, nudging Cailean forward. As they walked, the trickling of the stream grew more prominent until they finally saw the stream cutting through the trees. Brooke dropped the shirt which she'd been carrying and jumped into the water. Following her, Cailean knelt over the edge of the water and splashed some onto his ribs to wash away the blood. When they had both cleaned themselves up adequately enough to avoid strange looks on the walk home, Brooke walked ashore and squeezed water out of her hair.

"We should get back to where we transformed. My father is probably looking for us," Cailean told her.

"I wonder if he had as much fun as we did last night," she pondered as she retrieved her shirt.

"Well, I doubt the two of us ate an entire deer ourselves."

"Maybe he's the one who ate the intestines."

"Whatever you need to tell yourself," Cailean teased. Brooke reached for Cailean's hand, intertwining her fingers with his. Despite the blood which would be horrible to clean from the hair on his legs and the less-than-ideal waking up situation, Cailean couldn't have imagined a better way to start the morning.

29 Days Until the Full Moon
Hayden

Blankly staring at the wall in front of her, Hayden allowed the warm water to race over her body. Glancing at her arm, she noticed a spot of blood which she had missed, but she failed to find the motivation to lift her hands and wipe it away. The blood seemed to spread, sliding down her bicep and trailing toward her forearm. When she blinked, though, the red vanished, leaving her pale arm free of blemish. The drops of water coating her skin reflected the light from the bulb above her, granting them an orange glow which she mistook for red. Averting her eyes from her wet arm, Hayden lowered her gaze and examined her hands in front of her. Regardless of the amount of time under the water or the copious amounts of soap applied, Hayden couldn't feel clean. Checking once again for blood underneath her fingernails, she spread her hand and carefully checked the back of each finger.

Satisfied with the absence of stains on her hands, she allowed them to fall to her sides and watched the liquid swirl down the drain. Water rained onto her head, travelling down her hair in every direction. A small stream poured from the top of her head, obstructing her view of her feet. Droplets raced down her shoulder as back, tracing the path of least resistance down her body and toward the acrylic of the tub beneath her.

For a moment, Hayden saw the red which had poured from her after the shower she'd taken the previous day. The feeling of blood matting her hair haunted her and she could still feel the force she'd had to apply when she scraped off dried, crusted chunks of Chase's blood. In her imagination, the water was mixed once again with oxygenated blood as the horrifying concoction formed a small vortex near the drain.

Vividly picturing that motion, Hayden felt nausea setting in once again. She tried to force the thought away blinking rapidly and shaking her head until the water appeared clear again. Finding the strength to raise her arms, she ran her fingers through thin strands of wet hair. Separating it into small groups, she felt for any chunks of hair which may still be glued together with the blood of her boyfriend. When her fingers caught on something, she stifled a scream and pulled her hand away. After building up the courage to check again, she found nothing more than a knot in her hair, which she brushed away with her fingers.

Every time she blinked, Hayden could see Chase's back split open. She couldn't accept the notion that the wound had closed so rapidly. The very next day, he'd told her that everything was normal. There was no possible way that what she had seen was legitimate and yet the image was seared into her mind. No amount of distraction could tear away the picture of his bare back with those four deep gashes trailing diagonally along it. Nothing could convince her that she hadn't seen the white bone through the wound. When she closed her eyes, she could see it clearly enough to count his vertebrae.

Biting her lower lip, Hayden continued to will herself not to scream. Though they had returned early from the camping trip, Hayden had taken a shower and cleaned herself off before her family had seen her. While she wasn't fond of hiding things from her mother, she also wasn't particularly interested in talking about what she had seen. Rather than answering any questions, she simply told them that they changed their minds about staying the entire weekend. If Hayden showed any signs of trauma, her mother would realize something was wrong, and she wasn't ready for that.

Instead, Hayden remained silent and fought the urge to blink for as long as she could. Tears welled up in her eyes, though, despite her best efforts. Part of the reason she stood in the shower was, of course, to wash up. The larger part, though, was because it was the only place she believed she could safely acknowledge those emotions.

Feeling defeated, Hayden slowly dropped to a seated position in the shower. She drew her knees to her chest and dropped her forehead onto them, rocking under the downpour. Behind her closed eyes, she saw Chase's impossible wound once again. The tears finally broke past her eyelids and streamed down her face, blending in with the water washing her.

❖ ❖ ❖

"Really, Hayden," Chase assured her. "I'm fine."

"How can that possibly be true?" Hayden pressed, growing annoyed with Chase. Men seemed to be allergic to admitting their own flaws and Chase – as friendly and humble as he was – was no exception to that rule. Even if her concerned psyche had over-exaggerated the wound, there was undeniably an injury of some sort. After the amount of blood that he'd lost the previous night, there was no excuse for him to be doing anything other than sleeping and recovering.

"To be honest," he shrugged. "I have no idea. It's true, though."

"I doubt it. You're probably just delusional. Blood loss has impacted your cognitive function."

"Come on now, you know it didn't have much to impact."

"That's not funny," she muttered. Sitting across from him at a picnic table at the park, Hayden leaned forward and rested her head in her hands. With a sigh, Chase reached out and placed a hand on her forearm.

"I feel fine. I promise," he reiterated. Hayden made no move to return his touch, but she didn't push him away. Motionless, she continued to rest her head in her hands and released a shallow sigh. Leaning back, Chase stayed quiet for a moment before finally conceding. "I'll tell you what, if it makes you happy, I'll go home and rest. I will make sure not to exert myself."

"Really?" Hayden asked.

"Yeah, sure. I could use a relaxing day to read, and who knows, maybe you're right. I wouldn't want to tear the wound back open."

"You're just saying that to make me happy," Hayden complained.

"Entirely," Chase agreed. "It doesn't mean it's not true. I don't want to worry you."

Conflicted, Hayden fell silent again. While she didn't want to be an overbearing girlfriend and try to control him, she also knew from the most basic understanding of first aid that she was right. After a wound like that, Chase shouldn't be walking around and acting like nothing happened. If being slightly controlling was the only way she could keep him safe and make sure he healed, maybe it was worth it.

"I can get some food," she offered, raising her head to look at him. Chase lifted his arms over his head as he stretched. Before he could put too much strain on his back, though, Hayden slapped his arm and he relaxed again, hiding his annoyance relatively well. "To preemptively reward you for being a good patient."

"Oh, yeah? Well, you should have said that earlier," he laughed.

"What do you want?"

"I don't know," he shrugged. "What are you in the mood for?"

"No, you're the one who's hurt. You get to decide."

"And I can't decide to make you happy?"

"That's a trap," she smiled. "What are you craving? Burgers? Soup? A sandwich? Pizza? Milkshakes?"

"Yes."

"Yes what?"

"Any or all of the above," he shrugged. Chase squinted as he thought and Hayden thought he was preparing to give her an actual answer. Instead, all he added was, "I actually am pretty hungry now that I think about it."

"You're not making this easy."

"Honestly, I would just be happy to eat with you."

"Alright, well, I don't think my allowance will accommodate all of those things…"

"We can also make something at my house," Chase offered.

"I'll just surprise you," Hayden finally conceded.

"Are you sure? I don't want you to feel like you have to spend money."

"I'm sure, but you can't be mad if it's sushi. That's what you get for not answering me."

"Okay, okay, then burgers," he groaned jokingly.

"Perfect. I expect you to be resting in bed when I get there though," she ordered, narrowing her eyes at him. After parting ways with a hug, Chase retreated toward his house – which wasn't far from the park – as Hayden tried to figure out how to hold true to her promise. Since nothing was too far away in town, she eventually decided just to walk to the diner.

❖ ❖ ❖

Lying on her bed, Hayden thumbed through one of her mom's textbooks. She had always assumed her mother was a hoarder for keeping every textbook from nursing school sitting on a bookshelf in her room, but as she sought answers, she learned to appreciate the practice. As she flipped through the pages and searched for anything related to wound healing, she realized that retaining all of the books was simply good planning on her mother's part. Aside from having them available in case Hayden or Caleb wanted them, it was beneficial for her to have the reference.

Flipping to the end of the book, Hayden found the index and searched for any mention of the words 'heal' or 'wound,' which led her to a large list of pages. With nothing better to search for, though, she began combing through the list slowly.

"Phases of wound healing," she read aloud, excited to finally find what she was looking for. Skimming the page, though, she didn't find any information which could support or even attempt to explain what she had seen. Judging from the photographs – which were enough to guarantee that she had no interest in following in her mother's footsteps – she concluded that Chase's wound was without question a laceration. The cut had sliced through every layer of skin and the bleeding was far too prominent to assume anything else. From what she'd seen at first, it was quite deep and should have required sutures and immediate medical attention.

Even if she accepted that she had overreacted and assumed it wasn't bad enough to require stiches, nothing lined up with what she witnessed. The book claimed that after clotting, which is what she had assumed was happening while she pressed against the wound, the inflammatory phase alone would last at least a few days. After that, new tissue should have formed as the cells differentiated, slowly filling the broken area.

Scar tissue, which was what already appeared to have formed on Chase's back, should have taken no less than a few weeks. Somehow, though, defying all logic, she had watched it appear on his back in a matter of minutes.

Failing to find any answers in the relevant section of that book, Hayden returned it to the shelf and retrieved another. Determined, she resolved to find some type of answer. Though she didn't want to admit it to him, Chase seemed completely fine. In fact, he almost seemed better than he had before he'd been attacked.

After hours of research, the only conclusion Hayden could possibly reach was that Chase was a superhuman. Even the healthiest of people shouldn't have any hope of recovering as quickly as he did. While it was vaguely possible that he was just extremely convincingly hiding the pain, it was far more likely that he'd healed somehow.

She found herself questioning whether the wound had even happened as she continued to read the books. The blood was undeniable, though. There was physical evidence that it hadn't been some horrible dream.

Hayden spent the entire night skimming her mother's entire library of medical textbooks and clinical research to no avail. There was preliminary research related to grafting to speed up the healing process and a mention of some type of scaffold which she couldn't fully understand, but none of it was even proven. Somehow, Chase had – without medical intervention – healed faster than the greatest researchers could even fathom.

"How?" Hayden whispered to herself, dropping the last of the books onto the bed next to her and staring up at the ceiling. Shaking the possibility of aliens out of her mind, she reached the end of rationality.

Chapter 5

16 Days Until the Full Moon
Cailean

As the bell rang to dismiss him from class, Cailean promptly stood and raced toward the door. Silently, he counted down the minutes until the end of the day. Unfortunately, that number was much higher than he'd like given the fact that first period had just ended.

"The bell doesn't dismiss you," the teacher growled at Cailean.

"That's exactly the bell's intended purpose, actually," Cailean argued, navigating around the desks toward the door. The annoyed teacher blocked his path, standing in front of the door equipped with nothing more than a stern look.

"I will not be disrespected in my classroom."

"That's why I'm trying to leave it," Cailean smirked, clicking his tongue and waving his hand theatrically.

"The entire class will be dismissed when you take your seat, Mr. Phoenix."

"Shall I cite the laws prohibiting illegal detention, or would you like to step aside and cut your losses?"

The teacher scowled at him, but he knew it was a losing battle. Resigned, he moved from the doorway and allowed Cailean to exit. Stepping into the emptiness of the hallway, Cailean triumphantly strode toward his next class. Faking his rude persona was becoming second nature, and Cailean barely even thought about it anymore. In fact, it was slowly taking the place of his natural responses. Moments like that left an impression, though, not only on the teacher but also the students who witnessed it. Rumors would spread like wildfire throughout the school, further helping to draw attention to Cailean. In middle school, he had adopted the abrasive attitude for that very reason – because his father always taught him that the best way to fit in was to stand out. Hunters would never expect a werewolf to place himself intentionally in the spotlight when he knew he was being hunted. Recently, though, Cailean found himself enjoying standing up for himself more and more.

On his way to class, something caught his attention. Though Cailean had no idea what it was, he knew there was something subtle that a part of him was able to perceive. Freezing in the middle of the hall, he allowed other students to pass him as they poured out of their classes. His heart rate climbed steadily but Cailean still couldn't put a name on what he sensed.

Inhaling deeply, he felt the wolf within him react to something in the air. With each breath, his pulse quickened and his senses heightened. A smell separate from the musty hallway and ample body odor emanating from the surrounding students demanded his attention. Blindly following his nose, Cailean nudged his way through the crowd and moved closer to the distinctive aroma.

At the end of his trail, though, he saw nothing spectacular. The scent was powerful, and somehow he knew he had found the source, but there was nothing special about anything he saw. There were just a few students walking in different directions as everyone scrambled to make it to the next class in the allotted minutes. A short redheaded girl wandered off alone in one direction. Walking in another was a smaller group, but Cailean's eyes were for some reason drawn to the blonde girl in the middle. Her wavy hair fell to the middle of her back and bounced with each step. Her thin legs crossed over one another in a gait which Cailean couldn't imagine was comfortable but caused her hips to sway rhythmically. Her pants and long sleeve shirt rendered her far more clothed than most of her peers, and her hourglass figure represented what many would consider the epitome of female beauty. While Cailean had never found himself attracted to any woman other than Brooke, he couldn't help but acknowledge a certain appeal in his mind.

For a brief moment, he allowed himself to be distracted in his thoughts. Although in his eyes, he was completely justified, he felt guilty for even considering her attractive. He quickly pulled his eyes from watching her move.

He finally noticed another hand wrapped around hers. Tracing the masculine arm, Cailean saw an impressive level of definition which he'd only seen matched by the best athletes on his team. The boy wore a tight-fitting shirt which clearly displayed his chiseled back, clearly tracing the lines of his latissimus dorsi. For some reason, Cailean was unable to take his eyes from him. He was the source of whatever smell Cailean had been chasing, and something compelled him to follow the couple.

The ringing of the bell which indicated one minute until the next class rang, pulling Cailean from his trance. While distracted, he watched the couple turn a corner. Instinctively, he took a step to follow them. Stopping himself, though, he turned and walked to class.

❖ ❖ ❖

"For the first time, I think I actually mean this: What are you staring at?" Brooke asked, cutting Cailean with her glare. Since the beginning of lunch, he had been distracted as he stared off at another table. Though he wasn't sure why, he wasn't able to get that other person out of his mind. Watching him eat, Cailean tried to work through any explanation as to why.

"Do you know that guy?" Cailean responded with a question of his own. Tracing his gaze, Brooke turned her head and found the table which held Cailean's attention.

"The guy?" She muttered.

"I'm serious," Cailean insisted.

"You sure you're not looking at that girl? She's hot, that's for sure. Is that why you want to wait? In case you find someone more attractive, like her?"

"Brooke," Cailean groaned. "This really isn't the time, but no, that's not why. I think you're far more attractive than her, and I'm also fond of your personality. I don't even know that girl."

"So it really is her boyfriend you're interested in?" She widened her eyes as she slowly formulated the question.

"Not like that," Cailean laughed. "I just… I can't explain it. There's something off about him."

"What do you mean?"

"You can't see it?" Cailean questioned. Once again, she looked behind her to the table where the two strangers ate together. Over the boy's shoulder, Cailean could see the obscene amount of food he had brought to school. If he ate like that, he without question would have to exercise at least daily to maintain his chiseled physique, but Cailean hadn't seen him in the gym.

"I mean, he looks… strong, I guess?"

"No, well I mean yes, but that's not it. I don't know," Cailean stammered, searching for the best way to explain himself to her. Apparently feeling their stares, the boy turned his head and caught Cailean's eye for a moment. Brooke quickly pivoted, turning her attention back to her food without thinking about the fact that the panicked retreat was more obvious than just staring. Cailean looked away as well, hoping the boy would interpret the gaze as one of another student staring into space rather than intentionally watching him eat.

Silently, Cailean and Brooke continued to eat their food. Cailean, though he tried to focus on Brooke for the remainder of lunch, found his eyes drifting back toward the odd couple across the lunch room. Overpowering all of the smells in the lunch room was that same discernable but unrecognizable scent of that one man.

"That's it!" Cailean exclaimed, slightly too loudly. Calming himself, he leaned toward Brooke and added, "Take a deep breath."

Following his instructions, Brooke opened her mouth and breathed deeply.

"No, through your nose," Cailean corrected with a sigh.

Trying once again, Brooke inhaled as Cailean intently watched her face. At first, there was no reaction whatsoever. After a moment, though, confusion spread across her face like a virus, slowly overtaking every other emotion. Cailean could practically see her thoughts forming as she took a few more breaths and tried to determine the source of the strange scent. Turning her head, she eventually reached the same conclusion he had.

"Okay, so he smells… weird," she admitted.

"I have been trying to figure it out all day," Cailean informed her.

"Honestly, Cailean, he's probably just wearing a pungent cologne." The thought hadn't actually crossed Cailean's mind before, so he gave himself a moment to toy with the idea. Breathing in and focusing, he was able to smell cologne from nearby people, but none of them shared the same unique aroma.

"I don't know," Cailean thought aloud. "I mean, our senses shouldn't be particularly enhanced right now. If it's strong enough for us to smell from over here, how is no one else reacting?"

"Well, I don't know," she accepted slowly, trying to formulate a better idea as she spoke.

"Something is weird about him, Brooke. I just can't figure out what."

12 Days Until the Full Moon
Hayden

Bored in the silence of her room, Hayden sat at her desk and tried to sketch to pass time. Failing to find inspiration she thumbed through her book. Searching through the previous pages, she found a dozen self-portraits which she had used to strengthen her skills, as well as quite a few drawings of other people from memory. With a groan, she decided against something which required too much focus. Of course, she could always go with something cliché such as a fruit bowl. There was a reason it was the first thing most people drew, and she could always practice the fundamentals. Another drawing of a cup of coffee was an option too. Having drawn that hundreds of times, it would be more for a fun distraction than to actually practice the skill.

Offering a quick glance to the drumset in the corner of the room, she toyed with the idea of trying to learn a new song. The thought proved to be fleeting, though, as she decided against making too much noise. Leaning back in the chair with a sigh, Hayden pulled out her phone and decided to try to spend time with Chase instead.

"Hey, what are you up to?"

"Not much," he texted back nearly instantly. *"I'm about to help someone with their math homework though."*

"Oh, who?"

"Steve."

"I didn't know you even knew a Steve," she responded, desperate to keep the conversation going to kill her loneliness.

"I don't, but he needed help."

"Ah, that makes sense." Chase was not the type of person to deny anyone anything if he could help it. Sometimes that was a desirable trait, but others it was exasperating. She would far rather be able to spend time with her boyfriend than know he was helping another student neither of them knew. Pushing the selfish thought from her mind, though, she tried to be happy for his kindness.

"Okay, no worries," she continued in another message. *"What about tomorrow?"*

"I'm actually helping someone tomorrow too. This is a pretty busy week actually. Haha. I've got basketball with some friends who needed another guy to make their numbers even. I can cancel something, I'd rather hang out with you."

"No, don't do that. I'll see you at school, you don't have to cancel your plans."

With a sigh, Hayden tossed her phone on the bed where she couldn't hear it vibrate. The last thing she wanted was to be a controlling girlfriend and demand all of Chase's attention, but it was exhausting working around his philanthropic schedule.

"You alright?" Caleb asked, surprising her as he appeared from the hallway. Her heart racing, Hayden turned quickly to face him.

"You scared me," she scolded.

"Sorry. I was just walking back to my room and I saw you toss your phone."

"It was just onto the bed," she laughed, trying to conceal her emotions. Embarrassed of feeling so annoyed at Chase, she didn't want to complain about it.

"I'll just go back to my room if you want," Caleb shrugged, backing away from the door frame. "I just know that sigh, so I know something is on your mind."

"Yeah," she muttered. With her mom working too frequently to care for the two of them, the parental advice role had often fallen onto her brother, despite their relatively small age gap. Over the years, he had grown capable of recognizing her emotions despite her best efforts. While it was impressive and appreciated, it also made wallowing on her own difficult.

"Do you want to talk about it?"

"I don't know," she sighed.

"That means yes," Caleb surmised. Stepping into her room, he dropped onto the bed and sat facing her.

"It's Chase," she explained. "I have just been feeling… conflicted."

"I like Chase," Caleb told her, smiling to try to ease the tension of the situation.

"I know," she groaned. "Everyone likes Chase. That's kind of the problem."

"You're not getting your familial disapproval fix?"

"No," she laughed, leaning forward and dropping her head. Finally able to formulate her thoughts, she took a deep breath and tried to explain herself, hoping her brother would have the same sage wisdom he often did. "No, it's not that. I just don't feel like a priority to him."

"What makes you say that?"

"I don't know, it's dumb."

"It's you, so I doubt that."

"Alright," she groaned playfully. Despite being overplayed, it was exactly what she needed to hear, and she appreciated her brother for that. "I was pretty bored, right? So I texted Chase and asked him if he wanted to hang out, but he is tutoring some guy tonight. A total stranger who just apparently knows he's good at math."

"That sounds like a kind thing to do."

"Then he's tutoring again tomorrow and he's also playing basketball with some people he doesn't know just because they needed more players."

"Wait, really? I'm not going to lie, that does sound a little frustrating."

"I just don't want to be overbearing, you know? But it seems like he would want to spend time with me instead of a bunch of strangers."

"That is a valid feeling. Have you talked to him about it?"

"No, I know what he'd do. He would just cancel all of his plans and then I'd feel bad about that."

"Well, maybe talk to him about it as a general trend instead of this specific instance."

"I guess."

"I promise you, any man would appreciate you simply being upfront and honest. People are dumb, men and women. Sometimes we all need things spelled out for us."

"Yeah, I guess," she chuckled softly.

"And hey, in the meantime, if you're bored, you could always spend time with your brother. I've heard he's way cooler than Chase anyway."

"You do set a pretty high bar," Hayden concurred.

"Alright, so let's keep you entertained. What do you want to do?"

"Honestly," Hayden answered slowly, allowing herself a moment to think. "I know it may sound boring, but do you think you could drive me to the library?"

"The library?" Caleb laughed.

"It's okay if not, I can ride my bike. I just thought if you're not doing anything you may want to come."

"No, that's fine," Caleb laughed. "You're just a nerd."

"I can't argue that point."

"Alright, let's go to the library. We're apparently going to read. Is there anything specific you're looking for?"

"Well, I've been really interested in learning about wounds recently."

"Wounds?"

"Yeah. Chase got a scratch while we were camping and it healed way more quickly than I thought it would, so that got me thinking about the healing process."

"Wow, you are so much like Mom," Caleb teased.

"You don't have to come," she reiterated.

"No, I already said I would. I've made my bed, now it's time to lie in it. Let's go be nerds."

❖ ❖ ❖

"What is the best way to search for a book?" Hayden wondered aloud, overwhelmed by the massive library.

"It's all split up into categories, I think," Caleb shrugged. "As far as I know, there is no universal system for sorting the books."

"That seems like something you'd think they would invent."

"I don't know, I learned in American history that there was something in place once, but after they lost the technology to effectively handle that amount of data, libraries just started trusting individual librarians to organize things."

"Well, at least that means someone will be able to direct me," she shrugged.

"I'm going to go look around," Caleb told her before walking toward the bookshelves. Hayden made her way to the front desk, but a label caught her eye on the way. A small plaque on the side of the shelves read *'Natural Sciences.'*

Pivoting, she walked into the aisle and scanned the titles of nearby books. The section seemed to have everything from physiology and anatomy to zoology, but all of the books were meticulously organized. Everything was alphabetical and further divided into subcategories which weren't labelled. Hayden wondered if the librarian took extensive care of the library or if those particular books simply hadn't been checked out since they were stocked.

Finding the medical section, Hayden searched for any books she hadn't already found in her mother's extensive library. Nothing promising blatantly jumped out at her, but she was determined to find her answers. There had to be some explanation as to how Chase could possibly have healed so quickly. Even if he was an anomaly to the healing process, someone must have documented a similar case.

"Hey, Hayden, check this out," Caleb greeted, turning the corner and waving a book in the air.

"What is it?"

"I doubt it will be helpful," he shrugged, "but it looks like fun."

"A Catalogue of the Supernatural," Hayden read. "There's no author name."

"I just thought it was cool," Caleb laughed.

"Yeah, it is," she agreed. Hayden had been through so many books describing the natural healing process of humans. Even with the best medical technology available, nothing was able to describe Chase's recovery. In opposition to all logic, she wondered if the answer could actually reside in that book. Refusing to accept the possibility, she shook her head.

"Alright, fine, I'll help you look for real books," he sighed, returning to replace the book. Hayden tried to convince herself not to follow him, but she couldn't quiet the nagging voice urging her to consider the supernatural a miniscule possibility. Nature failed to explain the phenomenon, so maybe that was her last option.

With a quiet sigh, she followed her instincts and stepped out of the aisle. Watching where Caleb turned, she moved toward that row. When she turned the corner, he was already leaving the other end of the aisle and searching for more useful books.

"Okay, Hayden," she muttered. "You've officially gone crazy."

Despite her own scolding, she found the book which Caleb had thoughtfully returned to its perfectly organized place. As she thought about Chase's wound, she saw the broken skin and fragmented bone behind closed eyes. Shaking the image from her head, she peered down at the book. Nothing normal could explain what she had seen. Maybe it was time to accept crazy.

"A Catalogue of the Supernatural," she read, unable to find the name of an author on the old leather-bound notebook. Giving up the search for a name, she thought, *"I guess it makes sense that*

they wouldn't put a name. Who would want to be associated with this?"

When she opened the book, she saw what appeared to be a journal which had been written, and maybe copied, by hand. Flipping through the pages, she saw that they appeared to be in alphabetical order. There was no index, though, and she had no idea what she was looking for anyway. Finding a picture of a strange half-tree half-man being, she decided that was as good a place as any to start, given that they had been in a forest. Briskly skimming the page for relevant information, she ran her eyes over the lengthy explanation.

"The Leshy. The Leshy was hailed as a deity in Slavic mythology – seen as the protector of the forest. In reality, the Leshy is a child of the forest, merely interested in protecting its home. They pose no threat to those who upkeep their territory, but see themselves as the rightful judge, jury, and executioner. For that reason, the Leshy should be handled with caution.

"Strengths: Ability to determine perception – can take on any humanoid shape. Manipulation of local wildlife: often use wolves and bears to do their bidding. Enhanced strength and thickened skin.

"Weaknesses: Feels the pain of the forest – damaging trees in its territory can cause physical pain. As it is closely tied to the forest, fire also poses a significant threat."

Hayden toyed with the idea of a supernatural creature being at fault for their attack. They were attacked by animals, and it was possible that the Leshy was not fond of their use of firewood or dirtying his forest. Shaking the thought away as the crazy idea it was, though, she flipped further into the book. Even in the unlikely event that anything in that book were true, it wouldn't explain how Chase had healed so quickly.

Finding another page showing what appeared to be a normal woman, Hayden stopped again. Although it was far from likely to help her, she skimmed that page as well. If the creature looked human, it may actually apply to Chase.

"The Siren. Typically depicted as female, although this is not a requirement. The siren's song has the power to entrance members of either sex and flood their brains with dopamine and

oxytocin. The sound of their voice is enough not only to convince humans that they are in love, but to drive them to act violently in defense of that love. The Siren was born in ancient times, as there are records of the creature singing Greek sailors to their deaths. Sirens should be treated with extreme caution, as they are highly deadly and vindictive.

"Strengths: Manipulation. Their song will entice any hearers to perform their will without question. It is powerful enough to destroy any logical thought of the listener, rendering them completely unable to act of their own free will.

"Weaknesses: Aside from its song, the Siren is essentially human. Any wound fatal to man would be fatal to this creature as well. Obstructing one's ability to hear takes all power from the Siren."

"Well, I can't pretend this isn't a fun read," Hayden muttered, skimming over the entry. Realizing that she was speaking to herself, she didn't bother finishing the thought about how useless it was. Trying to turn her attention to something more productive, she closed the book. As a precaution, and due to pure curiosity, she opened it again and quickly flipped through to look at the pictures.

"The Banshee. The Mermaid. The Wendigo."

Toward the end of the book, though, one page stole the breath from her lungs. The picture was a perfect representation of the creatures she had seen in the woods. A wolf the size of a bear, snarling viciously to bare its razor teeth.

"The Werewolf. The werewolf is by far the most dangerous of supernatural creatures. It only changes once monthly, on the night of the full moon. When in its wolf form, the beast is nearly invincible, but it has no control. Many werewolves attempt to hide from civilization, but if they change anywhere near people, they will murder everything in sight.

"However, the werewolf is dangerous due to the power it provides the human form. Even when it appears as a man, the wolf has enhanced strength and speed. These are both results of the incredible rate of cellular regeneration. The wolf can heal rapidly, any wound closing up in a matter of seconds. This also allows muscle tissue to repair more quickly, growing faster and stronger than in any man. If any man does survive an encounter with a

werewolf, a scratch will turn him into one of the beasts. Werewolves which aren't purebred (born as children of wolves) can be detected by this scar – the scratch leaves a scar on the otherwise unblemished body of a werewolf.

"The origin of werewolves is unclear, but many stories exist for the first beasts. A popular theory is the curse of a witch, giving powers to a group of men who then scratched others and passed on the curse. Many believe those ancient wolves still walk the Earth, and that they've obtained the capability to control when they transform. There is no evidence to support this hypothesis.

"Strengths: Enhanced strength and speed. When in wolf form, these strengths are even more greatly intensified. Regenerative capabilities. Halted aging process. Heightened senses, especially near the time of the full moon."

Almost dropping the book Hayden controlled herself and slowly closed it, returning it to the shelf. Her eyes widened as she backed away and processed the information, shocked by how many pieces of evidence seemed to line up. The regenerative capabilities explained not only how the beasts continued fighting, but also how Chase could have healed if a scratch had changed him. The evidence was almost enough for her to accept the unlikely accuracy. Refusing to accept that her entire worldview was flawed, though, Hayden closed the book and returned it to the shelf. As she turned to walk away, though, returning to the realm of reality, she couldn't help but think about how perfectly the details lined up. What if the supernatural truly was the only rational explanation?

Chapter 6

3 Days Until the Full Moon
Cailean

"Alright, I have an idea," Cailean whispered to Brooke as the two of them sat at the lunch table. Just before she responded, he heard footsteps and turned to see the suspicious boy and his girlfriend. Holding up a finger, he silently told Brooke to wait before they discussed anything further. Refusing to take his eyes off of the boy, Cailean sneakily watched as the couple walked into the cafeteria. When they sat on the other side of the lunchroom, he finally dropped the finger and turned his eyes back toward Brooke, though he still watched the stranger with his peripheral vision.

"Well, I was going to ask for what," Brooke groaned, not bothering to quiet herself down. "But I think you answered that."

"Oh, yeah," Cailean agreed, not registering her sarcasm until after he'd responded. Rather than reacting to it, though, he remained silent. If he was right, he didn't want the stranger to discover the plot.

"Cailean, you're obsessing over a weird smell."

"I'm telling you, it's more than that," he whispered.

"You can't possibly know that."

"I have a large enough suspicion to warrant further investigation."

"Fine, what is your plan?"

"Talk about him."

"What? We don't even know his name."

"That is indeed a hurdle. I just can't chase him around anymore, I need to know." Movement from the corner of his eye caught Cailean's attention. The boy had looked up and was scanning the room as if he'd heard something which caught his attention. Without speaking, Cailean nodded his head toward the boy. Following his gaze, Brooke watched as he looked around too.

"That was a coincidence," she assessed. Furrowing his brow in disagreement, Cailean clicked his tongue and toyed with the idea of a test for the suspected lycanthrope. Finally decided his curiosity had to be sated, he nodded to himself and inhaled slowly.

"Can you hear me?" Cailean whispered, unsure of whether the hope in his voice was for a response or a lack of one. The stranger's head shot around and he briefly made eye contact with Cailean. Looking away, he grabbed his head and rested his elbows on the table.

"Okay, I'll admit, that was a little strange," Brooke admitted hesitantly.

"I know what you are," Cailean whispered menacingly. The boy's head twitched, but he clearly tried to avoid looking back toward Cailean.

"You don't have to be a jerk about it," Brooke sighed.

"Meet me in the hallway," Cailean continued, changing his tone to a slightly friendly suggestion. "I just want to talk."

When the boy looked up, his eyes caught Cailean's and he looked confused. At first, he looked away, clearly trying to ignore what he'd heard. After a moment, though, he sighed and placed his hands on the table, pressing against it as he stood.

"I'll be right back," the stranger told his girlfriend. Cailean watched as he walked toward the exit. Allowing enough time to pass to avoid being suspicious, Cailean stood himself.

"Don't hurt him," Brooke pleaded.

"Am I that much of a brute?"

Her silent response was a stern look. Cailean opened his mouth to argue, but he quickly realized he had no ground on which to stand.

"I'll try not to hurt him," he agreed. Trying to contain his enthusiasm, he carefully monitored his pace as he trudged across the cafeteria toward the door through which the stranger had exited. As he walked through it, he saw that the boy was about to give up, turning back toward the lunchroom. Cailean allowed the door to close as they both stared at each other in silence. The stranger seemed surprised, so he was clearly having trouble formulating a greeting. Cailean, though he had planned that encounter for nearly a month, still found himself at a loss as well.

"What are you?" Cailean finally asked.

"My name's Chase," the boy responded, clearly mistaking Cailean's question.

"Oh, right. I'm Cailean," he responded. "Cailean Phoenix."

"Nice to meet you," Chase responded, cheerfully despite also being somewhat awkward.

"Who are you with?"

"I'm not sure I understand."

"Who is your pack?"

"My… pack?"

"Stop playing dumb, I know! I've seen all the clues, and I know you heard me."

"I'm sorry, Cailean, but I really don't know what you're talking about."

"We own this town," Cailean threatened, malice simmering in his voice. The pride he held in his father's territory was beginning to reveal itself to Cailean, who hadn't realized before that moment the he had even felt it. Suddenly, everything fell into place. The wolf had smelled another werewolf which wasn't in his pack and recognized it as a threat to his land.

"You what?" Chase laughed.

"You think I can't tell that you're a werewolf?" Cailean spat, rage boiling in his veins. He tried to no avail to calm himself down. For some reason, he saw the presence of another pack as an invasion and he couldn't stop himself from reacting passionately.

"Okay, is this some kind of joke?"

"I don't know," Cailean growled. "Are you joking? Or are you seriously trying to convince me that I'm wrong?"

"Cailean, werewolves don't exist."

"Alright, enough," Cailean snapped. In a quick motion, he threw his fist in a hook toward Chase's jaw. Connecting the blow, he felt the boy's jaw break from its hinge. In reaction, Chase dropped to the side and clutched his face, muttering expletives. Cailean's instincts told him to continue his attack, but he was able to reel himself in slightly as his opponent writhed on the floor.

"Tell your alpha to leave my town. If you don't, whatever happens is on you."

Cailean watched as Chase pushed his jaw back into place. The bones healed and Chase stood, backing away from Cailean.

"You're insane," Chase reiterated. "You could have broken something."

The fear in Chase's eyes would have been enough to convince Cailean if he hadn't just witnessed the boy healing at an inhuman rate. If nothing else, Chase was a good actor. Regardless, he had no place in Aldric's territory and it was Cailean's job to enforce that.

Chase fell through the door back to the cafeteria, retreating back to his seat. Not long after, Brooke found her way to Cailean in the hallway.

"How did it go?" She asked.

"Not well," he admitted. "But I mean, not the worst it could have gone. I guess."

Night of the Full Moon
Hayden

"Do you want to hear this new song I found?" Hayden asked, eagerly bouncing on the balls of her feet. For some reason, showing people music seemed to be one of the greatest joys in her life. Every time she introduced someone to a song they liked, she felt an admittedly unearned sense of accomplishment.

"Yeah, sure," Chase laughed quietly, rubbing his temples as she spoke. Trying not to be offended or take his action as an implication that her voice was giving him a headache, she turned and retrieved the record. After lifting the top of the record player, she carefully set the black disk onto the center and gently placed the needle on the edge.

As it began to spin, Hayden inched away and fell onto her bed. Chase, ever the respectful gentleman, sat on her desk chair. The chair was turned around backwards, and Chase was leaning forward resting on the back support with his head resting on his forearms. Finally, the needle slipped into the groove on the record and the quiet music surrounded them.

Visibly uncomfortable, Chase shifted in his seat. Selfishly, Hayden tried to ignore his apparent illness. If he had wanted to talk about it or use it as an excuse to avoid hanging out, he would have mentioned it to her. She tried not to let herself get annoyed at the fact that when they finally were spending time together, he was clearly battling a headache which was likely from the sleep deprivation brought on by his multitude of obligations.

As his discomfort grew, though, Hayden wondered if his perpetual rubbing his temples was an overt plea for her to address his pain. With a sigh, she sat up and crossed her legs beneath her. Chase was fully covering his ears and grinding his teeth as he struggled free from the position in which he'd trapped himself upon the chair.

"Are you alright?" She asked softly, her concern overcoming any selfish qualms. Generally, Hayden assumed that boys simply became infants when presented with the slightest inconvenience. Looking at Chase's face, though, she saw a genuine pain – almost agony – which deeply worried her.

"Please don't yell," Chase groaned, punctuating his request with a whimper.

"Chase, what's going on?"

"The music is just so loud," he struggled to formulate his thoughts. Hayden stood and moved toward the record player, which was already set to the lowest volume to avoid disturbing Caleb. Switching it off, she turned to face Chase skeptically.

"Why does your fan sound like it's moving so fast? The A.C. is screaming, and I can practically hear the water in the pipes. I've never noticed how loud your house is."

"Chase, I don't understand what you're talking about," Hayden responded slowly. Nothing seemed out of the ordinary to her, but Chase's biceps bulged as he firmly pressed his palms over his ears in attempt to drown out some perceived cacophony.

"My head is pounding," he finally concluded his complaints. Worried, Hayden stepped toward him and gently placed the back of her hand against Chase's forehead. Though the method was far from accurate, it didn't provide her with any reason to believe that he was running a fever.

"Maybe we should go for a walk to clear your mind," she offered.

"Yeah, that sounds nice," Chase nodded slowly. "Some fresh air might be nice."

Wrapping an arm around his waist, Hayden led him through her open bedroom door and toward the front of the house. As she passed Caleb's room, she peeked inside. Lying on his bed and flipping through a comic book with headphones over his ears, Caleb didn't notice her at first. When he finally sensed her movement, though, he looked up at her and slid one headphone back over his ear.

"What's up?" He greeted as he paused the music.

"Chase and I are going for a walk."

"Do you need a ride somewhere?" Caleb offered, spinning around and throwing his legs over the side of the bed.

"No, that's okay. We just want to get some fresh air."

"Okay," he nodded. "Make sure you bring your phone so you can call me if you need anything."

"Of course," she laughed. Hayden appreciated her brother's protective demeanor. It proved to her that he cared, and she felt safe knowing that he'd always be there to look out for her – even when she didn't need it.

Returning to Chase, Hayden resumed her walk with him toward the front door. As she turned the deadbolt, Chase winced in response to the loud click of the lock. The creaking of the door seemed to cause physical pain. The moment they were outside, though his shoulders fell slightly as his body relaxed.

"You already seem better," Hayden observed.

"Yeah, I think just a bit of fresh air helps. My head is still killing me, but there aren't quite as many noises competing for my attention out here."

"Really?" Hayden asked. Cars from a few streets over revved their engines and crickets awoke with the setting sun to begin singing their song, creating a symphony of noise all their own. If for some reason that was preferable to Chase, though, it was worthwhile to her.

"Those cars could stand to be a bit less obnoxious, though," he admitted, addressing her silent concerns. He winced again, but Hayden hadn't heard even the slightest sound.

"What happened?"

"You didn't hear that?"

"No, what?"

"The screeching? Someone slammed on their brakes I guess. How did you not hear that? It was deafening."

"I think you just have incredible hearing, Chase," Hayden shrugged. The two of them walked toward the edge of town in attempt to put as much distance between themselves and the sounds of the city as possible without actually venturing into the woods. After the events of the previous month, Hayden was not interested in returning to the dark grove which surrounded her home.

Even as the sounds slowly faded and the afternoon sun fell from the sky, Chase's pains didn't seem to dissipate. In fact, they only appeared to grow worse. Gripping his stomach, Chase came to a complete stop and grunted in pain. Slowly, the grunts became quick yelps as he dropped to his knees.

"Chase," Hayden screamed, trying to catch him but only succeeding to wrap her arms around his waist and fall with him. She was far from able to support Chase's dead weight.

"I'm sorry," he muttered, forcing the words out through gasps for air.

"What's going on? What hurts?"

"Everything," he replied, biting his lower lip to stifle a scream. When he looked back up at Hayden, she noticed his eyes shining a brilliant green in the light of the rising moon.

"Chase, your eyes…"

"What about them?" He questioned – each word clearly more difficult to utter than the previous.

"They're changing color."

"They feel weird," he acknowledged. "I don't understand, everything feels weird."

Hayden's mind wandered back to the book, but she refused to accept it as a possibility. The world of the paranormal belonged in fiction novels, not on the street in front of her. That stubbornness, though, was faltering as she watched Chase clutch his stomach and writhe in pain caused by some unseen force. Turning her eyes to the sky, she saw the full moon on the horizon, slowly pushing its way through the clouds.

"Hayden," he struggled, forcing her name out in a hoarse whisper. He failed to finish his thought, though, as he fell to the ground and convulsed. Fighting against that sensation, Chase stumbled to a kneeling position, barely able to support himself. Hayden leaned toward him, offering her shoulder for stability. Together, they rose to their feet and Chase rested part of his weight on her.

She had managed to get him onto his feet, but Hayden didn't have a plan for the next step. Without any way to gauge what was ailing Chase, she had no idea how to help him. Standing still, she just searched her head for any solution before finally settling on the simplest one.

"I'm going to call an ambulance," she suggested.

"No!"

"No? Chase, you can barely walk. We need help."

"Not an ambulance," he grunted, stumbling forward. Chase stepped one foot out to catch himself and distribute his weight, but his tumble was almost enough to send Hayden plummeting to the ground. She barely caught herself and was able to keep the two of them standing.

With Chase's refusal to accept help from medical professionals, Hayden was at a loss. She searched her mind for alternatives and tried to postpone her questions until after she could confirm his safety.

"I can call my brother or your parents," she offered,

"No," Chase declined, clutching his stomach again. Biting back another scream, he paused, but Hayden could tell that he was working toward offering a solution of his own. Despite every instinct screaming to her that she needed to act fast, she stood still and supported Chase until he was able to work up the strength to finish his sentence. “Take me to Cailean Phoenix. He’ll know what to do.”

Chapter 7

Night of the Full Moon
Cailean

Silently following his father into the woods once again, Cailean couldn't distract himself from the other werewolf encroaching on his father's territory. Assuming it wouldn't be an immediate problem, Cailean opted to withhold the information until he was sure his warning wasn't enough. As they trudged through the wilderness, though, he wondered where they were transforming and how long they had been there. Somehow, they had managed to avoid detection so long despite the vigilance of Cailean's father.

Brooke, clearly discerning his pensive expression, gave him a questioning look. Wordlessly, he waved the issue away and resolved to more carefully monitor the expressiveness of his face as he allowed his thoughts to roam. Brooke raised her eyebrows, unwilling to accept Cailean's dismissiveness.

Cailean lifted his upper lip and pointed to his canines, then threw his thumb over his back shoulder. Widening her eyes, Brooke pointed forward to Aldric and tapped her temple, but Cailean shook his head in response. Communicating through gestures and mouthed words, Brooke tried to convince Cailean to tell Aldric, but it didn't feel like the right time.

"What on Earth are the two of you doing?" Aldric demanded without turning around. Cailean wondered if he was hearing the displacement of the air as they swung their hands around, watching their shadows, or if he just had a sixth sense. None of those options would have surprised him, knowing his father.

Once again, Brooke encouraged him to talk about the issue, but Cailean found himself terrified of his father's response. He had thought he'd handled the issue, but Brooke's lack of confidence in that conclusion made him question himself. Dropping his shoulders dramatically, he finally accepted his fate.

"Father," Cailean mumbled, already bracing himself for the scolding he anticipated.

"Yes?"

"I have to tell you something," Cailean told him. Aldric stopped, turning in to face Cailean as he heard the guilty tone. His stern expression only hardened as he looked at his son.

"What?"

"A few days ago, I confronted someone in the hall at school. He's another werewolf. I scared him off and told him that this land belonged to another pack."

"That was reckless, Cailean," Aldric growled. "You didn't think this information was pertinent?"

"I was just trying to be helpful," Cailean defended, dropping his head. Aldric groaned and softened his scowl slightly as he turned his attention away, looking around the woods.

"I would have noticed another pack," he told Cailean, clearly biting back his anger. "You said you confronted him. Did he admit it?"

"No," Cailean admitted. "I suppose he could be alone."

"This isn't a game, Cailean," Aldric scolded him. "Our lives are at stake if the hunters discover us. Did it occur to you that he could have been a hunter?"

"No, I tested him. He could hear me from across the lunch room."

"Alright, at least that shows some insight," Aldric sighed. "Regardless, we don't know how desperate the hunters may be. They could recruit a werewolf to scout us out. Without more knowledge on the situation, you shouldn't have acted rashly."

"I'm sorry, Father. I won't do it again."

"Just consult me if there is ever anything which could even possibly be important, do you understand? I know you want to be helpful, Cailean, but you have fourteen years of experience. I have over thirty times that. Utilize it."

"Yes sir," Cailean nodded sheepishly. Aldric looked as though he was planning to continue reprimanding Cailean, but his words caught in his throat. Stumbling forward, he managed to catch himself by stepping his front foot into a good stance.

"We will continue this conversation later," Aldric growled. Cailean wasn't sure if his father was angry or in pain, but he chose to assume the worst.

Aldric turned on his heel and quickened the pace as they walked the last half-mile into the woods. When they finally reached their usual spot, he calmly removed his clothes and instantly began transforming.

"Well, that's going to be fun," Brooke muttered.

"I should have told him," Cailean acknowledged.

"Well, at least I'll be able to see you once a month while you're grounded."

"Funny," Cailean muttered, tossing his shirt to the ground.

"Maybe he'll forget that he's mad when he changes back," Brooke shrugged.

"You're really not being helpful."

"Well, maybe you shouldn't hide important information from the alpha."

Cailean muttered to himself as he dropped his head. Brooke wrapped her arms around him and kissed his forehead. For a moment, she rested her cheek on his shoulder.

"We're both still learning, Cailean. You thought it was handled, you tried to ease your dad's burdens, and you did what you thought was right. Now we know what's expected for next time. Don't beat yourself up."

"I just hope there is a next time," Cailean mumbled. "I'm scared I made a stupid mistake that we can't come back from."

Night of the Full Moon
Hayden

"Cailean Phoenix?" Hayden scoffed. "Why would he have any idea what's happening here?"

"I can't explain now," Chase grunted, barely able to muster the strength to form the words. His assertion was punctuated with a short fit of coughing as he struggled to hold back the sudden burst of pain.

"I don't even know where he lives," Hayden stumbled, panicking as she tried to think of any possible way to fulfill Chase's request. She couldn't drive, and he was in no condition to walk. Even if she had a vehicle, she had no idea how to find Cailean's house or who might have that information. She could ask Caleb to pick them up, but no story she could think of would explain to him why they so desperately needed to find his house.

As she thought, though, her mind began to filter out the fear and focus on finding a solution. She remembered the three years her brother had spent delivering newspapers around town. Back then, he would have been able to locate the home of any particular resident. If he still could, he would be their best option. Reluctant to call him solely because she couldn't think of an explanation, she wondered how difficult it would be to break into the post office. Shaking her head, she hesitantly accepted the fact that there was no other logical option.

"Chase," she whispered, briefing him as she planned to embark upon a covert operation. "Do you think you can hold yourself together for fifteen minutes?"

"Probably not," he admitted.

"You're going to have to. I have no idea what's going on, but honestly I don't want to involve my brother in it. Unfortunately, he is our only hope. We just can't let him think anything strange is afoot, or he'll try to help, and I'm scared he may hurt himself."

Although she had trouble admitting it, even to herself, Hayden was struggling to find any possible explanation which didn't involve werewolves. If there were such dark forces at work in the world, she wanted to keep her brother isolated from it. Caleb had always protected her and it was her turn to return the favor. Even if she tried to lead with a theory concerning lycanthropy, he was likely to waste precious time dismissing it as a joke. They desperately needed his help, but she knew she had to fabricate a different reason for it. Scrambling for the right words, she pulled out her phone and called her brother.

"Hey, Hayden. Is everything alright?" He greeted with apparent concern in his voice.

"Of course. You're always so paranoid," Hayden teased, forcing herself to sound playful and jovial.

"Sorry," he responded. "I just wouldn't have expected you to call me on your romantic walk unless there was a problem."

"No problem," she lied as Chase writhed on the floor at her feet, visibly biting his lip to prevent himself from screaming. As she spoke, Hayden felt the guilt welling inside of her, but she knew it was for the best. Whatever trouble they had found themselves in, she wanted him to have as little connection to it as possible. "We just realized that we have a group project meeting that we are supposed to get to, and I was wondering if you could pick us up and take us there."

"That's a strange thing to randomly remember," Caleb teased.

"Well, Cailean just texted us now," she stumbled.

"Where are you?" Caleb asked. Hayden was fairly certain she heard keys jingling in the background. Though she had always appreciated her brother's reliability, it had never been as much as in that moment. The second she called, he had dropped everything and was already on his way. As she looked for a street sign, she heard the front door close.

"We're on the corner of third and Seneca," she told him, squinting to read the green signs in the dim light of the streetlamps. The full moon barely provided any light as it peeked over the edge of the horizon, so they were mostly surrounded by darkness and the flickering yellow glow of those lamps.

"Oh, you didn't make it far," he observed. In the background, she heard the engine turn over. "I'll be there in just a second."

"Okay, thank you so much. Also, do you still remember where he lives?"

"Remember?"

"From your paper route, I thought you might know."

"Why didn't you just ask for his address?"

"That is a very reasonable point to which I have no response," she muttered slowly. Hayden was sure her story was loaded with holes, but she hadn't had much time to think of answers for any possible question. Something so obvious, though, left her stumped and slowly falling back into panic.

"It's fine," he laughed. "I'm sure I can remember how to get there. They're on the end of a street near the woods, so their house was distinct."

"Thanks, Caleb."

"No worries. I am going to go now because I shouldn't be talking on the phone. I'll be there in a few seconds."

"Thank you so much. I owe you one."

"One? Don't worry, that's what big brothers are for," he laughed. Giving her no time to respond, he ended the call and left her in silence with Chase. Looking down at him, she sighed deeply and squatted down.

"Alright, you just have to act cool in the car. Can you do that?"

"I feel like my organs are liquifying and every cell is simultaneously and intentionally dying, but I'm sure I can fake it," he coughed, failing to sound confident as every word was punctuated by a quiet groan.

"I'm sorry, Chase," she tried to comfort him.

"Don't be," he forced himself to say, fighting back the pain as he struggled to his feet. "If Cailean is right, we shouldn't alert him. Otherwise, I'm absolutely insane for trusting Cailean and I'm just dying."

"Whatever's going on, it's insane regardless of who you trust," Hayden asserted. Headlights peeked around the corner and Hayden wrapped her arm around Chase's waist to stabilize him. When Caleb pulled up in front of them, Chase pitched forward and caught himself on the car, fumbling to open the back door and throw himself inside. Falling into the car, Chase tried to mask the pain behind a smile. Between his dazed expression and aimless motions, though, he appeared intoxicated, which probably led to fewer questions than the truth.

Quickly, both to rush to their destination and to distract from Chase's display, Hayden pulled open the passenger door and jumped into the seat. Drawn to the rapid motion, Caleb turned his eyes toward the front of the car so he was at least not staring directly at Chase.

"Thanks again," Hayden told him. She realized that she was excessively thanking him which may be suspicious in itself. Of course, she was always grateful when he helped her, but she usually didn't express it repeatedly. Scolding herself for being too obvious, she bit her lip and turned to face forward. She realized, though, that her behavior may not seem suspicious to someone who didn't know that there was something of which to be suspicious.

"It's not a problem," Caleb assured her, waiting until they were both strapped in before driving down the road. They drove for a minute in silence as Caleb looked around the environment, trying to remember where he was going. Hayden watched as the moon slowly climbed. Glancing at Chase, she could clearly see the pain on his face, but he turned his head to look out the window and hide his expression from Caleb. With apparently great effort, he was able to remain stationary and appear thoughtful.

"So, what is this group project?" Caleb inquired as he took a left turn. Hayden watched as Chase fell onto the arm rest, unprepared for the change in direction. He winced as he tried to sit up, but in order to maintain the act he forced himself up once again. Trying to distract him from the scene in his back seat, Hayden searched for a reasonable response to her brother's question.

"Well," she muttered slowly. "It's for biology."

"Oh, that's interesting," he responded, raising his eyebrows but keeping his eyes glued to the road in front of him. "I didn't have any projects like that until senior year."

"It's new. We have to raise a caterpillar," she explained, attempting to sound natural but clearly selecting each word as she paused between them.

"Oh, studying metamorphosis?"

"That's the word I couldn't think of," she laughed, wondering if her brain had subconsciously chosen that subject due to the fitting comparison or if it was pure chance. In a sense, it was a study of metamorphosis.

"That seems a little patronizing to have three freshman team up to raise a caterpillar," he surmised, a tone of suspicion in his voice. Hayden panicked, even though there was no logical reason that his brain would connect the dots which led to Chase being scratched by a werewolf. Still, when she was hiding something, everything seemed catastrophic to Hayden.

"You know public school," she shrugged.

"You know, Hayden, if you're going to a party, I'm not going to rat you out."

"What?" She laughed awkwardly, drawing the word out as she decided whether to stick to her story or accept the alternative he'd presented.

"I just think that if I'm going to be an accessory to it, I deserve to know."

"Okay, I'm sorry I lied," she sighed, realizing that her best chance was to play along.

"I forgive you," he told her, patting her head with one hand. "I just want to make sure that you know that there's no reason to. I am not here to judge you. I went to a party or two at your age. And yesterday."

Laughing, she smiled in spite of the situation. Although he had no idea what was actually happening, Caleb was able to comfort her slightly.

"Just don't drink. It's stupid and pointless, and it only leads to problems."

"Trust me, you don't have to worry about that," Hayden promised, relishing her ability to tell the truth about something that night. The car pulled to a stop in front of a house Hayden had seen before but never walked inside. The porch light was on, but only a few windows shone yellow. Hoping the lack of commotion didn't bring her story into question, Hayden eagerly looked for any sign of life.

"This is it?"

"Yeah," Caleb shrugged. "At least, it was a few years back. They don't seem like the type to move, though."

"Do you know anything about them?"

"No, but I particularly enjoy making generalizations with little to no supporting evidence."

"I'll let you know if we're in the wrong place," she laughed. As calmly as she could, Hayden reached for the handle. As she pulled it back and pushed open the door, though, the shaking in her hands betrayed her. Climbing out, she tried to give the image that she held the door rather than using it for support. Chase practically leapt from the car before leaning back against the door as it closed, relying on it for balance. Hayden was annoyed at his lack of tact, but she couldn't hold it against him. Overall, she was impressed with how well he handled the pain and a few slipups were to be expected.

"You both seem really nervous," Caleb told Hayden, misinterpreting the tension and forcing her to hesitate as she tried to leave the car.

"You know," she told him, thinking quickly, "it's just that there will be a lot of popular people in there."

"You shouldn't be intimidated by popular people," Caleb laughed. "You want to know a secret about them?"

"I guess."

"They're people. Nothing more. Nothing to be afraid of," he smiled. Had he been right, it wouldn't have been bad advice, but Hayden had a feeling that Cailean Phoenix was a lot more than a person. Regardless, she smiled and nodded as she stepped out of Caleb's car. Feigning a romantic gesture, she wrapped her arm around Chase's waist.

"I love you, Caleb," she called, turning over her shoulder and reaching back with her free hand to close the door.

"I love you too. Call me when you need me." She nodded before turning and leading Chase toward the front door. The walkway was no longer than any other house on the block, but it felt like miles as the two of them staggered forward, trying to appear to be walking normally. Chase hunched forward for a moment but quickly straightened himself up, groaning in pain as he did so. The moon was climbing rapidly into the sky and Chase's pain only seemed to intensify.

Halfway up the concrete pathway, Chase finally lost his ability to walk. Hayden heard a disconcerting snap as one of his legs bent abnormally. Steeling herself, she bore all of his weight and still tried to appear unfazed. She hadn't heard the car leave and knowing her brother, he would wait until they crossed the threshold of the house. Generally, it was a caring gesture which she appreciated. In that moment, though, it was nothing more than frustrating.

One of Chase's arms rested over Hayden's shoulders and the other pressed against her stomach as he tried to stabilize himself. As he walked, she could feel the weight he placed on her fluctuating, alternating by the step. Her own legs shook beneath her, unaccustomed to working so hard simply to move.

Three-quarters of the way down the path, Hayden was convinced she didn't have any energy left. Ready to collapse, she tried to press on for Caleb's sake. If she didn't get Chase to the door, he would be there to witness what happened. Worse, he would undoubtably try to protect Hayden and injure himself in the process. Fortified with the thought of her brother's unknowing dependence on her, she pressed forward, practically carrying Chase as he fought the impending screams.

As they ascended the porch steps, Hayden heard another loud snap. At first, she thought the wood had cracked beneath them. When they didn't fall, though, she realized that the arm which was draped around her no longer pressed down on her shoulders. Chase's arm had broken, taking all of his motor function controls and leaving him dependent exclusively on her arm around his waist to stand.

Holding him, she could feel every muscle in his body which could still receive signals from his brain tense. Starting with his abdominals, which almost sent him falling forward, and moving to his arm. The hand on her stomach spasmed as well, tightly grabbing her. A sharp pain reverberated through her body as if she'd been pricked by needles, but she continued to lead Chase to the door. They were too close for her to give up, and the adrenaline gave her the strength she needed to persevere.

Finally, she was within reach of the door. Stretching her arm, Hayden knocked, dropping her weight against the wood. After a moment, she heard footsteps from within the house. Light flooded her surroundings as a middle-aged woman pulled the door inward. As quickly as it appeared, the smile vanished from her face and was replaced with terror and concern.

"We're looking for Cailean Phoenix," Hayden told her. "We think he can help us."

"He's not here," she informed them. "But come inside. I think I can help."

"No," Hayden argued, unwilling to put an innocent life in danger.

"I know what's happening," the woman assured her. "Just get inside."

"Okay," Hayden reluctantly agreed. "Thank you."

Turning around, she used the last of her energy to fake a smile and wave to her brother. The moment he drove off, though, her knees gave way. As she collapsed into the door, Chase fell forward as well. His fingers caught in her abdomen, tugging as he rolled away from her. Pressing her hand against her stomach, Hayden fell forward, face-planting into the floor. The woman closed the door as Hayden tried to catch her breath and recover from the ordeal. Chase groaned in agony, pulling Hayden's attention to him. She watched as he struggled to his hands and knees and his broken arm slowly grew, tearing at his shirt.

The woman grabbed the scruff of Chase's neck and dragged him toward a door a few feet from them. After she opened it, she disappeared into the darkness. Hayden heard a rhythmic banging as she pulled Chase down stairs.

Trying to stay near Chase, Hayden mustered her strength and climbed to all fours. Looking at the floor, she saw a growing pool of blood. A trail led toward the stairs. She hadn't even noticed Chase bleeding, but it made sense. As his body was tearing itself apart, it would have been more surprising if he hadn't bled.

Though she had never found herself to suffer from vasovagal syncope, the sight of blood was beginning to make her dizzy. Everything combined seemed to be taking a toll on her as the adrenaline wore off. The extreme physical exertion, the worry for

Chase, and the sight of his blood encompassing her were enough to make her feel weak.

The banging stopped and Hayden forced herself to her feet. Her eyes fluttered as she took a step, but she summoned an unknown energy reserve to keep them open. The paranoid part of her was terrified that the woman's idea of fixing the problem would involve hurting Chase, and she had to get into that basement to stop that from happening.

Hayden only managed to take one step before collapsing. Pain radiated around her body, but it was centralized in her core. She wondered if the muscles were merely exhausted from carrying Chase, but the pain only grew more intense. The blood continued to spread and the pool appeared to grow despite the lack of a source. Hayden rolled over, looking up at the ceiling and begging herself to go help Chase.

Hearing footsteps coming up the stairs again, though, she started worrying for herself. If she knew too much, the woman could be planning to kill both of them. Her body refused to react, though, and she accepted the fact that she had no more options. Lying in a pool of her werewolf boyfriend's blood, all she could do was hope for the best. The only movement she could bring herself to perform was setting her hand limply on her abdomen.

As she did so, Hayden realized that she was completely drenched in blood. Beyond that, though, she felt something strange about her skin. Finally, the pieces started to fall together in her mind. Lifting her hand over her face as if it would confirm her suspicions, she only saw a bright red outline of her own palm as her vision blurred.

"Oh," she muttered, dropping her arm to the ground. The footsteps seemed to increase in urgency until they stopped next to her ear. Hayden saw triple as the woman fell to her knees near her.

"Stay with me," the woman ordered.

"I don't feel good," Hayden mumbled incoherently. She felt herself quickly growing tired and finally allowed herself to close her eyes. As she did, she felt a burning sensation as the woman slapped her face, but it didn't entice her to open her eyes.

"This is really going to hurt," the woman warned. Too tired to process the warning, Hayden simply tried to open her eyes to look at her. Suddenly, agony exploded through her entire body as the wound in her stomach was torn open wider. The sudden sensation gave her the strength to open her eyes and lift her head to see the woman's hand plunged inside her stomach. She tried to force out words, but the indescribable pain limited her vocal cords to agonized screams.

"Just bear with me," she pleaded, firmly grabbing something as the pain receptors in Hayden's abdomen screamed their protest. "I have to hold the artery closed until you can heal yourself. It's going to get a lot worse before it gets better, but it will get better."

For what felt like an eternity, Hayden moaned as the pain reverberated through her body. Finally, though, the woman released her hold and Hayden felt a strange sensation as she pulled her hand from the wound in her stomach. The relief, though, was fleeting, as a new wave of agony washed over her. The pain, though, was exponentially more intense than it had been before, exactly as the woman predicted. Hayden's bloodcurdling screams reverberated throughout the walls of the house as she became fully aware of every individual piece of her body through its respective level of pain.

"Your entire genetic sequence is rewriting itself," the woman explained. Hayden was only partially able to process the information with her brain completely overwhelmed by the rapid fire of neurons. Eventually, her screams faded as her throat became unable to produce the sound, so the only thing demonstrating her pain was her eyes, which she could feel widening and pouring water.

"This will be the most painful thing you've ever experienced, but it won't last forever. Just stay with me. This will pass."

The words weren't particularly comforting, but they did make Hayden feel less alone. She felt as if a string had been laid across the wound in her stomach. That string was soon joined by a few others, which began forming an interconnected web over the wound.

"It's almost over. Stay strong."

If Hayden had the capability, she would have laughed at the concept. The last thing she felt in that moment was strong. In fact, she had never felt weaker in her entire life. The crippling torment of whatever was changing within her left her cowering like an infant. In that moment, she would have gladly given anything – including her life – for a second of relief.

The web seemed to spawn more strings of its own, slowly encompassing the entire wound. As that sensation faded away, the pain slowly left with it. Over the course of a few minutes, Hayden's pain faded from unimaginable to unbearable to inconvenient and eventually to nonexistent.

"Who are you? What is Chase? Where is Cailean? What's happening?" Hayden asked, panting and pausing between each question as she tried to catch her breath.

"My name is Linda Phoenix," the woman responded. "I know we have a lot to discuss, but for now you should go home so no one worries about you. Get some sleep. Tomorrow after school, we will address all of your questions."

Chapter 8

30 Days Until the Full Moon
Cailean

Cailean quickly jumped to his feet as he awoke to the sound of an alarm blaring from within his bag. Though he typically hated waking up in the morning, he understood the necessity of rising early after a full moon. Missing school every month just after the full moon would raise suspicion, so he couldn't risk oversleeping.

Over the years, that time had grown slightly earlier as well. Cailean was no longer convinced he was getting any sleep at all. To him, it seemed that the moment he regained his human form, the alarm summoned him. While he had never bothered to verify that claim, he believed in its validity based solely on the unparalleled exhaustion.

Stretching, Cailean found his way back to the source of the ringing. He removed the battery-operated alarm clock from his bag as the earsplitting sound overwhelmed his senses. Switching it off, he dropped it back in the bag and gave his ears a moment to recover. Digging through his clothes, he donned the same attire he always wore to transform. Granting himself a moment to rest, he leaned against a tree as he waited for the others.

A rustling in the leaves alerted him to a presence. The fact that any noise was made at all assured him that it was Brooke, so he retrieved her shorts and shirt from the bag. Stretching her arms toward the sky, she appeared from the dense foliage and approached him.

"Here," Cailean offered, holding the shorts out toward her.

"Thanks," she laughed, accepting them and sliding them up her legs. Checking the watch on Cailean's wrist, she threw her head back in protest. "It's so early."

"We still have to get home, shower, and get ready for school –" he began to explain, though he knew she understood the importance as well as he did.

"I know, I know," she interrupted. Taking the shirt from him, she pulled it over her head. Placing one hand on the back of her head and another on her chin, Brooke turned her head in either direction to crack her neck.

"Let's find my father," Cailean ordered. Though they still had more than enough time, tardiness was something he had grown cautious of. Cailean wanted to make sure that there was absolutely no doubt that they would be at school.

"When have you ever been the one to find me?" Aldric asked harshly as he emerged from the woods behind Cailean. Turning over his shoulder, Cailean raised his fists in surprise and prepared himself for a fight. Exhaling, he relaxed and shook his head. Despite his father's tone, that was the closest he had come to a joke in a long time.

"I can keep trying," Cailean laughed.

"Please do," Aldric challenged. "That will help me ensure that you don't oversleep."

"Should we get going?" Brooke suggested. Cailean had never known Brooke to be intimidated by anything before she'd met Aldric. In general, she was self-assured and outgoing, but as she asked the question her quiet, uncharacteristically sheepish voice shook. Her confidence seemed to wash away. Cailean's father had that effect on people.

"Lead the way," he ordered. Brooke turned on her heels and began walking out of the forest. Having returned to their usual spot with the threat of campers removed, she navigated through the woods with ease until they emerged into the light of the rising sun. Continuing along the streets, she led them to the point where their paths diverged.

"I'll see you at school, Cailean," she hugged him tightly. Cailean's father passed the two of them, but he stopped to wait for Cailean just a few feet in front of them. Brooke glanced at him, clearly censoring her word choice with Cailean's father so near. Cailean wondered if he'd worried her by mentioning his father's ability to hear everything in their house, and he could practically sense her thoughts as she wondered what provocative things Aldric had heard her say to his son.

"He's not as scary as he seems," Cailean assured her.

"Yes, I am," Aldric countered, his gaze still glued to the path ahead.

"See? He's a big joker."

"Right," she laughed, shaking her head. Brooke looked around uncomfortably, still holding Cailean in an embrace. Finally, she leaned in and whispered, "I love you."

"I love you too," he told her, kissing her gently before pulling away. "I'll see you at school."

Aldric remained silent for a while as the two of them continued walking toward their house. Cailean listened to Brooke's footsteps as she walked the other direction. The moment her footsteps faded away, his father turned to look at him.

"You love her?" He asked cautiously.

"There are different kinds of love, Father," Cailean sighed.

"Watch your tone."

"Yes, sir. I'm sorry."

"I'm just trying to..." Aldric trailed off. Turning his head away, he lifted his chin slightly and sniffed the air around them. Without another word, he sprinted away. Cailean, having never seen his father react in such a way, was filled with concern. As his body reacted to that fear, he was able to pick up on the smell of blood toward which their alpha had run. Spurred on by the scent, Cailean chased after him.

Aldric had always taught him to carefully avoid sprinting where they could be seen. Due to the strength of the muscles in their legs, werewolves were naturally good runners. At a jog, Cailean could keep pace with the best human athletes alive. Running any faster than that would invariably destroy any cover they may have established. Tossing caution to the wind, though, Cailean risked discovery to reach his mother's side as quickly as possible.

Arriving moments after his father, Cailean burst in through the door, terrified of what he'd find. Cailean's parents stood a few feet in front of him on a freshly cleaned floor. Though his mother looked perfectly healthy – aside from being sleep deprived – her expression was uncharacteristically grim. Carefully, Cailean stepped toward them and observed his surroundings.

The overwhelming smell of ammonia attempting to cover the blood assaulted his nose, overtaking his other senses. As he adjusted to it, though, he heard movement from somewhere else in the house. In order to avoid alerting any potential attackers, Cailean kept his head perfectly still as he looked around the house. There was no sign of anyone else, but he heard a thumping sound which convinced him that someone was hiding. As he tried to pinpoint the source, he determined that the thumping and footsteps were coming from beneath him.

"Mother, are you alright?" He finally asked.

"I'm okay. I'm sorry, I tried to clean everything so you two wouldn't be worried."

"That's good to hear," Cailean nodded. "So, follow-up question: Why is there a man in our basement?"

30 Days Until the Full Moon
Hayden

Hayden stood in front of the bathroom mirror, trying to convince herself to put on her clothes and get ready for school. After everything that had happened the previous night, though, she couldn't imagine actually focusing on anything else. The fingers of her right hand gently traced the four lines on her abdomen. Any degree of logic would dictate that the wound would be nowhere near that stage of healing, but she could see and feel the results. As she pressed against it more firmly, there was no residual pain. She had made a complete recovery from a wound which quite possibly could have been fatal.

Nothing felt different to her, of course. She had awakened with ease, which wasn't particularly normal, but it wasn't impossible. Nothing ached or was sore from the previous night, but nothing felt strange. She didn't feel stronger or faster than she had been. She didn't even feel healthier. Nothing about her, aside from the new scar, looked particularly different either. Somehow, though, she was a completely different woman than the one who had looked in that same mirror just one day prior.

Slowly, Hayden pulled her pants on and buttoned them. She could hear Caleb moving around as he prepared for school, and she knew it wouldn't be long before he insisted that they leave. All she wanted to do was tell her mother she was sick and avoid going to school, but that was far too problematic to be considered a solution. Even if she could convince her mother, a nurse, that she was sick – she was explicitly told that she had to avoid suspicion. Linda hadn't given her much detail, but she was adamant that Hayden attend school.

Leaning forward, Hayden pinched her earlobe between her fingers. Unable to find the hole, she gently tugged at her ear to stretch the tissue. Her earlobe stretched as one unified piece, as if it had never been pierced. Hayden tried to blink the illusion away, but was finally forced to accept the validity of what she saw.

"How?" She muttered under her breath, caressing her healed earlobe. Backing away from the mirror, she stared at herself in amazement and dropped her hands to her sides. Shaking her head, she pulled her focus back to the task at hand.

Hayden reached for her shirt, but she stopped herself before she put it on. Once again, the scar caught her attention and left her enraptured. Grazing her fingers along it once more, she wondered again how it could have healed so quickly.

The glint of the bathroom light reflected from a razor on the counter before her. Hayden couldn't help but contemplate the limits of her healing. As if compelled by a strong external force, she slowly reached her hand toward the razor.

"Hayden," Caleb's voice called, freeing her from her trance. Feeling as though she had been caught in the middle of a crime, Hayden quickly pulled her hand back and looked around for a witness.

"Yeah?" She finally replied.

"Are you almost ready to go?"

"I am, sorry!"

Finally covering the scar, Hayden pulled the shirt over her head and opened the door. Caleb, standing close to the door as he waited for her, stumbled backward as he was clearly surprised by her prompt exit.

Hayden moved past him to put her shoes on and get her backpack. Following Caleb to his car, she prepared for a day of pretending to pay attention to anything other than the fact that her entire perception of the world had been flawed.

❖ ❖ ❖

"Will you tell me what's going on, now?" Hayden asked impatiently. Having rushed to Cailean's house immediately after school, she sat across from his mother before Chase or even Cailean had arrived. Though her first instinct had been to wait for Chase, Hayden didn't believe any part of the explanation would feel redundant if she heard it a second time. She had seen it with her own eyes, but it was still going to take time to convince her brain that she wasn't trapped in a very elaborate nightmare.

"Of course," Linda sighed, leaning back into her chair. Leaning forward on the edge of the couch, Hayden rested her palms on the coffee table as she awaited a more detailed response. Linda rubbed her eyelids as she tried to determine where to start. With a full day to prepare her speech, Hayden had assumed Linda would have prepared a speech, but she simply remained silent for a full minute.

"Do you want me to handle this?" Her husband offered, entering from a door on the other side of the room. On his face was a scowl which didn't match his tone and Hayden wondered if it was simply the only expression which he knew how to display. Between his imposing figure and the confidence and power he exuded, she couldn't picture the intimidating man wearing a smile.

"You can have the next one," Linda smiled, catching Hayden's gaze before she turned her head over her shoulder to decline his offer. Glancing down at his watch, he wandered into another room.

"Thanks," Hayden sighed, realizing that Linda had been attempting to make her as comfortable as possible with the situation.

"He can be scary at first," she replied dismissively. "He's been through a lot, but the steely exterior is a defense mechanism. Beneath it all, he's just a big teddy bear."

"Somehow I doubt that," Hayden muttered, dropping her eyes.

"It's pretty deep," Linda admitted.

"So…" Hayden urged, eager to have her answers.

"You were scratched by a werewolf," Linda started, breaking the news quickly. When Hayden didn't react, a look of confusion briefly crossed her face. Pausing for a moment, she probably assumed Hayden simply needed a moment for the gravity of that sentence to affect her.

"I know," she nodded.

"You know?"

"I did some research. I didn't believe it at first, but after what I saw there isn't another explanation."

"I see," Linda nodded slowly.

"I just… I have so many questions."

"I'll answer anything I can, but I think I should also try to prepare you for what this means." She spoke slowly, carefully selecting each word as if dancing around something she didn't want to say.

"This means I'm a werewolf, doesn't it?"

"Yes. That you will be, at least. Have you started your period?"

"I'm sorry?" Hayden choked.

"The transformation doesn't begin until puberty. For young women who are scratched, that is the simplest indicator for when it will begin. If you haven't, you won't transform until the full moon after you do."

"Oh…"

"So, I just ask to know how best to prepare you."

"Yes, I have," Hayden spoke quickly as she tried to move on.

"Okay, I have another question which will be uncomfortable, but I need you to bear with me."

With a groan, Hayden braced herself. Talking about her personal life with strangers wasn't something of which she was particularly fond, especially when she hadn't had time to prepare. She expected the meeting with Linda to simply answer her questions rather than to involve prying into Hayden's life.

"Have you and Chase been intimate?"

"Okay, do we really have to do this?"

"I'm sure you've heard that wolves mate for life," Linda explained. "The same is true of lycanthropes. You see, when you sleep with someone, you are actively making the decision to be with that person for life. Humans are able to move on if a relationship doesn't work out. If the two of you have been intimate, I am just suggesting that you wait for a while before doing so again. I don't know you or Chase, and I'm not saying you shouldn't be together, but I'm saying that it is a big decision."

"So if I sleep with him now that I'm a werewolf, that means I'll never love anyone else?"

"Love is a strange word," Linda struggled for a good explanation, looking up and to the left as if the answers were written in her peripheral vision. "Functionally, of course you can love. True love is the act of putting someone else's needs before your own; it's making the active choice to care for them. Conventionally, though, how we tend to define love, you can't. That feeling that you get in the pit of your stomach, or even just a basic attraction, will never be felt for someone else. Essentially, the wolf compels you to act in a loving way toward your partner, but it also prevents the secretion of certain chemicals which could ever possibly draw you to another."

"The wolf? You act like it's something different from me.

"We talk like it is. Honestly, it makes it easier. Conceptually and emotionally."

"I see," Hayden nodded, still trying to unpack the information which was being thrust upon her. Closing her eyes, she tried to picture her future with Chase. The idea of choosing one person with whom she would be forced to spend her entire life was terrifying. She had always thought of that as something which would happen when she was older, and marriage became a viable option. Panic set in as she realized that she was far too young to be making such a decision. The fact that her entire life was about to change as a result of a scratch from a werewolf was overwhelming enough. Her mind reeled and her head pounded as she desperately tried to come to terms with the novel information.

Hayden tried to speak but stumbled over her words. There were more questions she wanted to ask, but she was completely petrified. When she opened her mouth, nothing more than a few croaks passed her lips. Just as she was finally about to work up the nerve to speak, the front door opened and her mind was overloaded with a barrage of voices.

"Sorry I punched you," Cailean said as he walked into the room. "I thought you were from another pack."

"That's fine, I just thought you were insane," Chase responded with a chuckle.

"Everything makes a lot more sense now, I guess."

"But how did you know I was a werewolf?"

"You could hear me from across the lunchroom, you started shedding fat despite what you were eating and never being at the gym, and you… smelled like a wolf, I guess? I don't know, you weren't really hiding it."

"Wait, you can smell other werewolves?"

"I don't know, it isn't something that I can explain. It's just like how you can smell the difference between a human and a dog, but there is no particular human smell, you know?"

"I really don't, Chase laughed. "I don't generally make a habit of sniffing animals."

"Whatever. You're the weird one here, not me," Cailean asserted. Apparently hearing the commotion, Aldric emerged once again and met them in the living room.

"Oh, hey Hayden," Chase greeted, kissing her on the top of her head. Hayden was dumbfounded by how quickly Chase and Cailean seemed to be talking as if they'd known each other for years. She knew Chase had a way with people, but Cailean had a reputation for being a tough bully who would never associate with people like her and Chase. Still, somehow he had broken through that in less than a day.

"Good, you're here," Aldric interrupted curtly before Hayden had a chance to return Chase's greeting. Intimidated by his tone and stature, Hayden remained silent and turned her attention toward him. "We have a lot to discuss."

"That's great," Chase chirped. "I have so many questions."

"I'll start with an introduction. My name is Aldric Phoenix, and as the alpha of this pack, it is my responsibility to ensure your safety. Part of that duty is to educate you on the basics of what you're becoming."

"I'm Chase," Chase greeted with a smile. Hayden stumbled over her words for a moment, so he intervened and introduced her as well. With a grateful sigh, Hayden dropped her shoulders.

"Great," Aldric nodded, waving a hand toward the couch. Obediently, Chase and Cailean joined Hayden on the sofa. Despite his attitude, Hayden could tell that Chase was at the very least uncomfortable.

"So you've both accepted the reality of the situation. You understand that you're werewolves. When the moon is full, you will walk in the skin of the wolf. Along with that comes changes to your body and perception, but it also brings a new set of risks. A group exists, aptly named the 'Hunters.' Their purpose is to eradicate all paranormal and supernatural creatures. It is vital that you not only understand my teaching, but heed my advice. Before I try to explain all of this to you, are there any questions?"

Chase's hand slowly rose into the air.

"Yes?" Aldric asked, clearly regretting opening the floor. Hayden's mind swam with dozens of questions of her own, but she knew that he would more than likely have a plan to address the all.

"You said they hunt more than just werewolves? What else exists?"

"A lot," Aldric replied, annoyed.

"Do ghosts exist?"

"No."

"Vampires?"

"No."

"Mermaids?"

"Probably."

"Zombies?"

"Not anymore."

"What about like, bird people?"

"I don't know," Aldric replied. His cold demeanor broke for a minute as he chuckled, offering Hayden a glimpse at the smile she hadn't thought he could muster. "Can we move on?"

"Wait a minute," Chase muttered, looking toward Hayden as he finally pieced together what she had been avoiding telling him. "Hayden, why are you here?"

"I was scratched too," she admitted. The brief silence which followed seemed to stretch for an eternity as Hayden watched Chase's face fill with dread.

"When?" He asked slowly, as if afraid to hear the answer. "Why didn't you turn like I did?"

"In the woods, with you," she lied. "It wasn't as deep as yours, so I wasn't too concerned. But Linda just told me that I wouldn't transform until I..."

She wasn't sure why mentioning it made her so uncomfortable, but it did, so she trailed off. Chase, leaning forward, dropped his head into his hands. With a quick glance toward Hayden, Linda nodded, demonstrating a silent understanding of her decision.

"I'm so sorry. You wouldn't have been out there if it weren't for me."

Regardless of what she had told him, Chase would have blamed himself. It was far better, though, if he believed he indirectly cause her scratch. Knowing that he was directly responsible would have broken him. Since telling him wouldn't change the result, Hayden decided to bear the burden of that truth alone.

Chapter 9

29 Days Until the Full Moon
Cailean

Sitting with Hayden and Brooke, Cailean gently tapped the table as he waited for Chase to arrive. Contrary to the emphasis his father placed on remaining inconspicuous, he had insisted that Hayden and Chase start eating lunch with Cailean and Brooke. In his eyes, the comradery formed in that time spent together was worth the risk of breaking daily routine. Cailean, although he trusted his father completely, was annoyed with the decision. Most of his time was spent pretending to be someone he wasn't in order to draw attention to himself. Lunch had become a break from that because he'd managed to convince his friends that Brooke – the demanding girlfriend – had insisted that they spend time together.

With a new girl at the table, though, Brooke seemed intent on fostering that friendship. Cailean couldn't blame her for trying to make the new wolves feel welcomed. He wasn't quite as quick to accept new additions to the group as she was, but they were his brother and sister now. Bound by a secret stronger than blood, the four of them shared a key characteristic which, in his eyes, made them worth his time. Regardless, he couldn't pretend that he didn't miss the time alone with Brooke. Listening to her and Hayden bond as he rested his jaw on his open palm was not an ideal way for him to spend his time.

"I like to draw, I guess," Hayden shrugged, responding to yet another of Brooke's probing questions. Brooke tried to make the conversation appear natural, but Cailean could see that she was desperately searching for some way to relate to her new friend. To Cailean, Hayden was a sister, but she hadn't earned friendship yet. Brooke just seemed ecstatic to have another female to talk to.

"Oh, that's fun! I've never been good at anything artistic, but I try," Brooke responded. Cailean finally spotted Chase as he approached the group and breathed a sigh of relief. If nothing else, at least he would no longer be outnumbered.

"I mean, I'm not that great either, but I just practice," Hayden humbly clarified.

"I'm sure you're great," Brooke confidently asserted. "So, what about your parents? What do they do?"

"My mom's a nurse," Hayden answered quickly. Cailean could hear the sadness in her voice as she hesitated to answer the rest of the question. A deep inhale implied that she had more to say, but she allowed the breath to silently pass her lips. That delay answered everything either Cailean or Brooke needed to know.

"That's cool!" Brooke exclaimed, trying to brighten Hayden's day with her positivity. Despite his annoyance at the general situation, Cailean found himself smiling as well. One of the many things he loved about Brooke was her emotional intelligence. Had her father been something Hayden wanted to discuss, he was sure Brooke would have noticed and taken the conversation in a completely different direction.

"Sometimes," Hayden chuckled.

"What do you mean?"

"Well, it's a bit exhausting at times. If I try to do anything mildly dangerous – like ride a bike – she had so much advice. Also, if I do somehow get an injury, there is no chance I'm going to get to take the easy approach in treating it."

"She's just looking out for you. Trust me, I can beat that. My mom is a teacher."

"Oh, that is rough," Hayden admitted, cringing subtly.

"Yeah. I can't get away with not doing homework, that's for sure. Sometimes she even makes me do extra because she isn't happy with what I'm learning in school. And, worst of all, guess who was in her class."

"You?"

"No, I think that's a conflict of interest or something. But Cailean was."

"I like her," Cailean shrugged.

"Oh, I love her," Brooke defended. "I'm just saying sometimes her career is exhausting."

"Yeah, I get that. I am so grateful for my mom," Hayden assured them. "It's just nice to complain sometimes."

"Why?" Cailean muttered.

"To vent," Brooke scoffed as if the answer should have been obvious. Finally, Chase took a seat at the table. Cailean subconsciously breathed a sigh of relief.

"Vent about what?" Chase joined.

"Their mothers caring about them," Cailean sarcastically answered.

"Oh, that's the worst," Chase replied hesitantly, glancing toward the others.

"Don't mind him, Cailean is just grumpy when he meets new people," Brooke teased.

"Oh, we're not new," Chase laughed, patting Cailean's back. "We go way back. Remember when you threatened to kill me?"

"What?" Hayden spat.

"That technically happened," Cailean admitted. "I did think you were a threat, though."

"Seriously? Actually, you know what, I'm not surprised," Hayden growled, slamming her hands on the table and standing. Cailean glanced around the cafeteria, concerned with the scene she was making.

"Hayden, sit down," he ordered.

"No," she retorted. "I don't have to put up with this. You're crazy, and you can't justify that with lycanthropy."

"Lower. Your. Voice."

"You're cruel, you're a bully, and everything people say about you is true. I'm not going to pretend to be your friend just because I got scratched," she ranted, ignoring his stern commands.

"Hayden," Chase finally pitched in. "It was a weird circumstance. I was just messing with him, no harm done."

"No harm done? Tell that to all of the victims of his bullying."

"I've already told you," Cailean hissed, growing more infuriated by the second, "I do what I have to in order to stay unnoticed. Efforts which you, by the way, are not helping."

"He hasn't actually hurt anyone," Chase agreed. "I understand why you'd be upset, but there's a lot we have to learn about this life. I'm sure we'll understand better as we get more experience."

"Of course you're defending him," Hayden groaned. "Why take my side here? Why support your girlfriend when you can defend a total stranger?"

"Hayden," Chase whispered.

"You need to learn that you can't always appease everyone," she scolded. "Sometimes, people are just wrong."

Without waiting for another response, she turned and stormed away. Brooke glared at Cailean, who defensively furrowed his brow and waved his hand.

"I'll go talk to her," Chase offered.

"No, please don't," Brooke stopped him. Standing up, she added, "you've already done enough damage. Both of you. Cailean, I know I took it well, but you have to understand that adjusting to this life is hard. I'll try to convince her to give this group another chance but please, play nice."

16 Days Until the Full Moon
Hayden

"Hayden, don't forget…" Her mom's voice resonated throughout the house. Before she even spoke, Hayden could hear her inhale as she prepared to raise her voice and demand her daughter's attention. Though her mind swirled as she once again found herself trapped in the dark web of mysteries which shrouded her newfound powers, she was able to maintain enough presence of mind to call out a reply before her mother could finish her sentence.

"I know, mom," she replied, trying to sound cheerful and appreciative. "I'm on it."

"I'm sorry," her mother added in a hushed tone as she appeared in the doorway to the kitchen. Hovering there for a moment, she drummed on the doorjamb as she searched for a way to connect with her daughter. "I'm trying to be more subtle."

"It's okay, Mom," Hayden smiled, pushing her seat backward and standing. Before leaving the room, she set her plate in the sink and met her mother. "Thank you for looking out for me."

"That's my job," she shrugged. The smile tugging at the corner of her mouth betrayed the nonchalant response behind which she hid. Hayden wrapped her in a tight embrace only to quickly loosen her grip when she heard her gasp for air.

"You give good hugs," her mom laughed, once again failing to conceal her true feelings as she coughed slightly. "Maybe take it easy on your poor old mom, though."

Hayden blushed, backing away more quickly than she'd intended and bumping into the island in the center of their kitchen. Distressed, she pulled her fingers through her hair before resting her hand on her cheek, as if that would somehow make her appear more collected. Realizing it was futile, she dropped her palm onto the island and tried to act natural.

"I'm just joking," her mother comforted, expressing concern in both her tone and the way she moved forward and placed a hand on Hayden's shoulder.

"Sorry," Hayden sighed. "I guess I'm jumpy today."

"Is everything alright?"

"Yeah, I'm fine," Hayden assured her, hugging her again. Taking more caution, Hayden gently embraced her mother. Though she was far from a weak woman, the gap in physical prowess between her and her daughter was already widening drastically. Kissing her mom's cheek, Hayden pulled away and slid past her to move toward the bathroom. As it often did, the urge to dress well for school had come over her that morning, and it was especially important to her that she fulfill it. With Aldric's lessons, she was becoming paranoid about the hunters, and the last thing she wanted was to break any type of routine which she'd established.

Wishing to avoid pushing her brother to rush, Hayden had intentionally awoken long before him. Leaving the kitchen, she heard his soft footsteps leading him in the opposite direction for breakfast. When she turned the corner, they met in the hallway and he jumped back in surprise. Though it had only been a few weeks since her ears had started changing, Hayden was already having trouble remembering normal human hearing. Seeing the startled expression on his face, though, it dawned on her that he hadn't heard her approach like she'd heard his.

"Sorry," she finally told him, pulling herself away from her thoughts.

"It's fine," he laughed. "I just forget what you look like before makeup."

"Very funny," she groaned. "That wasn't even a good cover-up, we eat breakfast together every day."

"Yeah, well, I'm tired and I didn't want to admit you startled me. It's not manly."

"Don't worry, Caleb," she consoled, patting his shoulder as she walked around him to continue to the bathroom. "No one has ever accused you of being manly."

She walked into the bathroom and turned to close the door, but he turned quickly and caught her eye.

"Hayden," he stopped her, stalling as he tried to find the right words to accompany the sudden change in his tone. "That was nice."

"What?"

"Mom. I heard you. I'm sure she appreciated it."

"She's not trying to embarrass me," Hayden shrugged. "Anyway, I'm starting to realize it isn't that big of a deal."

"I'm glad. You're catching on much more quickly than I did."

"Yeah, it's normal. It just means my reproductive system is functioning properly," she pondered, feigning deep thought as she pursed her lips slightly, furrowing her brow and turning her gaze toward the ceiling.

"Right," Caleb agreed, sounding slightly less sure of himself than he had previously.

"I mean, it's just a little blood," she continued.

"Okay," Caleb nodded. "I'm glad you're at peace with that."

"What's the difference if it comes from my arm or…"

"We can stop this now," Caleb playfully complained, turning back around. "Remind me not to compliment you anymore."

"I won't let you forget," she teased as she closed the door. Though she felt at least as awkward as her brother about the entire situation, it somewhat appeased her discomfort to create his. Hayden turned her attention back to preparing for the day. Though she was annoyed that nothing seemed confidential in her house, she took solace in the fact that she had more privacy there than in the world of werewolves. After only a few conversations with Linda, she had quickly learned that no conversation was off-limits, even for complete strangers, if it vaguely related to lycanthropy.

Examining her face in the mirror, she leaned forward and distracted herself by wondering which pair of earrings she should wear. Absentmindedly massaging her earlobe with a cotton ball, she searched through her jewelry. Finally settling on a simple pair, she pressed the stud against the tender tissue of her earlobe. Confused, she slid the blunt end of the stud around in search of the hole before pulling it away and stretching the skin. Not for the first time, she groaned as she remembered that the holes had closed. Setting the earring down on the counter in front of her, Hayden found a safety pin which she'd started keeping with her jewelry. Holding her earlobe firmly between the thumb and forefinger of her left hand, she used her right to swiftly plunge the pin through her ear. The pain, while not completely negligible, was far from the worst she'd experienced. As a small stream of blood trickled from the makeshift, she quickly retrieved the stud and replaced the safety pin as the wound closed around it. After repeating the piercing on the other side, she washed off the blood in the sink and examined her ears, which had already healed. Years of habitual behavior kept Hayden in the same ritual of removing her earrings at night, but she resolved to try to simply leave the studs in overnight and avoid re-piercing her ears daily.

Hayden plugged the curling iron into the socket next to her and allowed it to warm up as she continued to examine her earlobes.

As many times as she had watched her own wounds heal, she still found it hard to believe. Slowly, she leaned back and lifted her shirt slightly, examining her abdomen. Though she had already been thin, she could see the definition appearing as her core mysteriously strengthened each day. The Phoenixes had explained all of the changes which would accompany her lycanthropy so she was able to grasp the theory. Rapidly differentiating cells would ensure that muscles repaired quickly and efficiently, resulting in hypertrophy and growth. During a transformation, every cell was, as Aldric described, chemically reverted to a stem cell state and stimulated to the required form. Through that type of reconstruction, she could understand how her body would change. What she hadn't been prepared for, though, was how the minimal damage through daily use would be repaired and display such results.

Tracing over the scar on her stomach, Hayden remembered the deep wound which had caused it. A wound which would have been fatal had it been inflicted by anything other than a werewolf. In fact, even that wouldn't have saved her if it weren't for Linda's intervention. Regardless, she stared at completely healed scar tissue which was barely rough to the touch.

A knock on the door pulled her mind back from its depths. Dropping her shirt, she looked toward the curling iron again. Her mind still on the scar, she caught herself wondering if permanent damage was possible to her new body. The scar from the first time she'd burned herself on that iron had vanished, but could she create a new one?

"I'm almost ready," she assured Caleb.

"Are you curling your hair again?" He jokingly groaned.

"It's the price of beauty."

"Your beauty comes at no price."

"I don't know if that was as kind as you meant it to be."

"Whatever, you got it," he muttered, his voice growing quiet as he retreated down the hallway. With a sigh, she shook her head and cleared her mind before getting to work on her hair. Bit by bit, she wrapped it around the iron and dropped the curls over her shoulders. When she finished, she quickly brushed her teeth and looked back over herself in the mirror. Her flawless skin shone in the yellow light emanating from the bulb as she examined her face for any blemishes. Though the lycanthropy eliminated the need, she quickly rubbed a thin layer of foundation on her skin to maintain a sense of normalcy and avoid suspicion.

Just before she grabbed the doorknob, Hayden remembered her mother's warning. She opened the cabinet under the sink and slid a few extra tampons into her back pocket, just in case. Finally convinced she hadn't forgotten anything, she opened the door and raced to meet Caleb in the living room. Adopting his typical position, he waited for her with his feet propped on the table and his hands folded behind his neck.

"You and I really need to align on what 'almost' means," Caleb jokingly scolded as he dropped his feet to the floor. Continuing onto his feet, he bent his knees and grabbed his backpack. As he rose, he swung it over his shoulder.

"To be fair, I would think you'd have learned by now," Hayden shrugged.

"You're not wrong," Caleb admitted. He picked up Hayden's bag and tossed it toward her. Somehow, although it was far from the first time he'd given her the backpack in the same manner, she was still caught off guard. Instinctively, she reached her hand forward to catch it as it raced toward her. Clenching her fist around the top of the bag, she stopped its momentum and held it in one hand. After a brief moment of hesitation, she overcame her surprise and pulled the straps over her arms.

"I guess you got the books out of there," Caleb joked, the shock apparent on his face.

"Disappointed?" She scoffed.

"I'm your big brother. It's my job to knock you over with things. That's my singular role in life."

"Don't say that. You also get to drive me around."

"You know," he muttered, narrowing his eyes at her. "It's a good thing I love you, because otherwise, you'd be walking."

"You wouldn't do that to me – you're too good of a person."

"Hey, don't mistake my weakness for kindness," he snapped jokingly.

"I'm pretty sure –"

"I know what I said," he interjected, rubbing her freshly curled hair before leading her to the door. Following her brother outside, Hayden briefly allowed herself to forget the fact that her life was changing faster than she could comprehend. For that moment, she allowed herself to simply be a sister.

❖ ❖ ❖

Snapped back to the presently tumultuous life which she led outside of home, Hayden glumly ascended the stairs toward her school. Wandering through the halls as she made her way to her first class, Hayden was unable to pretend life was normal any longer. With Aldric and Linda's warnings ever-present in the forefront of her mind, she began to see every student as a potential threat. Every action was a calculated attempt to guarantee that she was acting exactly as she had before she'd changed.

To make matters worse, she found herself running low on confidants. Cailean's mother tried to be available, but Hayden found the generational gap too vast for her to comfortably navigate. Aldric was terrifying and Cailean was abrasive, so seeking any wisdom from them was not an option. Every time she considered talking to Chase, she was assaulted by uncertainty. Rather than add another slew of questions to her already troubled mind, she tried her best to turn her focus from that particular issue.

As cruel as it felt, Hayden was grateful that Brooke had been scratched so long ago. Though she only had a few more years of knowledge regarding lycanthropy, it was enough for Hayden to have one person in whom she could confide. Though talking to a relative stranger about personal issues had made her uncomfortable at first, necessity had pushed her to become fast friends with Brooke.

Out of the corner of her eye, Hayden saw Chase's bright smile as he waved a hand to grab her attention. As slyly as possible, she ducked around a corner and pretended not to notice. Avoidance was a temporary solution, of that she was well aware. Even if the four of them didn't eat lunch together daily, it wouldn't be long before she was forced to interact with her boyfriend.

As she collapsed into her seat in class, Hayden dropped her face into her hands. On some level, she blamed Linda for the doubts in her mind. She had been happy before Cailean's mom had introduced any reason to wonder. The task of choosing the person with whom she'd spend her entire life was daunting, and far more pressure than any fourteen-year-old could handle. Dwelling on every event throughout her entire relationship as class droned on, though, she knew there was more to the issue than a simple warning about her changed nature as a werewolf. Though her intentions had been her best, she couldn't shake the concern that her relationship with Chase would forever have to live in the shadow of her lie. She didn't want him to assume that she resented him, but he had dragged her into that new world, and that wasn't something she could forget.

"Miss Faye," her teacher reprimanded. Hayden looked up to see the older woman standing near her desk, her left shoulder slightly elevated and her knee bent as she set her weight upon her right foot. A quick glance around the room informed Hayden that the two were its sole occupants. The confusion on her face clearly spoke more than any words she could formulate, as her teacher continued in response. "I let it slide when you were clearly distracted through class, but I don't know if your next teacher will be as lenient if you're late."

"Class is over?" Hayden muttered, silently scolding herself the moment the words left her lips. Though the teacher's assessment had been completely accurate, she wished she'd had the forethought to avoid confirming it.

"Yes, it is," she chuckled sadly, rolling her eyes as she turned to walk away. Hayden noticed that the chalkboard was completely filled with equations and definitions before dropping her eyes to the desk in front of her. There was no hiding the fact that she had neglected to retrieve her textbook, or even notes, from her bag.

"I'm sorry," Hayden sighed as she stood and moved toward the door, dropping her eyes to the ground. She debated adding a defense about how much she had on her mind but ultimately decided against it. Instead, she tried to just keep her head down and resolved to do a better job of acting composed in her next class.

"Hayden," the teacher called just before Hayden had made her escape. Brushing her hair to the side, she turned and fabricated a smile. Realizing that a smile didn't quite suite the situation, she wondered if that made her more suspicious. Concern quickly became panic as her paranoid mind became certain that she'd just given herself away to a hunter. Anxiously, she awaited the next sentence, but everything seemed to be happening in slow motion. "If you ever need to talk…"

"Thank you," Hayden interrupted. "I appreciate it. I'm sorry, I'm okay, really. I just didn't get much sleep last night."

"I know the look of teenage angst," the teacher teased. "I know it from years of seeing it in the mirror and raising three daughters. You can talk to me, or I can tell you where to go. Or you can work through it on your own. Just try not to do that during class, alright?"

"It won't happen again," Hayden assured her.

"I know you do most of your studying at home," she continued, although it seemed clear to Hayden that the point had already been made, "but at least pretend. Otherwise it makes me look bad."

"Yes ma'am," Hayden nodded. Quickly, she turned on her heel and forged her way toward her next class. Before she could safely reach the room, though, and avoid human interaction for another hour, she felt delicate hands firmly wrap around her shoulders. Startled, Hayden stopped abruptly but failed to convince herself to look over her shoulder.

"This dingy floor should not have the honor of admiring your eyes. Keep your head up," Brooke greeted, resting her head on one of Hayden's shoulders.

"That was cheesy," Hayden laughed quietly, turning to face her friend.

"Whatever," Brooke retorted. "Your heart would be fluttering if Chase had said it."

At the mention of Chase's name, Hayden averted her eyes slightly. Within a second, she was able to recover, but Brooke squinted one eye and tilted her head, assuring Hayden that she'd picked up on the microexpression.

"You must be highly confident in your abilities to recognize people from the backs of their heads," Hayden teased, desperately trying to prevent the conversation from taking the obvious turn.

"Are you kidding? I would recognize those bouncy golden curls from a mile away."

"They're closer to bronze than gold," Hayden mused, grabbing a strand of hair and holding it in front of her face pensively.

"Depends on the light," Brooke countered. The thoughtfulness in her eyes as she tried to accurately describe Hayden's hair color assured Hayden that her distraction had been successful. "In brighter light the yellow seems to stick out more, but the darker brownish hues are clearer in this dull interior lighting."

"That actually just helped prove my point."

"No, it didn't. You're blonde, it's amazing, it's rare, love it, your hair is majestic, but it won't save you from talking to your friend about your drama."

"What drama?"

"Come on, Hayden," Brooke urged, pulling her around a corner and leading her to a less densely populated stretch. "If we can't talk to each other, who do we have? I want to help you. I know how hard it is."

"How do you know you want to be with Cailean forever?" She finally asked.

"Oh," Brooke smiled sadly.

"I really do like Chase, but I just don't know. Sometimes I get annoyed with him, or I think he should prioritize me more, I guess? He always tries so hard to make everyone happy that he just spreads himself thin. I don't know, it's selfish."

"No, it isn't."

"Forever is just a long time. I want to know I've found the perfect person."

"No one is perfect," Brooke laughed. "You have no idea how often Cailean frustrates me. He can't make a decision to save his life. That or he's afraid of commitment. He complains about spending time with the other athletes, but he never tries to stop. Deep down I feel like he likes the attention. I don't know, I'm ranting. The point is, he's frustrating and he's immature, as all boys tend to be."

"Then how do you know?"

"It doesn't sound like good advice, but you just do. When you know, you know," Brooke shrugged.

"What if I don't?"

"Well, I guess if you don't know, you still do."

❖ ❖ ❖

Minutes stretched on for hours, and each class became a veritable eternity as Hayden counted down the time until lunch. With Brooke's words resounding in her mind, she had finally accepted the conclusion she'd subconsciously reached weeks ago. Though Chase was a great friend, he wasn't her forever. The looming conversation terrified her because she still had no desire to hurt him. However, in one sense it excited her. The chance to finally feel liberated from the weight which she bore was enticing.

As the bell rang, though, she realized how completely unprepared she was. Seeing Chase as she walked into the cafeteria, she began questioning herself once again. How could she be sure that she wasn't making an incorrect decision due to the flurry of emotions caused by the past few days? Doubting herself, she froze as he approached.

"Hey, Hayden," Chase greeted with a smile and a hug. Weakly hugging him back, she found herself unable to formulate any type of response. Overwhelmed by the contradicting thoughts polluting her mind, she just backed away as he released her.

"What's wrong?" He asked, furrowing his brow with concern as he noticed the conflicted emotions painted on her face.

"What?" Hayden asked, trying to smile. Even she wasn't certain what exactly she had meant to ask, but it was the only word which could pass through her lips. Steeling herself, she tried to build up the strength to hold the conversation. It would be best for both of them if they could simply move on from it.

"Your eyes get brighter when you're sad," Chase explained, smiling weakly as if he already knew what was coming. "And you've been avoiding me all day."

"I didn't mean to," she lied, as if his believing that would somehow lessen the pain she was preparing to inflict.

"Is everything okay?"

"No," she finally admitted as tears welled up in her eyes.

"Talk to me," Chase urged.

"I'm scared," she told him, finally allowing herself to be honest. Though the words were still difficult to form, it became easier as she stopped trying to hide.

"Of what?"

"Everything. Us, what we've become, what we have to run from, our new lives. Aldric," she ranted, punctuating the name of their alpha with a quiet laugh.

"I know it's a lot to handle."

"I'm just not sure of anything anymore. I don't know who I am, or what I am. And I'm so scared that I'm going to hurt you. You're my best friend, and I don't want to lose you."

"You couldn't," Chase assured her. In the silence that followed his assertion, though, he apparently began to understand the context of the situation, because his perpetual comforting smile faded from his lips.

"I need to find answers before I try to find them with someone else," she finally said. "I think I just need to figure all of this out."

"Alone," Chase muttered, more to himself than to her. Grief and disappointment flashed through his eyes only to be replaced with something far more confusing: joy and relief. Though Hayden knew him well enough to see through his guise, even through her own tears she could acknowledge that it was a valiant effort. Chase's inability to displease anyone once again shone through as he tried to smile through his first breakup.

"I'm sorry," Hayden choked.

"No," Chase consoled her. "No, don't be. You're right. I'm so glad that you agree with me. Honestly."

If Hayden didn't know better, she may actually have fallen for Chase's ploy as well. The glimmer of sorrow behind the feigned twinkle of happiness in his eye, though, confirmed that he had already thought through the same things and reached a different conclusion.

"Linda told us that we can only love once, and that it's forever. We're just so young, it would be crazy to try to make that decision right now," Chase asserted.

"Yeah," Hayden agreed sadly. Though she knew he was only pretending to be okay for her benefit, she was also aware that no good could come of arguing with him. With a shaky breath, Hayden set aside the confusion and uncertainty regarding the future of her relationship and followed Chase to an awkward lunch with their pack.

Chapter 10

One Year Later
Cailean

Before the alarm sounded, Cailean stirred from his fitful sleep. The moon had fallen, but the sun was still barely replaced it at the edge of the horizon. Only a few rays of light penetrated the dense foliage, and those which did were scattered by the surrounding fog. Rubbing his eyes, Cailean tried to understand and will away the soreness which overwhelmed his tired body.

Slowly, he rose to a seated position and blinked away the fatigue. As he bent his abdominals, an unfamiliar sensation erupted throughout his body – almost as if he'd been attacked. Fighting through it, though, he managed to remain upright as the pain dulled. With every passing moment, he felt his muscles waking up after him and strength slowly replaced the aching. The unsettling feeling of weariness crept away as he healed from the unseen injury.

Cailean could still practically see the world of his dreams in the mysticism of the fog. He could see an older version of himself wandering alone, scrambling for answers and safety only to fall to his knees in the leaves. That fear was still within him even as he pulled himself away from the sleeping world. Looking around, he found himself in complete isolation as the dense mist and relative darkness obscured his vision of anything more than a few feet before him.

The first thing to regain full functionality was Cailean's mind, as if it were already awake and summoning the rest of his body to catch up. As he struggled to his feet, his legs elicited a similar feeling as his abs had. Even his arms, which he pressed into the ground to stand, felt heavy and protested movement. His head dropped, leaving his eyes glued to the floor while the pain prevented him from raising them.

Never in his life had Cailean experienced any such internal tenderness, and as he tried to find a rational explanation, panic began to set in. Scanning the area, he searched for any familiar face. His father would have answers, he was sure. Even Hayden or Chase would be comforting, because the solitude was beginning to suffocate him. Despite the logical part of his mind screaming for his father, though, only one name came out in a hoarse whisper as he stumbled forward, dropping all of his weight on a weak foot. "Brooke."

Guided by instinct alone, Cailean moved weakly through the fog. Inhaling deeply, he hoped to find her scent. Nothing recognizable presented itself, though, as he was far too overwhelmed with the confusion. Finally, his strength gave way and he fell forward, barely catching himself on his palms. As he landed, pain reverberated through the muscle fibers in his arms, radiating to his shoulders. It wasn't pain like he was used to, though. Rather, it was more closely related to the feeling of trying to lift something which was too heavy to budge.

Finally, a unique smell wafted into his nostrils. Crawling on protesting limbs, Cailean moved toward the comforting smell. When he approached, he found Brooke, lying supine on the ground. Her chest rose and fell peacefully as she slept. The sight of her alone was enough to calm Cailean and almost managed to remove his pain entirely. Toying with the idea of waking her, Cailean sat on his heels and watched her for a moment. As much as he wanted her advice, he decided against requesting it of her. Instead, he moved closer to her and fell to his side, resting his head on her breast.

As he relaxed, Cailean felt a far more familiar sensation wash over his body. Torn muscles began piecing themselves back together, growing stronger than ever before. Somehow, he had awoken before he had completely healed from his transformation.

It had never happened before, but he was sure that was the only logical explanation.

"Hey," Brooke muttered, stirring quietly and gently placing her hand on his head. She didn't move him, though. She simply rested her palm on the back of his head, running her fingers through his hair.

"Sorry," Cailean replied, though he wasn't entirely certain why he felt the need to apologize.

"It's okay," she replied, gently caressing him. He felt her move slightly as she looked around the woods. "What time is it?"

"I don't know," he admitted.

"Did I miss the alarm?"

"No."

"Why am I so sore?" She complained.

"Sore?" Cailean asked, laughing quietly.

"Yeah."

"I didn't have a word for it."

"What do you mean?"

"Werewolves don't get sore. We heal too fast," Cailean explained. He moved his hand and rested it on her abdomen, slowly tracing the lines with his finger.

"I beg to differ," she laughed.

"No, that's why it's so weird. I think I woke up too soon after the change. Then I woke you up."

"That's weird. Why would that happen?" She wondered.

"I don't know," he admitted. "I think I was dreaming."

"Oh? About what?"

"It isn't important," Cailean told her, finally lifting his head and turning to face her. Even in the sparse light, her eyes shone brightly and the sweat on her skin glistened. "You want to hear a story?"

"I guess?" She humored him.

"When I woke up, I was scared. I thought I was dying, honestly. I've never felt like that before."

"You're being dramatic," she teased.

"Maybe, but it really was terrifying. I mean, to hurt when I move? How do people get over that?"

"I don't know, they get used to it, I suppose."

"Anyway, I looked for the one person I thought could help me. My father, right? He would know how to save me, or at least be able to tell me whether or not to be concerned."

"Okay?"

"But I didn't look for him. I looked for you. You were the one I needed, and when I found you, I was at peace. I knew everything was going to be okay."

Brooke didn't respond, but Cailean could see a gleam as tears formed in her ears. Her mouth tugged upward, forming her thin lips into a smile. Cailean, resting on an elbow, brought a hand to her cheek and gently brushed a strand of hair from it.

"You are my peace, Brooke. You are my love and my life. In the darkness, you are my light, and you will always be what I run to. Without you, I know I would have been overwhelmed by the darkness. I would have truly become what I pretend to be. You see the good in me, and you are the only one I believe can bring it out. If love is anything but this, I don't want it."

"I love you," she choked through the tears. Lowering his lips to meet hers, Cailean finally allowed himself to accept the truth his heart had known for years. What the wolf demanded was inconsequential. With or without its approval, his love already belonged to Brooke Cassidy.

Hayden

One last look over her desolate room finally convinced Hayden that she'd emptied it completely. With a sigh, she turned off the light and closed the door behind her, moving to meet her family in the living room. Most of their belongings had already been moved to the other house, but they'd saved a few large pieces of furniture and boxes of miscellaneous items, which were piled in the corner of the room, for last.

For a decade, Hayden had lived in that home with her mother and brother. A feeling of emptiness overwhelmed her as she realized that the last of everything she owned sat in boxes waiting to be moved. One last trip to their new home would mean the end of the old one. Once the rented truck was loaded up with the sofa, loveseat, end tables, coffee table, and those five boxes, she would leave that house for the last time.

Since she'd been a child, Hayden had known the day would come when she'd leave. Her mother's approach toward emotional trauma was to try to leave it behind. When Hayden's father had died, her mother had insisted that they find a new home for the three of them as she was unable to move on while she lived in the house she'd shared with him. As Caleb prepared to move to college, then, it only made sense that she'd use the same excuse to search for a new abode for herself and Hayden.

Of course, Hayden knew there was more beneath the surface. Her mother had never allowed them to need, and she always struggled to shield them from any financial difficulties. A single mother raising two children, though, was unlikely to be financially secure. Each house was slightly smaller than the previous because they no longer needed the extra space. Her mother would never admit it, but Hayden knew that in part the purpose of their move was to save money. Watching her mother and brother lift the table and carry it through the door, though, she resolved never to mention that knowledge.

Focusing on helping her family, Hayden picked up a stack of two boxes from her room, both of which were loaded with books. With ease she lifted the two heaviest boxes which she'd packed and carried them to the truck. Over the past year, her family had noticed her increasing strength, but she'd always been careful not to overdo it. In order to remain somewhat inconspicuous, she chose the boxes with concealed goods rather than hefting the entire couch over her shoulder.

Climbing up the ramp into the truck, she watched as her mom and brother set the table on its side against the wall. Her mother was breathing heavily, clearly worn out from exerting herself all day. While Hayden had been at school, she had taken the day off work to ceaselessly pack and move in order to minimize the amount of effort required of Hayden. Caleb, though he had spent the day helping her, was younger and far less affected by the continuous strenuous activity.

"You need help?" Caleb offered, turning his attention to Hayden and offering his assistance too late as she set the boxes in a corner.

"I'm alright," she laughed. "It was just a few light things."

Without a verbal response, he nodded and retreated into the house. Between the three of them, they were able to bring the last of the furniture into the truck within a matter of minutes. Hayden reached up to grab the handle of the rolling door. Recognizing a hint of concern in her brother's face, though, she realized that it was something he considered to be a difficult task. Feigning effort, she tugged at the cord once before doubling down her efforts. The second pull was enough to dislodge the door from its locked position and gravity did most of the work from there.

Hayden's mother climbed behind the wheel of the truck and Hayden and Caleb joined her in the cab. Hayden, being the smallest, was automatically designated to sit in between them. Attempting to take up as little space as possible and avoid getting in her mother's way, Hayden pressed her knees together and placed her elbows on them, holding her arms straight over them. Her mother was visibly uncomfortable driving the massive vehicle and Hayden didn't want to give her any reason to struggle with it more. Though the drive to their new house was reasonably short, the discomfort of her position made it drag on longer.

"You don't have to be an egg," Caleb told her, inching himself closer to his window.

"I'm okay," she assured him.

"Come on," Caleb argued, wrapping his arm around her shoulder and pulling her a bit closer to him. With more space to occupy, Hayden allowed herself to breathe and relax a bit. She could see that her brother was pressed against the door, but he was far too stubborn to allow her to be the uncomfortable one.

"Thanks," she smiled, resting her head on his shoulder as the truck drove down the bumpy road.

"I'm so glad that my kids get along," their mother mused, tears welling up in her eyes as she briefly glanced toward them before returning her eyes to the road in front of her.

"Mom," Hayden sighed. Without a follow-up, though, she fell silent and allowed her mother to enjoy the moment. When Caleb moved, those close family experiences would be far scarcer.

As they pulled into the driveway, Hayden noticed a door across the street opening. Caleb exited the cab first, but Hayden was close on his heels. Their mom took a bit longer as she carefully engaged the emergency brake and turned off the engine before opening her door, holding the handle on the side, and climbing out.

A stranger crossed the street, quickly closing the distance between them with a smile painted on her face. Her brown hair was tied back in a ponytail and her green eyes shimmered in the sunlight. Something about her looked familiar, but Hayden was confident she had never seen the woman before.

"Hi," she greeted, waving toward Hayden and her family. Hayden's mother moved from the other side of the truck to intercept her.

"Hello," Hayden's mother replied. "I'm Grace Faye. This is my son Caleb and my daughter Hayden. We're just moving in."

"I can tell," the woman teased, nodding her head toward the moving truck from which they'd all just disembarked. "Audrey. I live across the street and I saw the truck. I thought you may need some help."

"Oh, no I couldn't ask that," Hayden's mother quickly declined. "We've only a few more things in the truck, and I wouldn't want my first impression on my new neighbors to be inconveniencing them."

"Please," Audrey sighed, rolling her eyes playfully. Without waiting for an acceptance of her offer, Audrey moved toward the truck and lifted the rolling door, securing it at the top of the track. "It's my job."

"You work with the moving company?" Caleb skeptically asked.

"Okay, so it's not exactly my job, but I take protect and serve literally."

"Well, if you insist, we could use the help," Hayden's mom admitted. "Thank you."

"Don't mention it. My son will be home soon, I will rope him into it as well," Audrey joked as she lowered the ramp. Looking into the back of the truck, she whistled and dropped her hands onto her hips. Aside from the few things they'd had left when Hayden had made it home from school, her family had already loaded up a small assortment of dressers and nightstands, as well as a bedframe.

Audrey and Grace became fast friends as they talked about work and shared various embarrassing stories of their children's youth. Hayden tryied to ignore the conversation and focus on bringing things inside. Glancing at Caleb, she was rewarded with a knowing smile and a shrug.

"It's nice for mom to have friends," he shrugged when the two women had gone inside and left Hayden alone with her brother.

"I just don't understand why embarrassing their children is a requirement of bonding for adulthood," she complained.

"Don't you bond with your friends by talking about your life?" Caleb countered.

"I guess."

"Well, we're her life. I'm pretty honored by that."

"Quit being logical and let me mope," Hayden groaned as she turned away and climbed up the ramp to retrieve a box. On her way inside, she passed Audrey, who smiled and stepped to the side to allow her to pass. Just as she set the box down in her new room, she heard a car door slam from outside.

"Garrick!" Audrey shouted, presumably summoning her son. "Come help us out. I want you to meet this girl."

Hayden felt her face redden and she ducked behind her doorway, feeling a sudden urder to hide. Regardless of kind intentions, Hayden was not interested in meeting anyone in that manner. Parents introducing their children was always the single most awkward experience, and she wanted no part in it. Knowing full well that it was unavoidable, though, she sighed and sulked outside.

When she walked back into the bright light of the sun, she blinked a few times as her eyes adjusted. She tried to catch a glimpse of her new neighbor before his mother inevitably introduced him to her. The only visible person, though, was Audrey, so Hayden surmised that all of the others were hidden within the truck. At the very least, she could introduce herself and minimize the awkwardness of the encounter.

Quickly, she made her way toward the truck. As she did, she saw the neighbor boy's shaggy brown hair. From the back, nothing about him seemed impressive. Dressed very plainly, he held one side of the couch with shaky arms as Hayden's mother supported the other end. His scrawny legs quivered as he took a step backward, leading the way down the ramp. When he reached the end, he tripped over himself and dropped the couch on his toe. Hayden's mom was able to support the other side, but she almost fell forward with the momentum.

"Smooth," Hayden teased as she walked up behind him. The boy lifted the couch just enough to pull his foot free. Turning to face her, he tried to smile to hide the embarrassment on his burning red face. Something about his smile, along with the fact that he'd taken the brunt of the uneasiness of their meeting upon himself, set Hayden at ease.

"Hayden Faye," she greeted. Taking pity on the neighbor boy and smiling gently, she reached out her hand toward him. Defeated, he accepted her hand and tried to grip it firmly. Unwilling to make him feel even more uncomfortable, Hayden was careful not to outmatch the strength of his handshake too much.

As she gazed into his eyes, Hayden felt a stirring in her stomach she had never experienced before. Something within her was calling to the boy standing before her. Though his eyes were a dull green like his mother's, the way the sun reflected from them made them shine and appear bright blue. Entranced by his eyes, she barely noticed as his stance seemed to strengthen and he straightened his shoulders. Respect was the most accurate word for her feeling, but even that failed to qualify the sensation which encompassed her.

"I'm Caleb," her brother blurted out, pulling her from her trance. Looking down, Hayden realized that her hand was still in his, and she wondered how long she'd been standing there.

"I'm Garrick," the neighbor boy spoke up. A strange but unmistakable power in his voice resonated through Hayden's entire being. She didn't know what, but she had no doubt there was something special about Garrick Elliott, and she knew that whatever it was, she wanted to be a part of it. For the first time in her life,

Hayden understood what Brooke meant. She finally grasped the advice which at which she'd always scoffed. She knew.